SIMON SPOTLIGHT
An imprint of Simon & Schuster Children's Publishing Division
1230 Avenue of the Americas, New York, New York 10020
This Simon Spotlight edition September 2022
Copyright © 2022 by Simon & Schuster, Inc. All rights reserved, including the right of reproduction in whole or in part in any form.
SIMON SPOTLIGHT and colophon are registered trademarks of Simon & Schuster, Inc.
YOU'RE INVITED TO A CREEPOVER is a registered trademark of Simon & Schuster, Inc. For information about special discounts for bulk purchases, please contact Simon & Schuster Special Sales at 1-866-506-1949 or business@simonandschuster.com.
Designed by Nicholas Sciacca. Text by Matthew J. Gilbert. Based on the text by Ellie O'Ryan. Art Services by Glass House Graphics. Pencils & Inks by Onofrio Orlando. Colors by Giusi Lo Piccolo, Color Assistants Nataliya Torretta, Francesca Ingrassia and Santino Triolo. Lettering by Giuseppe Naselli/Grafimated Cartoon. Supervision by Salvatore Di Marco/Grafimated Cartoon. The illustrations for this book were rendered digitally.
Manufactured in China 0522 SCP
10 9 8 7 6 5 4 3 2 1
ISBN 978-1-6659-1564-9 (hc)
ISBN 978-1-6659-1563-2 (pbk)
ISBN 978-1-6659-1565-6 (ebook)
Library of Congress Catalog Card Number 2022934417

YOU'RE INVITED TO A CREEPOVER

THE GRAPHIC NOVEL

TRUTH OR DARE...

WRITTEN BY P. J. NIGHT
ILLUSTRATED BY ONOFRIO ORLANDO
AT GLASS HOUSE GRAPHICS

SIMON SPOTLIGHT
NEW YORK   LONDON   TORONTO   SYDNEY   NEW DELHI

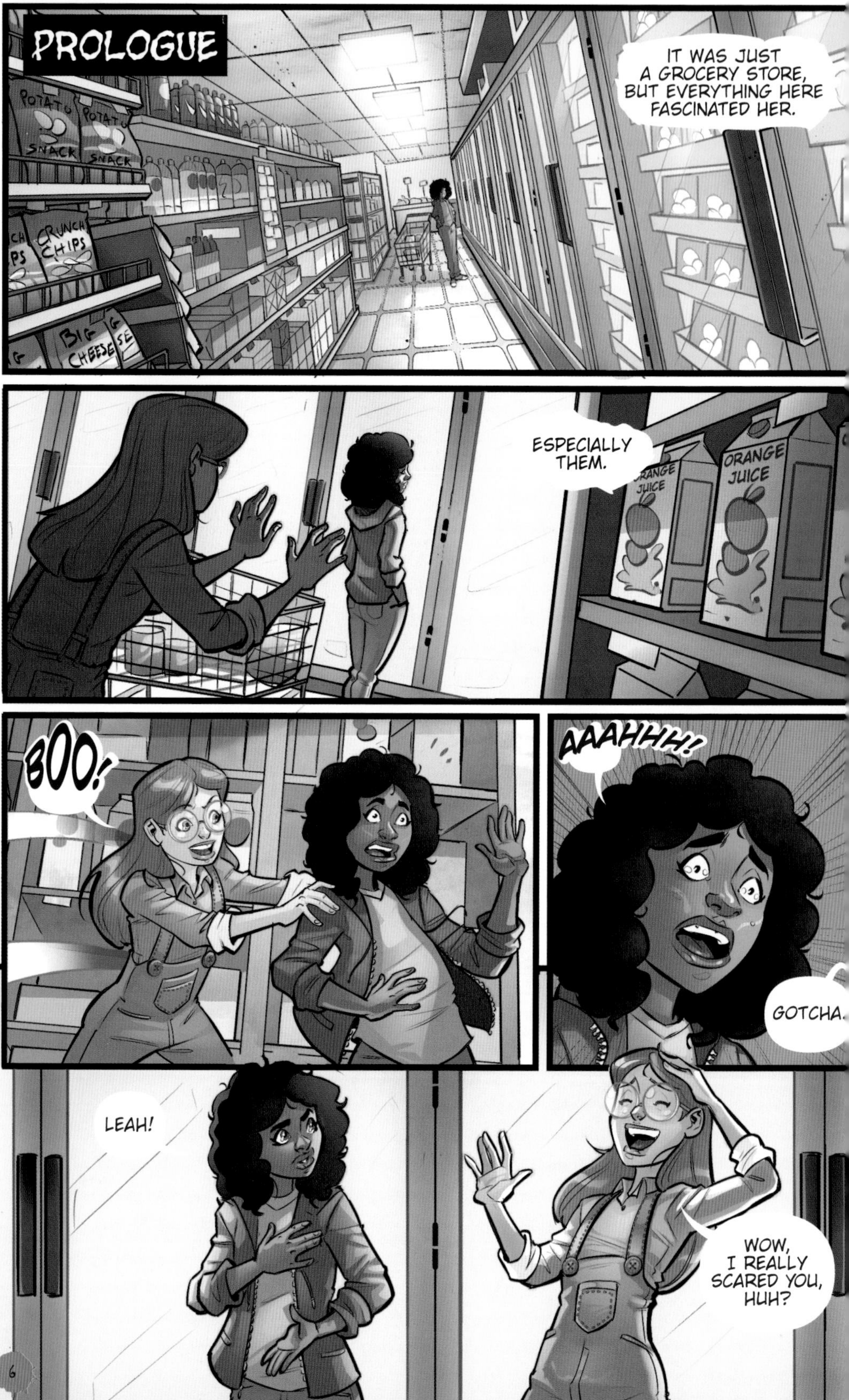
PROLOGUE
IT WAS JUST A GROCERY STORE, BUT EVERYTHING HERE FASCINATED HER.
POTATO SNACK
POTATO SNACK
CRUNCH CHIPS
BIG CHEESE
ESPECIALLY THEM.
ORANGE JUICE
ORANGE JUICE
BOO!
AAAHHH!
GOTCHA.
LEAH!
WOW, I REALLY SCARED YOU, HUH?

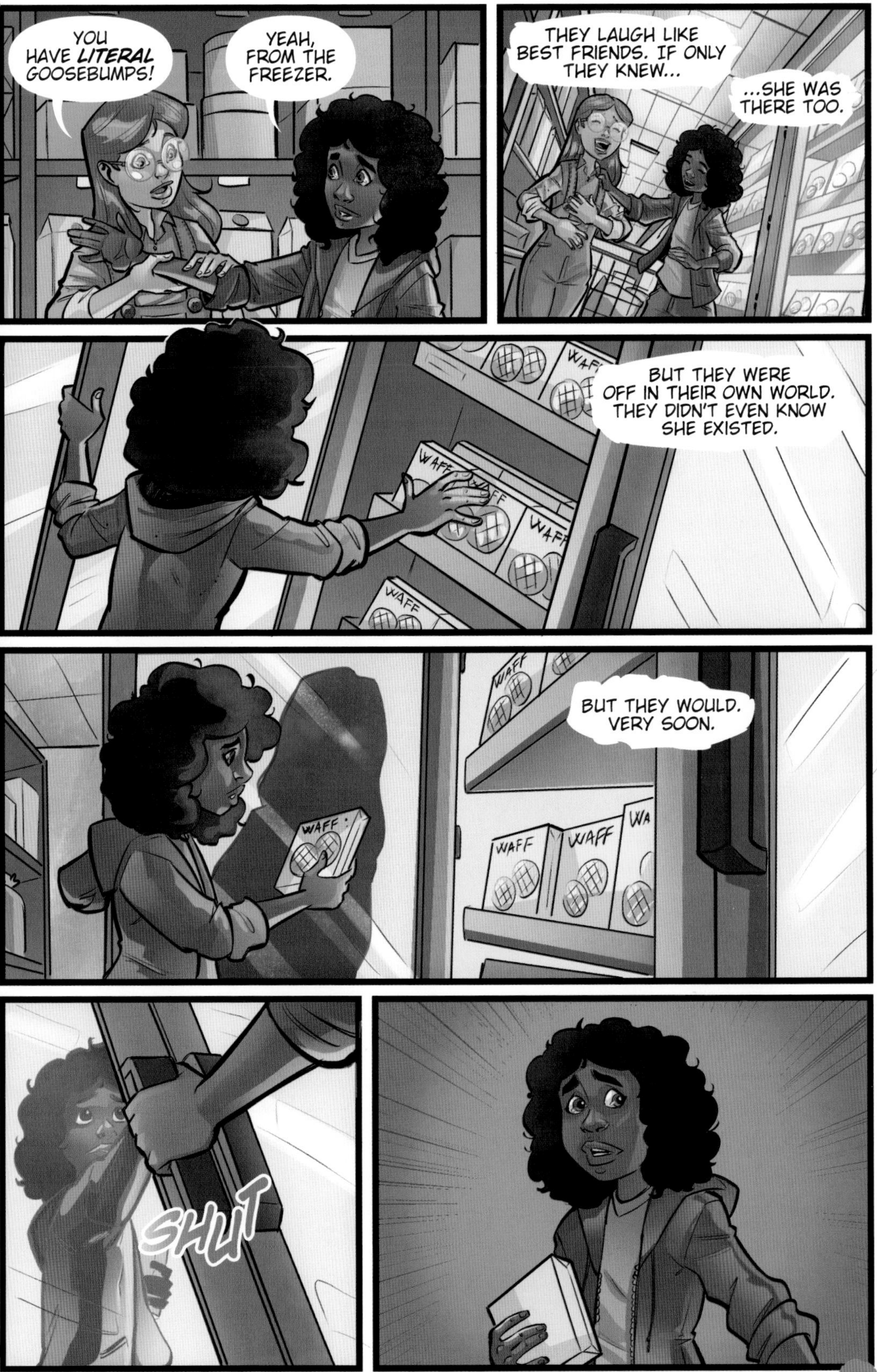
YOU HAVE *LITERAL* GOOSEBUMPS!
YEAH, FROM THE FREEZER.
THEY LAUGH LIKE BEST FRIENDS. IF ONLY THEY KNEW...
...SHE WAS THERE TOO.
WAFF
BUT THEY WERE OFF IN THEIR OWN WORLD. THEY DIDN'T EVEN KNOW SHE EXISTED.
WAFF
BUT THEY WOULD. VERY SOON.
SHUT

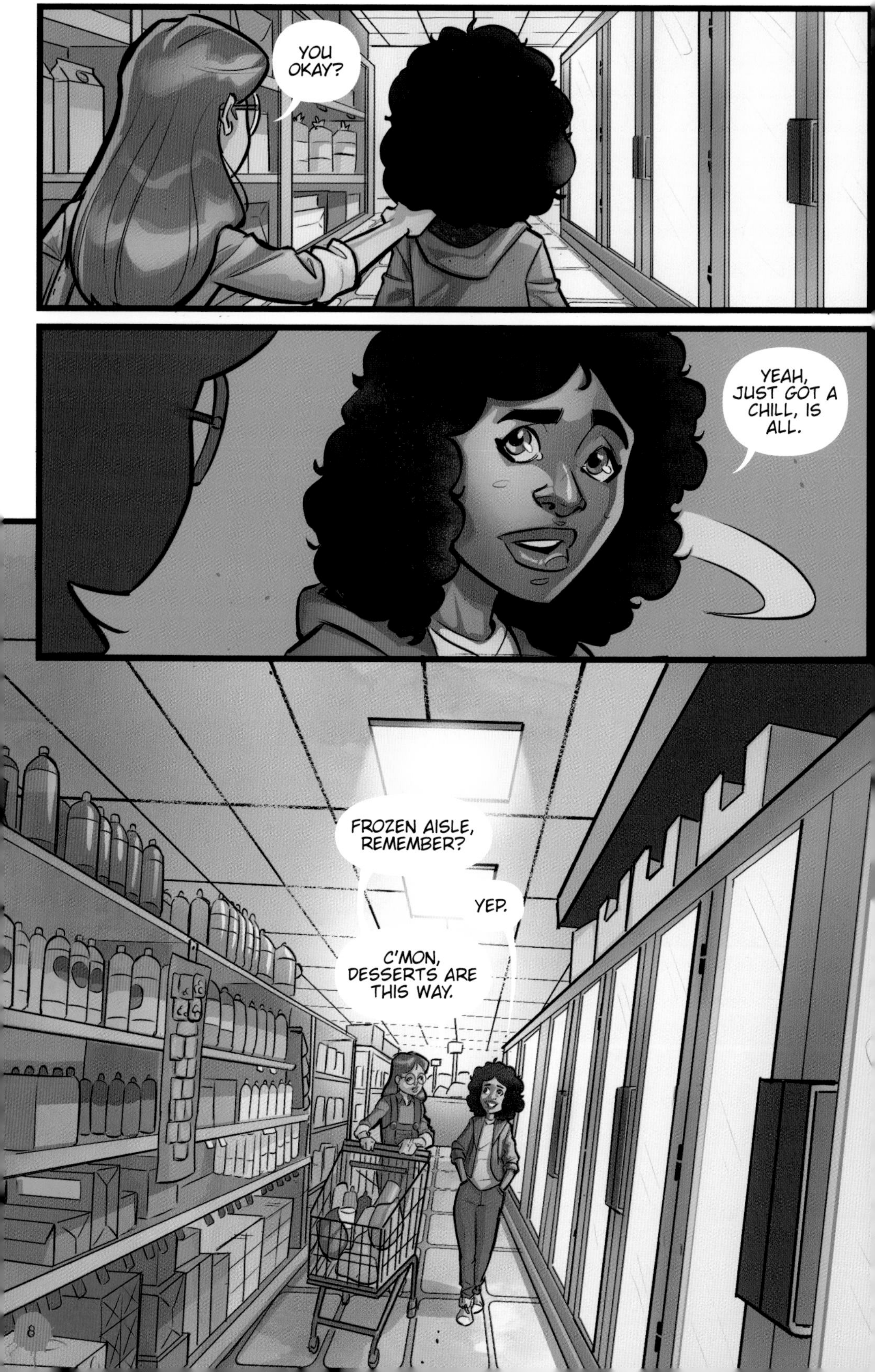
YOU OKAY?
YEAH, JUST GOT A CHILL, IS ALL.
FROZEN AISLE, REMEMBER?
YEP.
C'MON, DESSERTS ARE THIS WAY.

CHAPTER 1

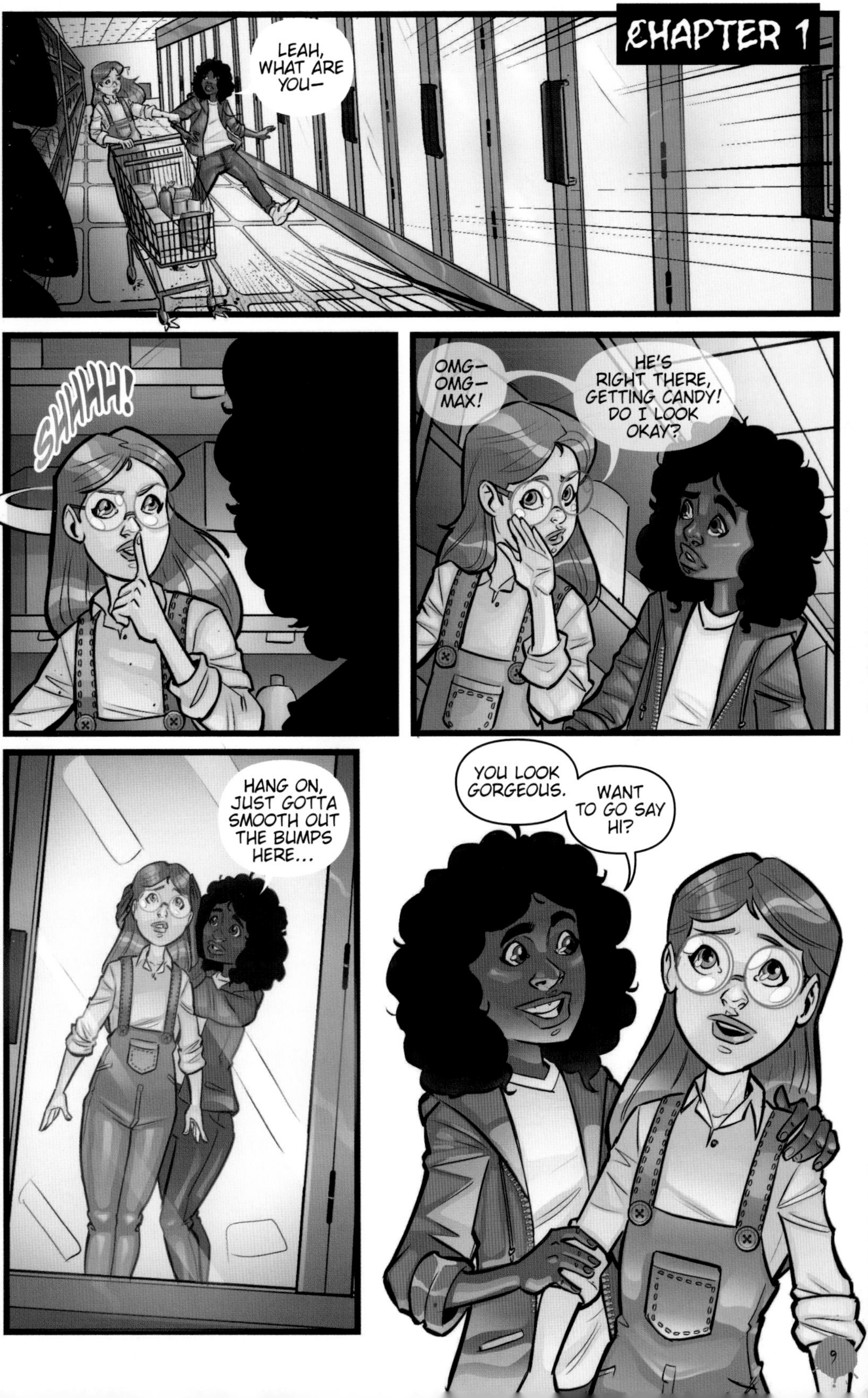

LEAH, WHAT ARE YOU—
SHHHH!
OMG— OMG— MAX!
HE'S RIGHT THERE, GETTING CANDY! DO I LOOK OKAY?
HANG ON, JUST GOTTA SMOOTH OUT THE BUMPS HERE...
YOU LOOK GORGEOUS.
WANT TO GO SAY HI?

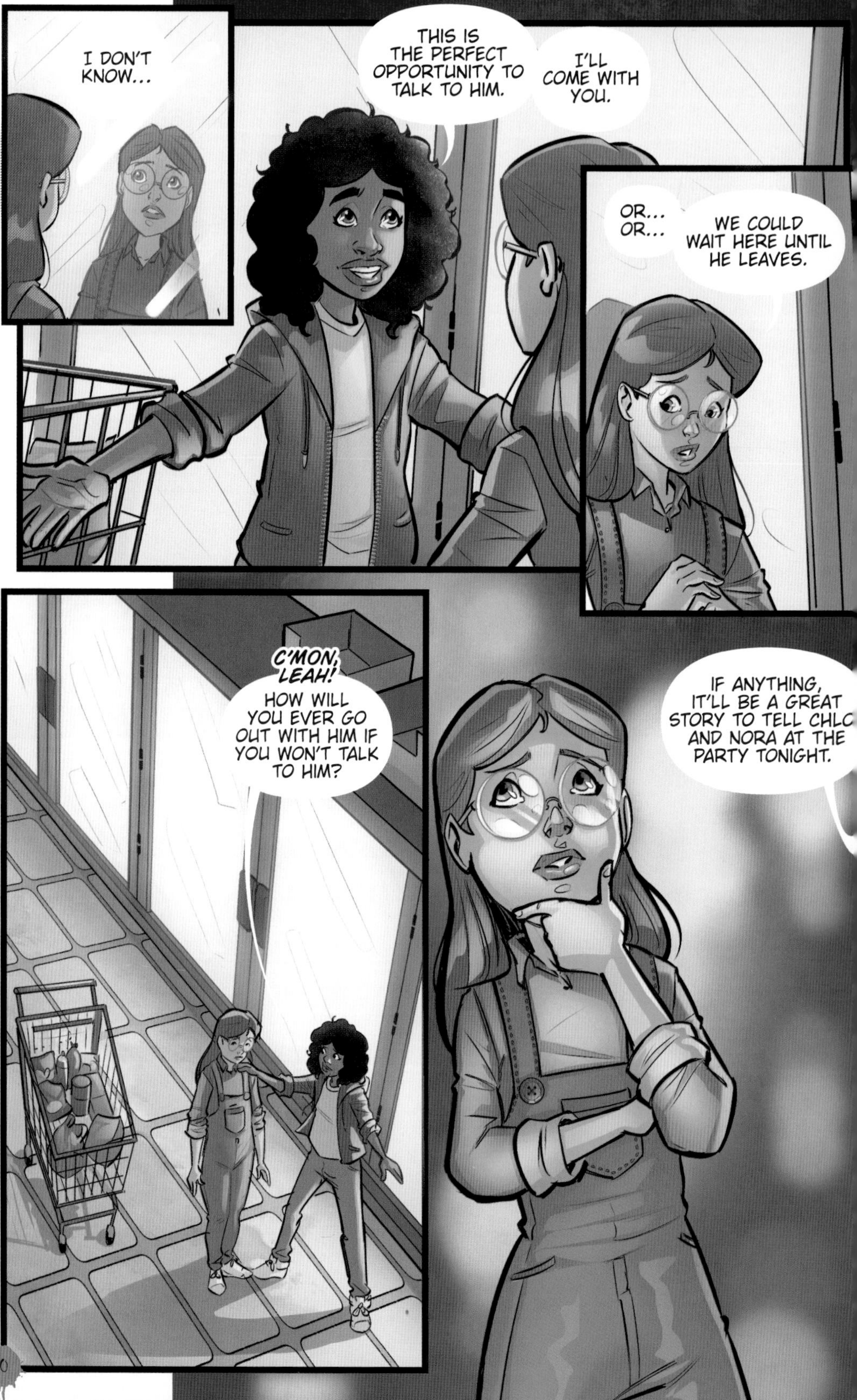
I DON'T KNOW...
THIS IS THE PERFECT OPPORTUNITY TO TALK TO HIM.
I'LL COME WITH YOU.
OR... OR...
WE COULD WAIT HERE UNTIL HE LEAVES.
C'MON, LEAH!
HOW WILL YOU EVER GO OUT WITH HIM IF YOU WON'T TALK TO HIM?
IF ANYTHING, IT'LL BE A GREAT STORY TO TELL CHLO AND NORA AT THE PARTY TONIGHT.

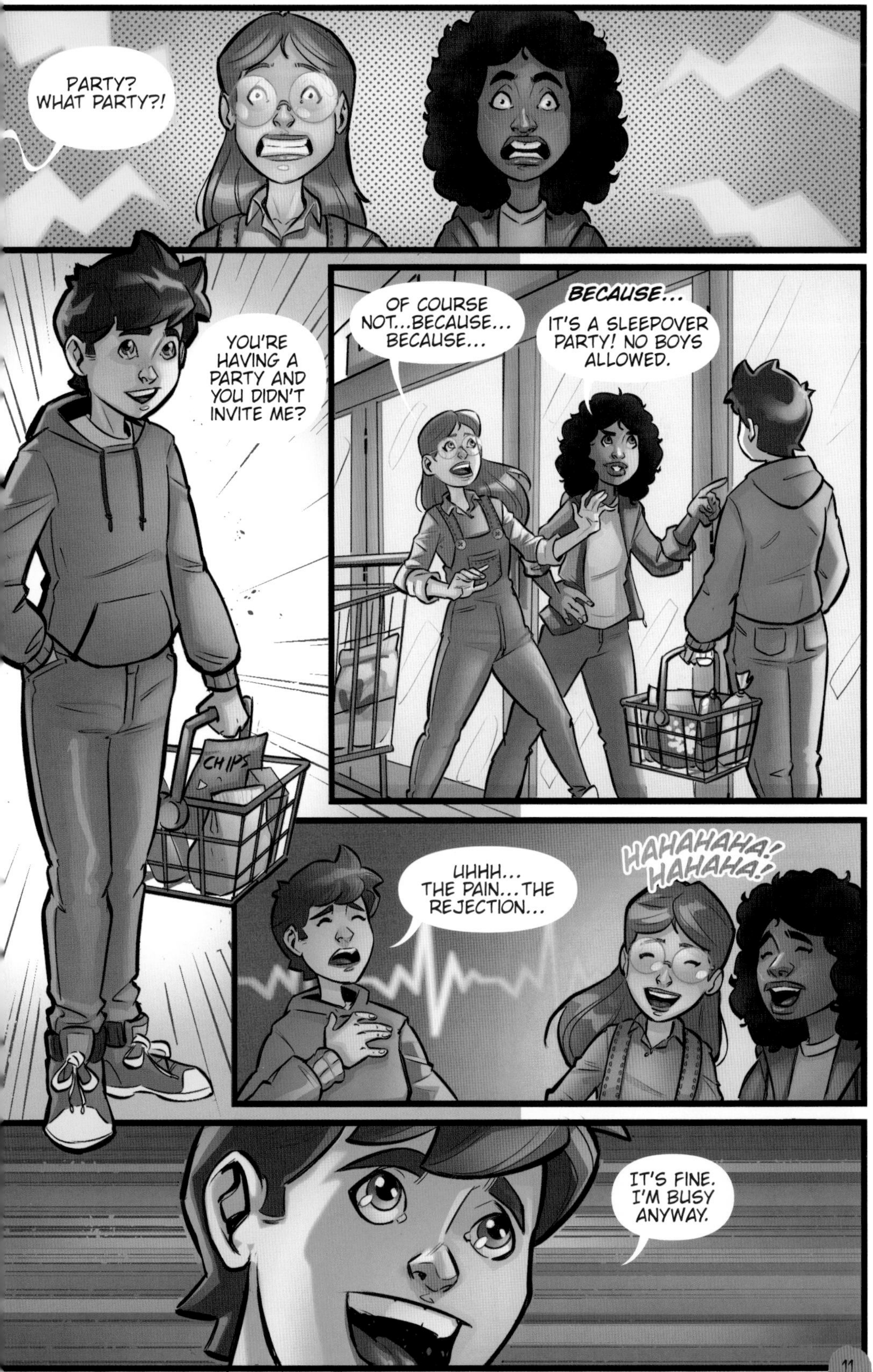
PARTY? WHAT PARTY?!
YOU'RE HAVING A PARTY AND YOU DIDN'T INVITE ME?
CHIPS
OF COURSE NOT...BECAUSE... BECAUSE...
BECAUSE...
IT'S A SLEEPOVER PARTY! NO BOYS ALLOWED.
UHHH... THE PAIN...THE REJECTION...
HAHAHAHA! HAHAHA!
IT'S FINE. I'M BUSY ANYWAY.

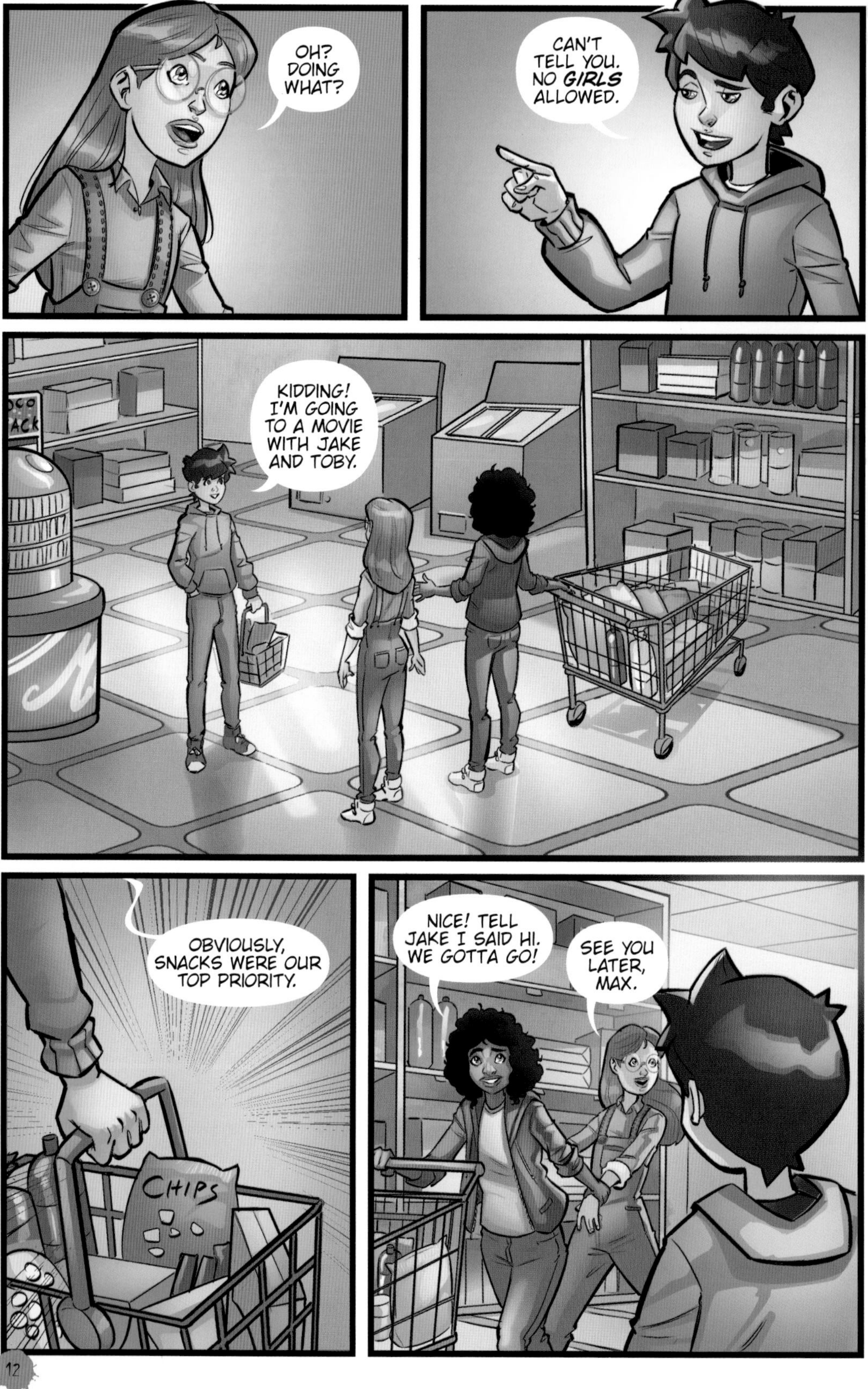
OH? DOING WHAT?
CAN'T TELL YOU. NO **GIRLS** ALLOWED.
KIDDING! I'M GOING TO A MOVIE WITH JAKE AND TOBY.
OBVIOUSLY, SNACKS WERE OUR TOP PRIORITY.
CHIPS
NICE! TELL JAKE I SAID HI. WE GOTTA GO!
SEE YOU LATER, MAX.

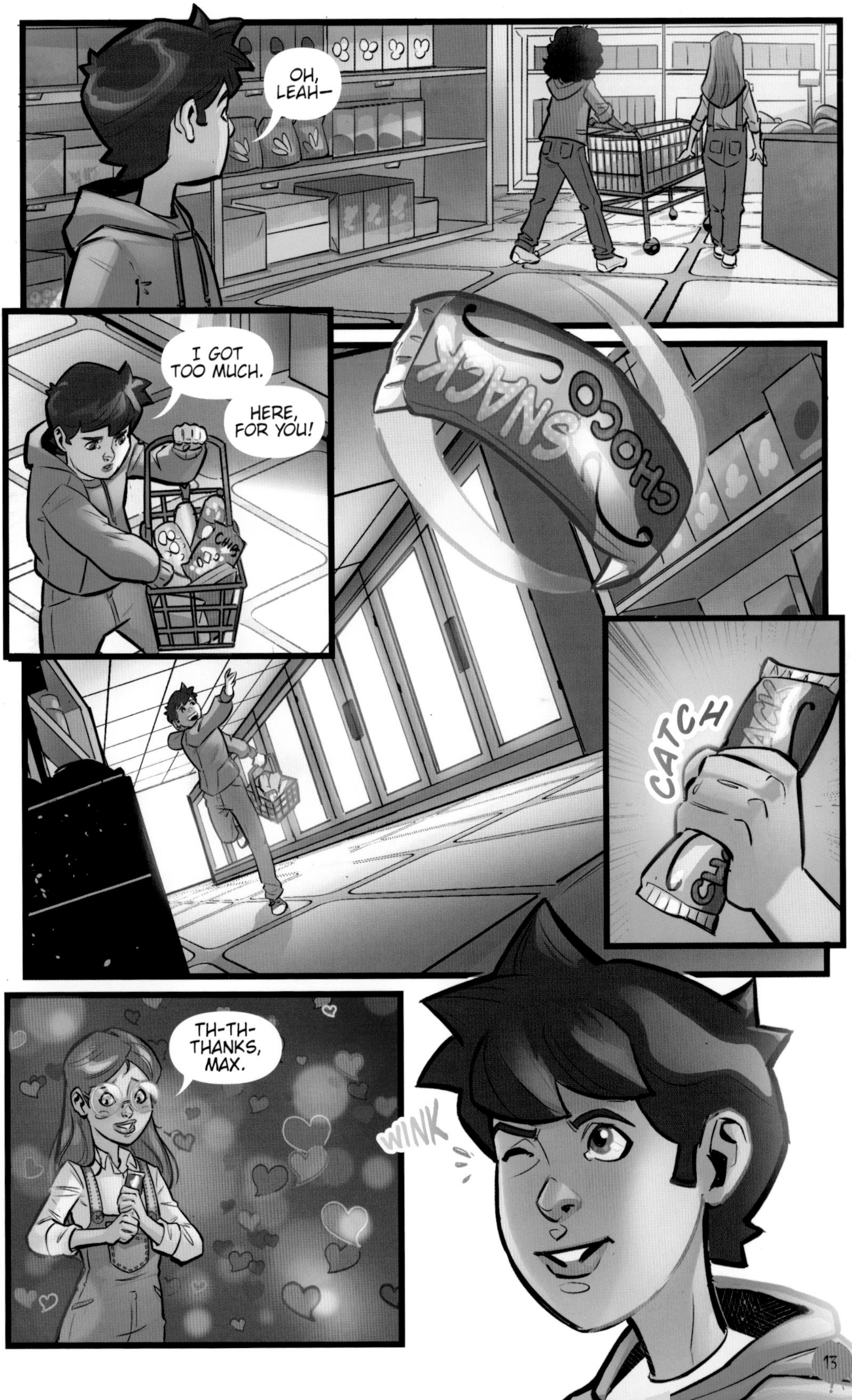
OH, LEAH—
I GOT TOO MUCH.
HERE, FOR YOU!
CHOCO SNACK
CATCH
TH-TH-THANKS, MAX.
WINK

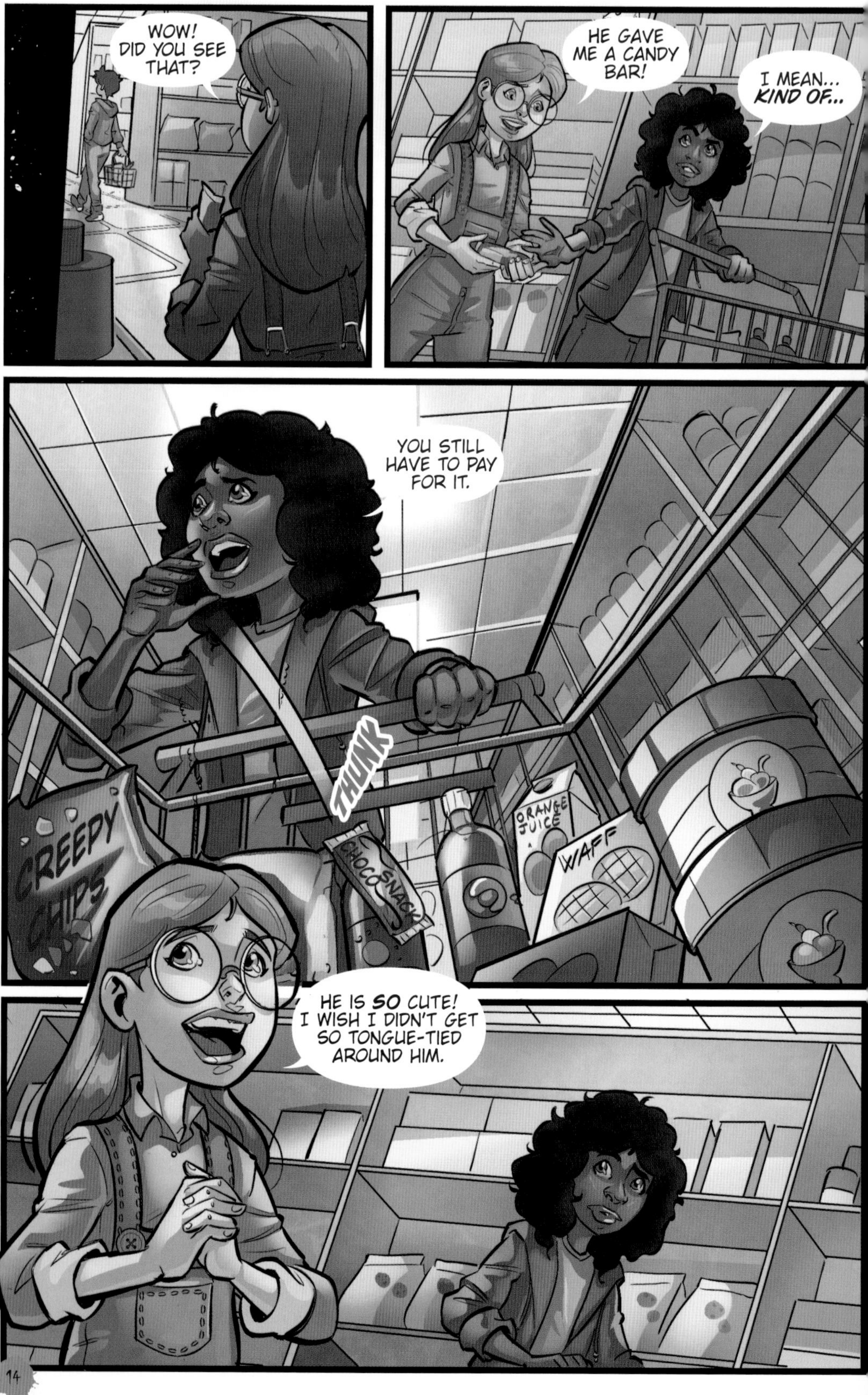

WOW! DID YOU SEE THAT?
HE GAVE ME A CANDY BAR!
I MEAN... KIND OF...
YOU STILL HAVE TO PAY FOR IT.
THUNK
CREEPY CHIPS
CHOCO SNACK
ORANGE JUICE
WAFF
HE IS SO CUTE! I WISH I DIDN'T GET SO TONGUE-TIED AROUND HIM.

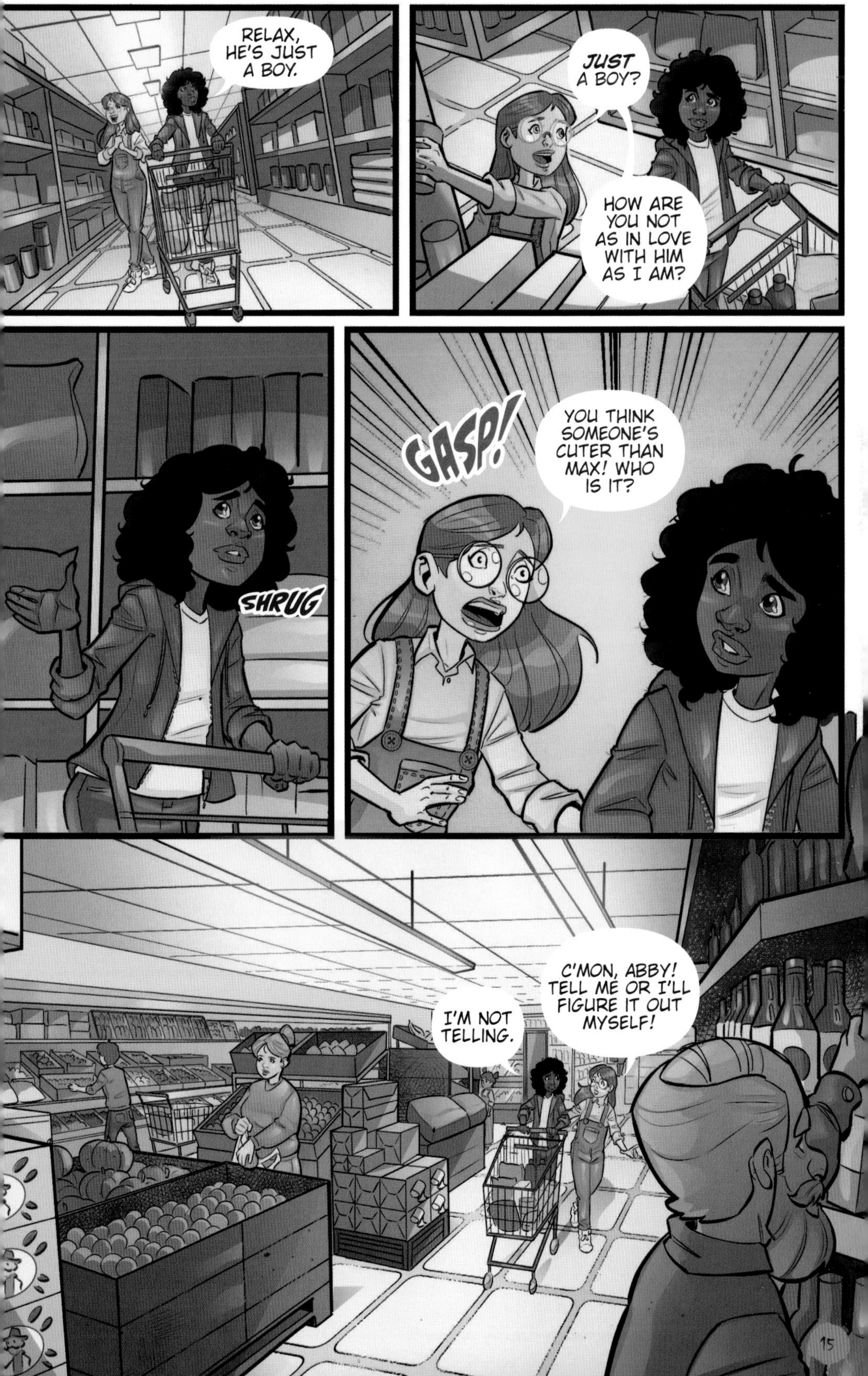
RELAX, HE'S JUST A BOY.
JUST A BOY?
HOW ARE YOU NOT AS IN LOVE WITH HIM AS I AM?
SHRUG
GASP!
YOU THINK SOMEONE'S CUTER THAN MAX! WHO IS IT?
I'M NOT TELLING.
C'MON, ABBY! TELL ME OR I'LL FIGURE IT OUT MYSELF!

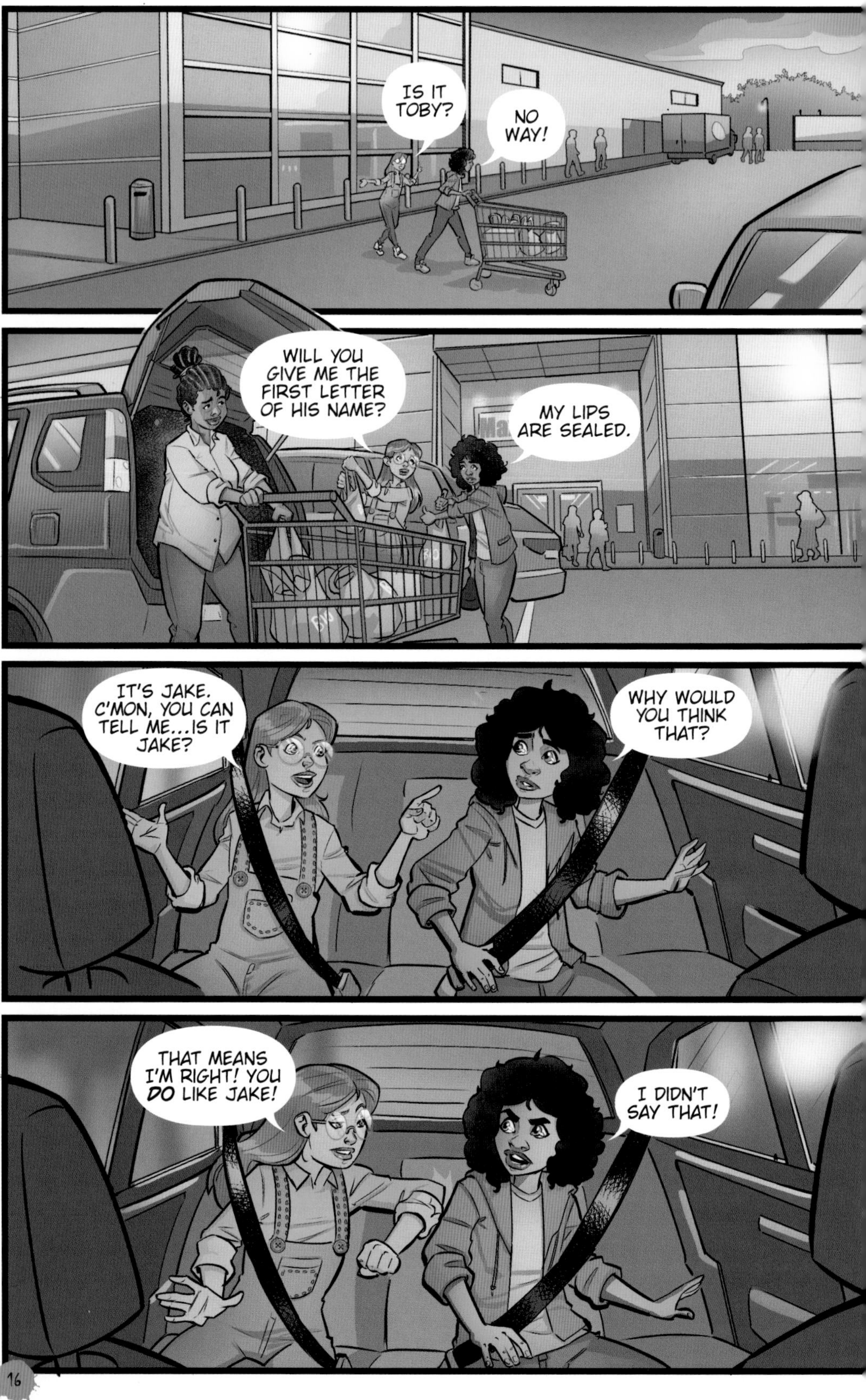
IS IT TOBY?
NO WAY!
WILL YOU GIVE ME THE FIRST LETTER OF HIS NAME?
MY LIPS ARE SEALED.
IT'S JAKE. C'MON, YOU CAN TELL ME...IS IT JAKE?
WHY WOULD YOU THINK THAT?
THAT MEANS I'M RIGHT! YOU DO LIKE JAKE!
I DIDN'T SAY THAT!

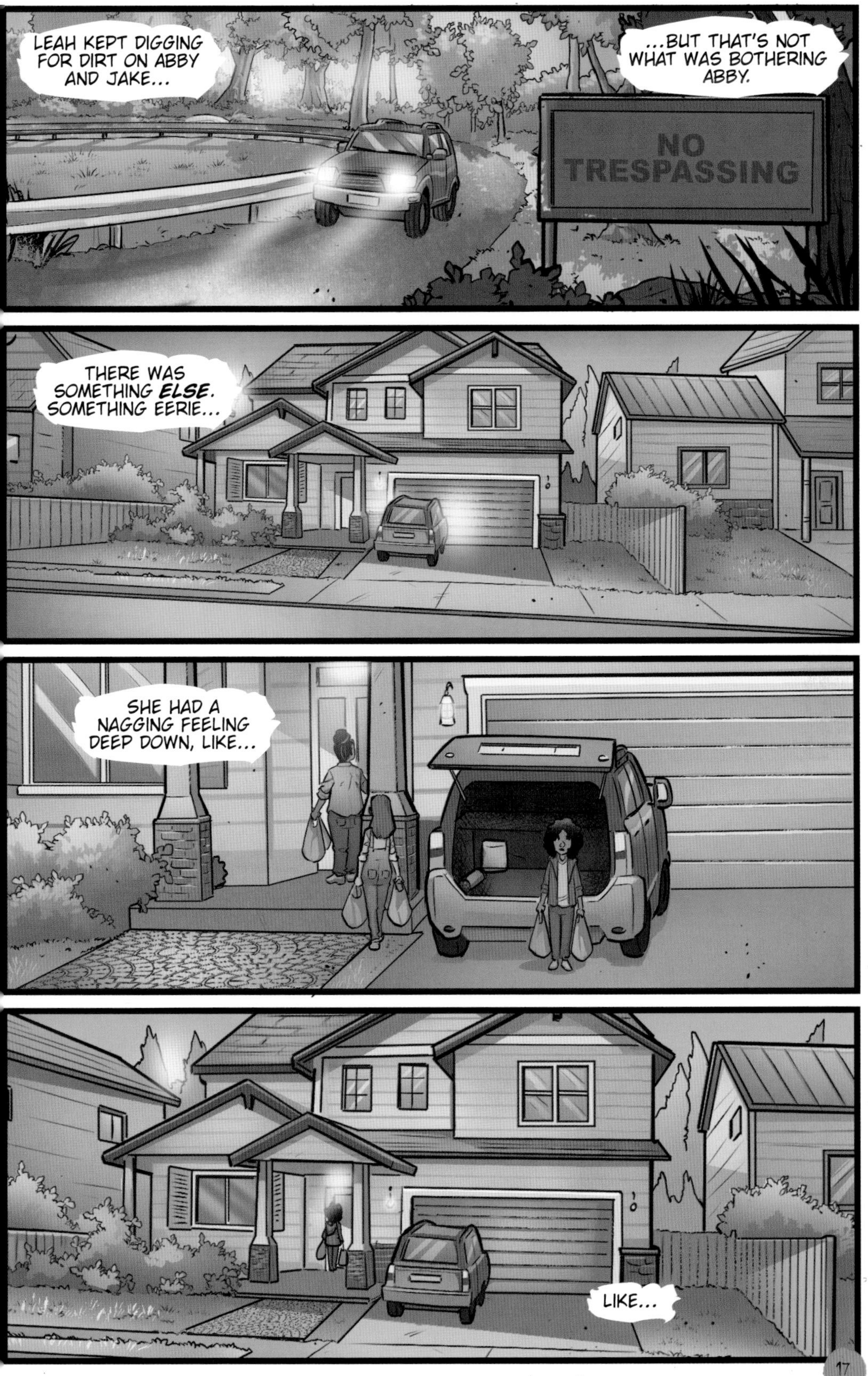
LEAH KEPT DIGGING FOR DIRT ON ABBY AND JAKE...
...BUT THAT'S NOT WHAT WAS BOTHERING ABBY.
NO TRESPASSING
THERE WAS SOMETHING *ELSE*. SOMETHING EERIE...
SHE HAD A NAGGING FEELING DEEP DOWN, LIKE...
LIKE...

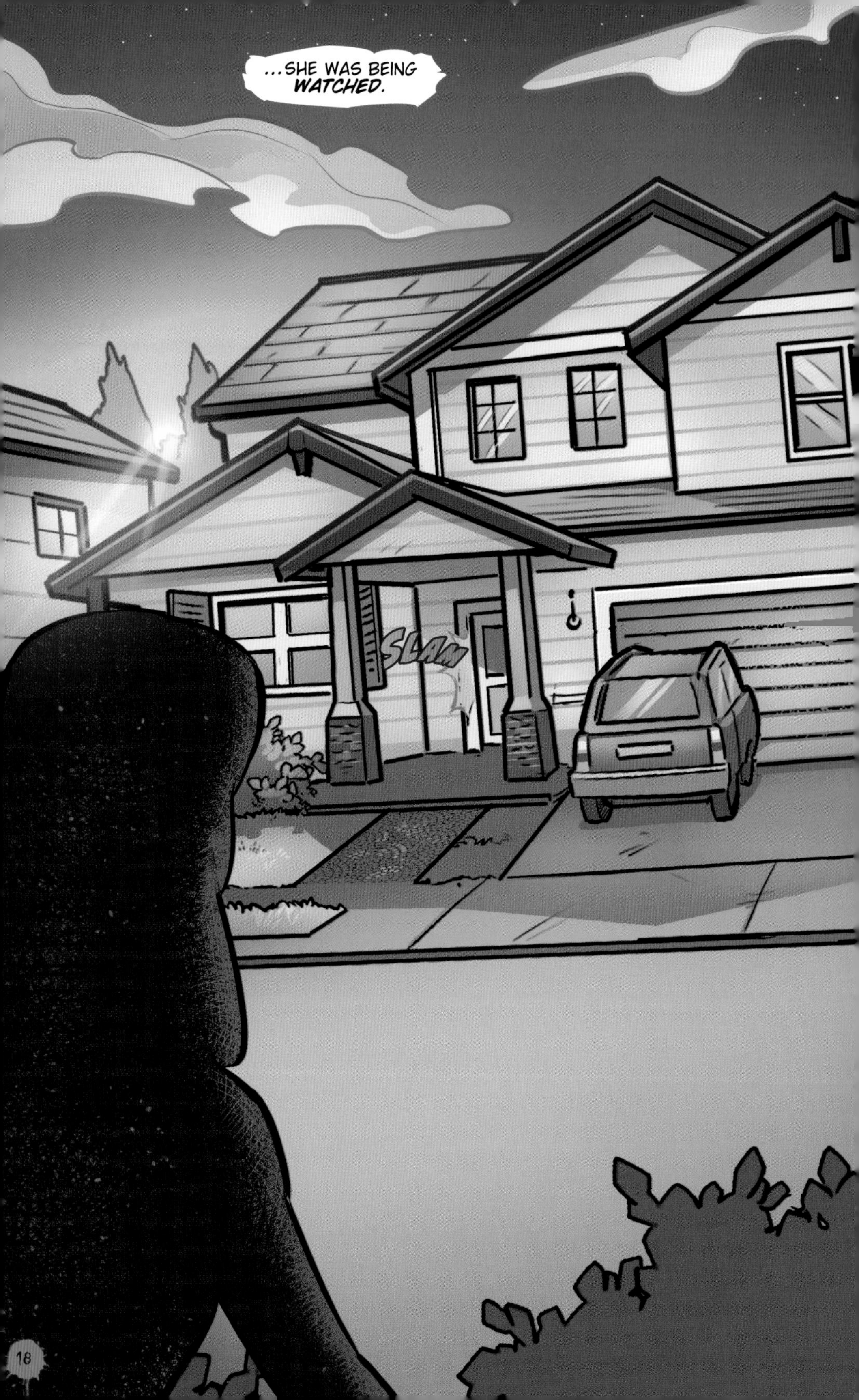
...SHE WAS BEING WATCHED.
SLAM

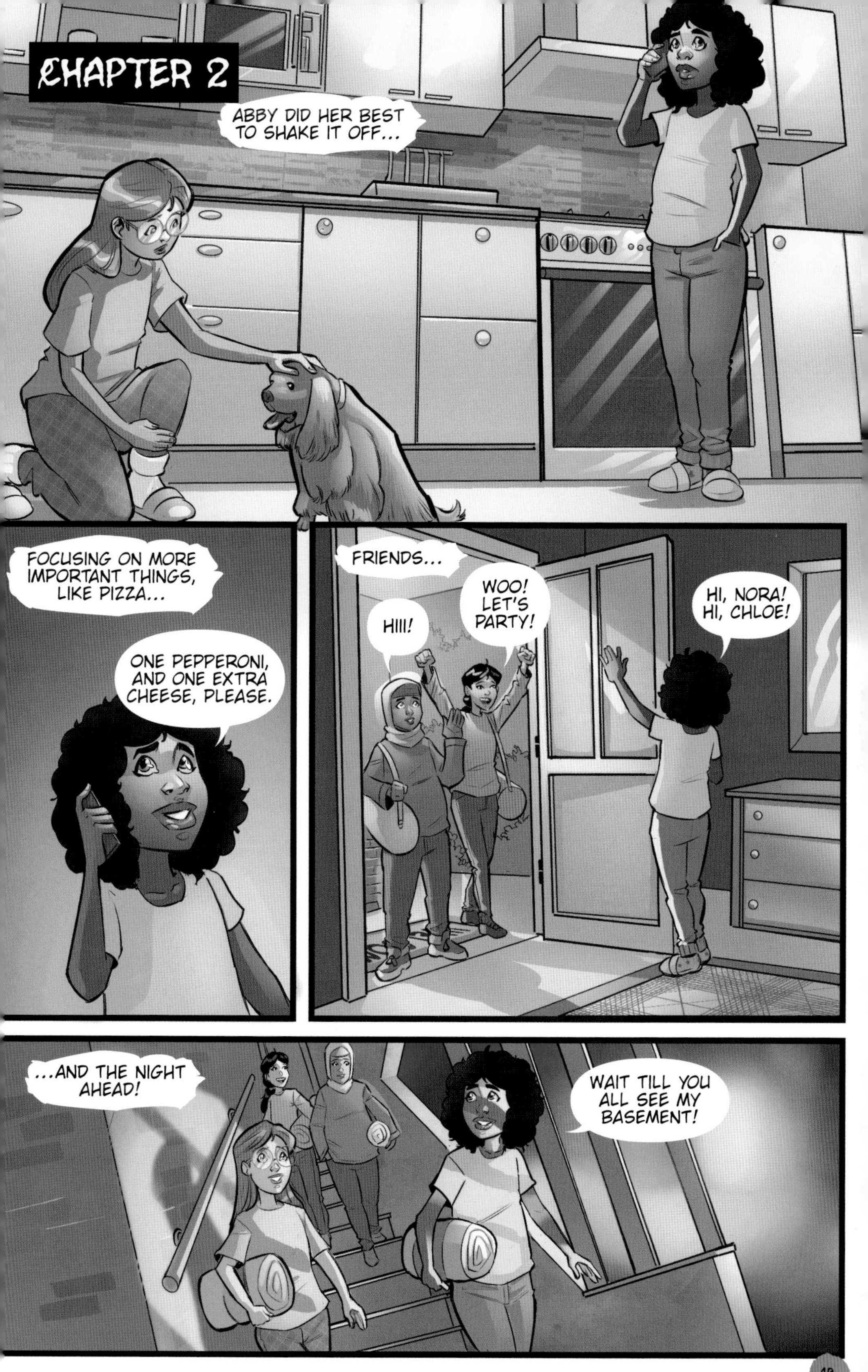
CHAPTER 2
ABBY DID HER BEST TO SHAKE IT OFF...
FOCUSING ON MORE IMPORTANT THINGS, LIKE PIZZA...
ONE PEPPERONI, AND ONE EXTRA CHEESE, PLEASE.
FRIENDS...
HIII!
WOO! LET'S PARTY!
HI, NORA! HI, CHLOE!
...AND THE NIGHT AHEAD!
WAIT TILL YOU ALL SEE MY BASEMENT!

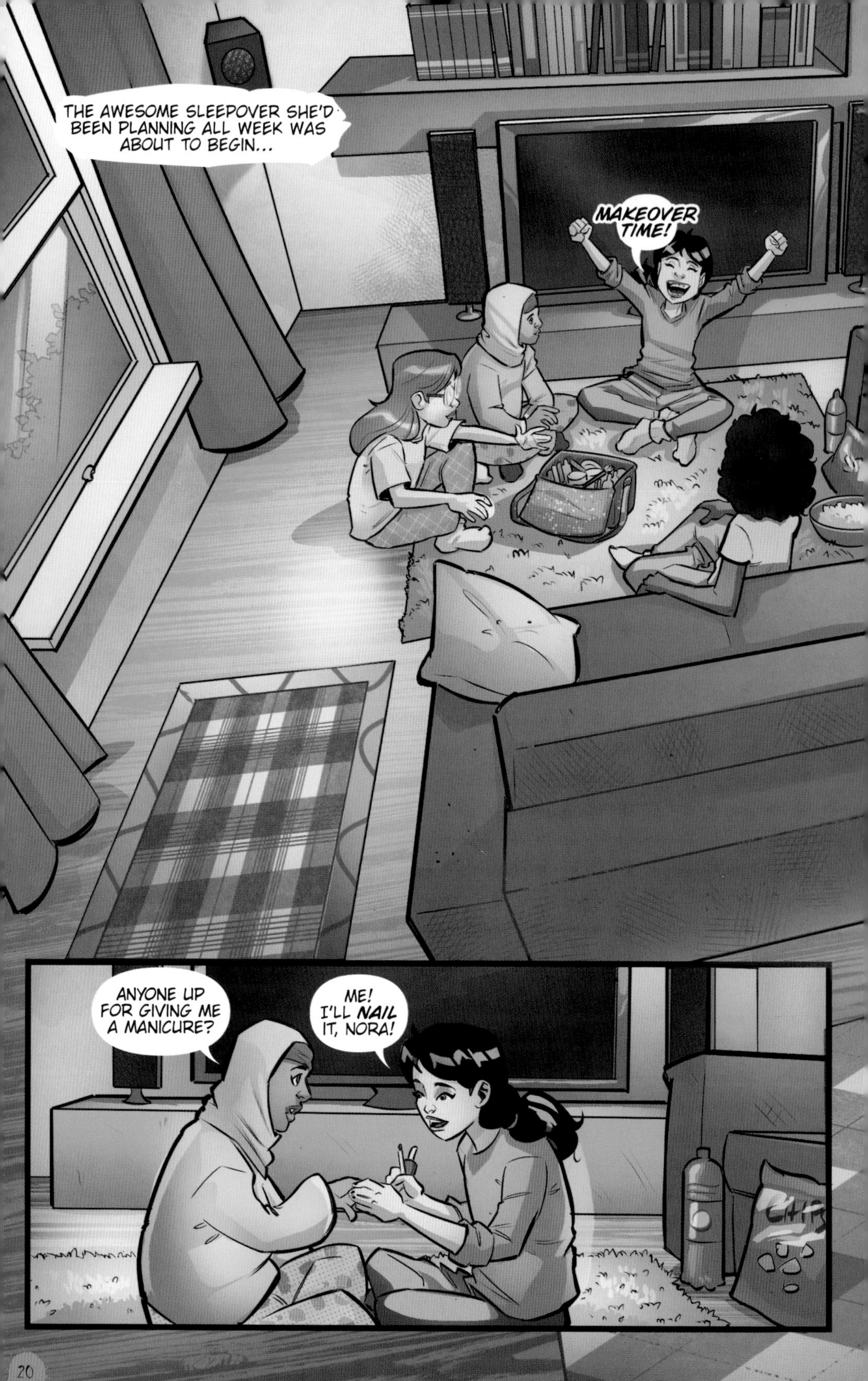

THE AWESOME SLEEPOVER SHE'D BEEN PLANNING ALL WEEK WAS ABOUT TO BEGIN...
MAKEOVER TIME!
ANYONE UP FOR GIVING ME A MANICURE?
ME! I'LL **NAIL** IT, NORA!
CHIPS

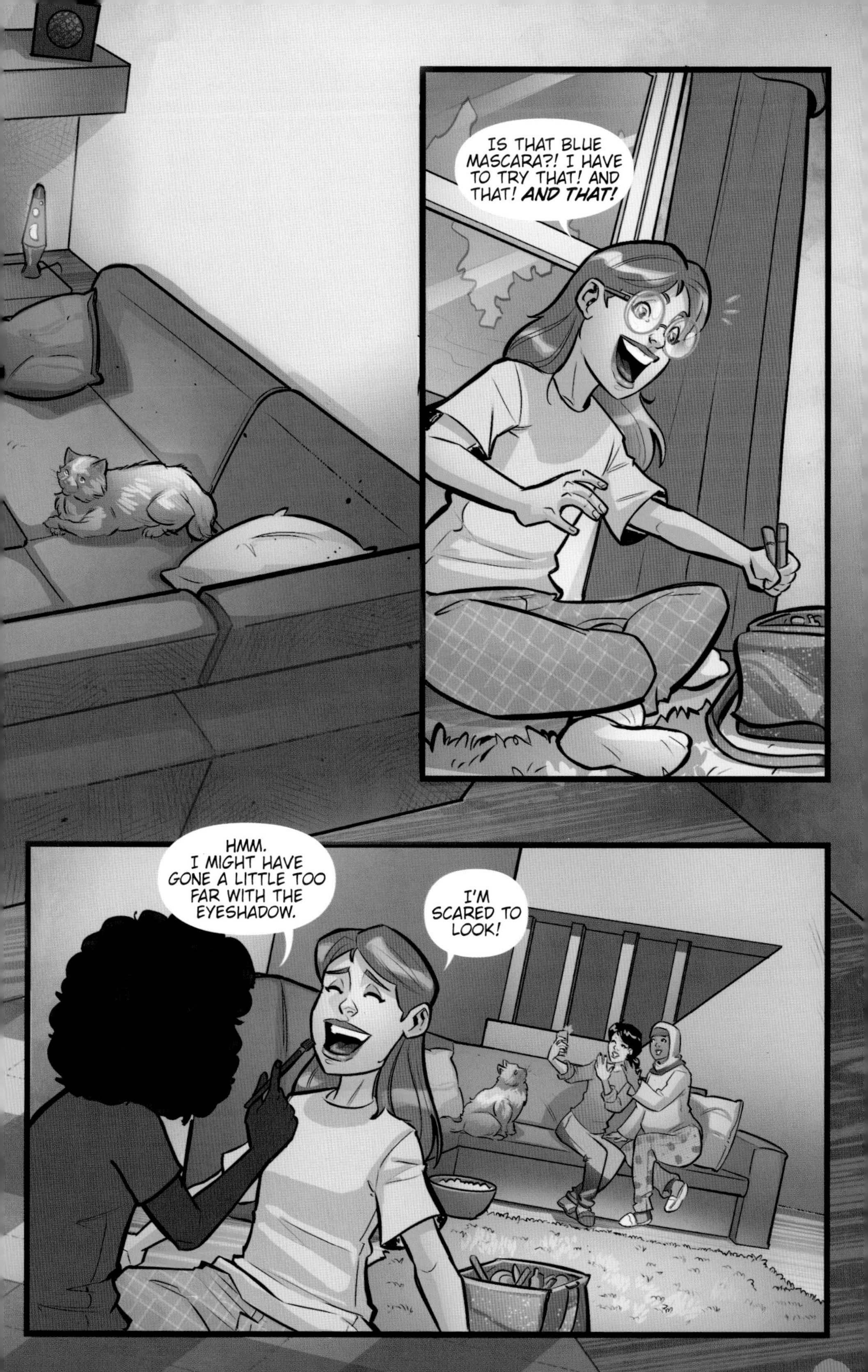
IS THAT BLUE MASCARA?! I HAVE TO TRY THAT! AND THAT! AND THAT!
HMM. I MIGHT HAVE GONE A LITTLE TOO FAR WITH THE EYESHADOW.
I'M SCARED TO LOOK!

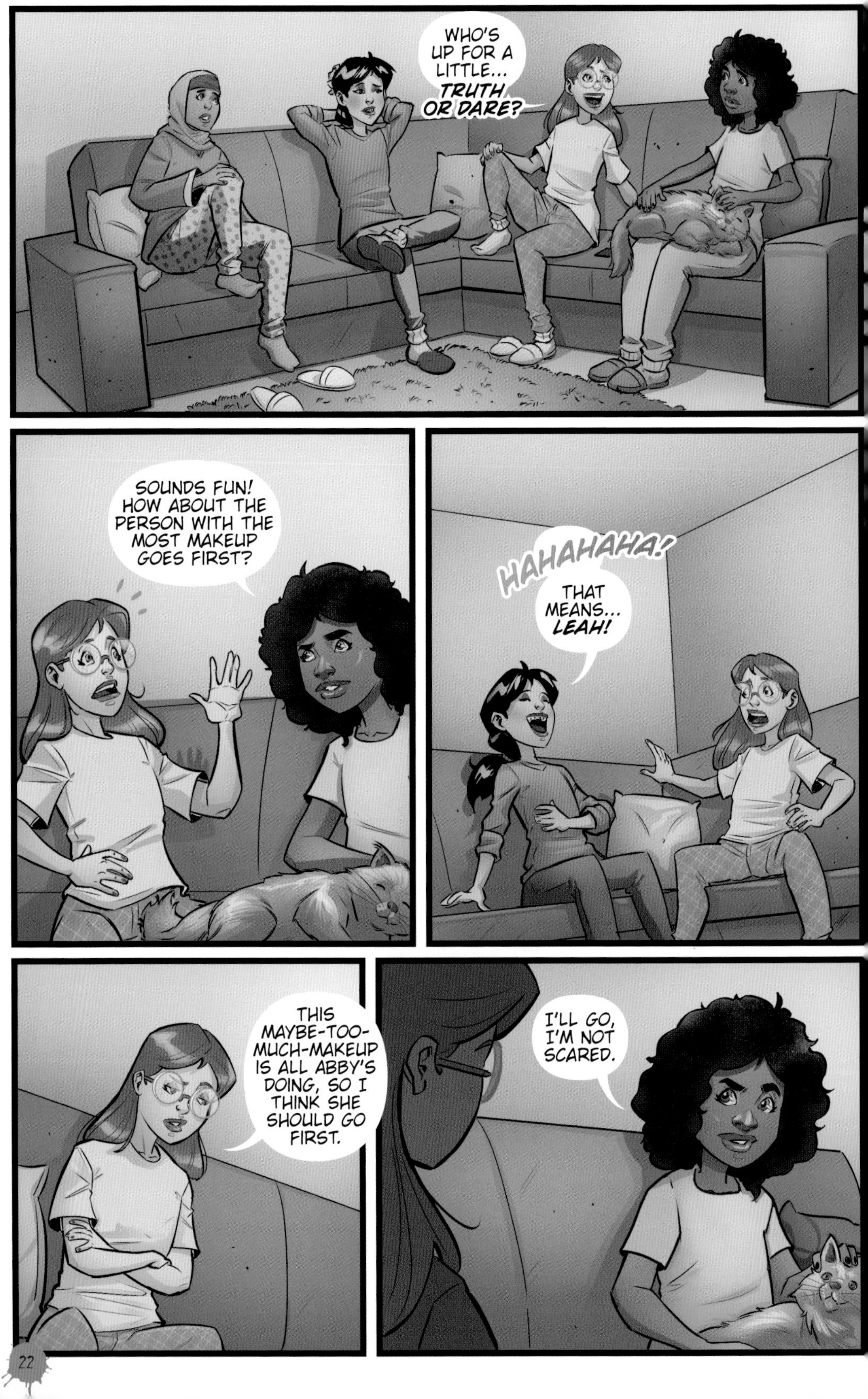
WHO'S UP FOR A LITTLE... TRUTH OR DARE?
SOUNDS FUN! HOW ABOUT THE PERSON WITH THE MOST MAKEUP GOES FIRST?
HAHAHAHA!
THAT MEANS... LEAH!
THIS MAYBE-TOO-MUCH-MAKEUP IS ALL ABBY'S DOING, SO I THINK SHE SHOULD GO FIRST.
I'LL GO, I'M NOT SCARED.

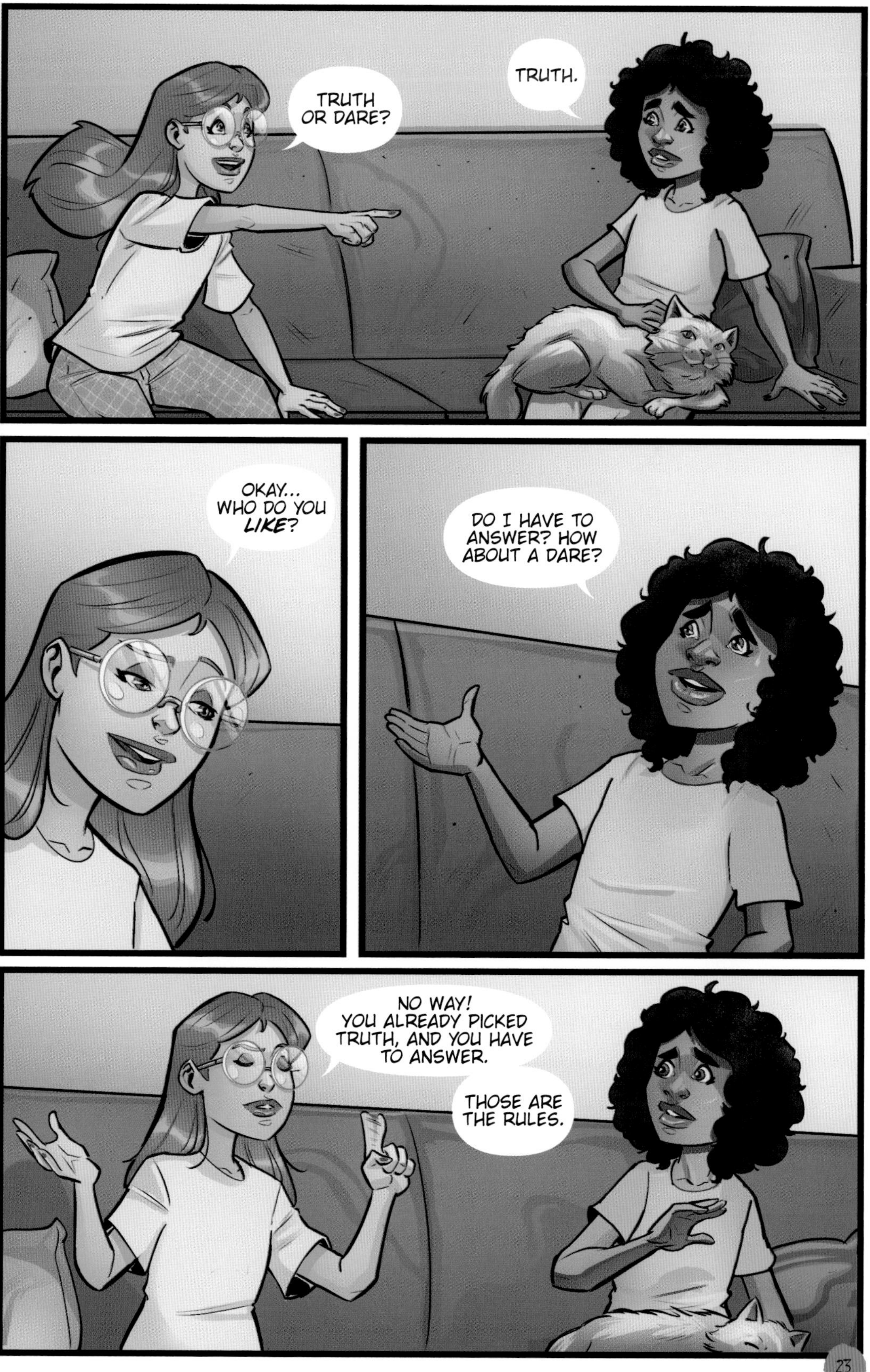
TRUTH OR DARE?
TRUTH.
OKAY... WHO DO YOU *LIKE*?
DO I HAVE TO ANSWER? HOW ABOUT A DARE?
NO WAY! YOU ALREADY PICKED TRUTH, AND YOU HAVE TO ANSWER.
THOSE ARE THE RULES.

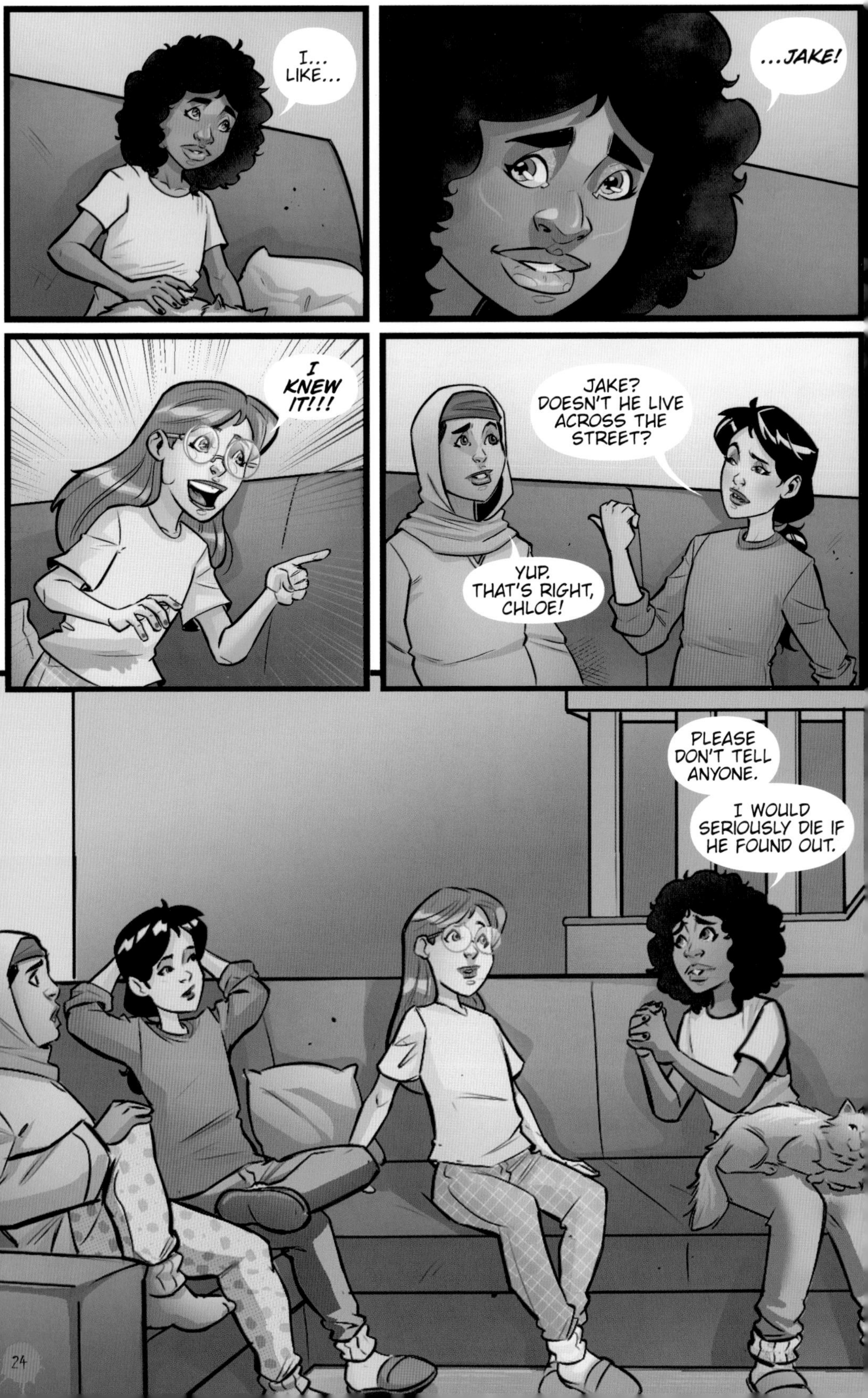
I... LIKE...
...JAKE!
I KNEW IT!!!
JAKE? DOESN'T HE LIVE ACROSS THE STREET?
YUP. THAT'S RIGHT, CHLOE!
PLEASE DON'T TELL ANYONE.
I WOULD SERIOUSLY DIE IF HE FOUND OUT.

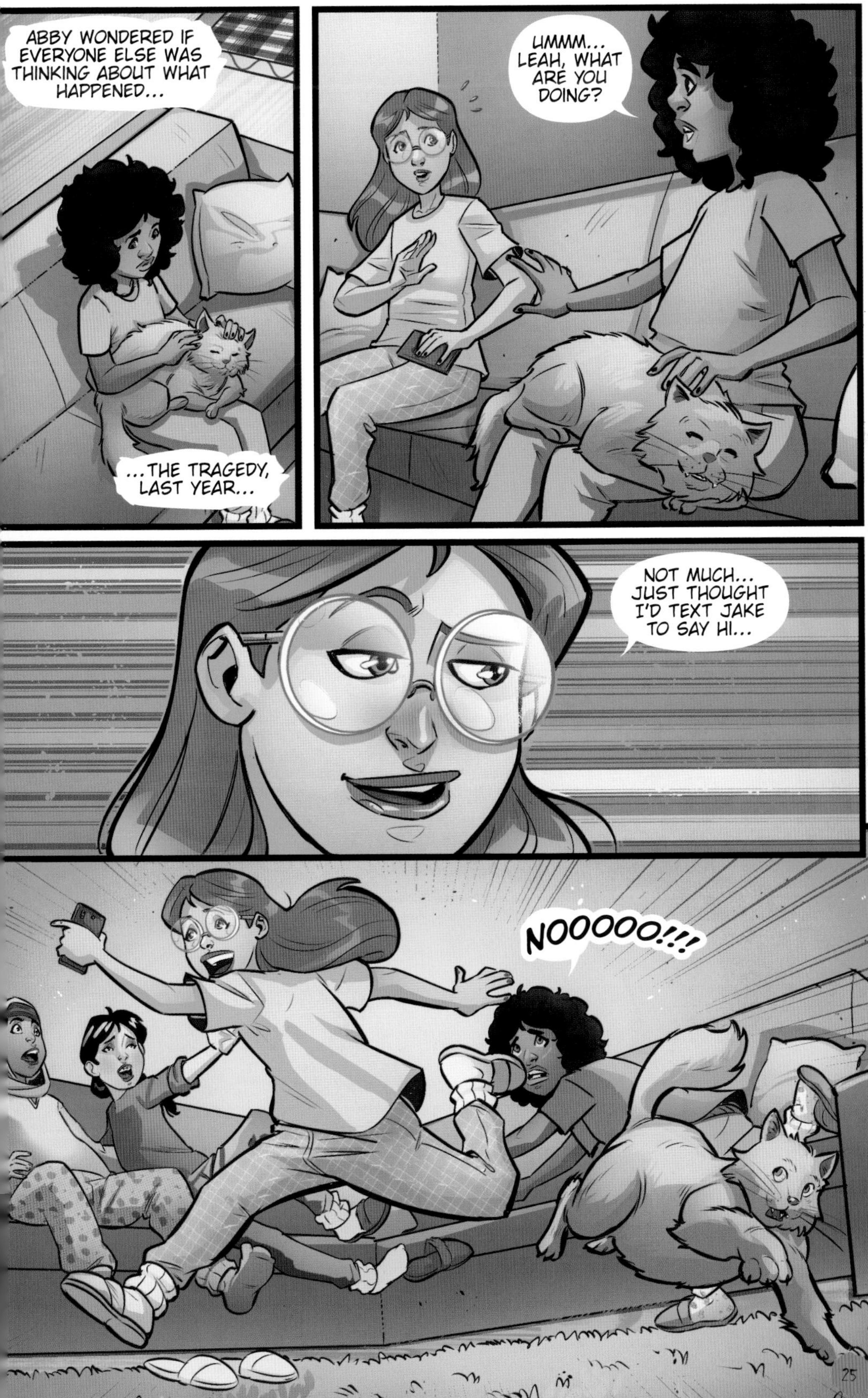
ABBY WONDERED IF EVERYONE ELSE WAS THINKING ABOUT WHAT HAPPENED...
...THE TRAGEDY, LAST YEAR...
UMMM... LEAH, WHAT ARE YOU DOING?
NOT MUCH... JUST THOUGHT I'D TEXT JAKE TO SAY HI...
NOOOOO!!!

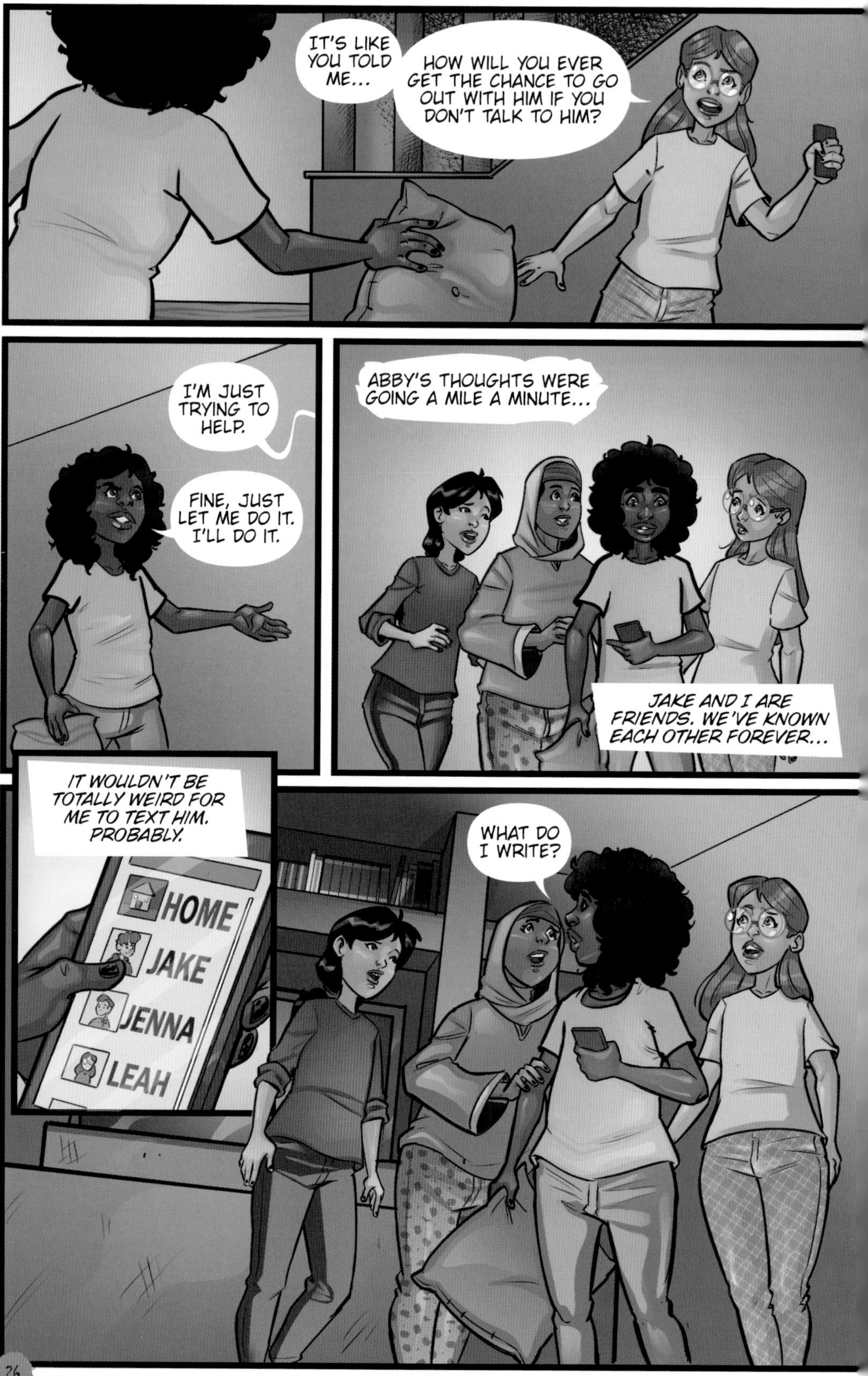

IT'S LIKE YOU TOLD ME...
HOW WILL YOU EVER GET THE CHANCE TO GO OUT WITH HIM IF YOU DON'T TALK TO HIM?
I'M JUST TRYING TO HELP.
FINE, JUST LET ME DO IT. I'LL DO IT.
ABBY'S THOUGHTS WERE GOING A MILE A MINUTE...
JAKE AND I ARE FRIENDS. WE'VE KNOWN EACH OTHER FOREVER...
IT WOULDN'T BE TOTALLY WEIRD FOR ME TO TEXT HIM. PROBABLY.
HOME
JAKE
JENNA
LEAH
WHAT DO I WRITE?

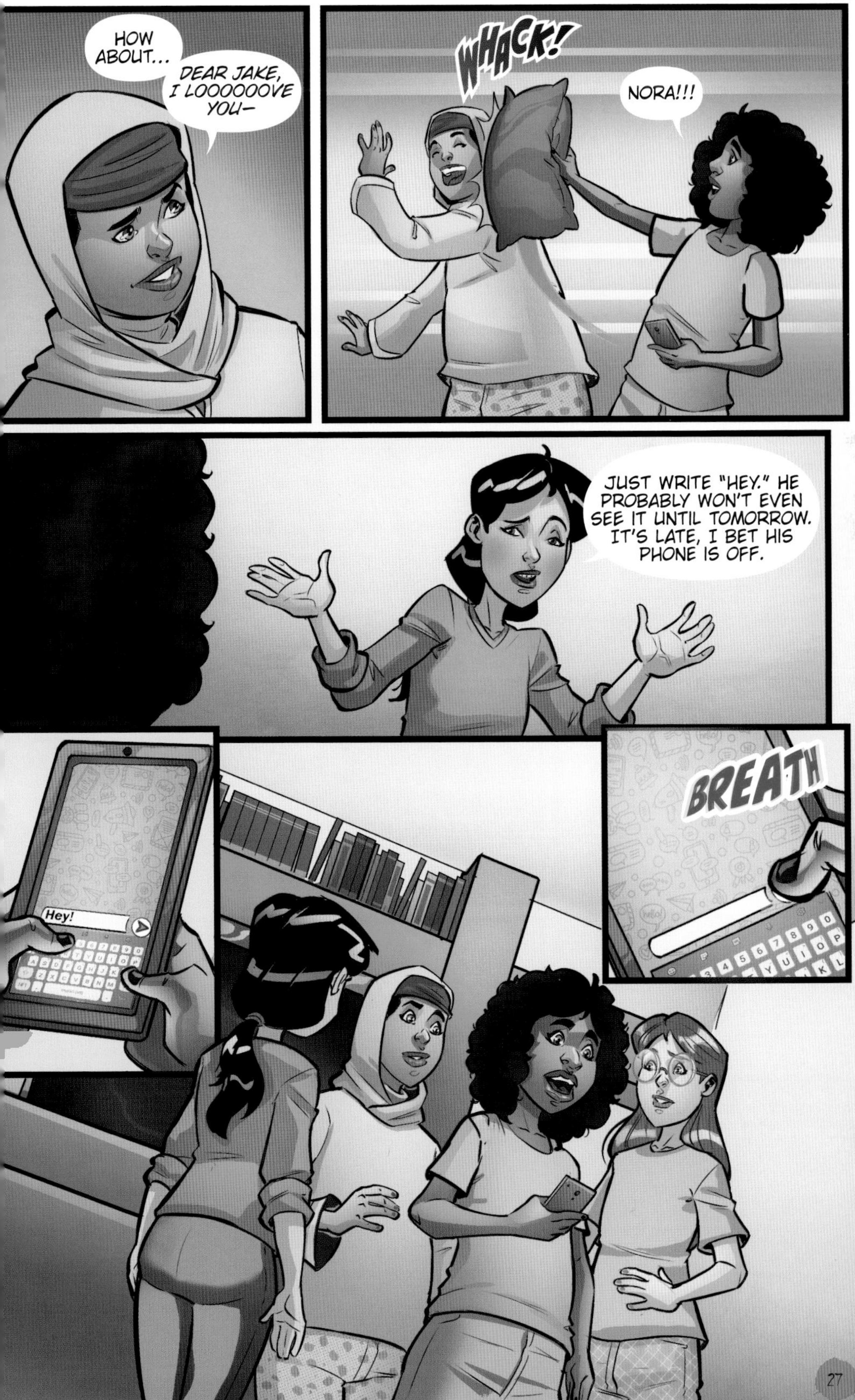

HOW ABOUT...
DEAR JAKE, I LOOOOOOVE YOU—
WHACK!
NORA!!!
JUST WRITE "HEY." HE PROBABLY WON'T EVEN SEE IT UNTIL TOMORROW. IT'S LATE, I BET HIS PHONE IS OFF.
Hey!
BREATH

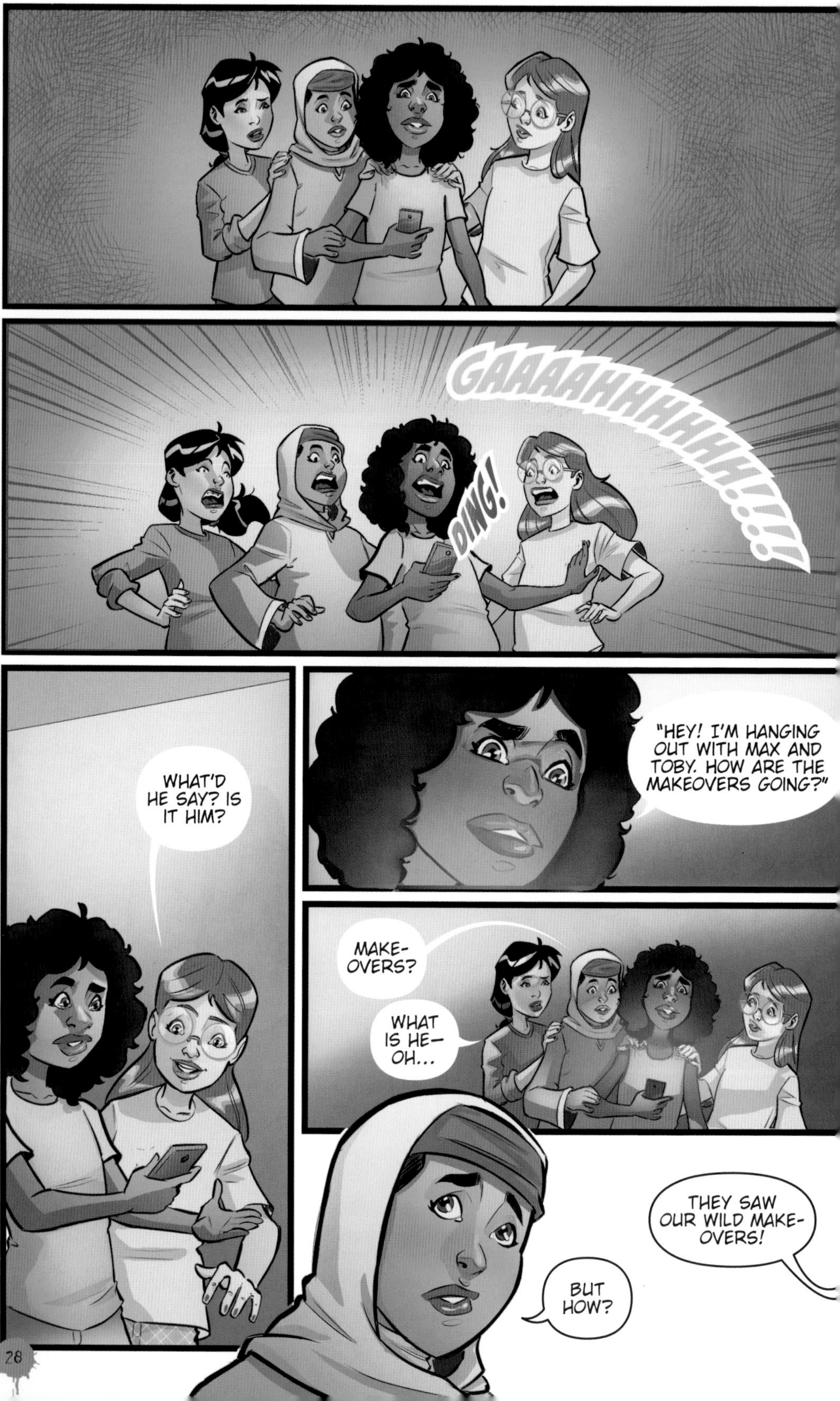
GAAAAHHHHH!!!!!
DING!
WHAT'D HE SAY? IS IT HIM?
"HEY! I'M HANGING OUT WITH MAX AND TOBY. HOW ARE THE MAKEOVERS GOING?"
MAKE-OVERS?
WHAT IS HE— OH...
THEY SAW OUR WILD MAKE-OVERS!
BUT HOW?

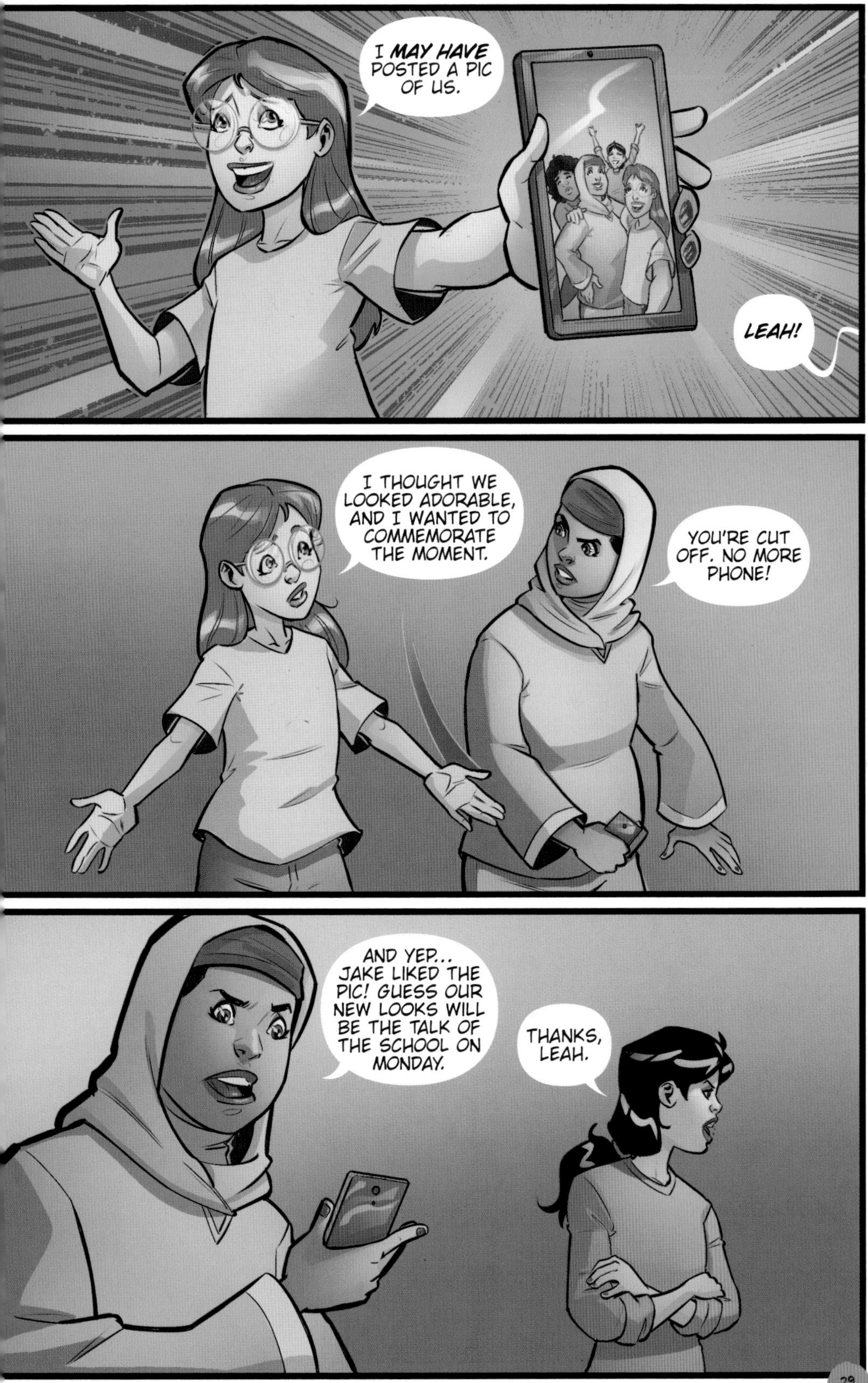
I MAY HAVE POSTED A PIC OF US.
LEAH!
I THOUGHT WE LOOKED ADORABLE, AND I WANTED TO COMMEMORATE THE MOMENT.
YOU'RE CUT OFF. NO MORE PHONE!
AND YEP... JAKE LIKED THE PIC! GUESS OUR NEW LOOKS WILL BE THE TALK OF THE SCHOOL ON MONDAY.
THANKS, LEAH.

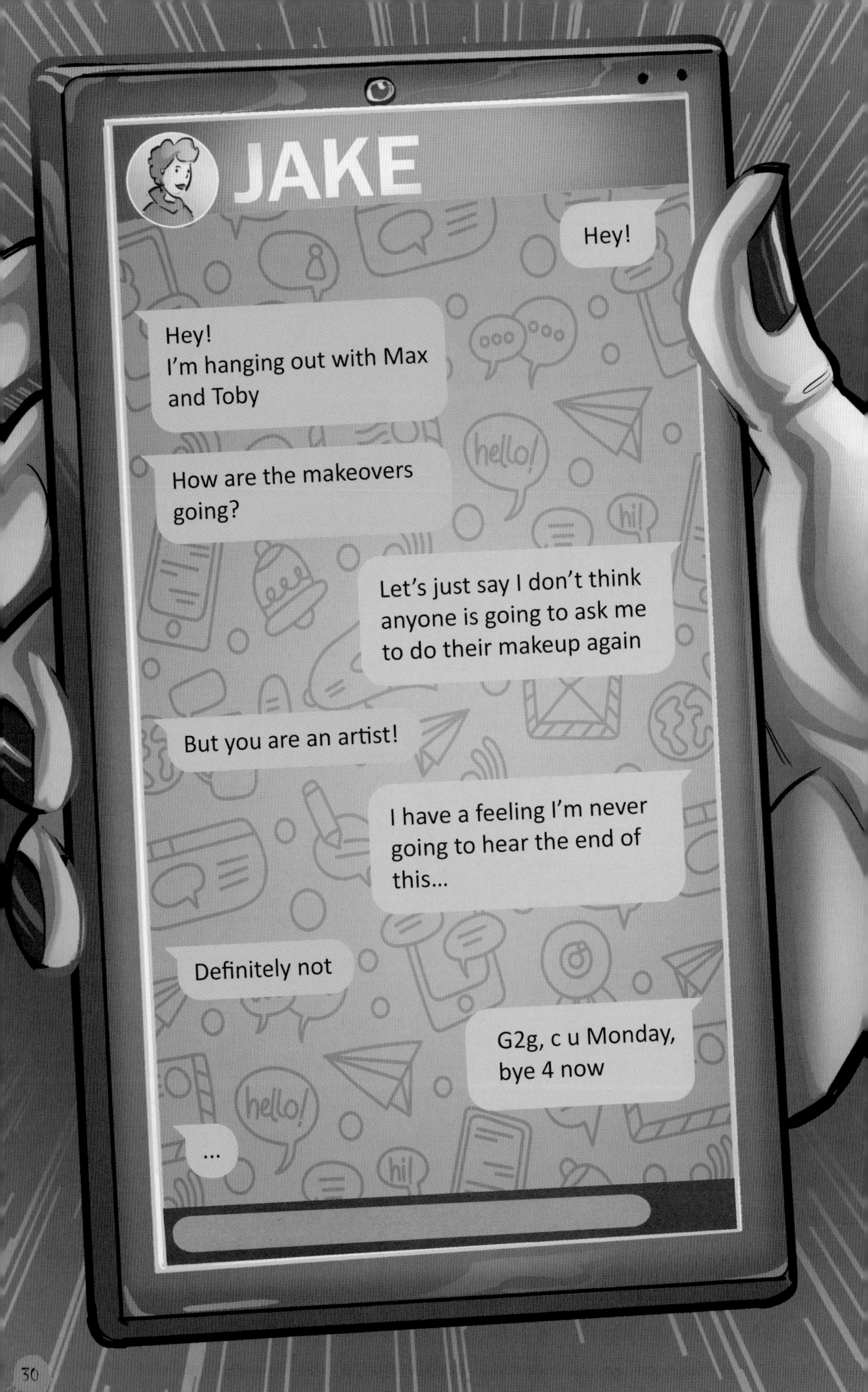
JAKE
Hey!
Hey!
I'm hanging out with Max and Toby
How are the makeovers going?
Let's just say I don't think anyone is going to ask me to do their makeup again
But you are an artist!
I have a feeling I'm never going to hear the end of this...
Definitely not
G2g, c u Monday, bye 4 now
...
hello!
hi!

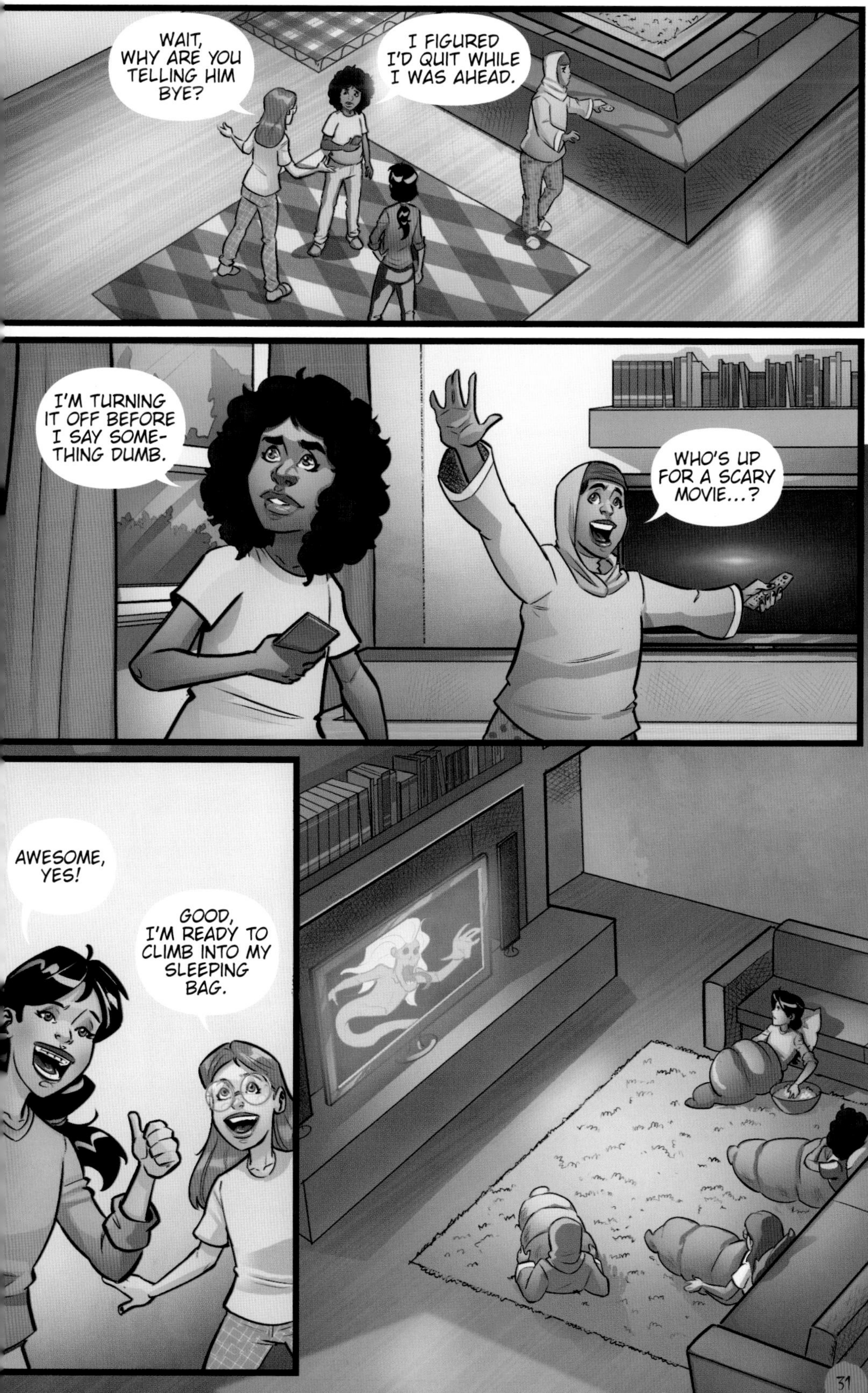
WAIT, WHY ARE YOU TELLING HIM BYE?
I FIGURED I'D QUIT WHILE I WAS AHEAD.
I'M TURNING IT OFF BEFORE I SAY SOME-THING DUMB.
WHO'S UP FOR A SCARY MOVIE...?
AWESOME, YES!
GOOD, I'M READY TO CLIMB INTO MY SLEEPING BAG.

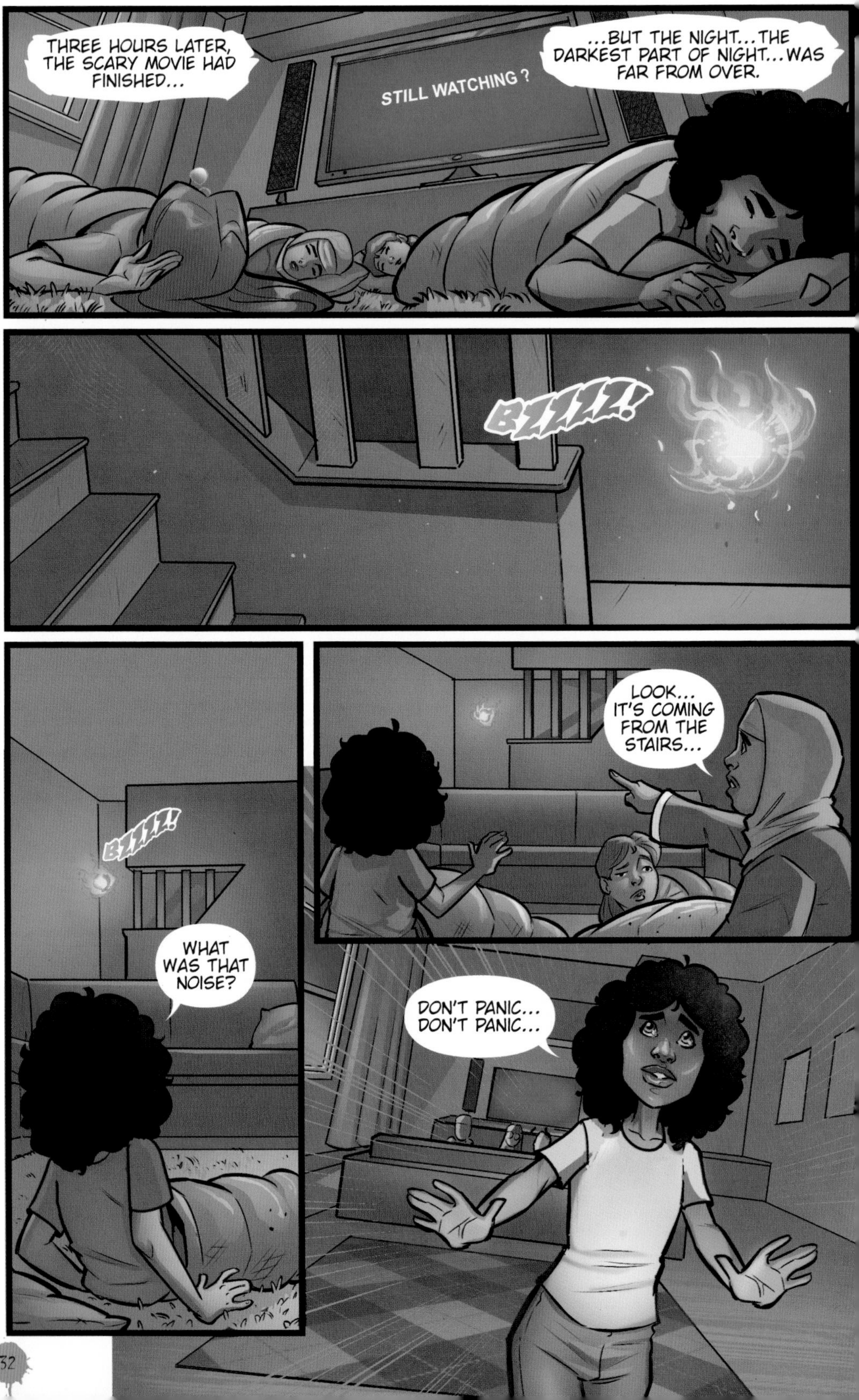
THREE HOURS LATER, THE SCARY MOVIE HAD FINISHED...
STILL WATCHING ?
...BUT THE NIGHT...THE DARKEST PART OF NIGHT...WAS FAR FROM OVER.
BZZZZ!
BZZZZ!
WHAT WAS THAT NOISE?
LOOK... IT'S COMING FROM THE STAIRS...
DON'T PANIC... DON'T PANIC...

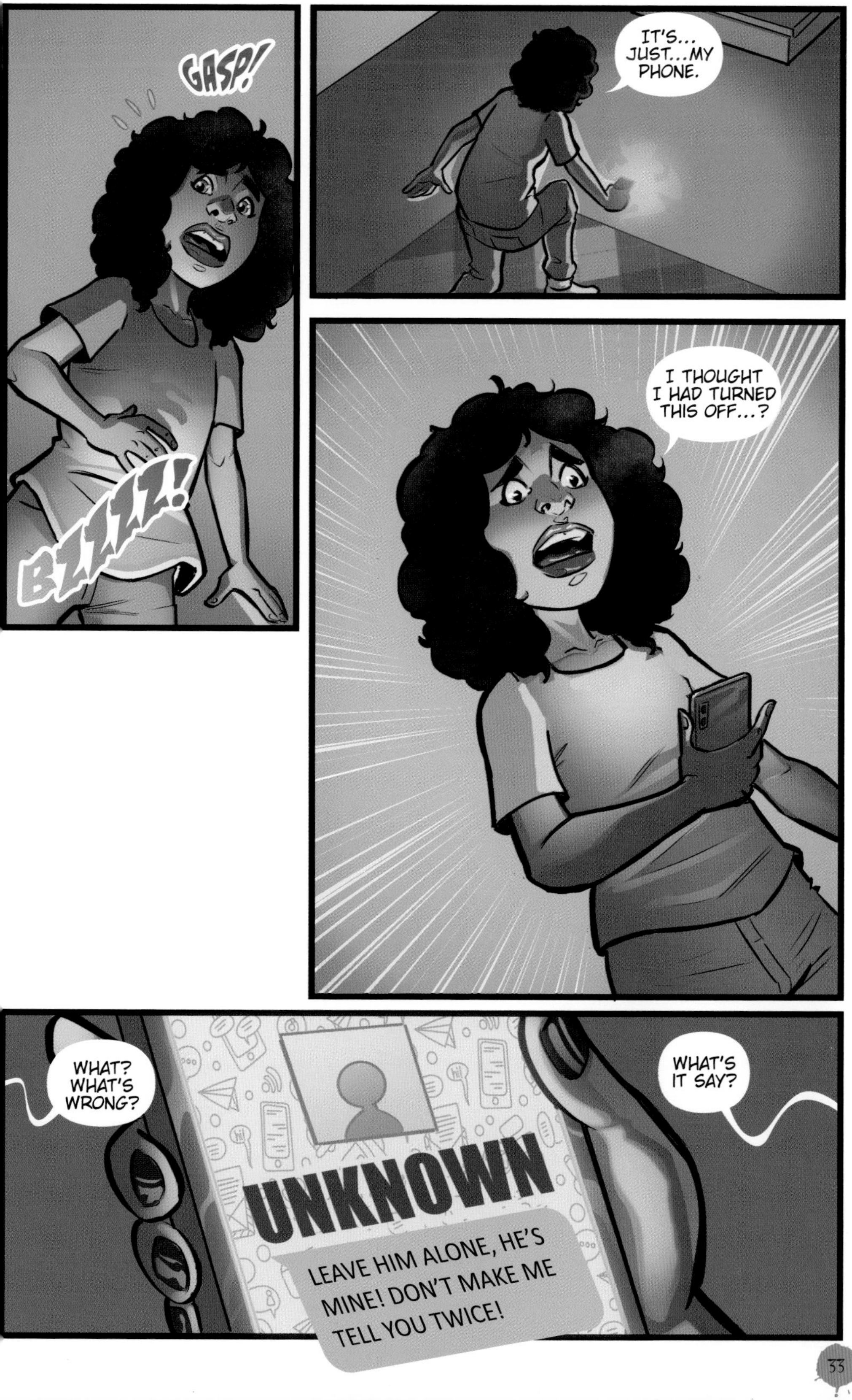
GASP!
BZZZZZ!
IT'S... JUST...MY PHONE.
I THOUGHT I HAD TURNED THIS OFF...?
WHAT? WHAT'S WRONG?
WHAT'S IT SAY?
UNKNOWN
LEAVE HIM ALONE, HE'S MINE! DON'T MAKE ME TELL YOU TWICE!

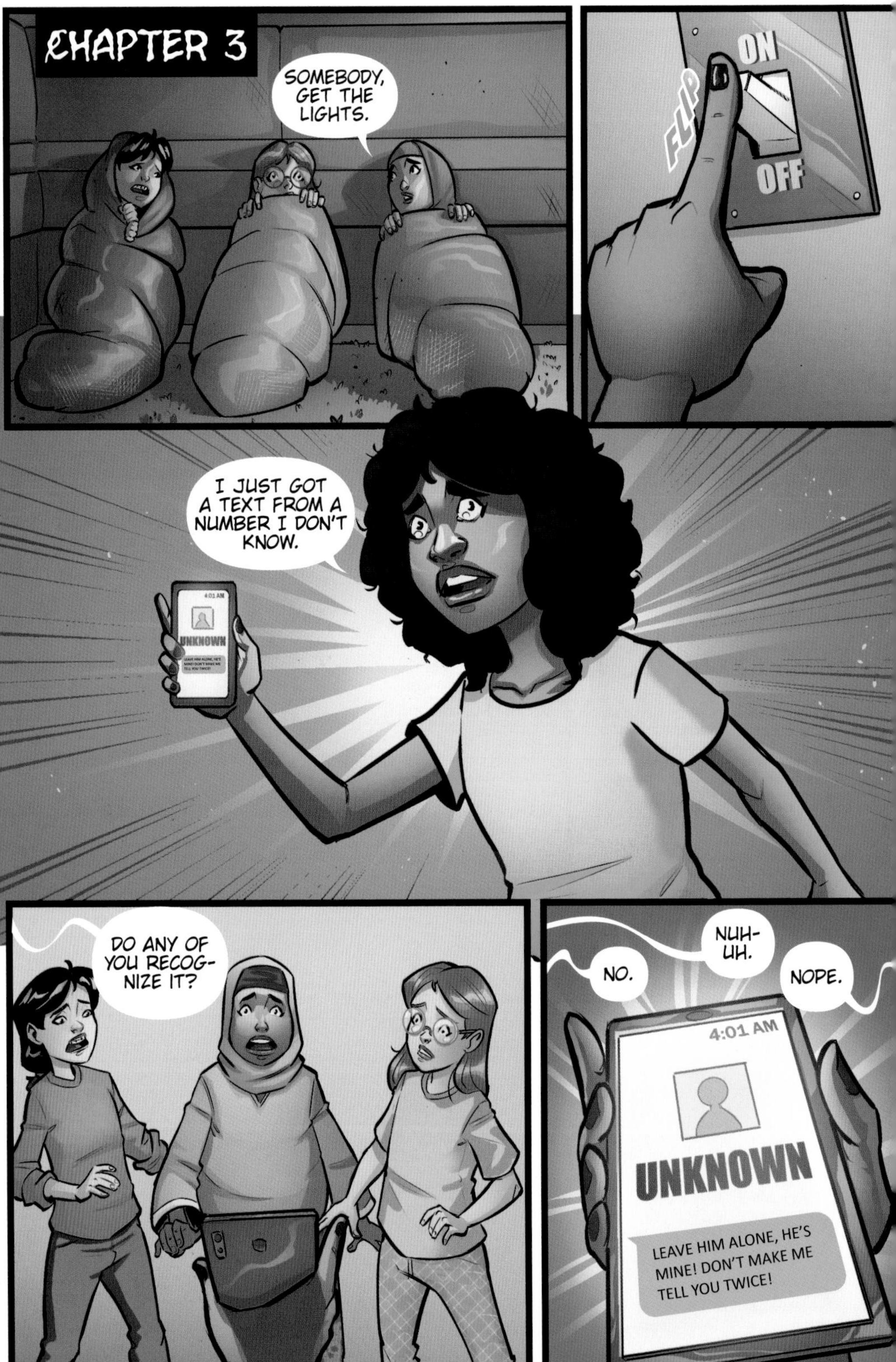
CHAPTER 3
SOMEBODY, GET THE LIGHTS.
FLIP
ON
OFF
I JUST GOT A TEXT FROM A NUMBER I DON'T KNOW.
4:01 AM
UNKNOWN
LEAVE HIM ALONE, HE'S MINE! DON'T MAKE ME TELL YOU TWICE!
DO ANY OF YOU RECOG-NIZE IT?
NO.
NUH-UH.
NOPE.
4:01 AM
UNKNOWN
LEAVE HIM ALONE, HE'S MINE! DON'T MAKE ME TELL YOU TWICE!

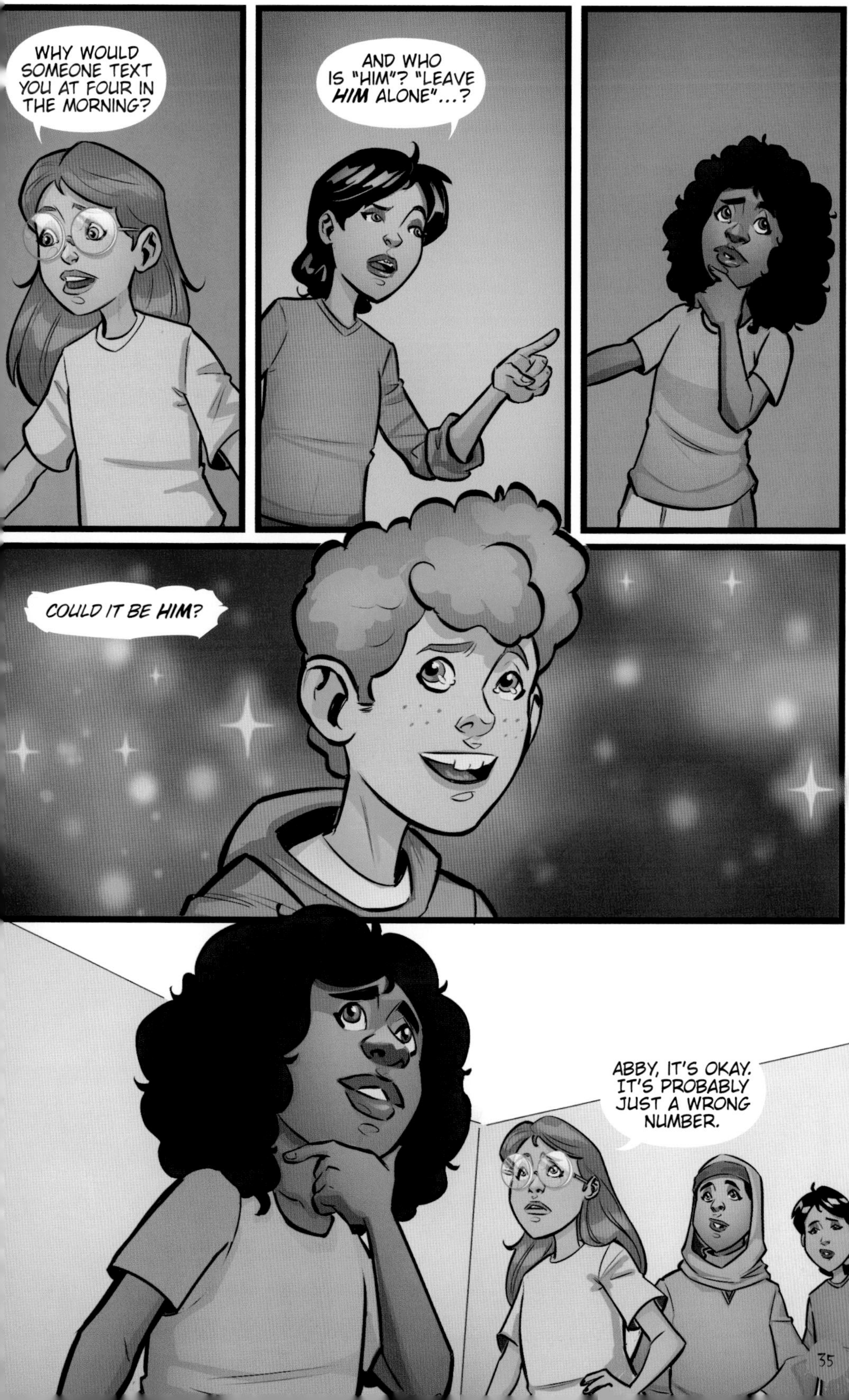
WHY WOULD SOMEONE TEXT YOU AT FOUR IN THE MORNING?
AND WHO IS "HIM"? "LEAVE *HIM* ALONE"...?
*COULD IT BE **HIM**?*
ABBY, IT'S OKAY. IT'S PROBABLY JUST A WRONG NUMBER.

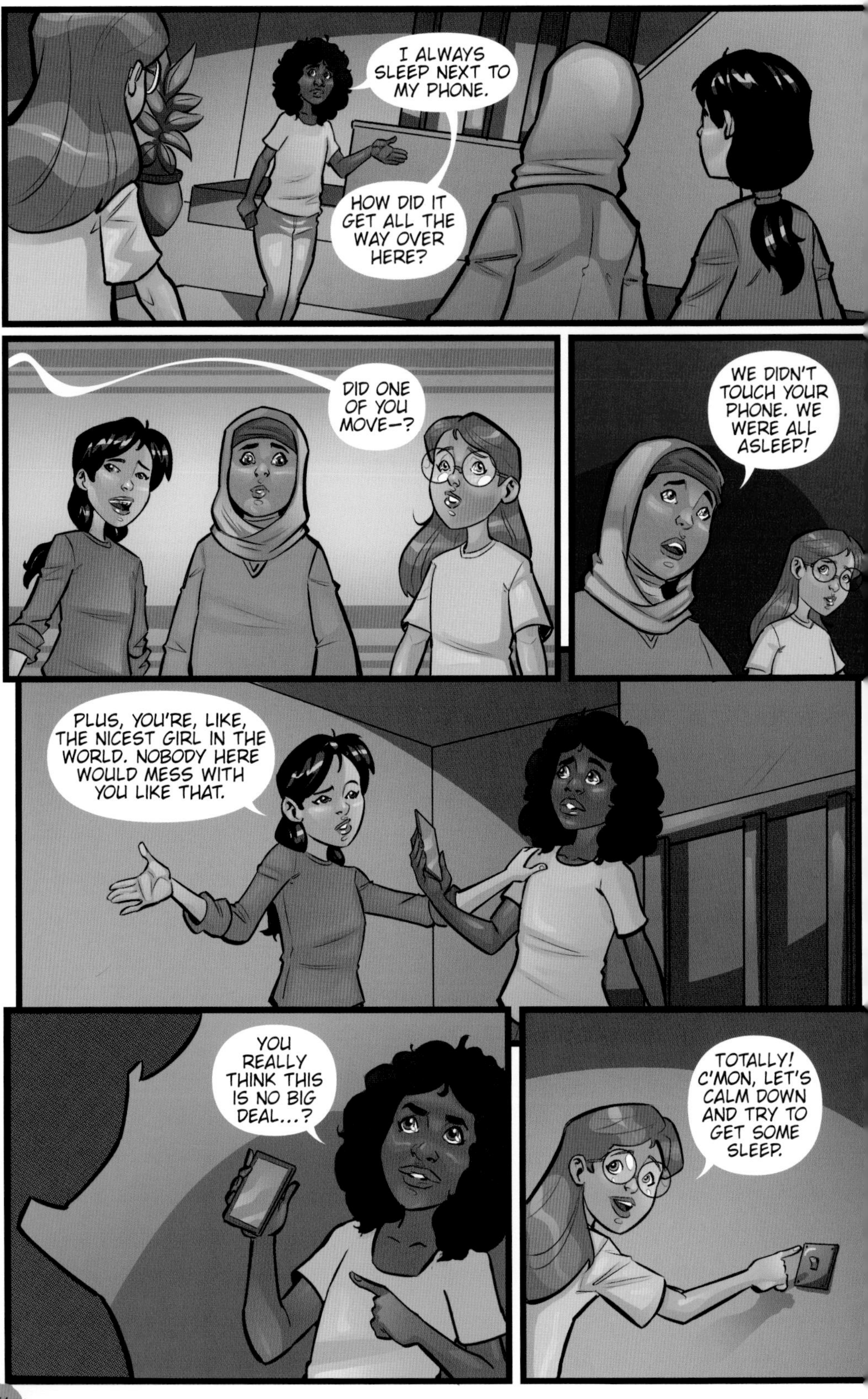
I ALWAYS SLEEP NEXT TO MY PHONE.
HOW DID IT GET ALL THE WAY OVER HERE?
DID ONE OF YOU MOVE—?
WE DIDN'T TOUCH YOUR PHONE. WE WERE ALL ASLEEP!
PLUS, YOU'RE, LIKE, THE NICEST GIRL IN THE WORLD. NOBODY HERE WOULD MESS WITH YOU LIKE THAT.
YOU REALLY THINK THIS IS NO BIG DEAL...?
TOTALLY! C'MON, LET'S CALM DOWN AND TRY TO GET SOME SLEEP.

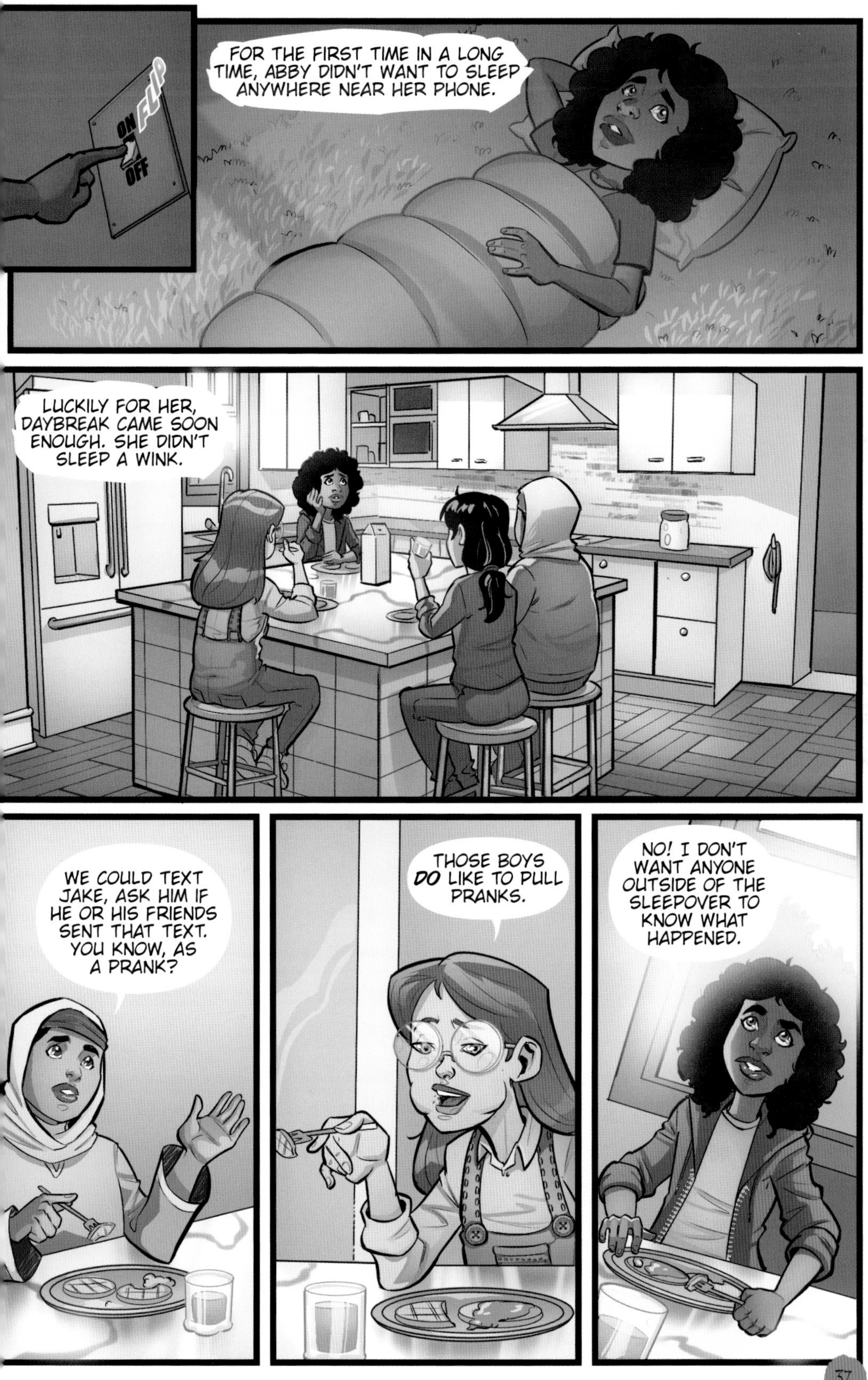
ON
FLIP
OFF
FOR THE FIRST TIME IN A LONG TIME, ABBY DIDN'T WANT TO SLEEP ANYWHERE NEAR HER PHONE.
LUCKILY FOR HER, DAYBREAK CAME SOON ENOUGH. SHE DIDN'T SLEEP A WINK.
WE COULD TEXT JAKE, ASK HIM IF HE OR HIS FRIENDS SENT THAT TEXT. YOU KNOW, AS A PRANK?
THOSE BOYS ***DO*** LIKE TO PULL PRANKS.
NO! I DON'T WANT ANYONE OUTSIDE OF THE SLEEPOVER TO KNOW WHAT HAPPENED.

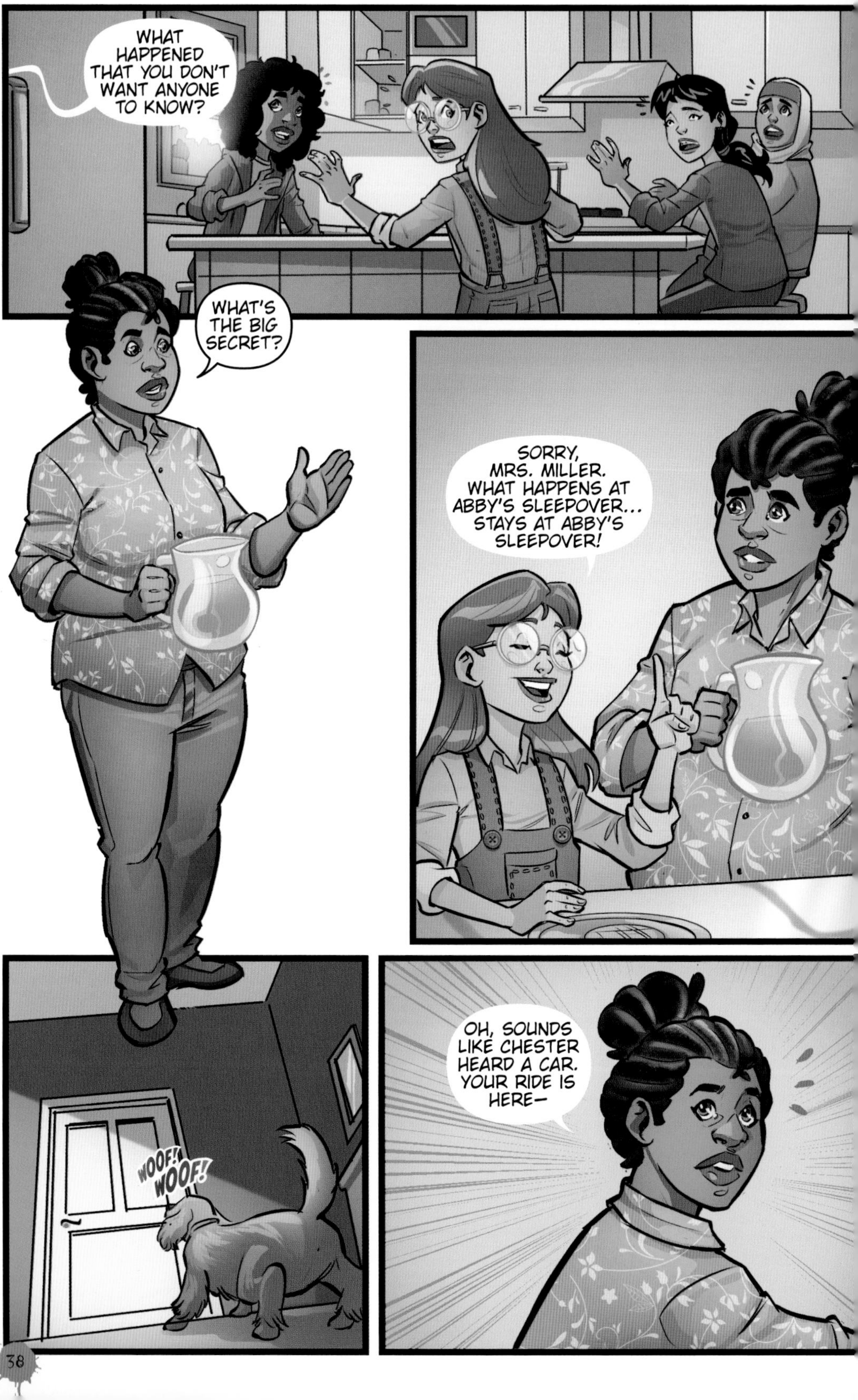
WHAT HAPPENED THAT YOU DON'T WANT ANYONE TO KNOW?
WHAT'S THE BIG SECRET?
SORRY, MRS. MILLER. WHAT HAPPENS AT ABBY'S SLEEPOVER... STAYS AT ABBY'S SLEEPOVER!
WOOF! WOOF!
OH, SOUNDS LIKE CHESTER HEARD A CAR. YOUR RIDE IS HERE—

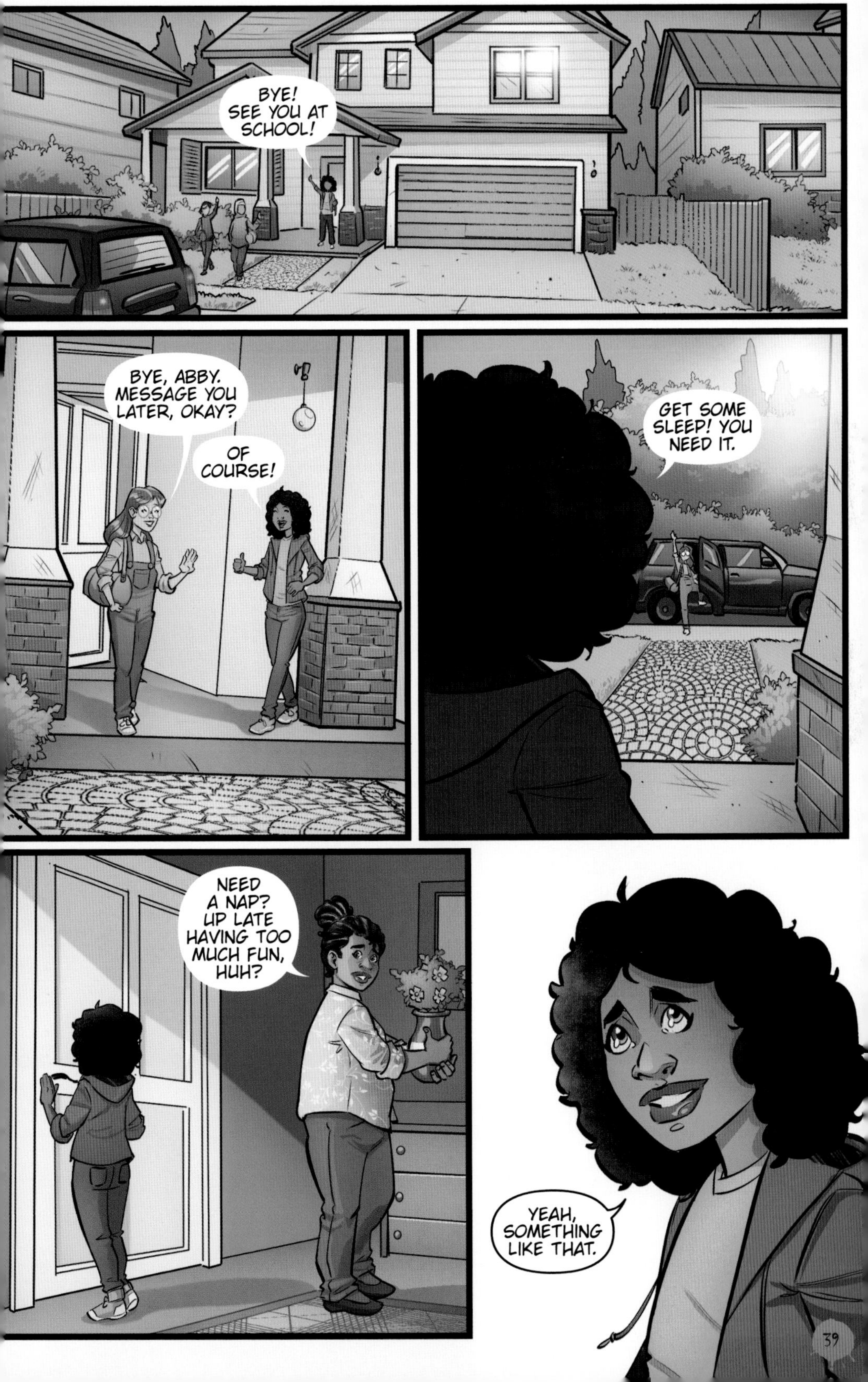
BYE! SEE YOU AT SCHOOL!
BYE, ABBY. MESSAGE YOU LATER, OKAY?
OF COURSE!
GET SOME SLEEP! YOU NEED IT.
NEED A NAP? UP LATE HAVING TOO MUCH FUN, HUH?
YEAH, SOMETHING LIKE THAT.

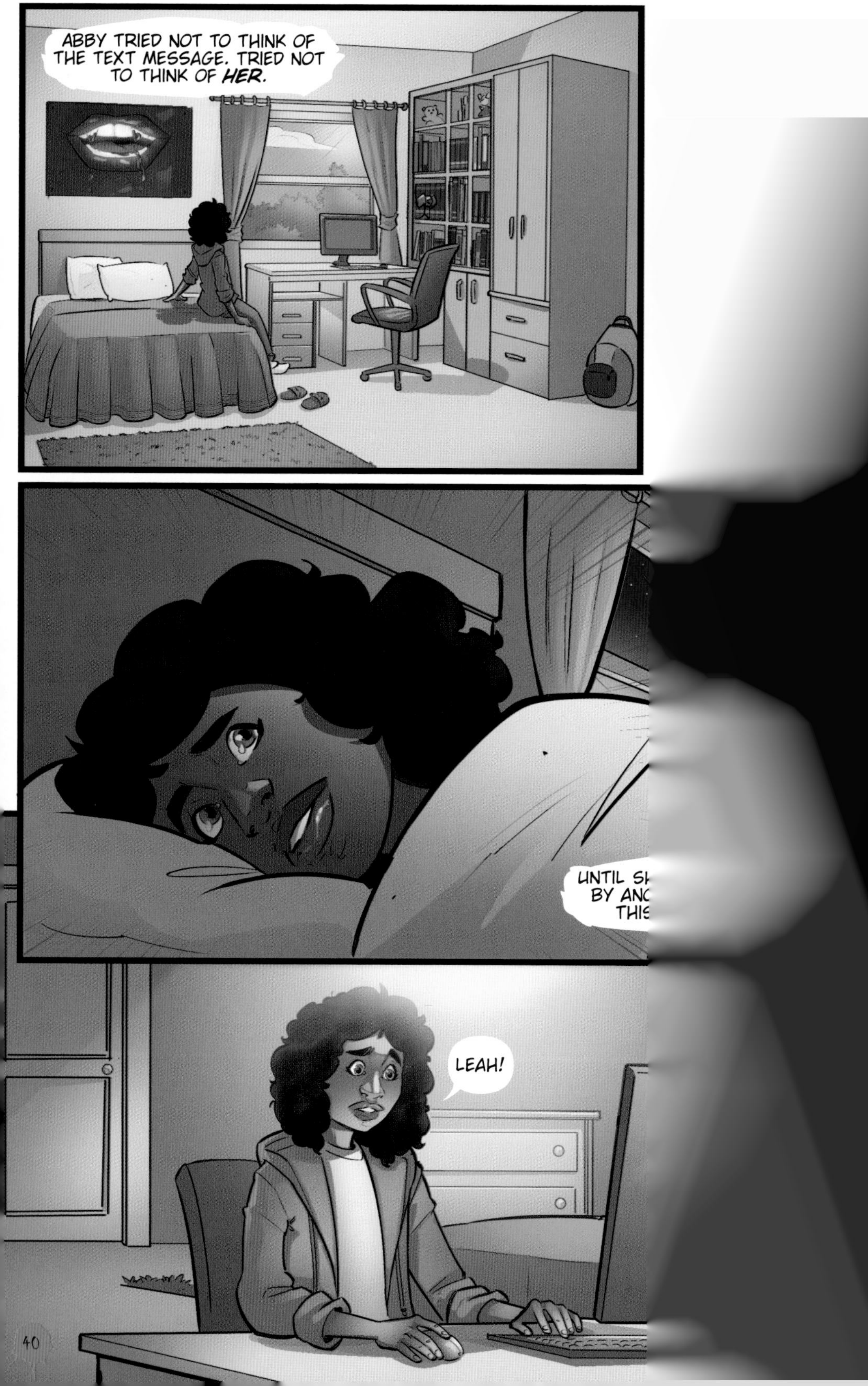
ABBY TRIED NOT TO THINK OF THE TEXT MESSAGE. TRIED NOT TO THINK OF *HER*.
UNTIL SH
BY ANO
THIS
LEAH!

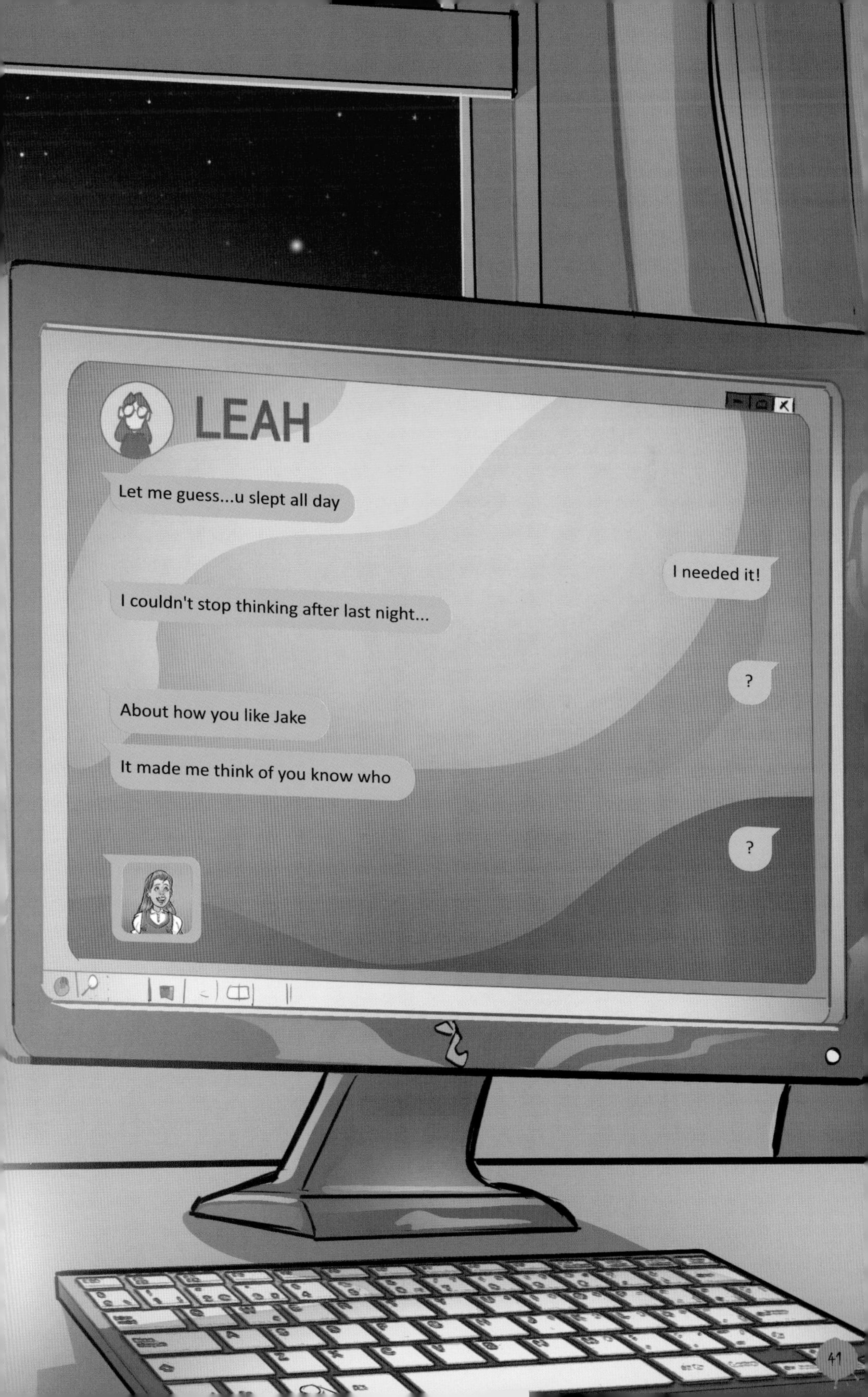
LEAH
Let me guess...u slept all day
I needed it!
I couldn't stop thinking after last night...
?
About how you like Jake
It made me think of you know who
?

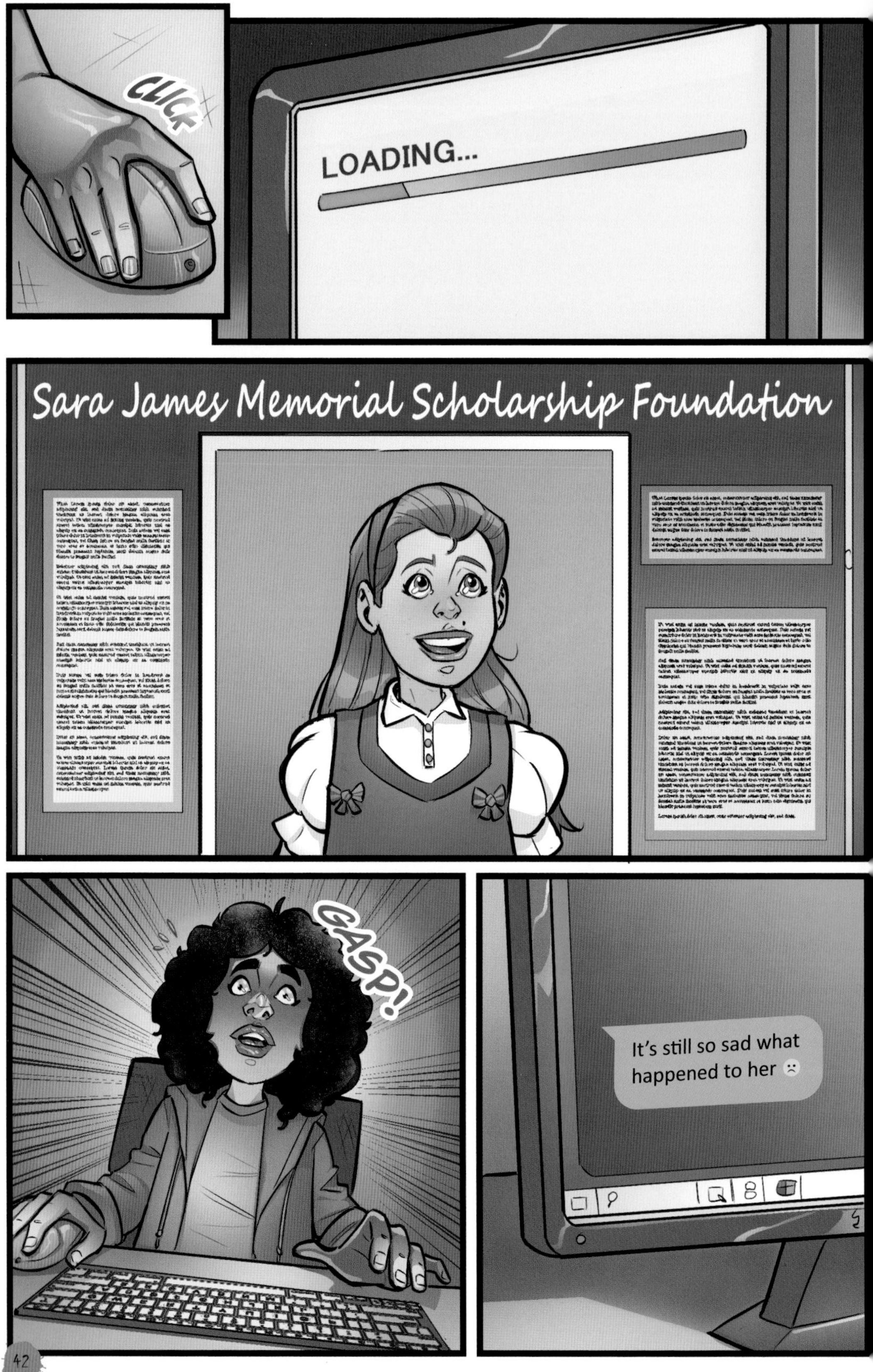
CLICK
LOADING...
Sara James Memorial Scholarship Foundation
GASP!
It's still so sad what happened to her ☹

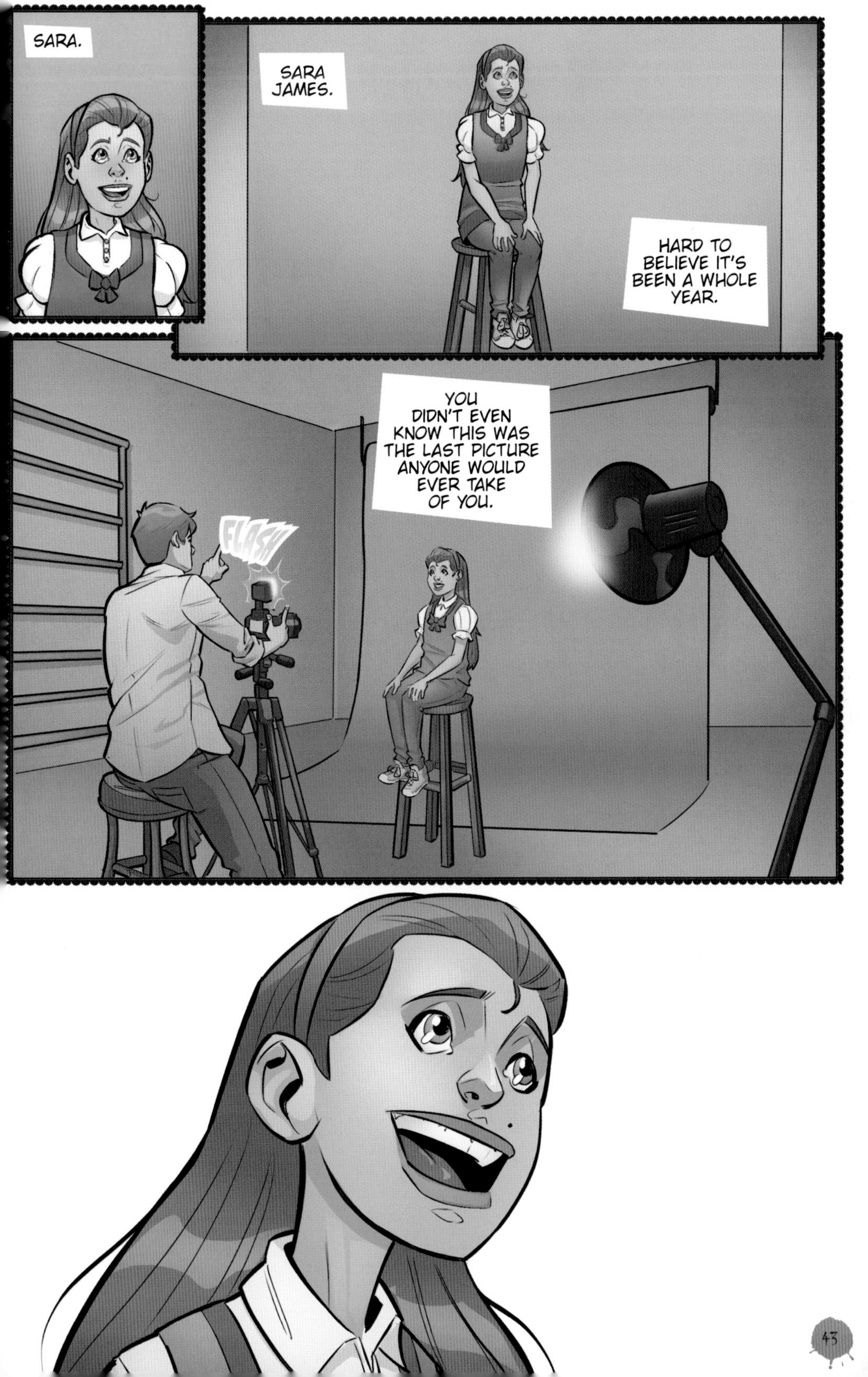
SARA.
SARA JAMES.
HARD TO BELIEVE IT'S BEEN A WHOLE YEAR.
YOU DIDN'T EVEN KNOW THIS WAS THE LAST PICTURE ANYONE WOULD EVER TAKE OF YOU.
FLASH

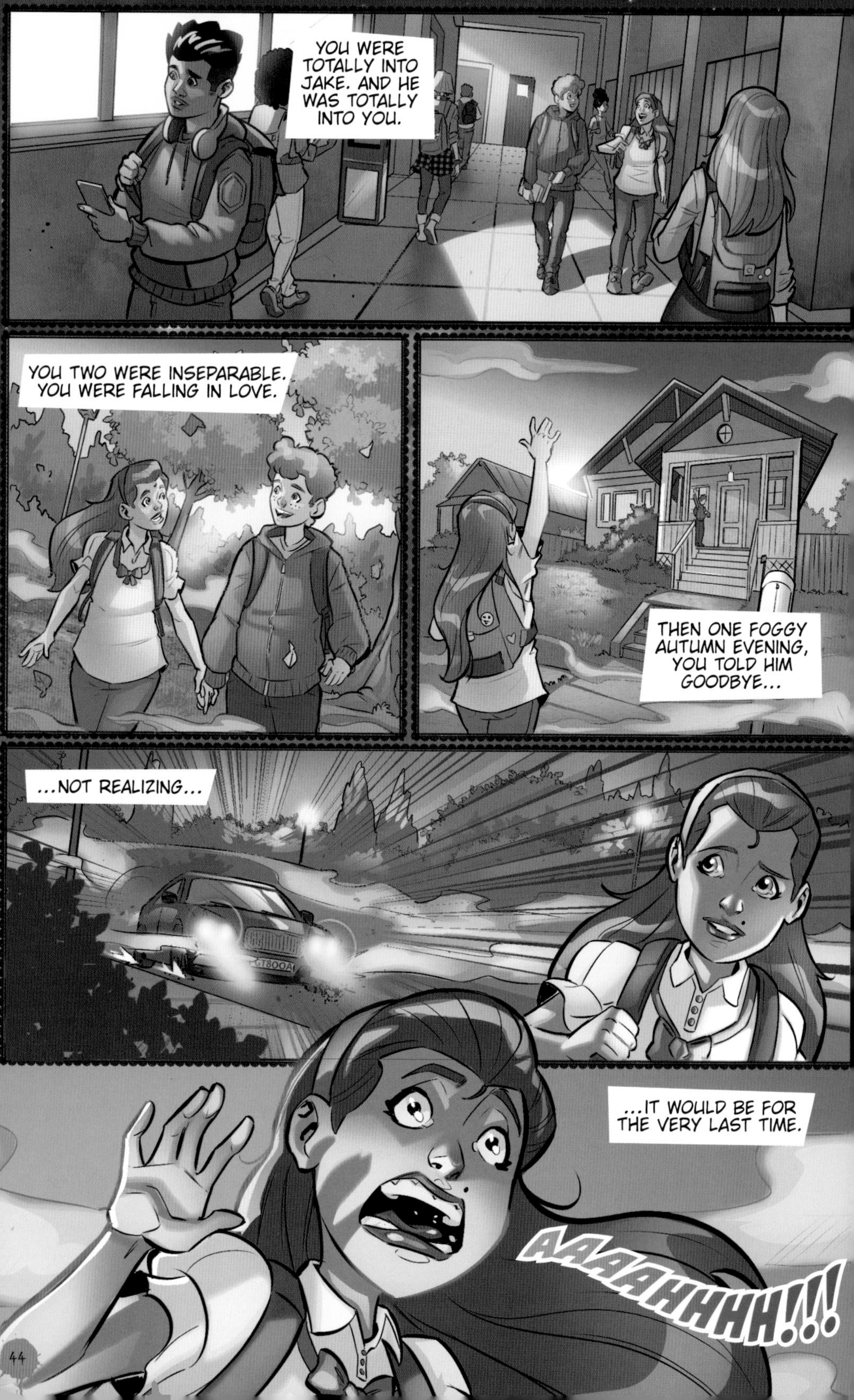
YOU WERE TOTALLY INTO JAKE. AND HE WAS TOTALLY INTO YOU.
YOU TWO WERE INSEPARABLE. YOU WERE FALLING IN LOVE.
THEN ONE FOGGY AUTUMN EVENING, YOU TOLD HIM GOODBYE...
...NOT REALIZING...
GT800A
...IT WOULD BE FOR THE VERY LAST TIME.
AAAAHHHH!!!!

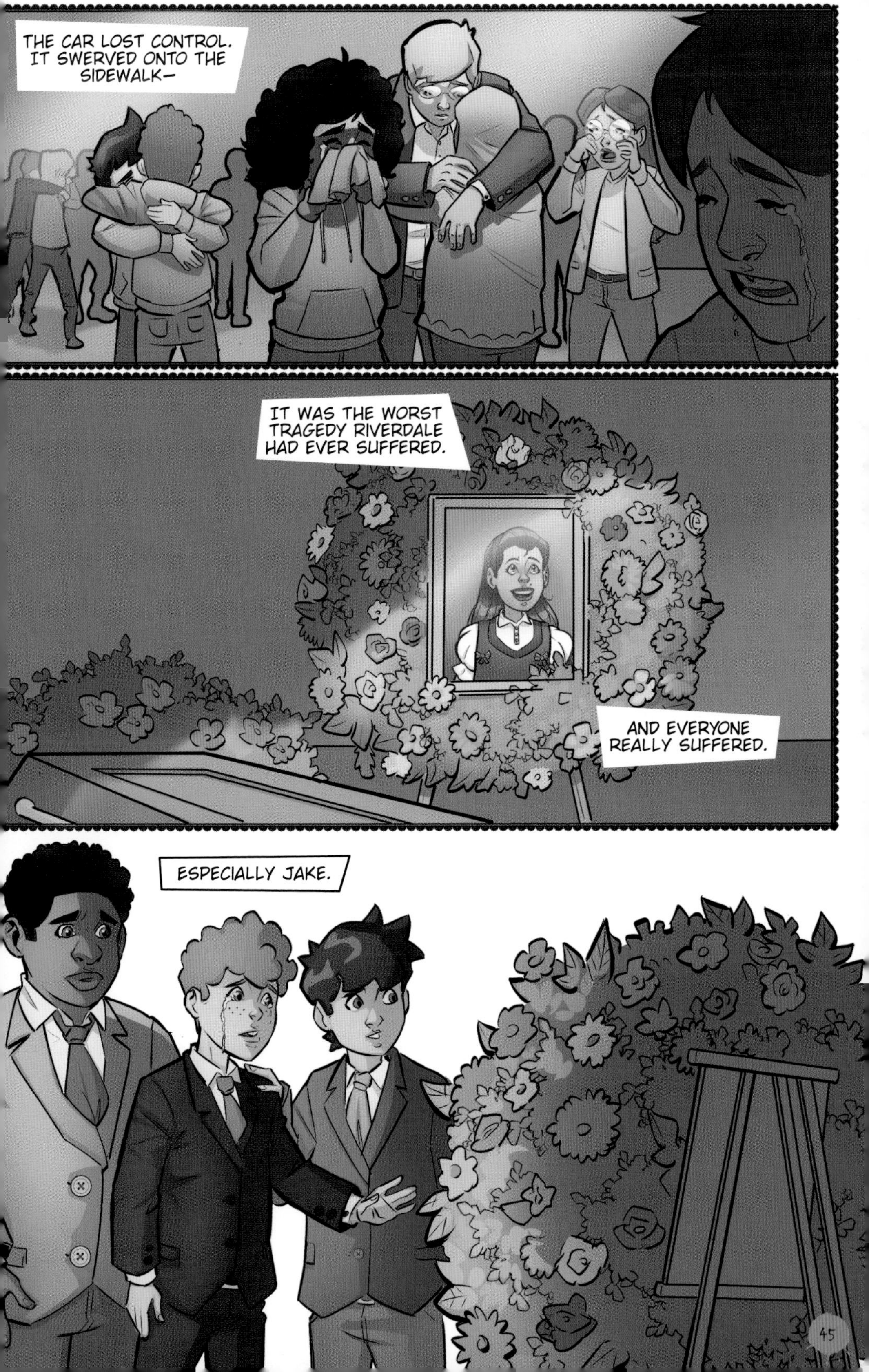
THE CAR LOST CONTROL. IT SWERVED ONTO THE SIDEWALK—
IT WAS THE WORST TRAGEDY RIVERDALE HAD EVER SUFFERED.
AND EVERYONE REALLY SUFFERED.
ESPECIALLY JAKE.

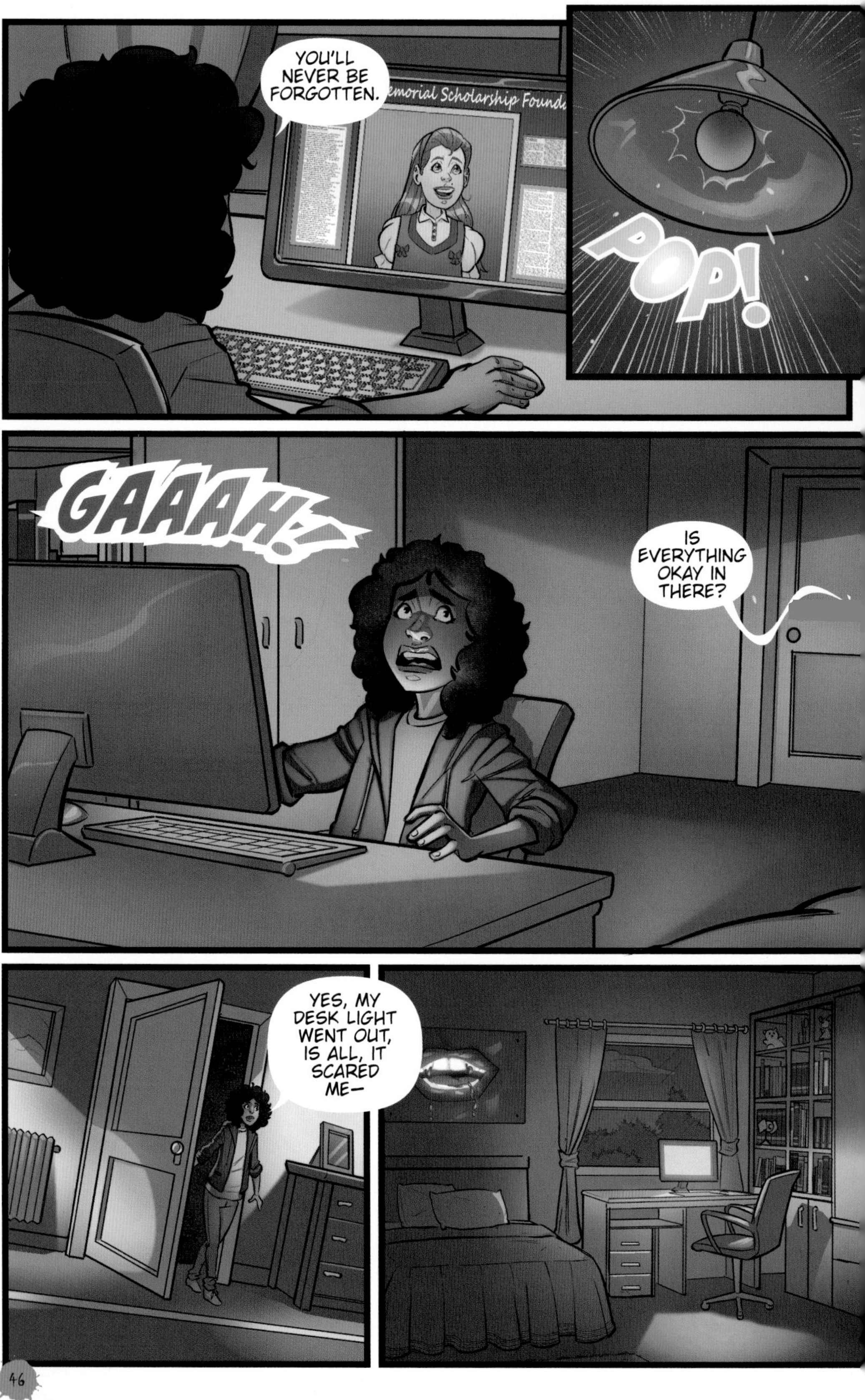
YOU'LL NEVER BE FORGOTTEN.
POP!
GAAAH!
IS EVERYTHING OKAY IN THERE?
YES, MY DESK LIGHT WENT OUT, IS ALL, IT SCARED ME—

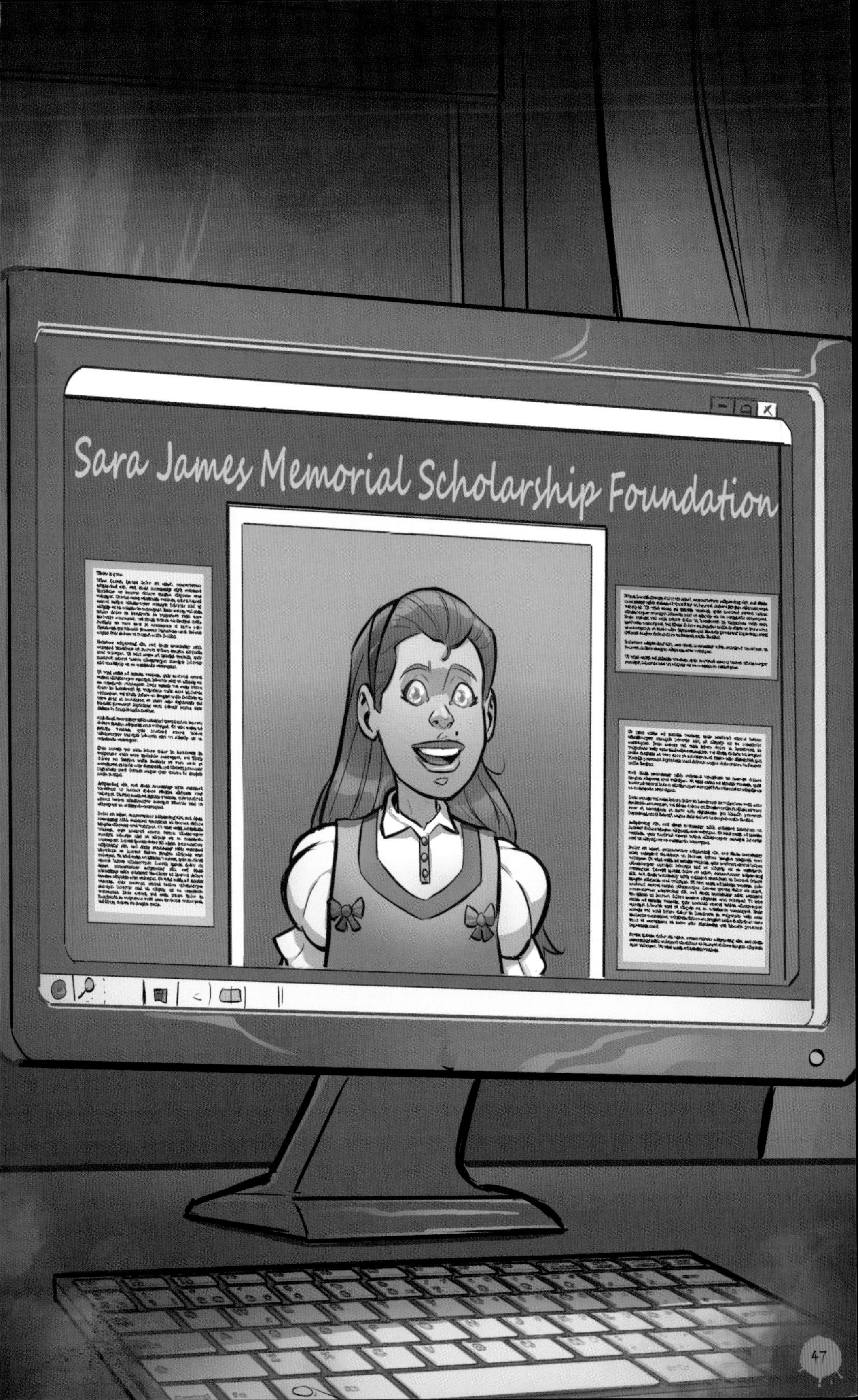
Sara James Memorial Scholarship Foundation

CHAPTER 4

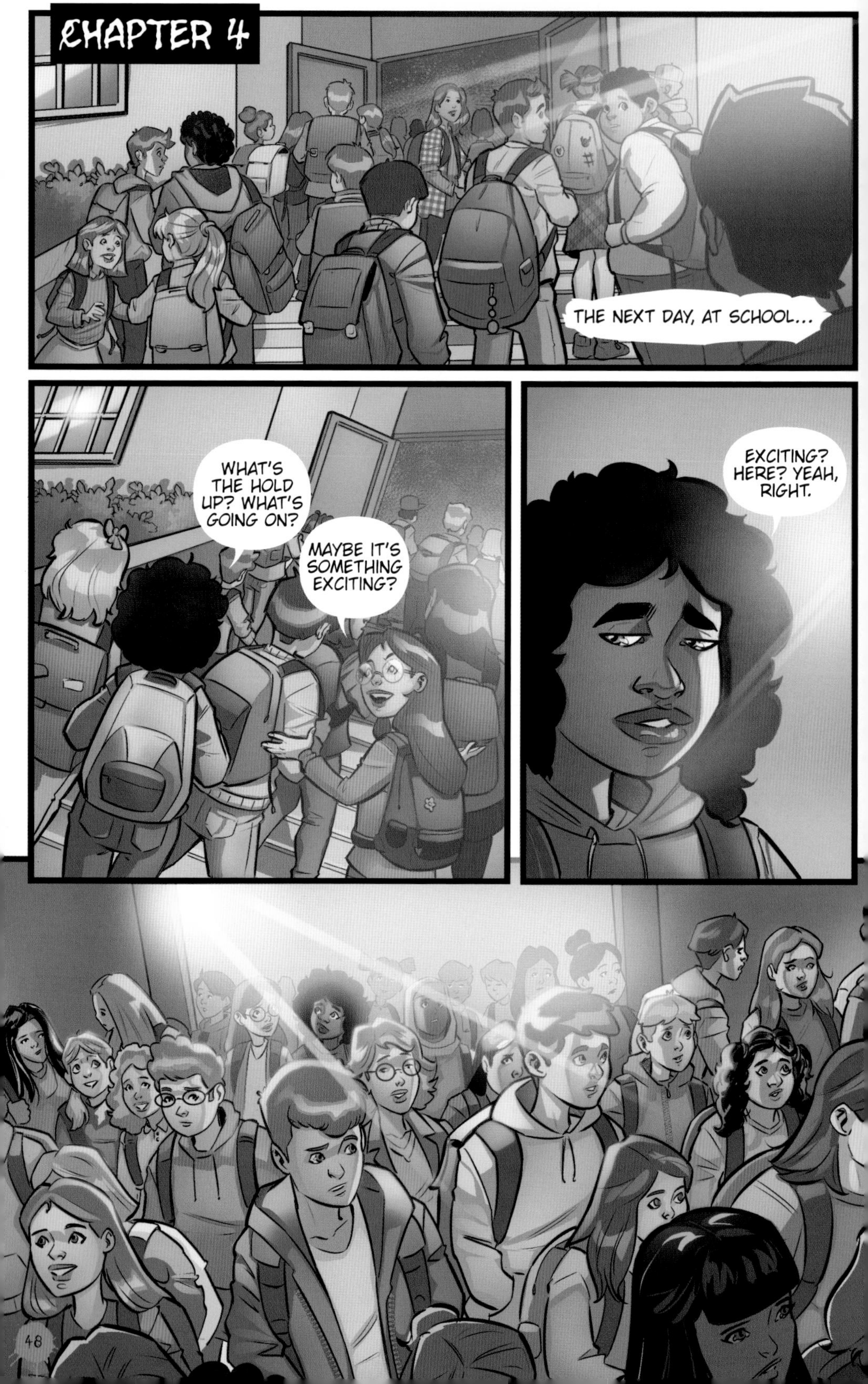

THE NEXT DAY, AT SCHOOL...
WHAT'S THE HOLD UP? WHAT'S GOING ON?
MAYBE IT'S SOMETHING EXCITING?
EXCITING? HERE? YEAH, RIGHT.

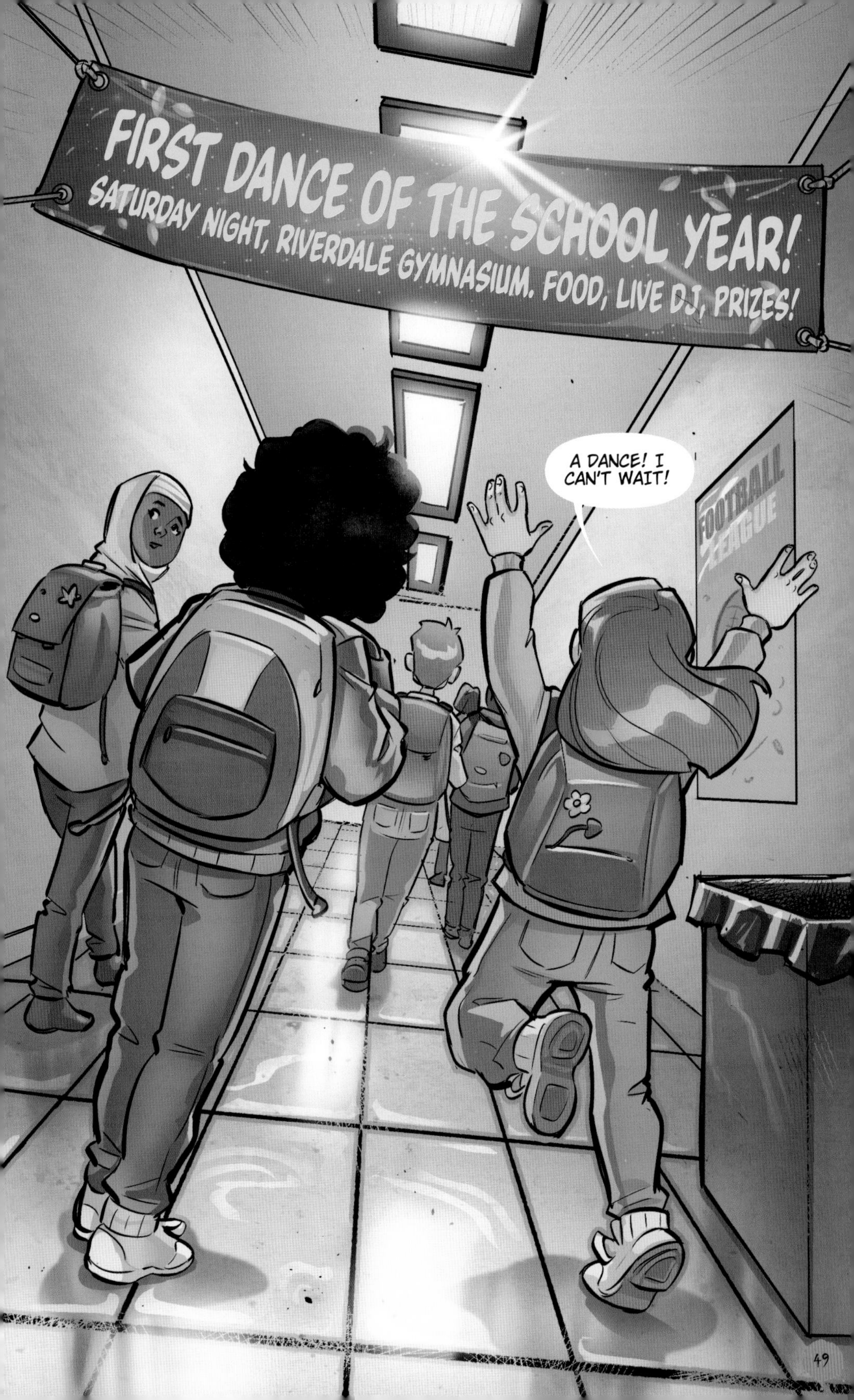
FIRST DANCE OF THE SCHOOL YEAR!
SATURDAY NIGHT, RIVERDALE GYMNASIUM. FOOD, LIVE DJ, PRIZES!
A DANCE! I CAN'T WAIT!
FOOTBALL LEAGUE

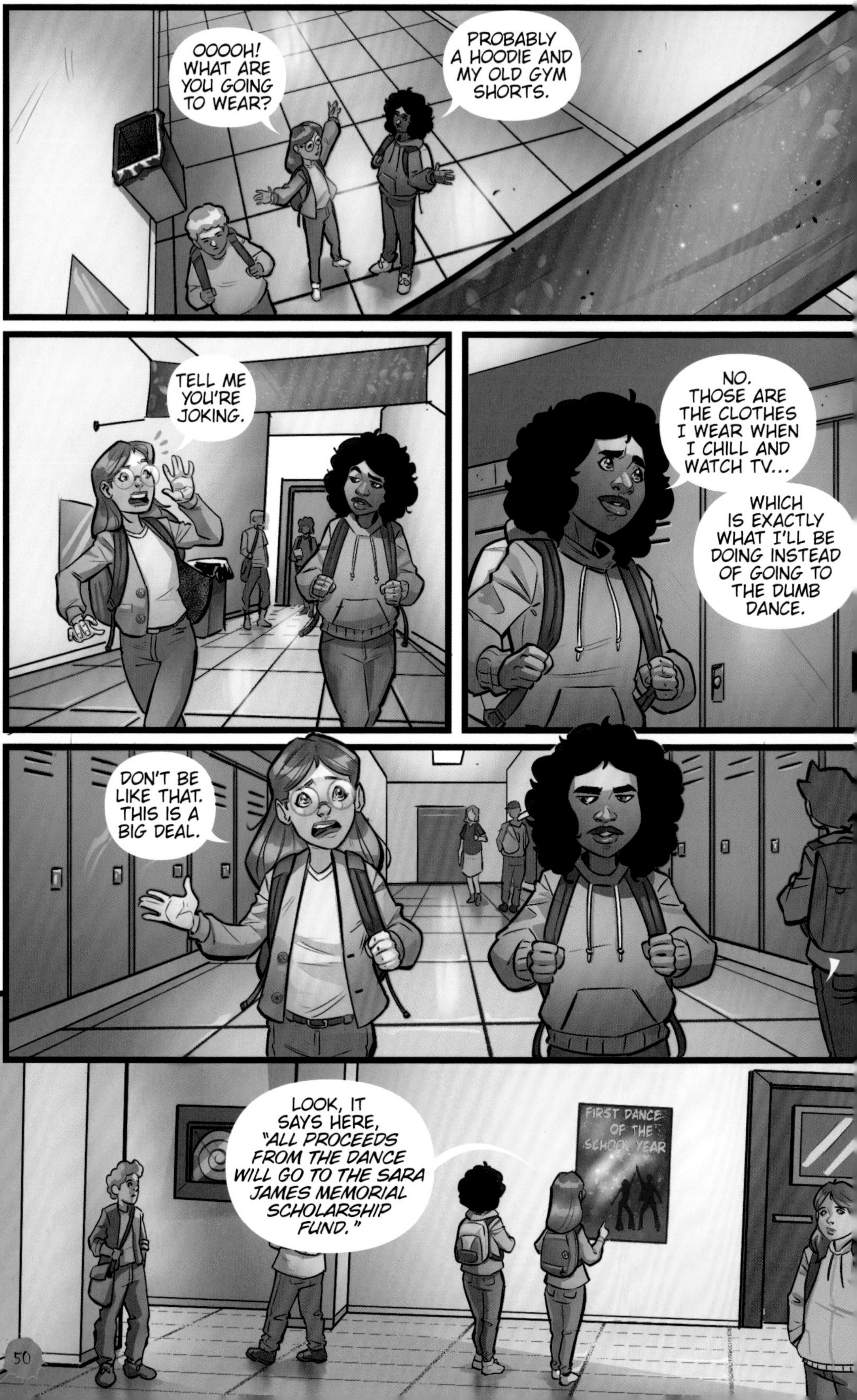
OOOOH! WHAT ARE YOU GOING TO WEAR?
PROBABLY A HOODIE AND MY OLD GYM SHORTS.
TELL ME YOU'RE JOKING.
NO. THOSE ARE THE CLOTHES I WEAR WHEN I CHILL AND WATCH TV...
WHICH IS EXACTLY WHAT I'LL BE DOING INSTEAD OF GOING TO THE DUMB DANCE.
DON'T BE LIKE THAT. THIS IS A BIG DEAL.
LOOK, IT SAYS HERE, *"ALL PROCEEDS FROM THE DANCE WILL GO TO THE SARA JAMES MEMORIAL SCHOLARSHIP FUND."*
FIRST DANCE OF THE SCHOOL YEAR

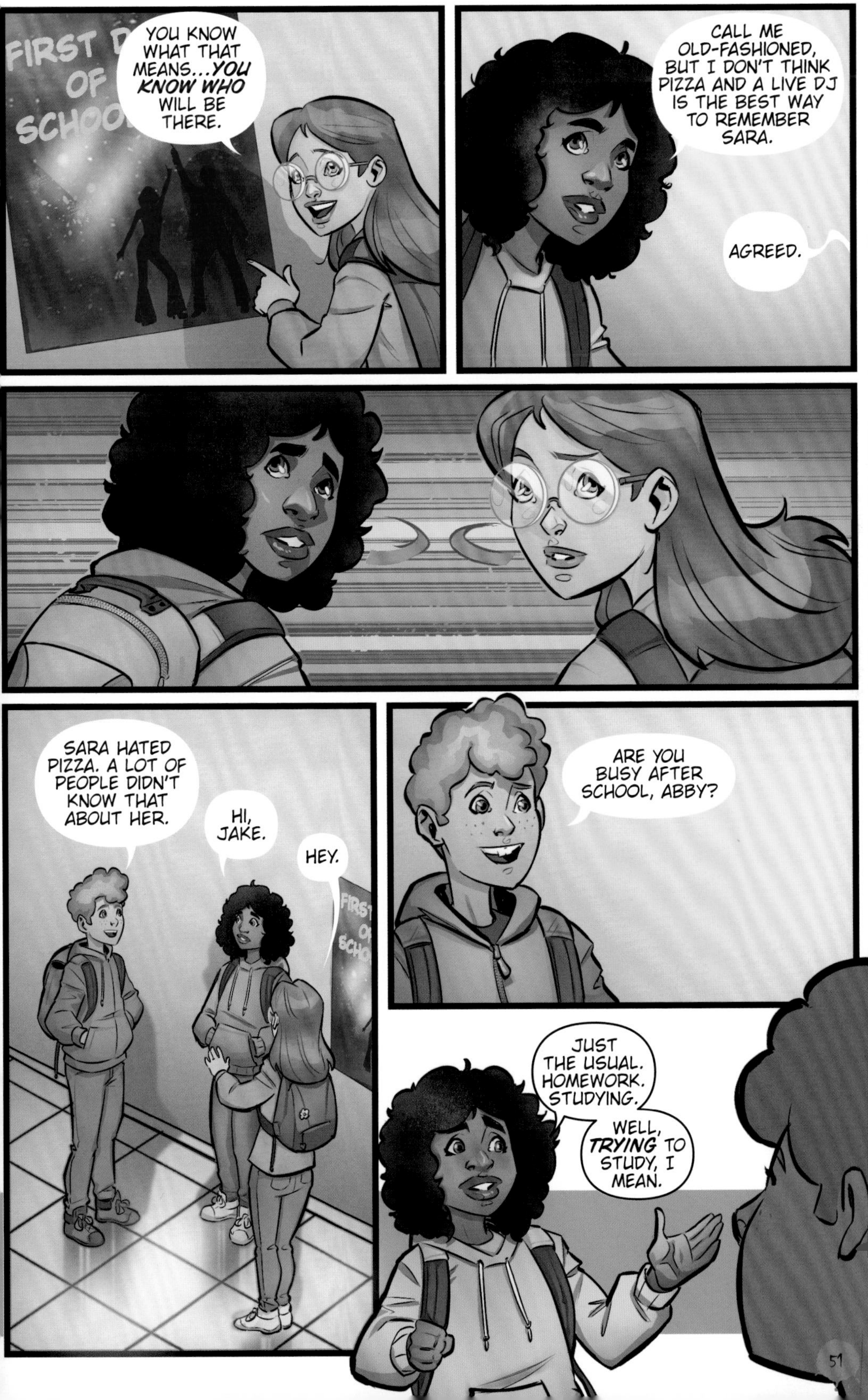
YOU KNOW WHAT THAT MEANS...*YOU KNOW WHO* WILL BE THERE.
CALL ME OLD-FASHIONED, BUT I DON'T THINK PIZZA AND A LIVE DJ IS THE BEST WAY TO REMEMBER SARA.
AGREED.
SARA HATED PIZZA. A LOT OF PEOPLE DIDN'T KNOW THAT ABOUT HER.
HI, JAKE.
HEY.
ARE YOU BUSY AFTER SCHOOL, ABBY?
JUST THE USUAL. HOMEWORK. STUDYING.
WELL, *TRYING* TO STUDY, I MEAN.

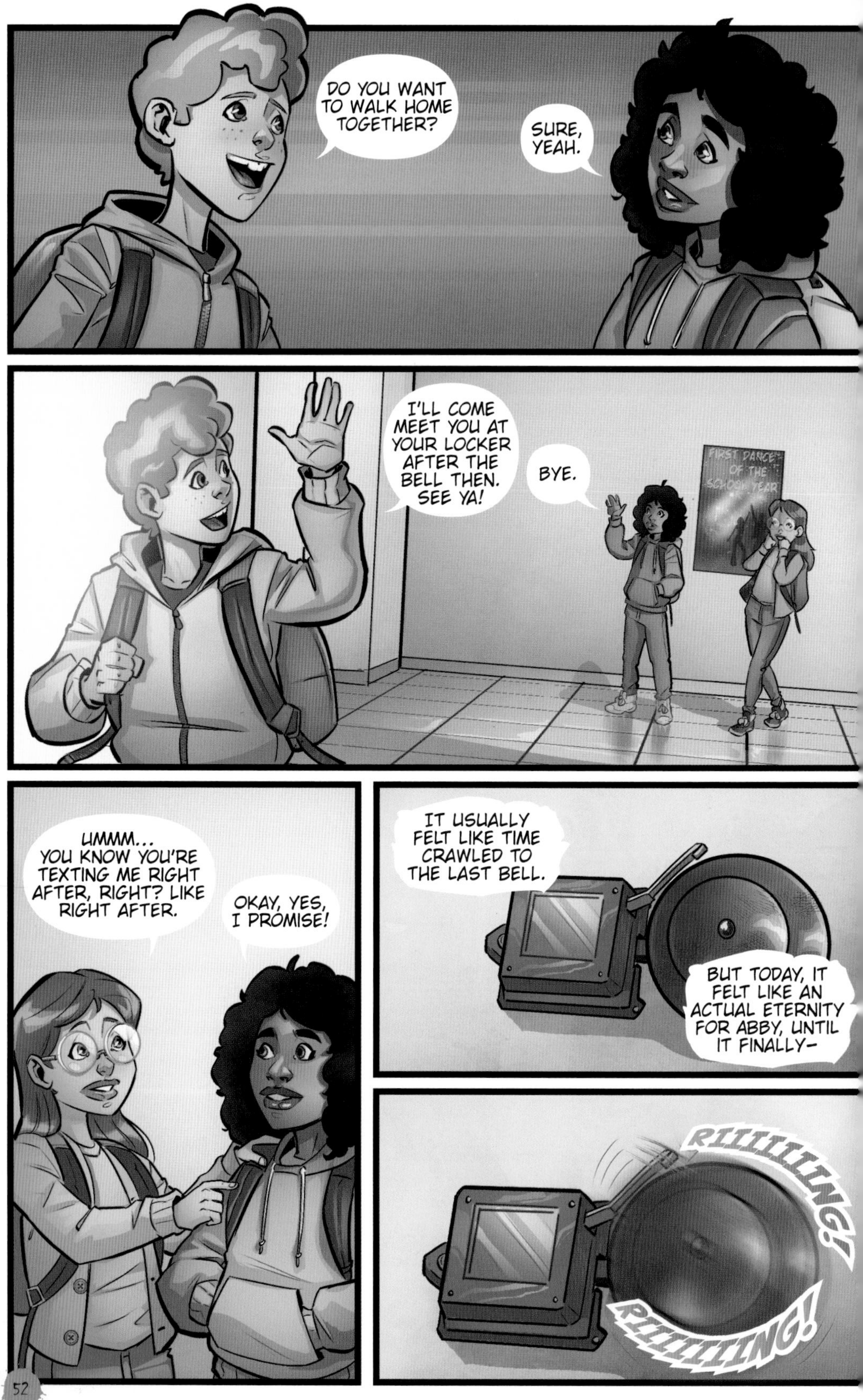
DO YOU WANT TO WALK HOME TOGETHER?
SURE, YEAH.
I'LL COME MEET YOU AT YOUR LOCKER AFTER THE BELL THEN. SEE YA!
BYE.
FIRST DANCE OF THE SCHOOL YEAR
UMMM... YOU KNOW YOU'RE TEXTING ME RIGHT AFTER, RIGHT? LIKE RIGHT AFTER.
OKAY, YES, I PROMISE!
IT USUALLY FELT LIKE TIME CRAWLED TO THE LAST BELL.
BUT TODAY, IT FELT LIKE AN ACTUAL ETERNITY FOR ABBY, UNTIL IT FINALLY—
RIIIIIIING!
RIIIIIIING!

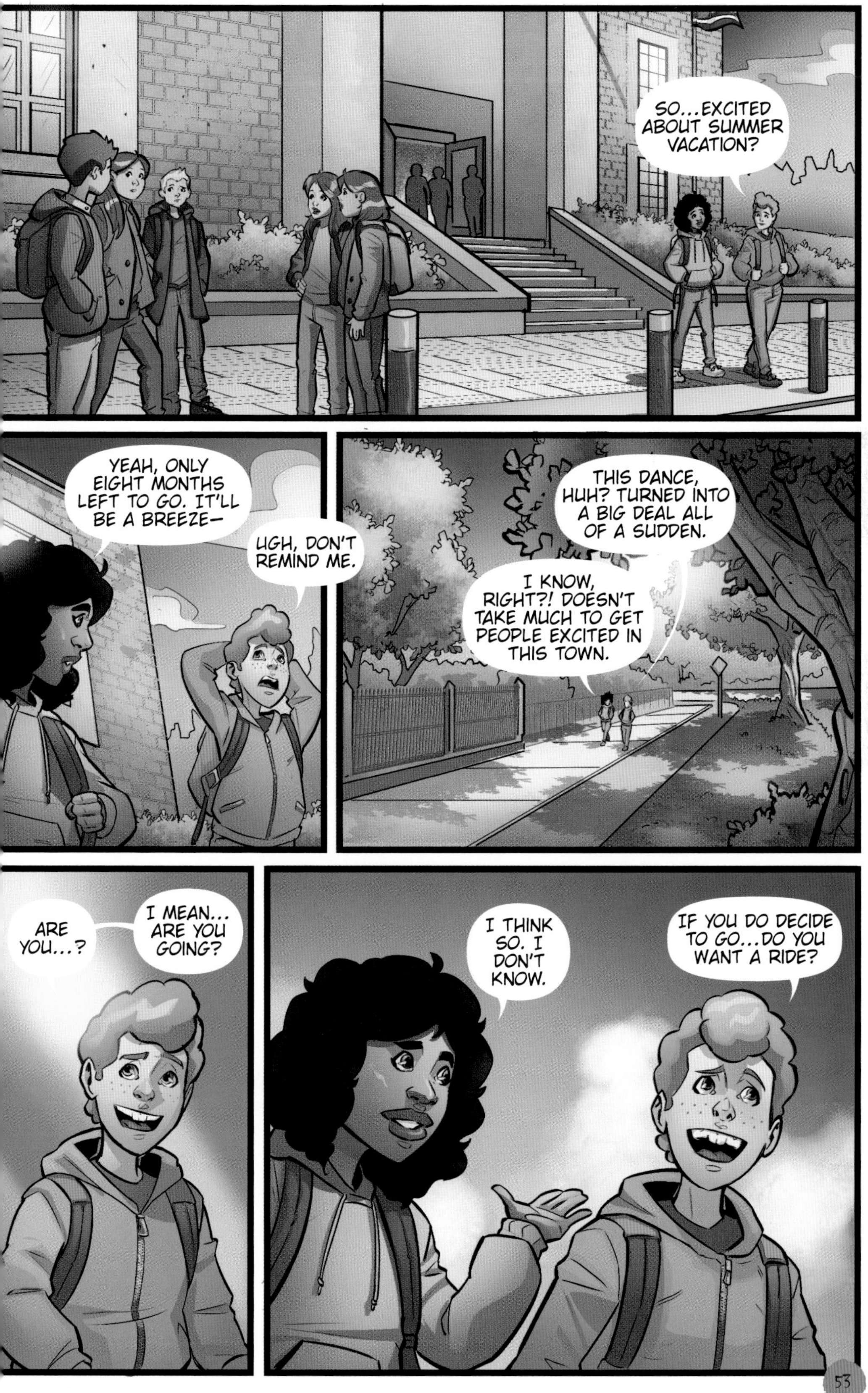
SO...EXCITED ABOUT SUMMER VACATION?
YEAH, ONLY EIGHT MONTHS LEFT TO GO. IT'LL BE A BREEZE—
UGH, DON'T REMIND ME.
THIS DANCE, HUH? TURNED INTO A BIG DEAL ALL OF A SUDDEN.
I KNOW, RIGHT?! DOESN'T TAKE MUCH TO GET PEOPLE EXCITED IN THIS TOWN.
ARE YOU...?
I MEAN... ARE YOU GOING?
I THINK SO. I DON'T KNOW.
IF YOU DO DECIDE TO GO...DO YOU WANT A RIDE?

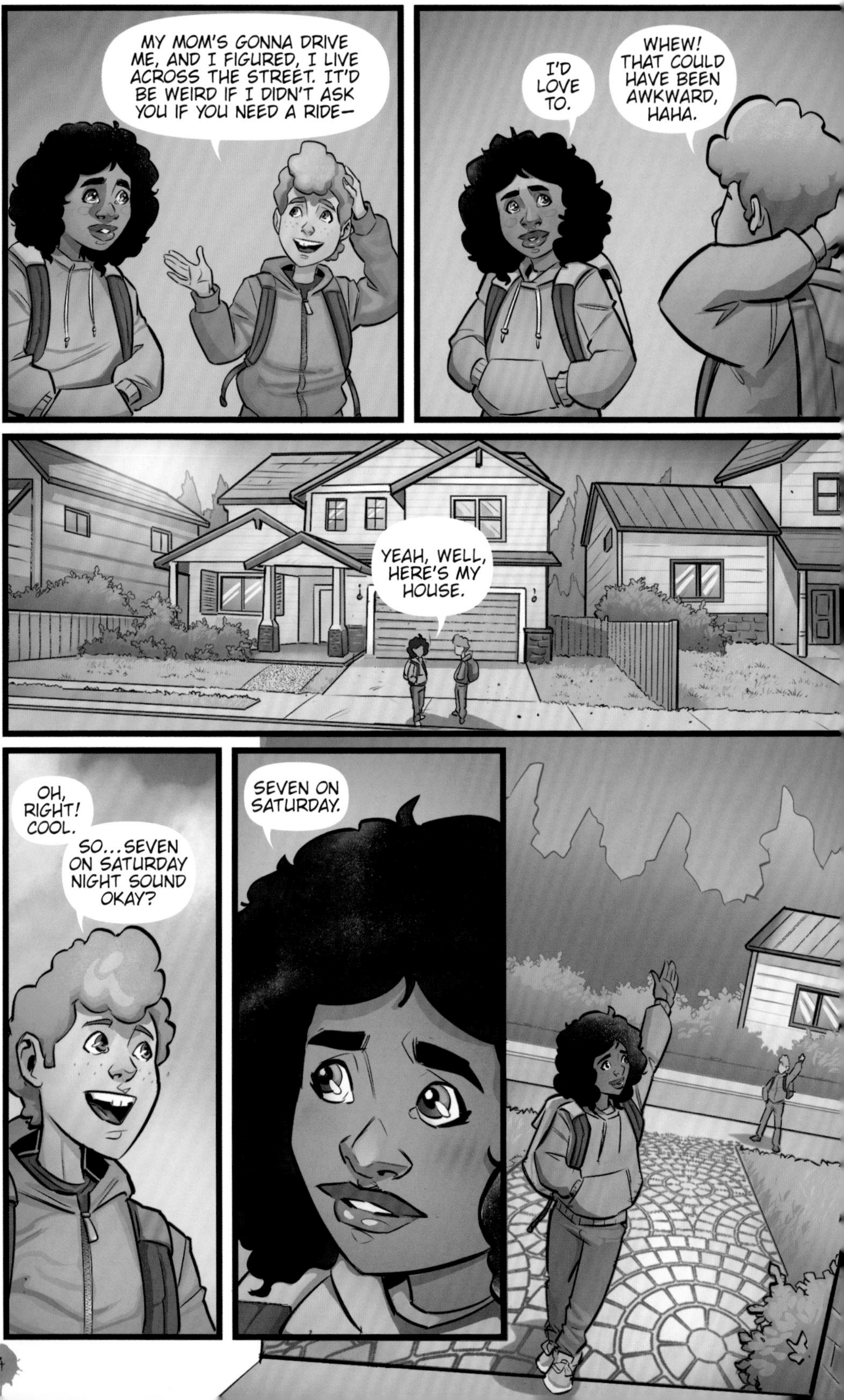
MY MOM'S GONNA DRIVE ME, AND I FIGURED, I LIVE ACROSS THE STREET. IT'D BE WEIRD IF I DIDN'T ASK YOU IF YOU NEED A RIDE—
I'D LOVE TO.
WHEW! THAT COULD HAVE BEEN AWKWARD, HAHA.
YEAH, WELL, HERE'S MY HOUSE.
OH, RIGHT! COOL.
SO... SEVEN ON SATURDAY NIGHT SOUND OKAY?
SEVEN ON SATURDAY.

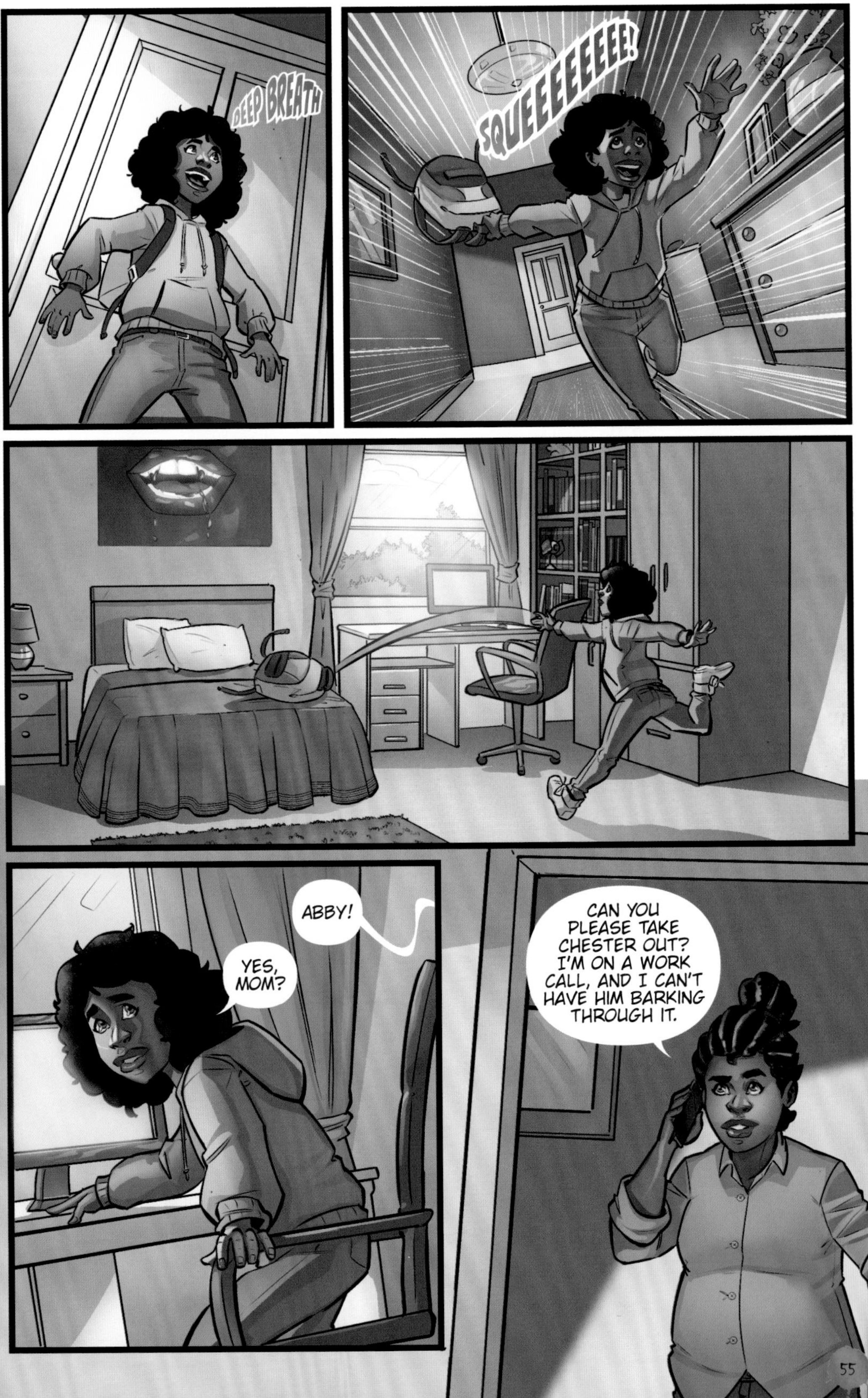
DEEP BREATH
SQUEEEEEEEEE!
ABBY!
YES, MOM?
CAN YOU PLEASE TAKE CHESTER OUT? I'M ON A WORK CALL, AND I CAN'T HAVE HIM BARKING THROUGH IT.

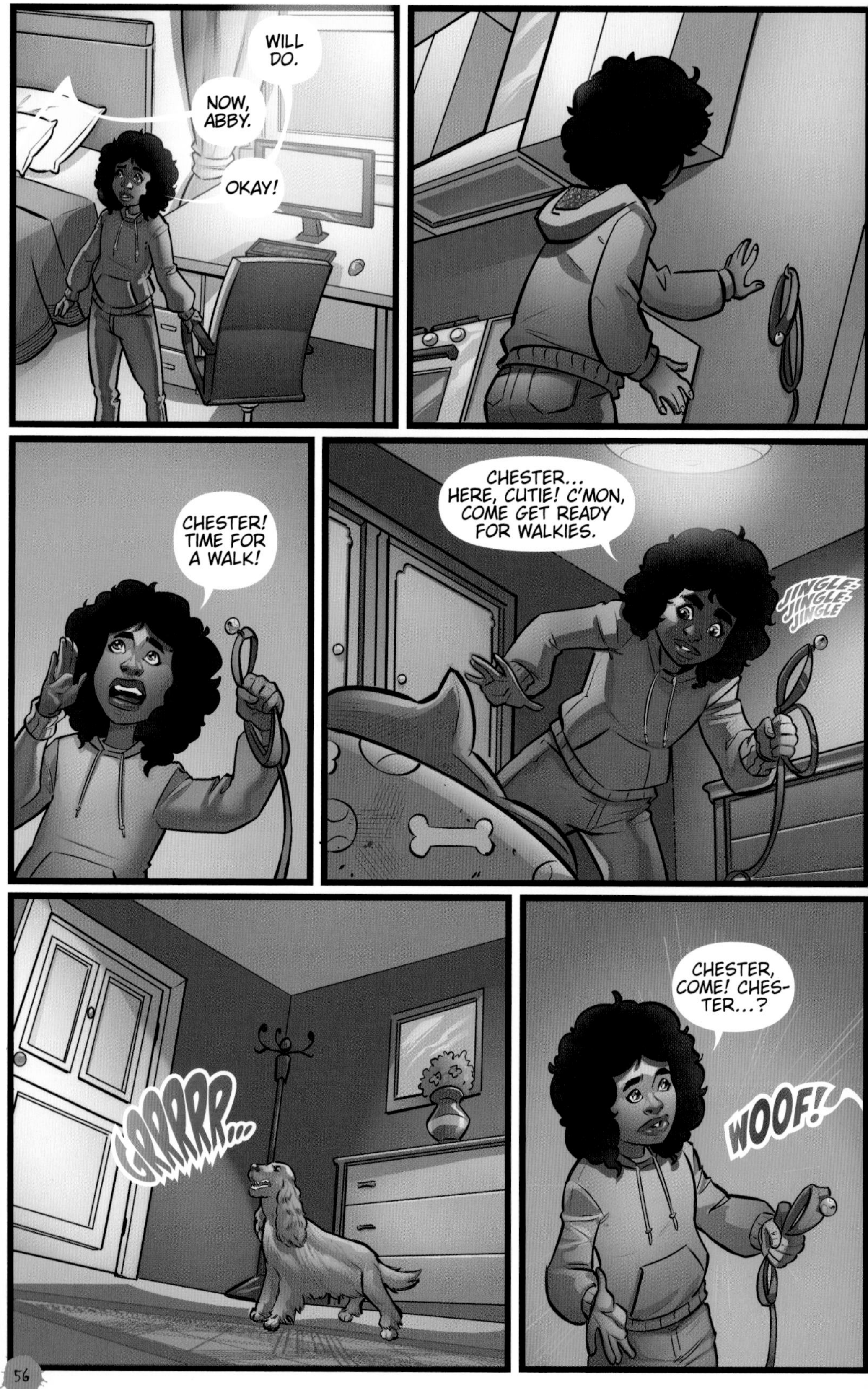
WILL DO.
NOW, ABBY.
OKAY!
CHESTER! TIME FOR A WALK!
CHESTER... HERE, CUTIE! C'MON, COME GET READY FOR WALKIES.
JINGLE-JINGLE-JINGLE
GRRRRR...
CHESTER, COME! CHES-TER...?
WOOF!

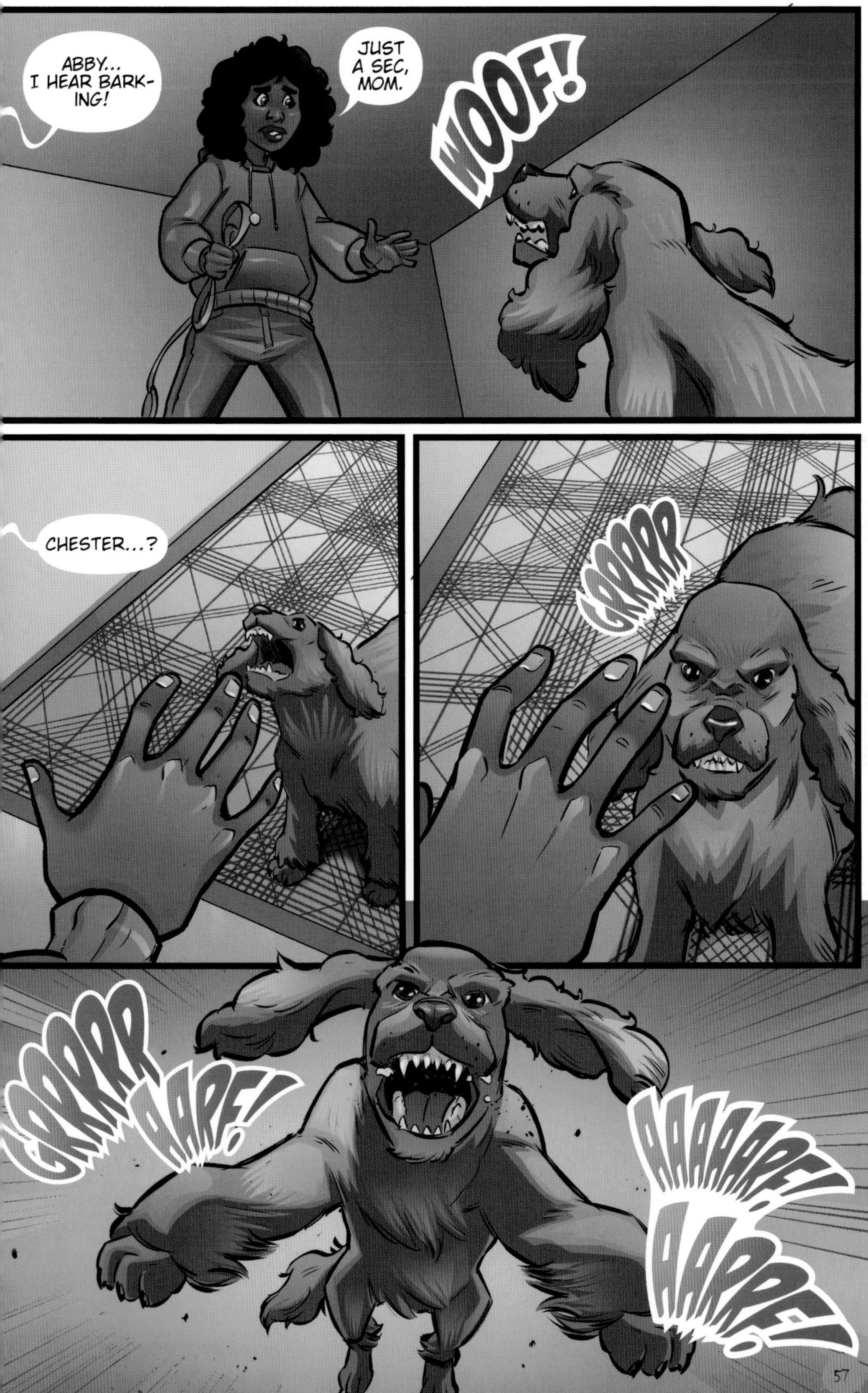
ABBY... I HEAR BARK-ING!
JUST A SEC, MOM.
WOOF!
CHESTER...?
GRRRR
GRRRR
AARF!
AAAARF!
AARRF!

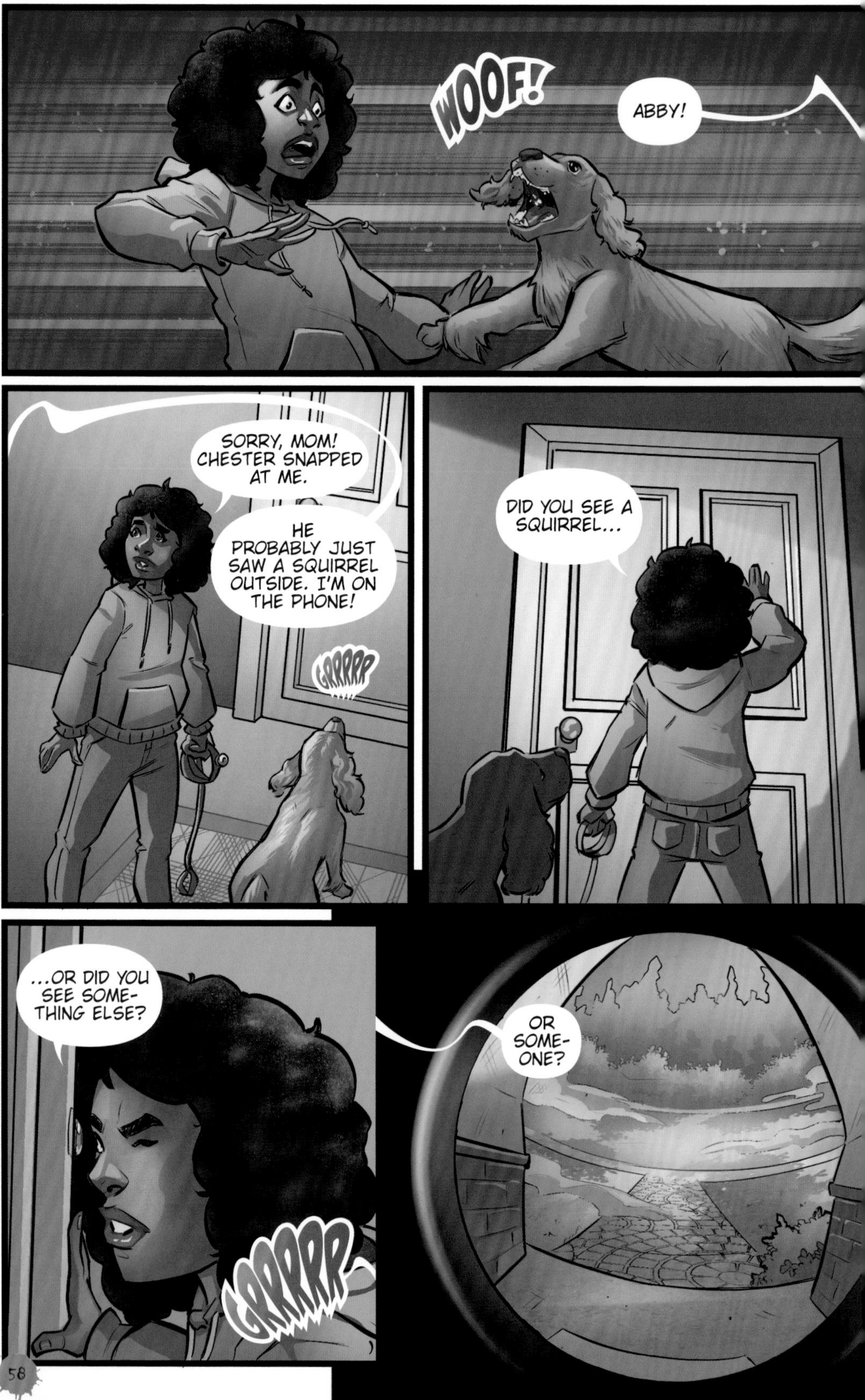
WOOF!
ABBY!
SORRY, MOM! CHESTER SNAPPED AT ME.
HE PROBABLY JUST SAW A SQUIRREL OUTSIDE. I'M ON THE PHONE!
GRRRRR
DID YOU SEE A SQUIRREL...
...OR DID YOU SEE SOME-THING ELSE?
OR SOME-ONE?
GRRRRR

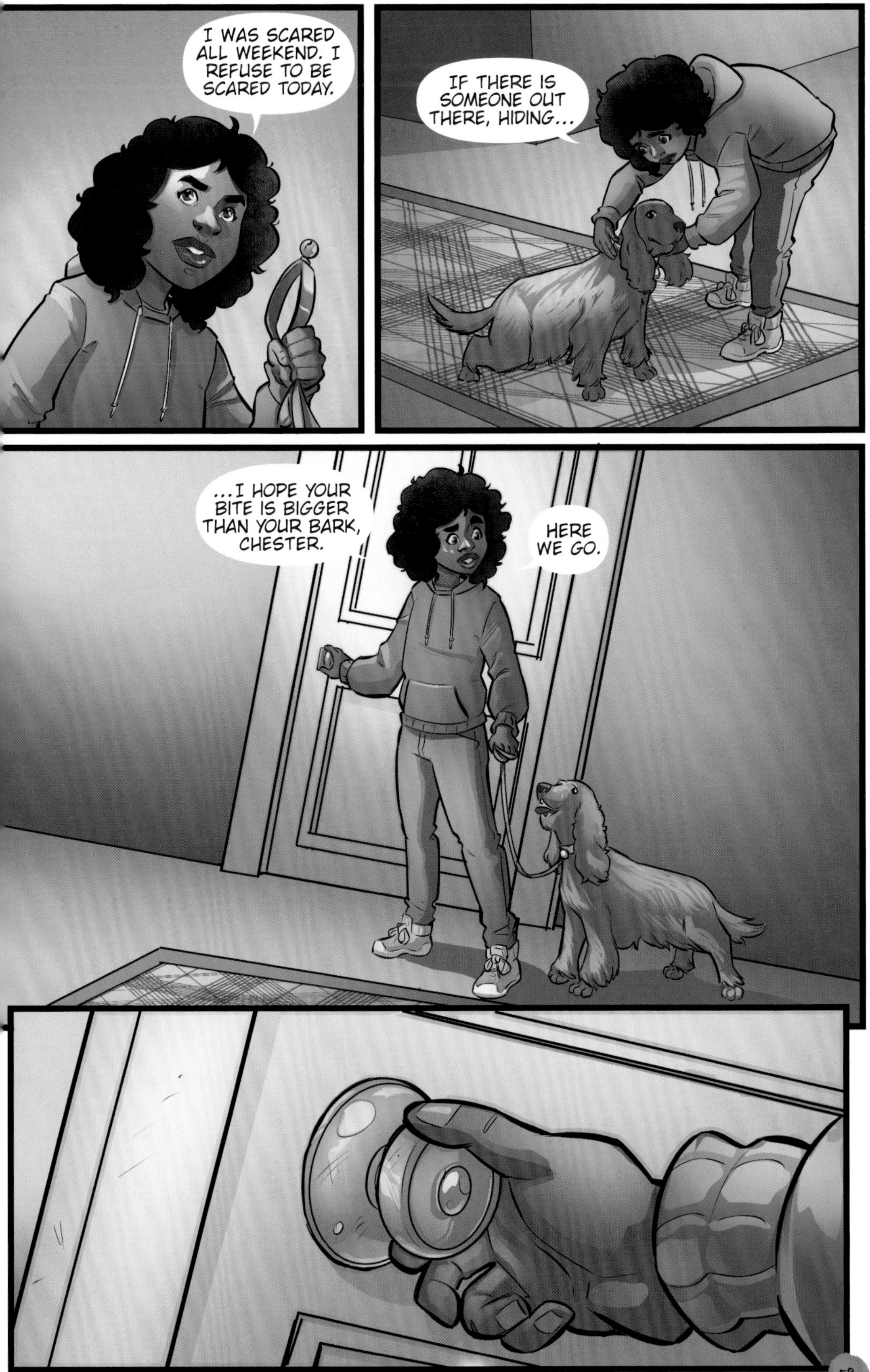
I WAS SCARED ALL WEEKEND. I REFUSE TO BE SCARED TODAY.
IF THERE IS SOMEONE OUT THERE, HIDING...
...I HOPE YOUR BITE IS BIGGER THAN YOUR BARK, CHESTER.
HERE WE GO.

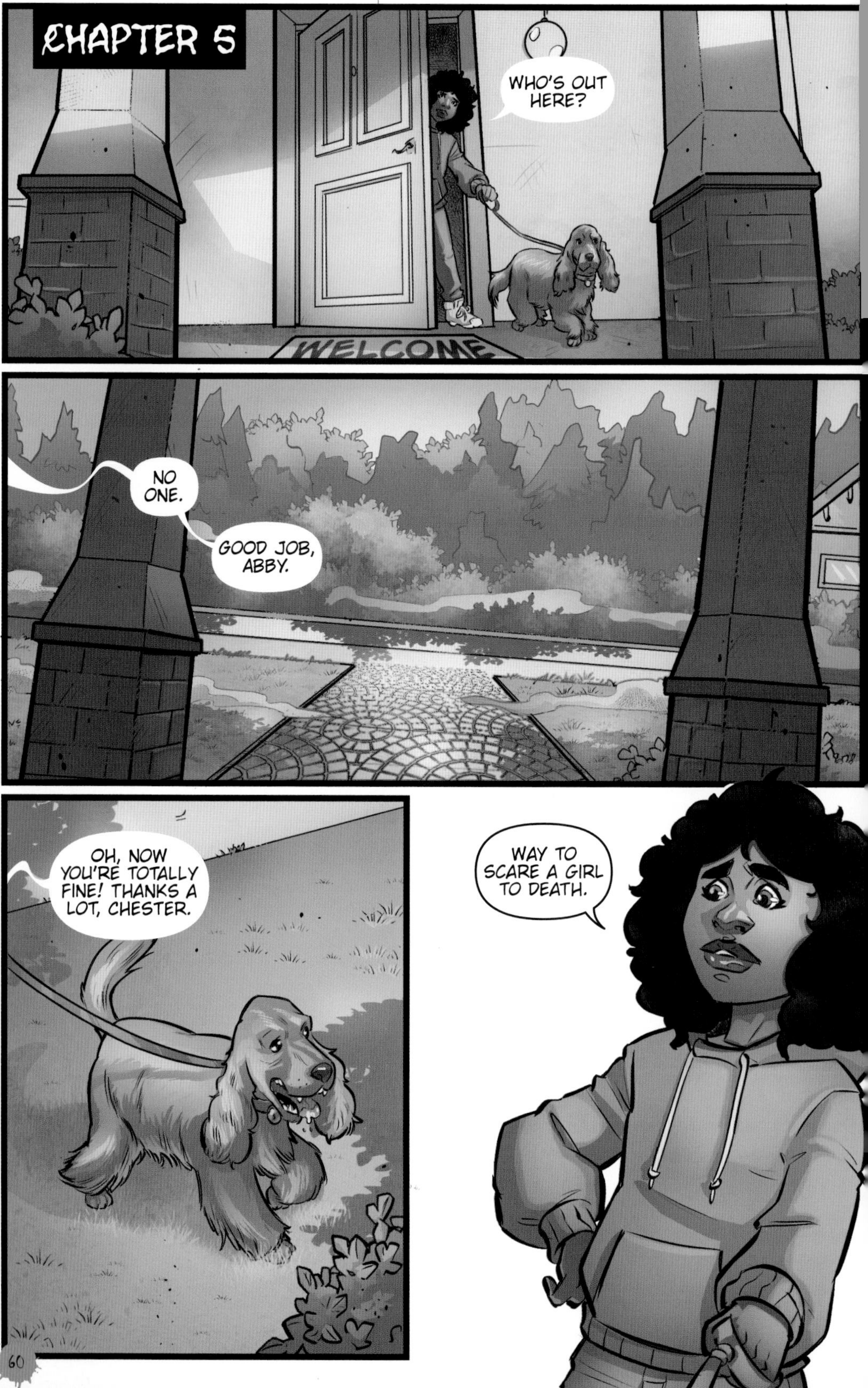
CHAPTER 5
WHO'S OUT HERE?
WELCOME
NO ONE.
GOOD JOB, ABBY.
OH, NOW YOU'RE TOTALLY FINE! THANKS A LOT, CHESTER.
WAY TO SCARE A GIRL TO DEATH.

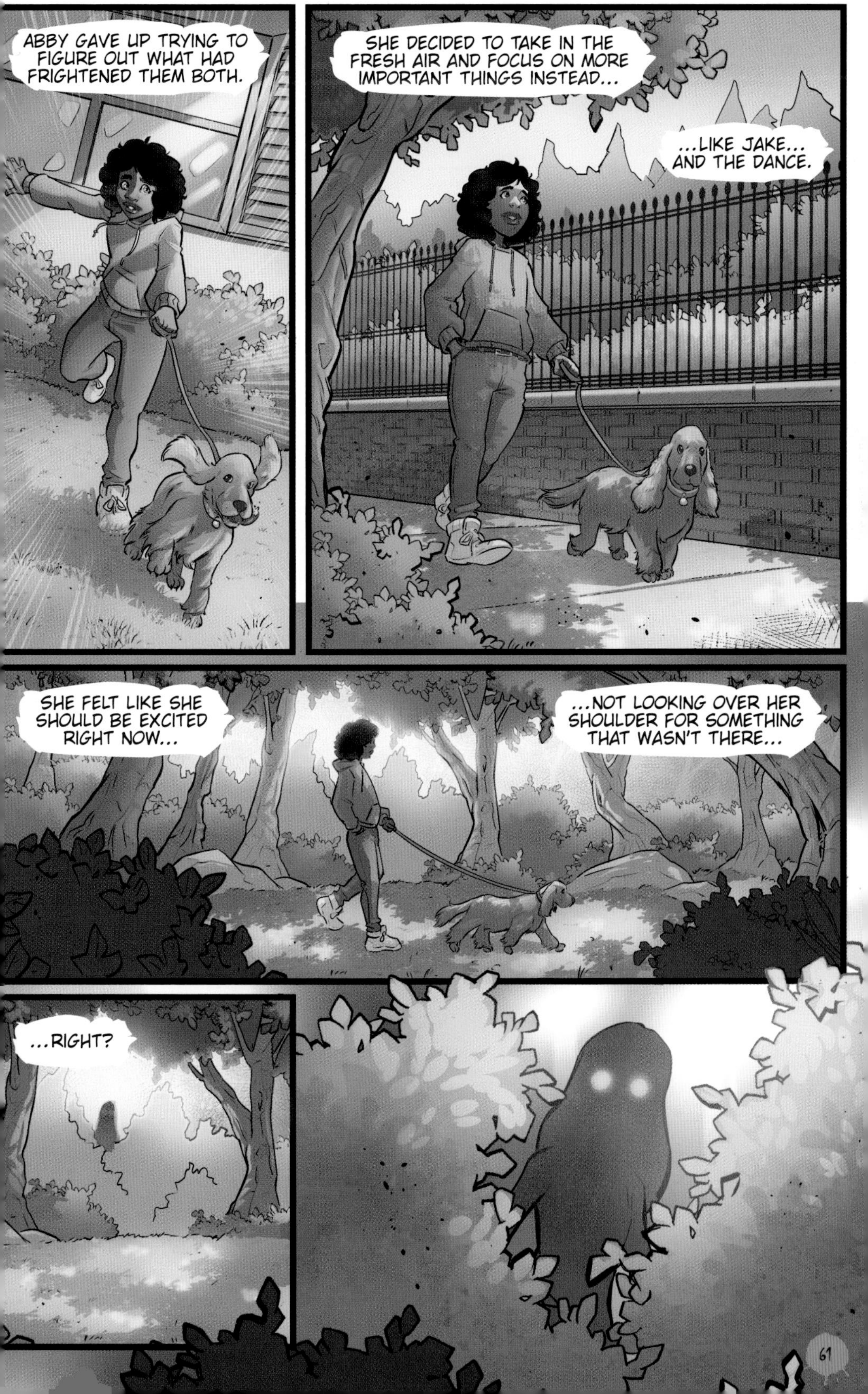
ABBY GAVE UP TRYING TO FIGURE OUT WHAT HAD FRIGHTENED THEM BOTH.
SHE DECIDED TO TAKE IN THE FRESH AIR AND FOCUS ON MORE IMPORTANT THINGS INSTEAD...
...LIKE JAKE... AND THE DANCE.
SHE FELT LIKE SHE SHOULD BE EXCITED RIGHT NOW...
...NOT LOOKING OVER HER SHOULDER FOR SOMETHING THAT WASN'T THERE...
...RIGHT?

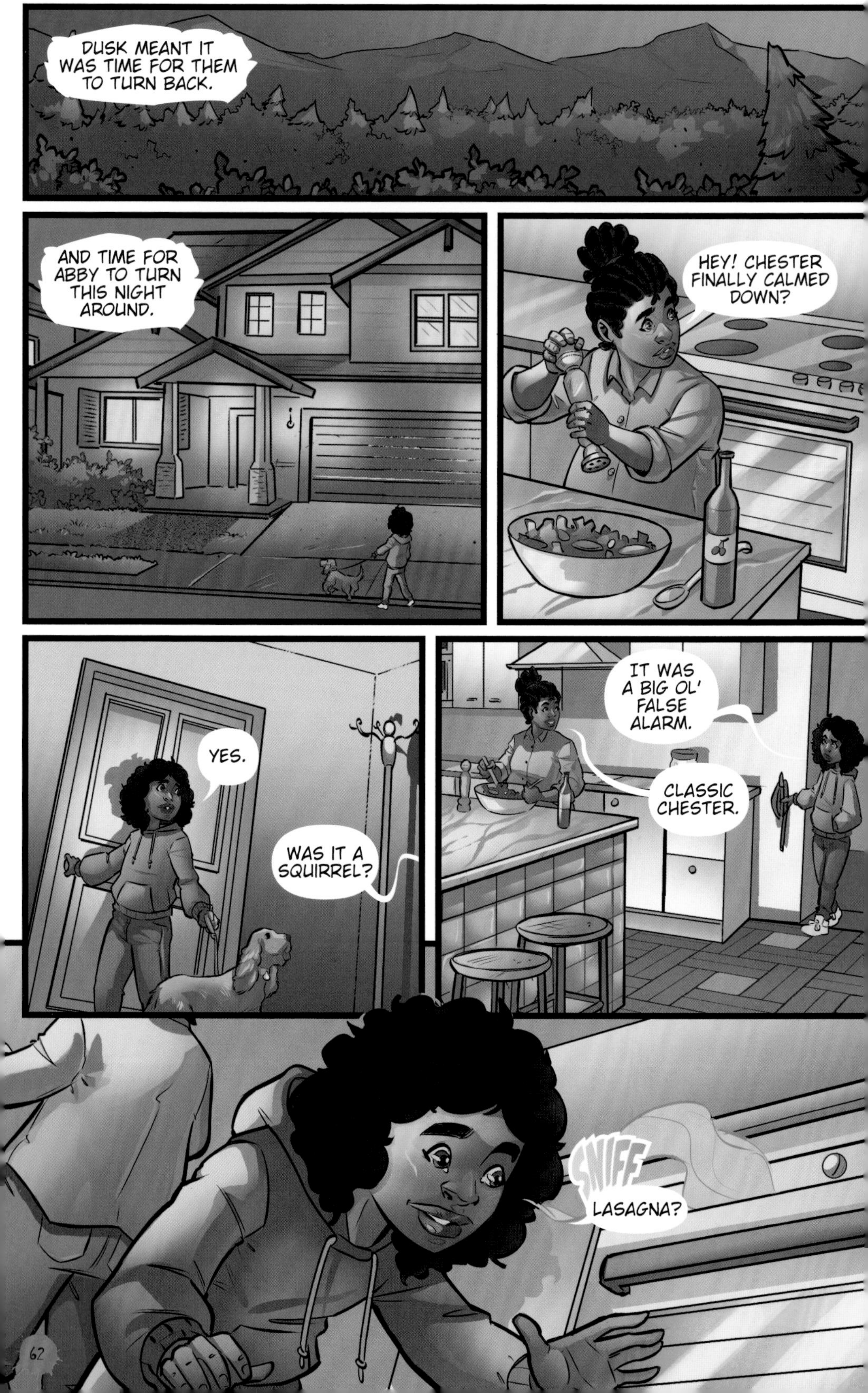
DUSK MEANT IT WAS TIME FOR THEM TO TURN BACK.
AND TIME FOR ABBY TO TURN THIS NIGHT AROUND.
HEY! CHESTER FINALLY CALMED DOWN?
YES.
WAS IT A SQUIRREL?
IT WAS A BIG OL' FALSE ALARM.
CLASSIC CHESTER.
SNIFF
LASAGNA?

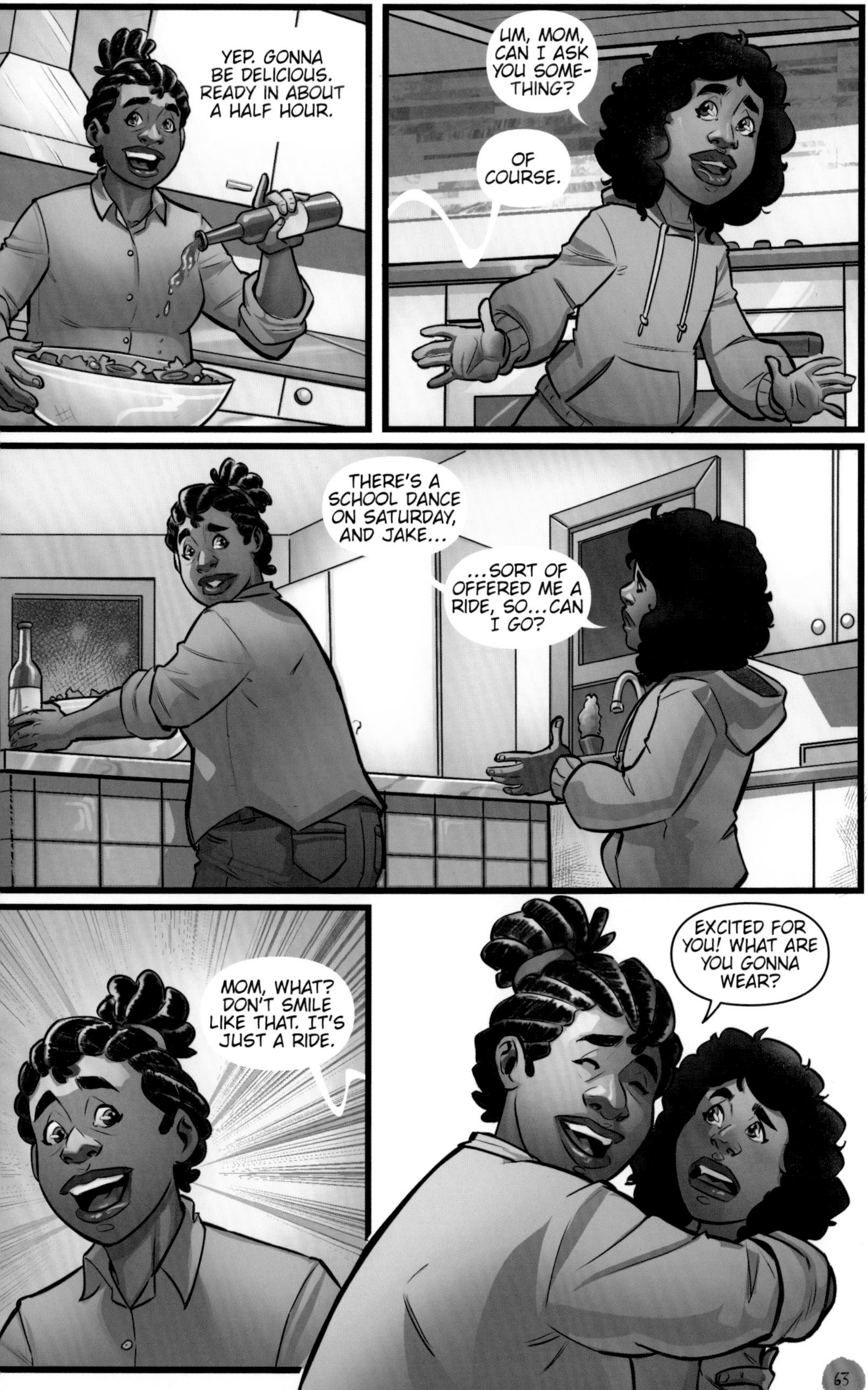
YEP. GONNA BE DELICIOUS. READY IN ABOUT A HALF HOUR.
UM, MOM, CAN I ASK YOU SOME-THING?
OF COURSE.
THERE'S A SCHOOL DANCE ON SATURDAY, AND JAKE...
...SORT OF OFFERED ME A RIDE, SO...CAN I GO?
MOM, WHAT? DON'T SMILE LIKE THAT. IT'S JUST A RIDE.
EXCITED FOR YOU! WHAT ARE YOU GONNA WEAR?

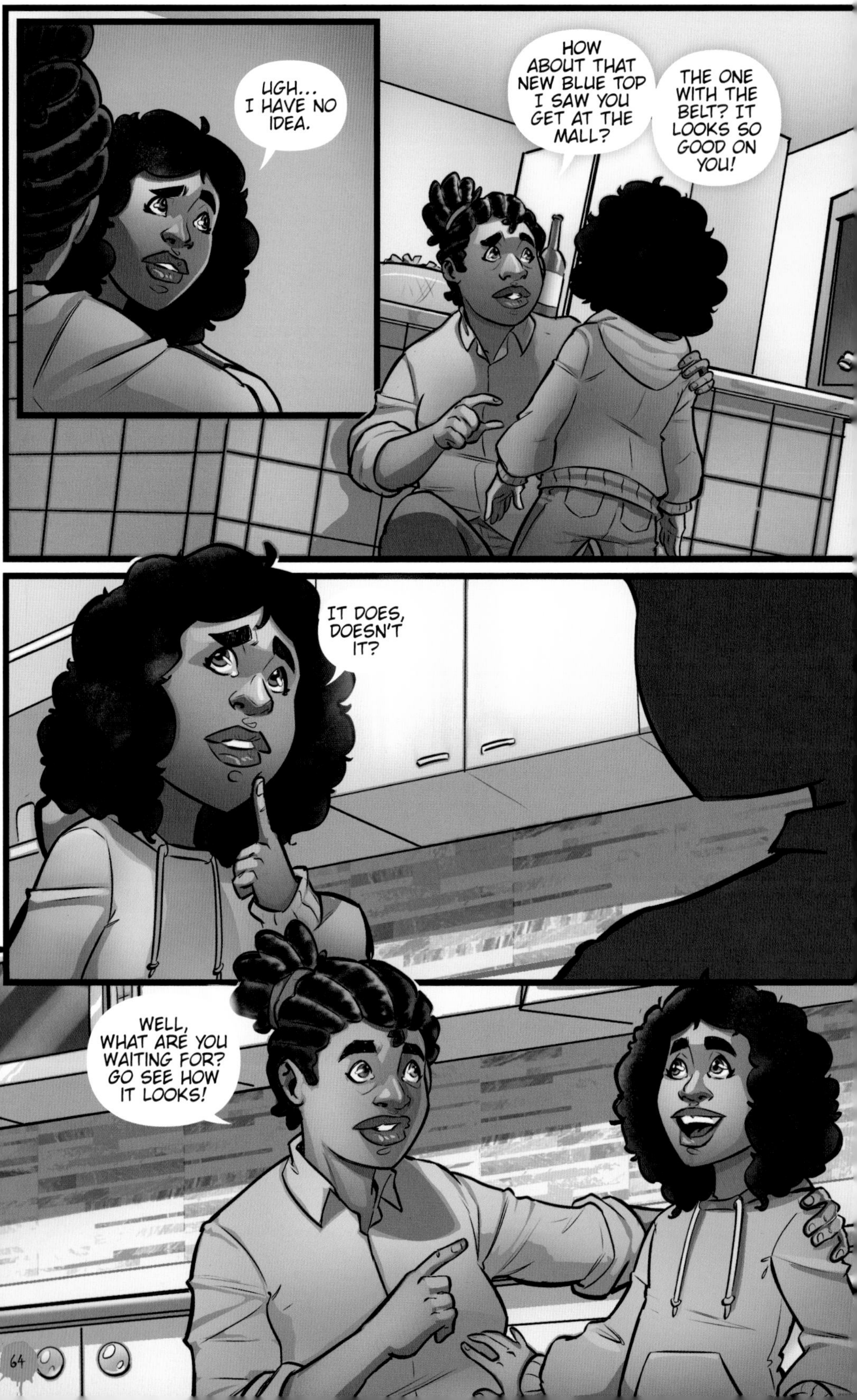
UGH... I HAVE NO IDEA.
HOW ABOUT THAT NEW BLUE TOP I SAW YOU GET AT THE MALL?
THE ONE WITH THE BELT? IT LOOKS SO GOOD ON YOU!
IT DOES, DOESN'T IT?
WELL, WHAT ARE YOU WAITING FOR? GO SEE HOW IT LOOKS!

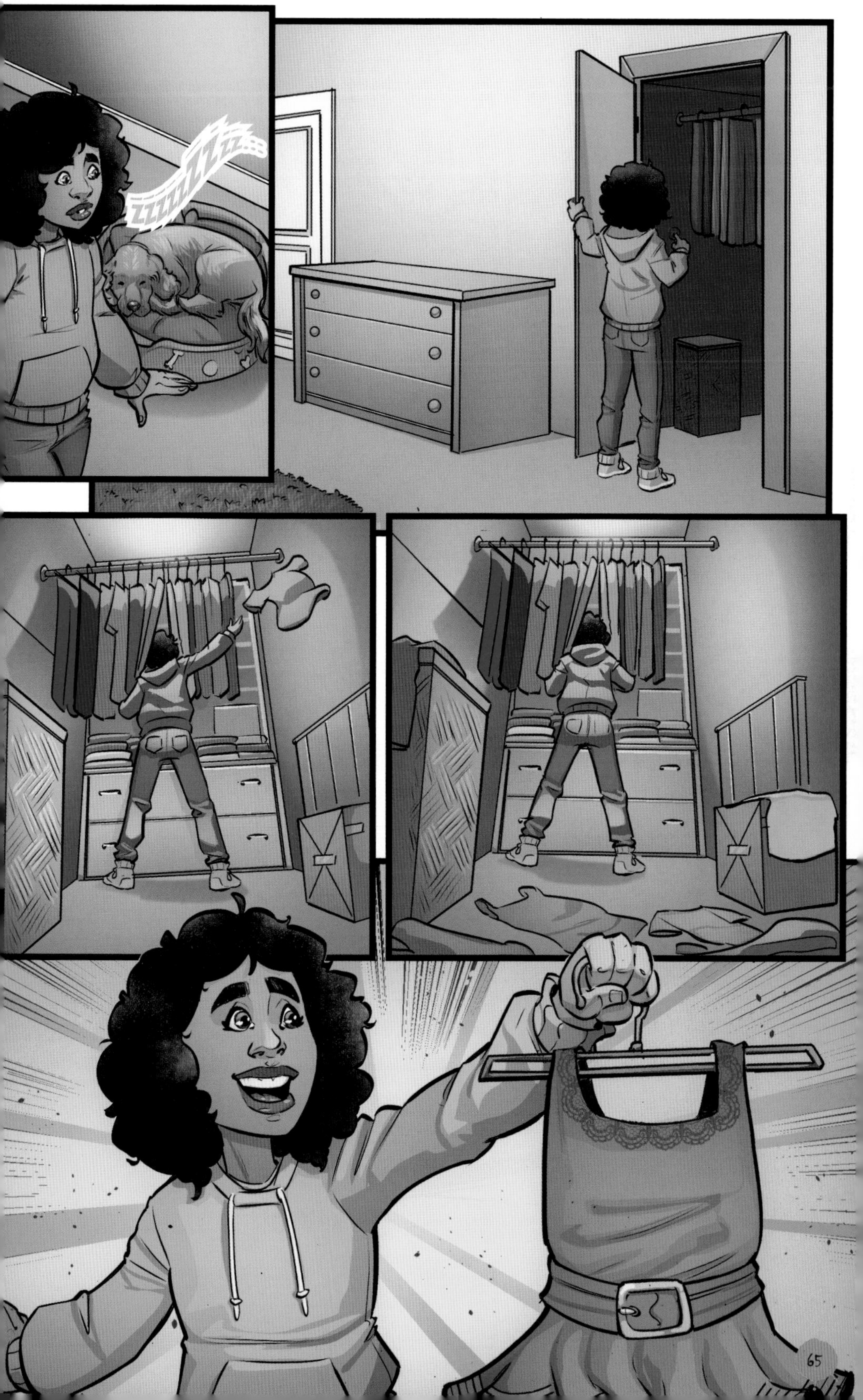
ZZZZZZZZZZzzz...

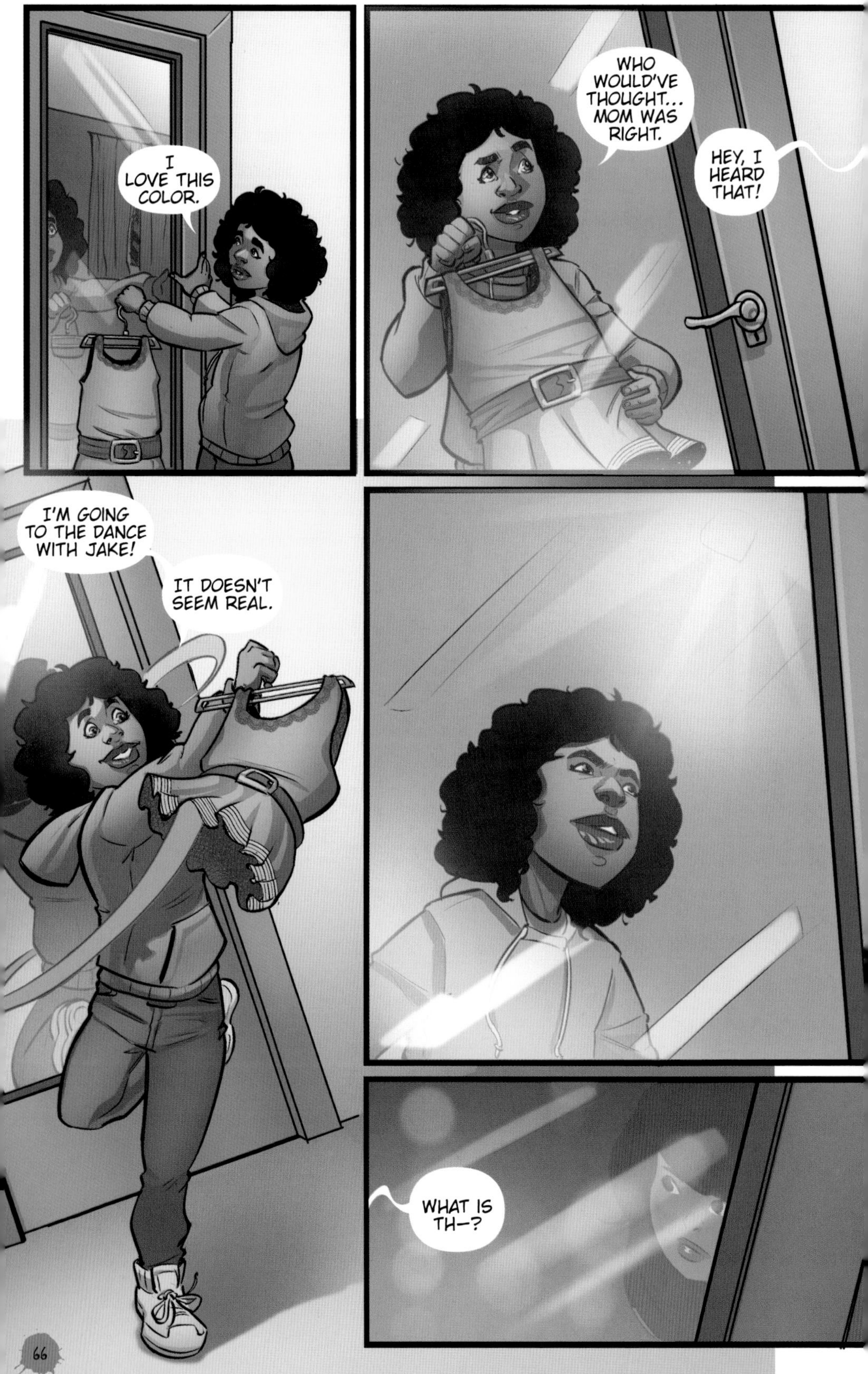
I LOVE THIS COLOR.
WHO WOULD'VE THOUGHT... MOM WAS RIGHT.
HEY, I HEARD THAT!
I'M GOING TO THE DANCE WITH JAKE!
IT DOESN'T SEEM REAL.
WHAT IS TH—?

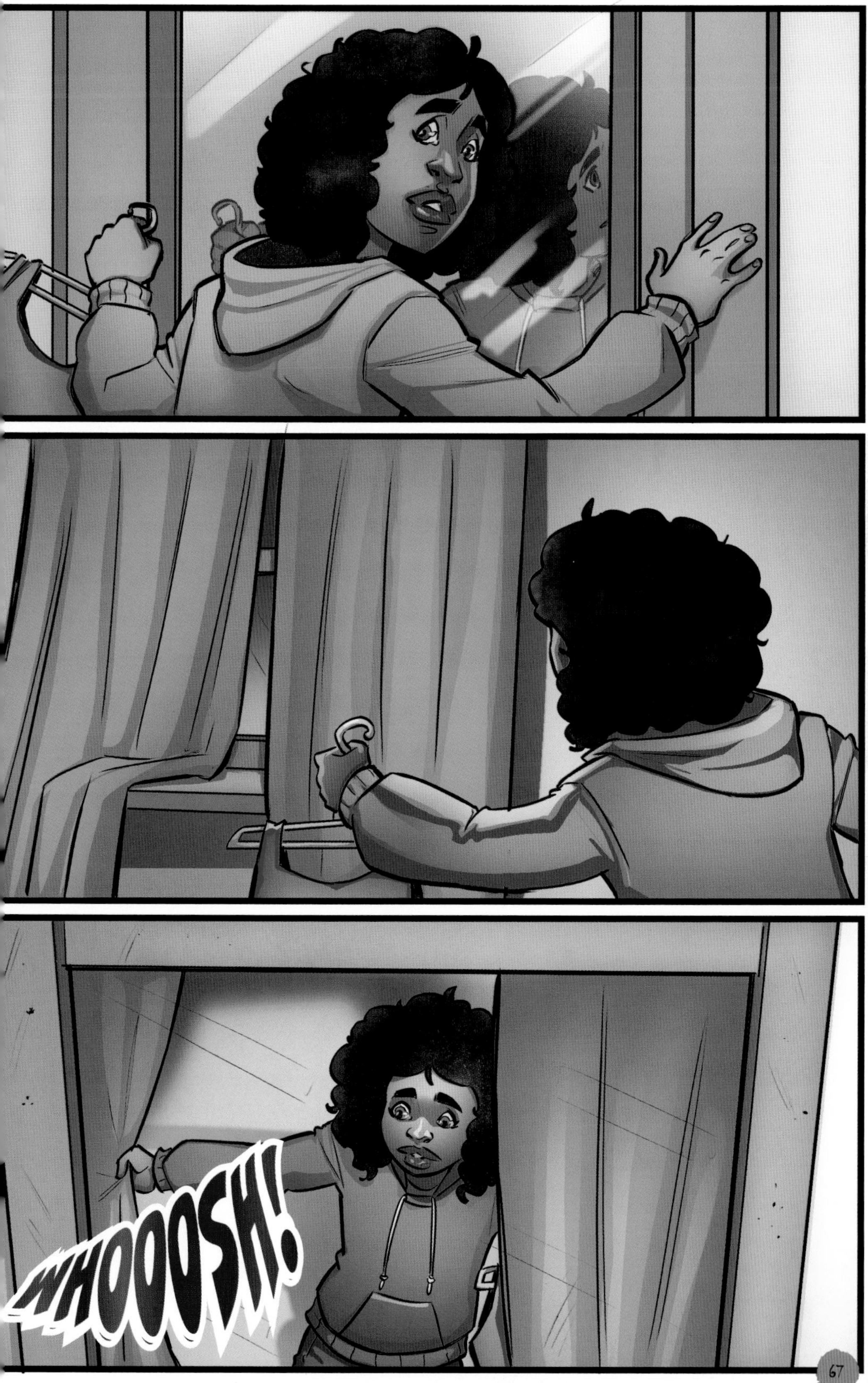
WHOOOSH!

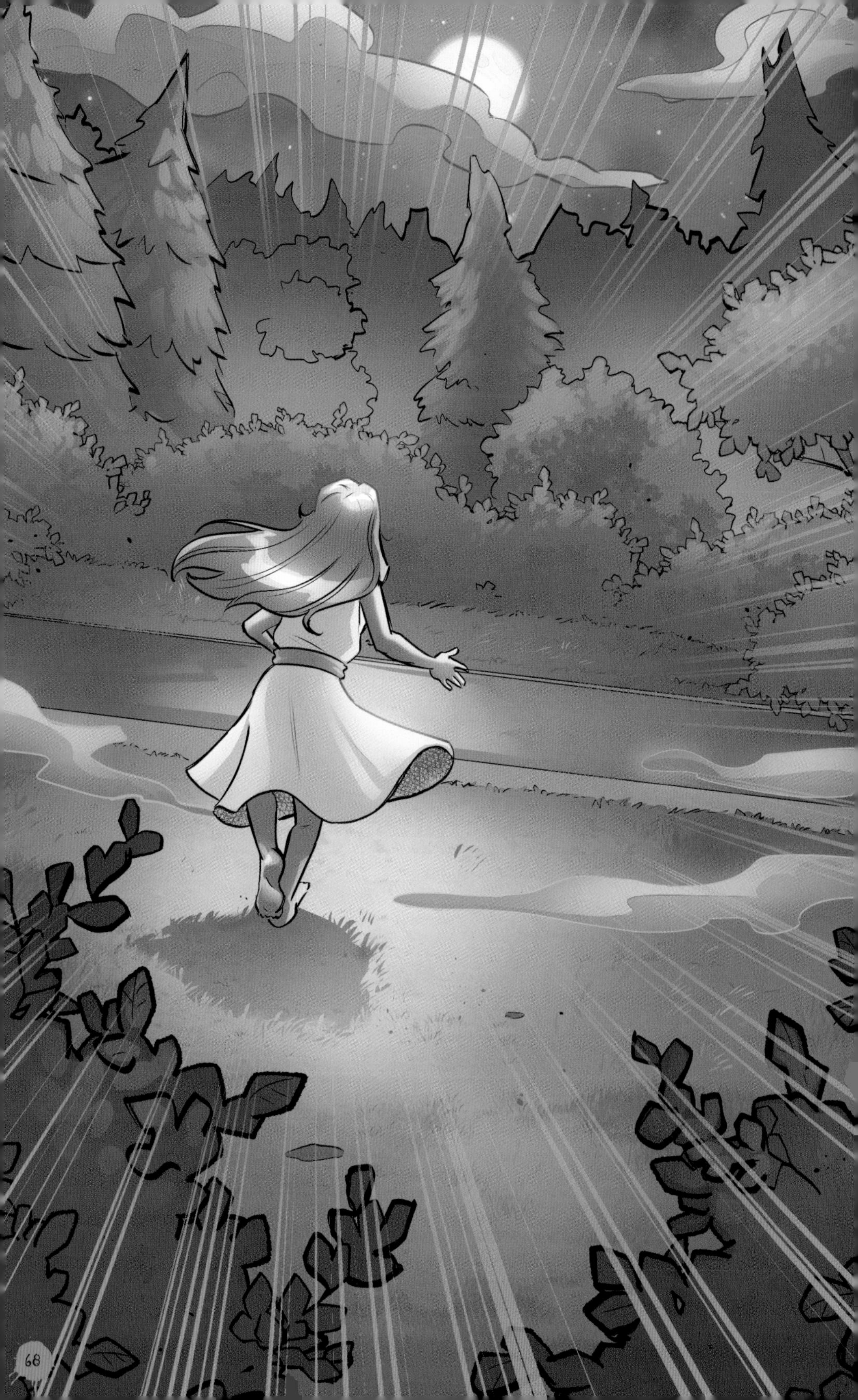

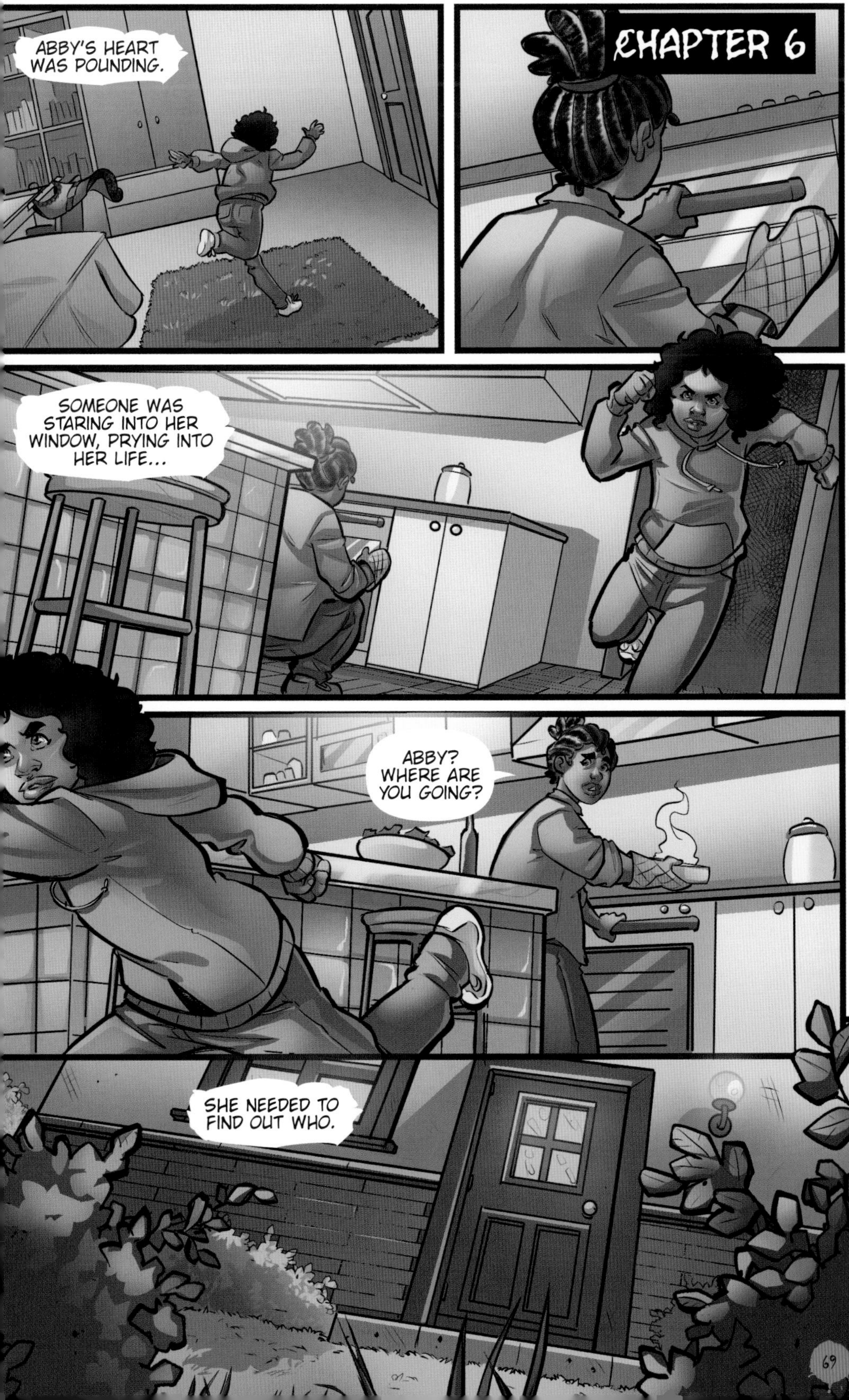

ABBY'S HEART WAS POUNDING.
CHAPTER 6
SOMEONE WAS STARING INTO HER WINDOW, PRYING INTO HER LIFE...
ABBY? WHERE ARE YOU GOING?
SHE NEEDED TO FIND OUT WHO.

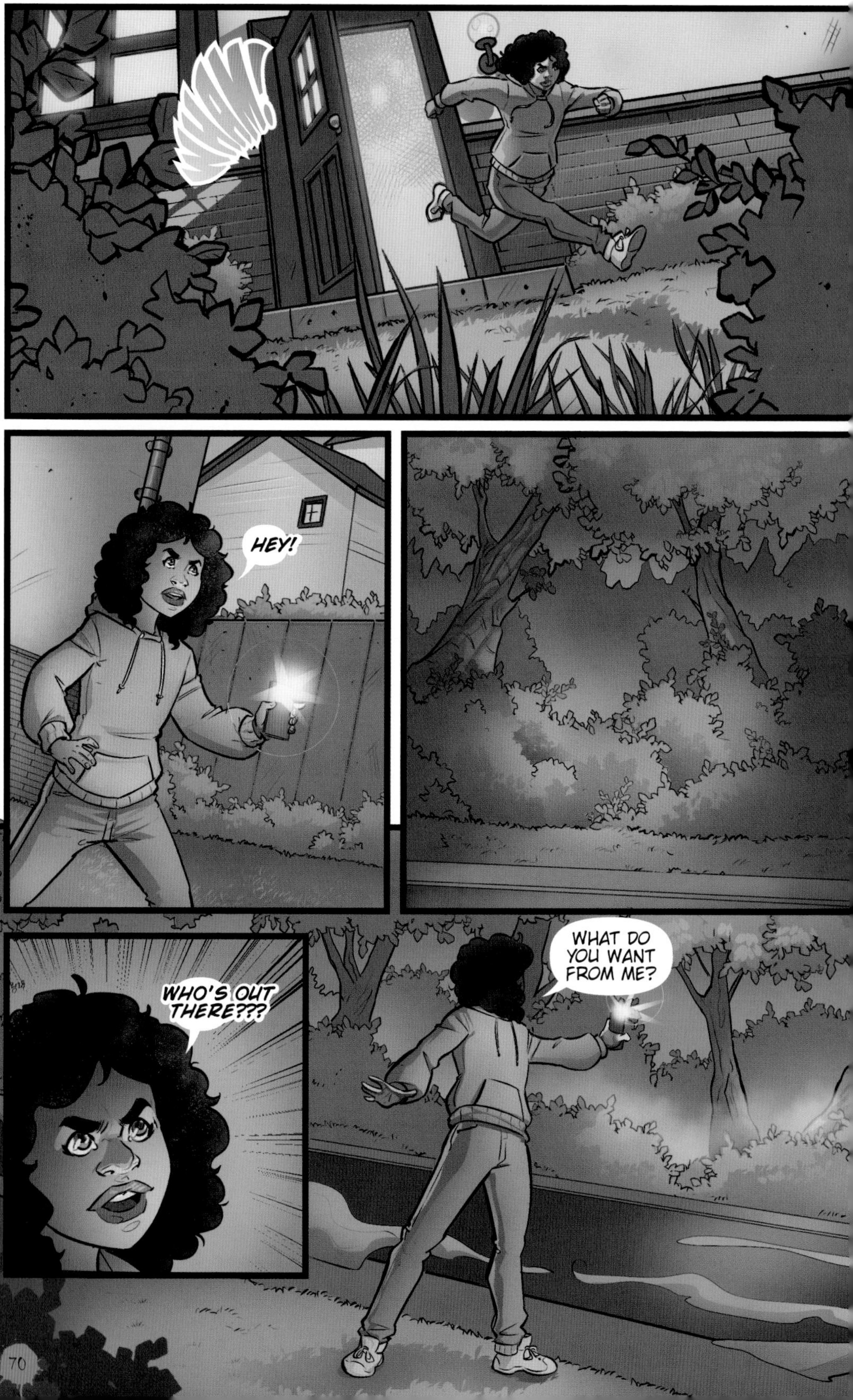
WHAM!
HEY!
WHO'S OUT THERE???
WHAT DO YOU WANT FROM ME?

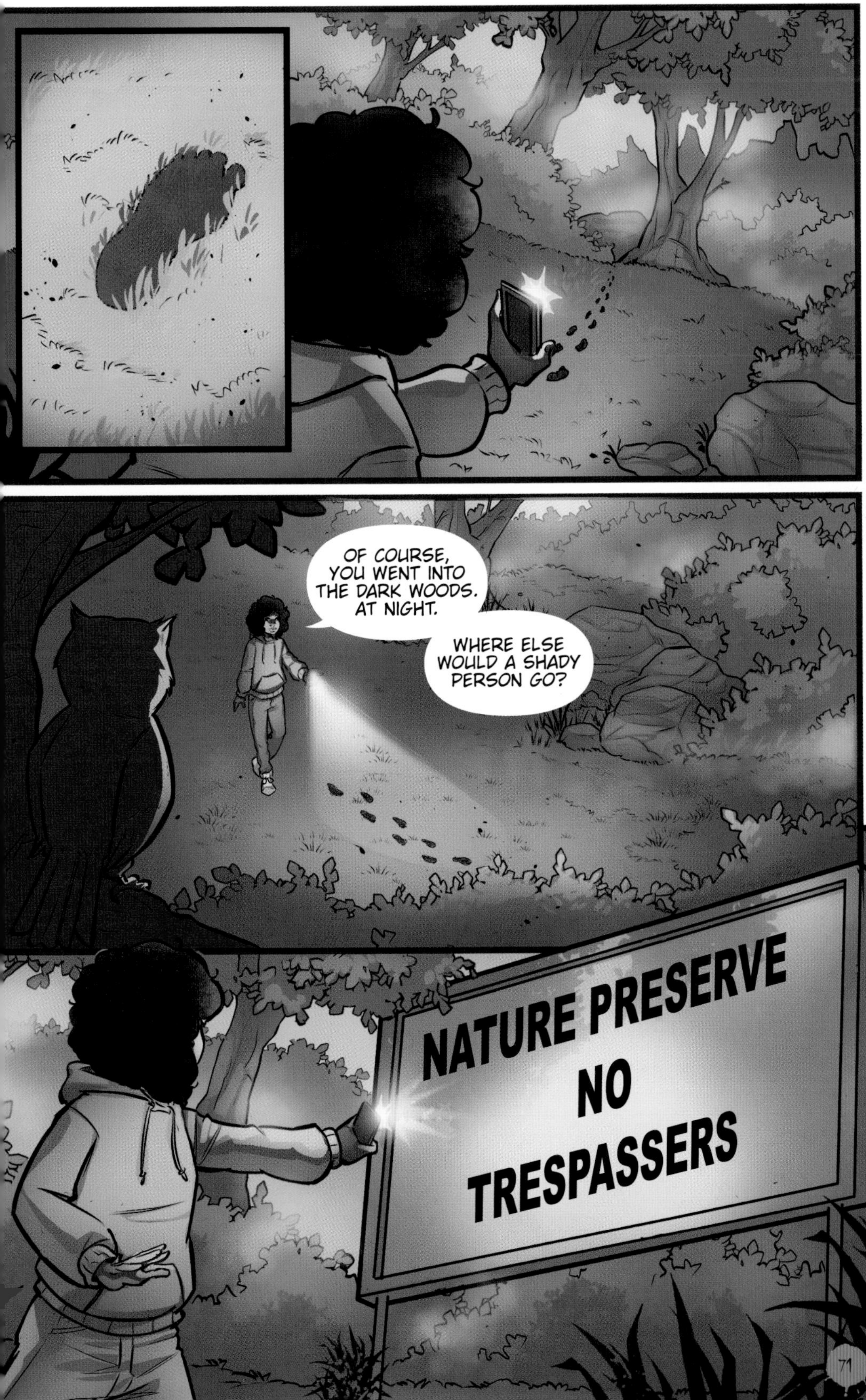
OF COURSE, YOU WENT INTO THE DARK WOODS. AT NIGHT.
WHERE ELSE WOULD A SHADY PERSON GO?
NATURE PRESERVE
NO
TRESPASSERS

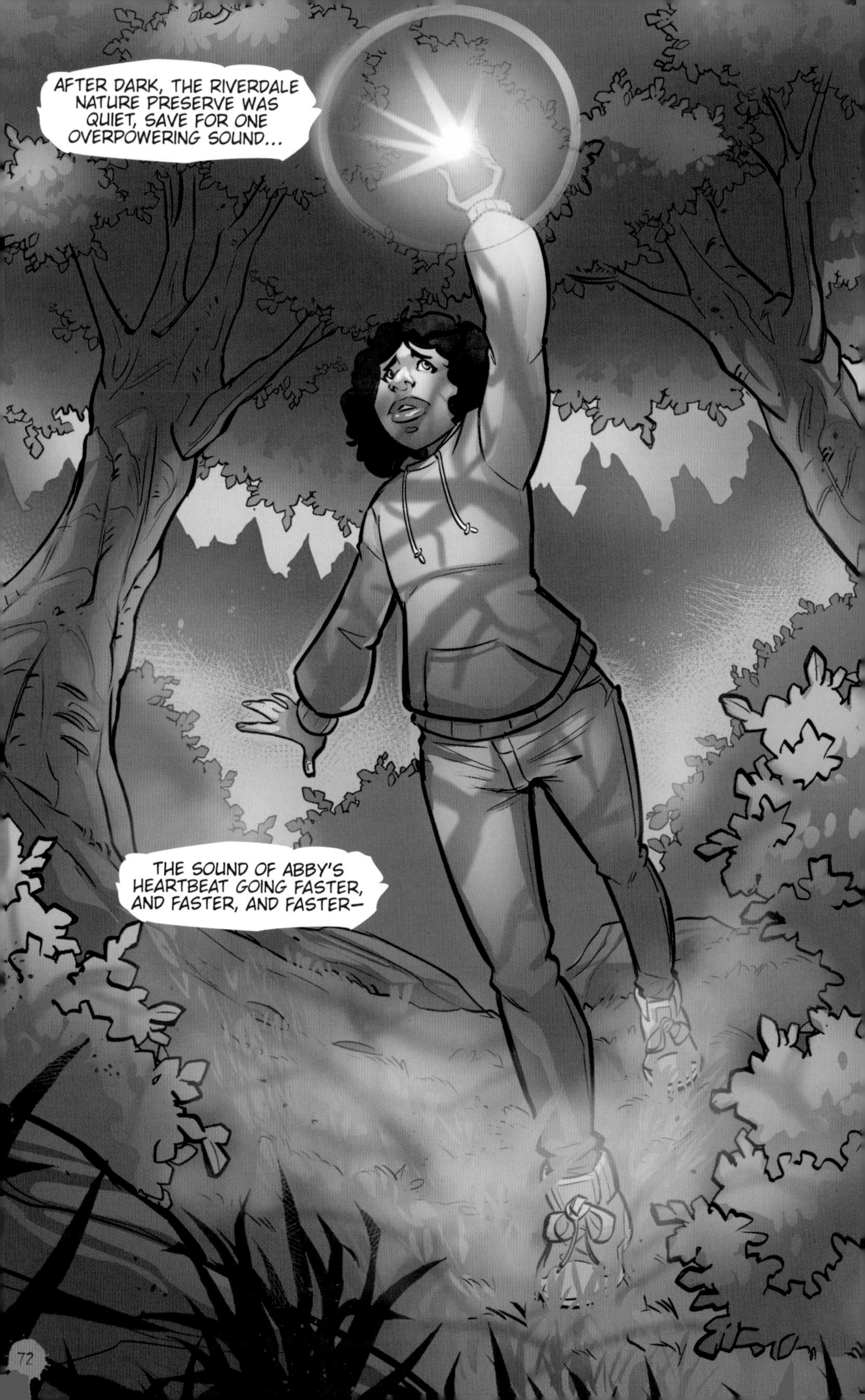
AFTER DARK, THE RIVERDALE NATURE PRESERVE WAS QUIET, SAVE FOR ONE OVERPOWERING SOUND...
THE SOUND OF ABBY'S HEARTBEAT GOING FASTER, AND FASTER, AND FASTER—

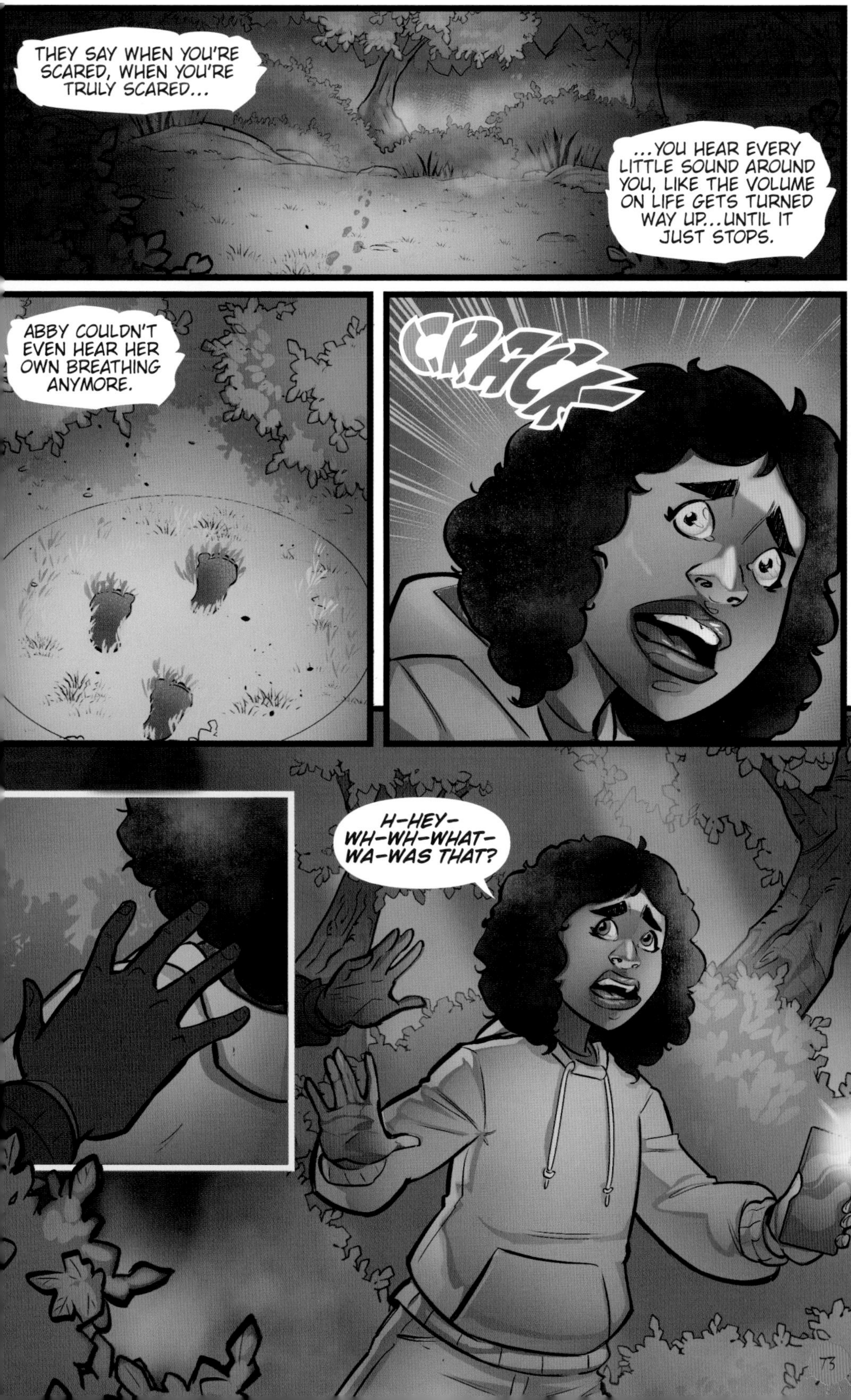
THEY SAY WHEN YOU'RE SCARED, WHEN YOU'RE TRULY SCARED...
...YOU HEAR EVERY LITTLE SOUND AROUND YOU, LIKE THE VOLUME ON LIFE GETS TURNED WAY UP...UNTIL IT JUST STOPS.
ABBY COULDN'T EVEN HEAR HER OWN BREATHING ANYMORE.
CRACK
H-HEY- WH-WH-WHAT- WA-WAS THAT?

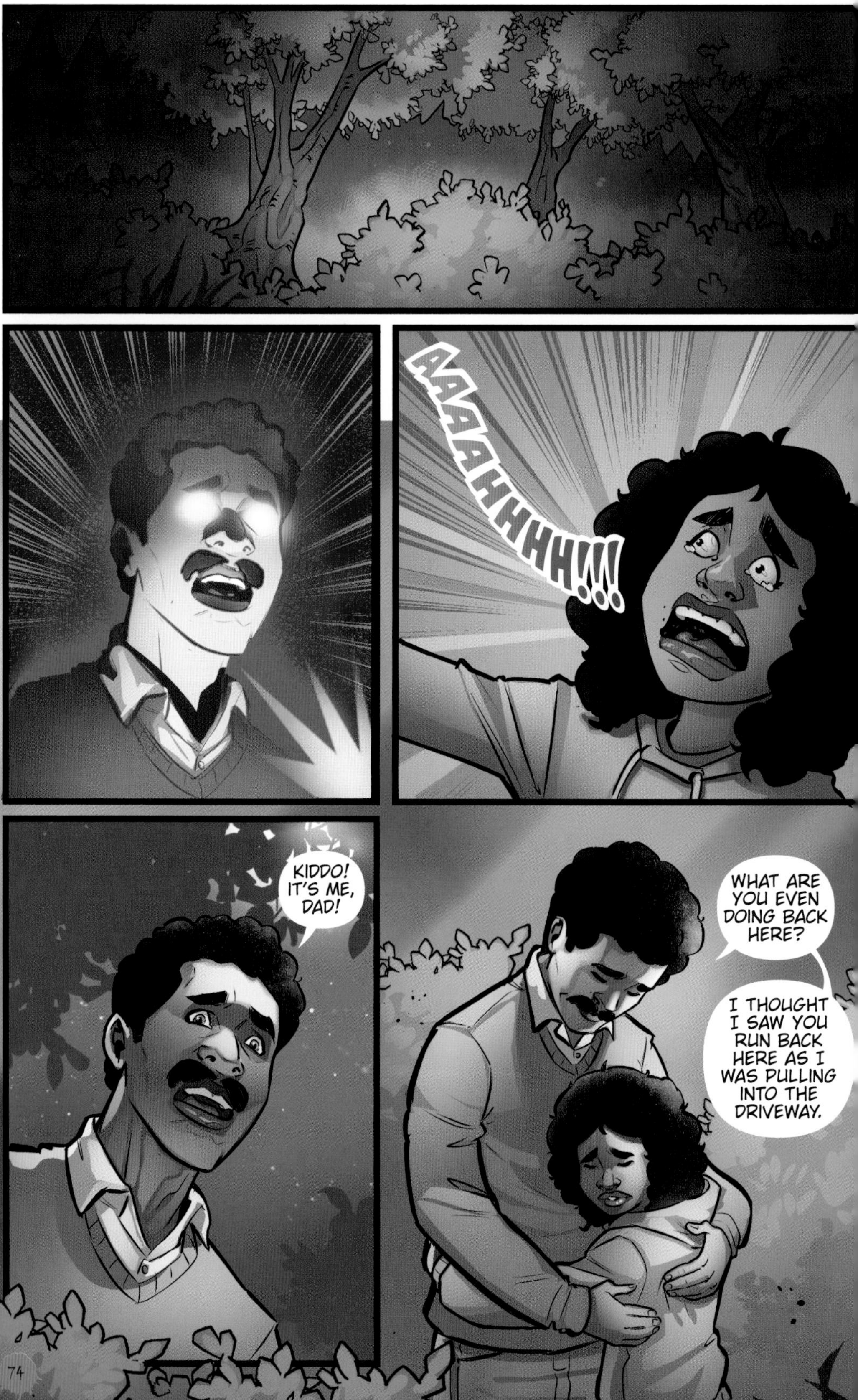
AAAAAHHHH!!!
KIDDO! IT'S ME, DAD!
WHAT ARE YOU EVEN DOING BACK HERE?
I THOUGHT I SAW YOU RUN BACK HERE AS I WAS PULLING INTO THE DRIVEWAY.

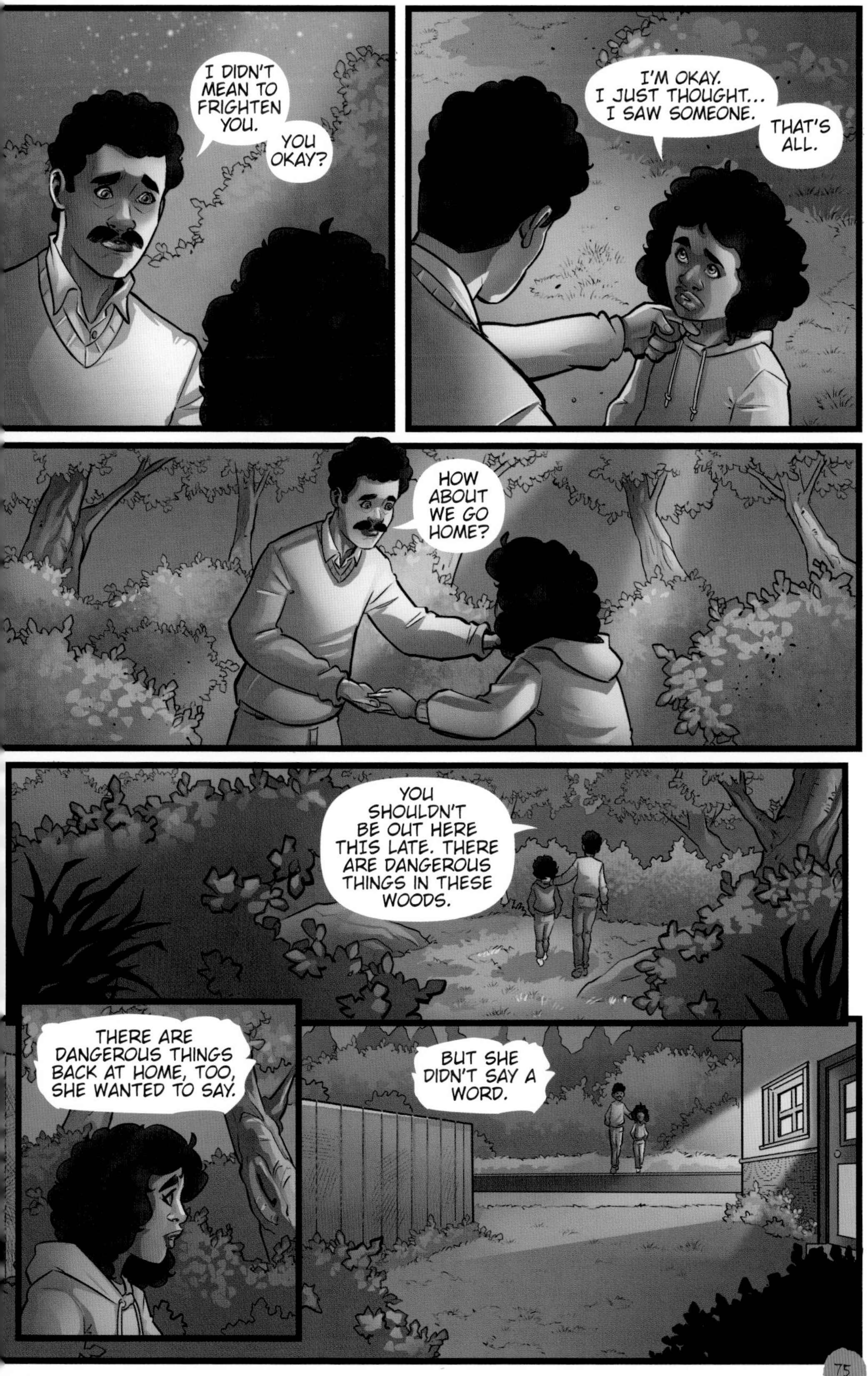

I DIDN'T MEAN TO FRIGHTEN YOU.
YOU OKAY?
I'M OKAY. I JUST THOUGHT... I SAW SOMEONE.
THAT'S ALL.
HOW ABOUT WE GO HOME?
YOU SHOULDN'T BE OUT HERE THIS LATE. THERE ARE DANGEROUS THINGS IN THESE WOODS.
THERE ARE DANGEROUS THINGS BACK AT HOME, TOO, SHE WANTED TO SAY.
BUT SHE DIDN'T SAY A WORD.

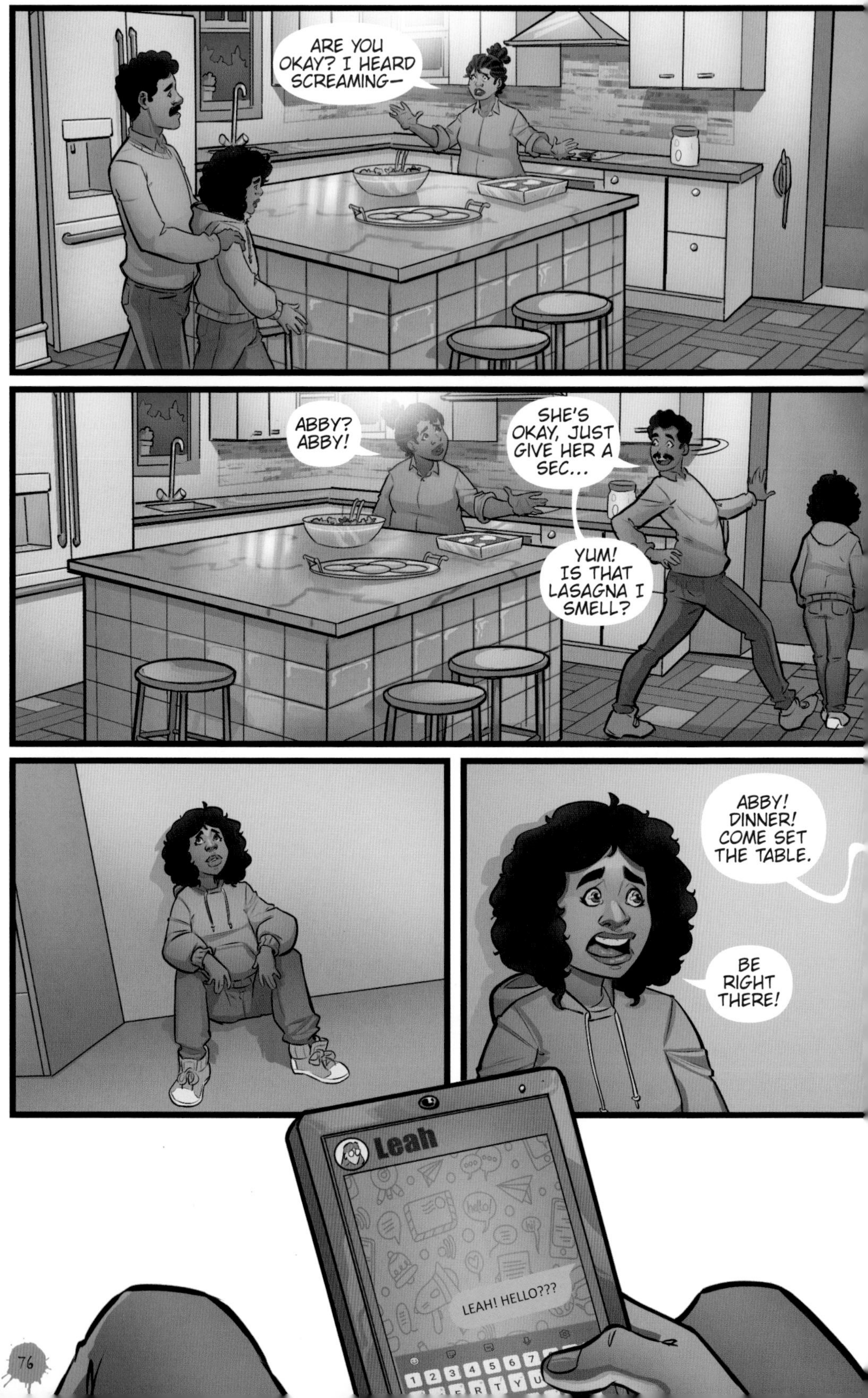
ARE YOU OKAY? I HEARD SCREAMING—
ABBY? ABBY!
SHE'S OKAY, JUST GIVE HER A SEC...
YUM! IS THAT LASAGNA I SMELL?
ABBY! DINNER! COME SET THE TABLE.
BE RIGHT THERE!
Leah
LEAH! HELLO???

Hey. What's up?

JUST CAUGHT A GIRL STARING IN MY WINDOW!!!!

WHAT???

I followed her into the woods, but she disappeared

Her hair looked just like...

??

I know it sounds crazy, but her hair looked just like...Sara's

I'm really freaking out

Take a breath. Relax.

Everybody has been talking a lot about Sara w/ the dance and all

And u might just be feeling strange bc you're going on a date

With Jake

I am sure you just imagined it

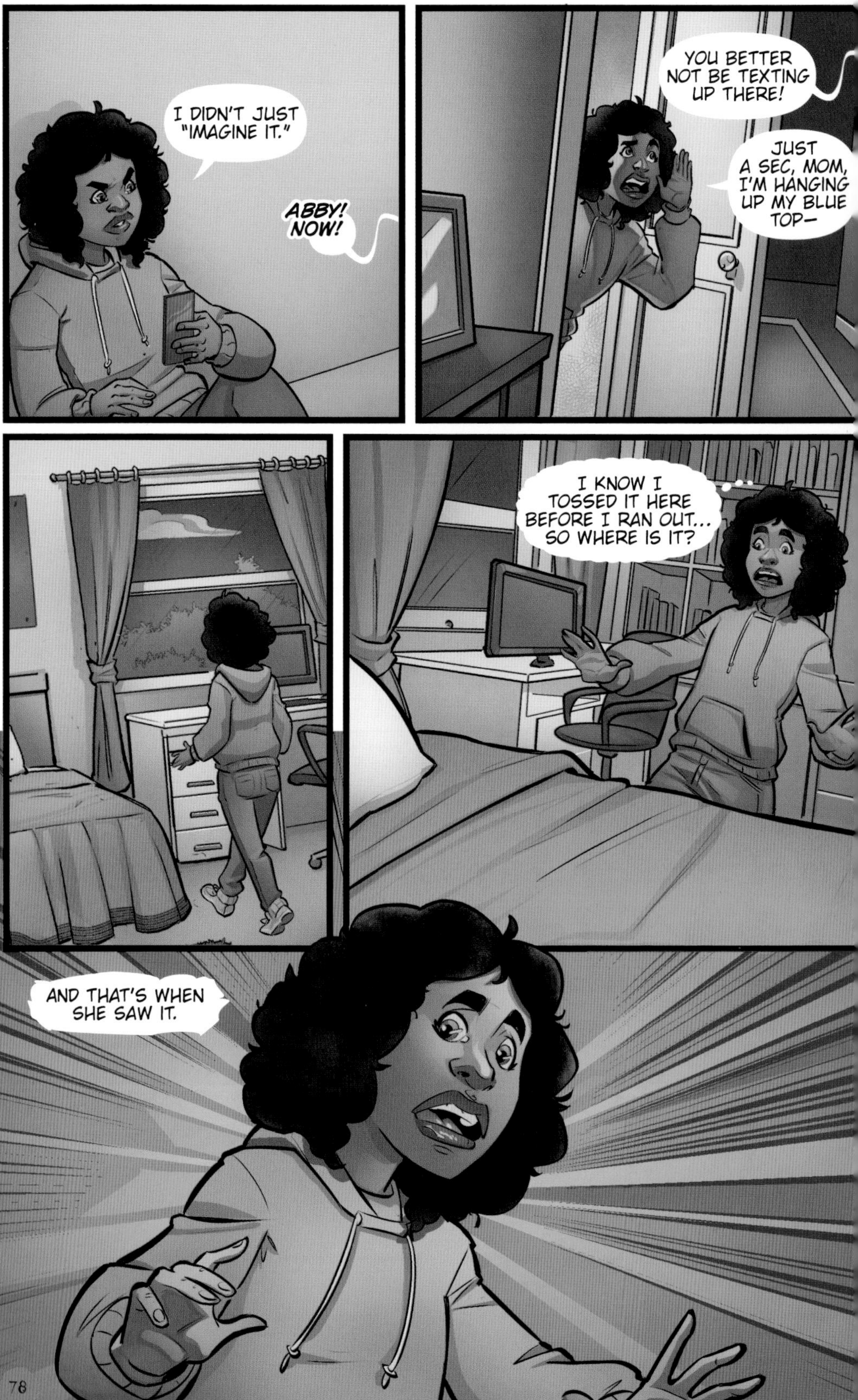
I DIDN'T JUST "IMAGINE IT."
ABBY! NOW!
YOU BETTER NOT BE TEXTING UP THERE!
JUST A SEC, MOM, I'M HANGING UP MY BLUE TOP—
I KNOW I TOSSED IT HERE BEFORE I RAN OUT... SO WHERE IS IT?
AND THAT'S WHEN SHE SAW IT.

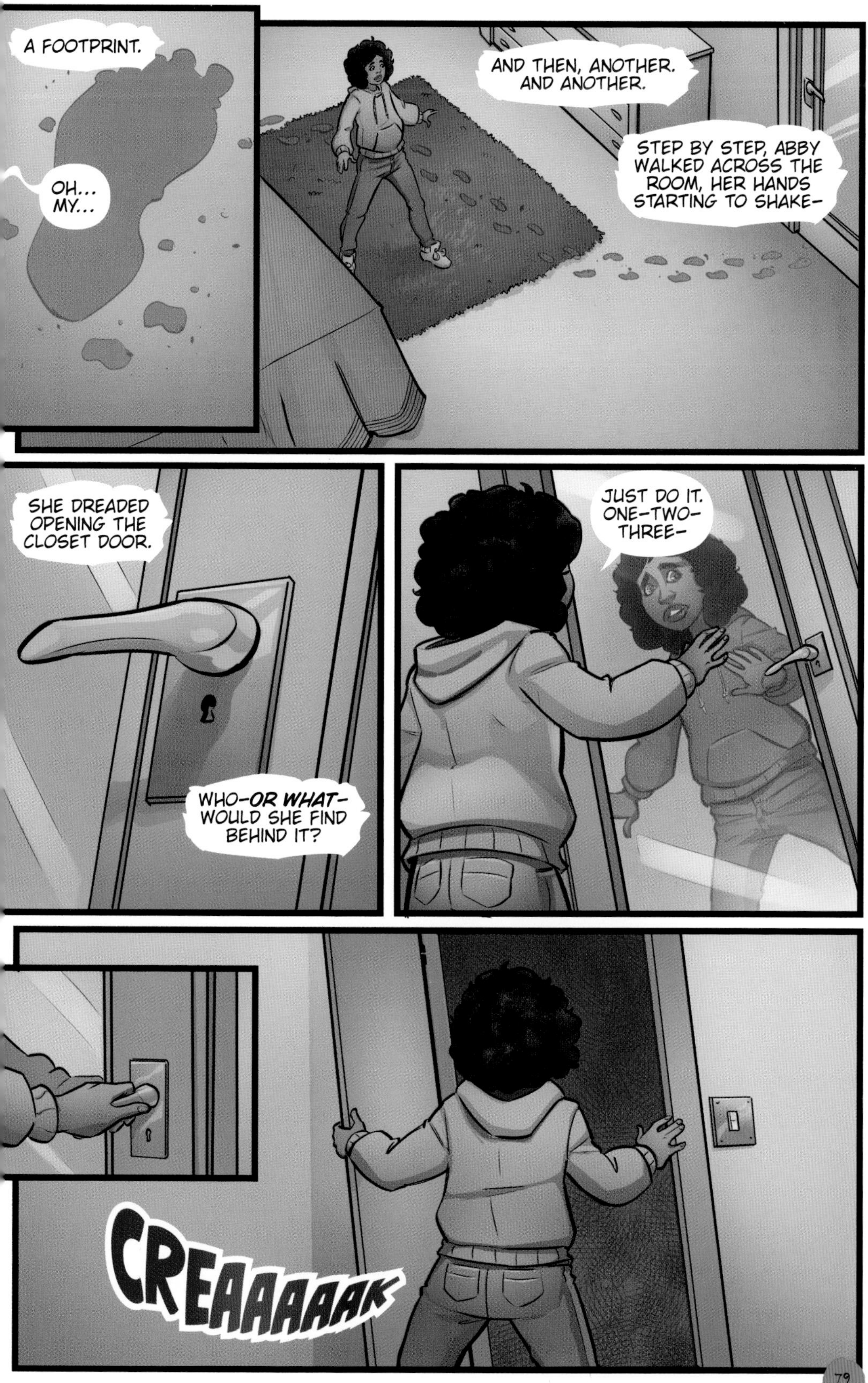
A FOOTPRINT.
OH... MY...
AND THEN, ANOTHER. AND ANOTHER.
STEP BY STEP, ABBY WALKED ACROSS THE ROOM, HER HANDS STARTING TO SHAKE-
SHE DREADED OPENING THE CLOSET DOOR.
WHO-**OR WHAT**-WOULD SHE FIND BEHIND IT?
JUST DO IT. ONE-TWO-THREE-
CREAAAAAK

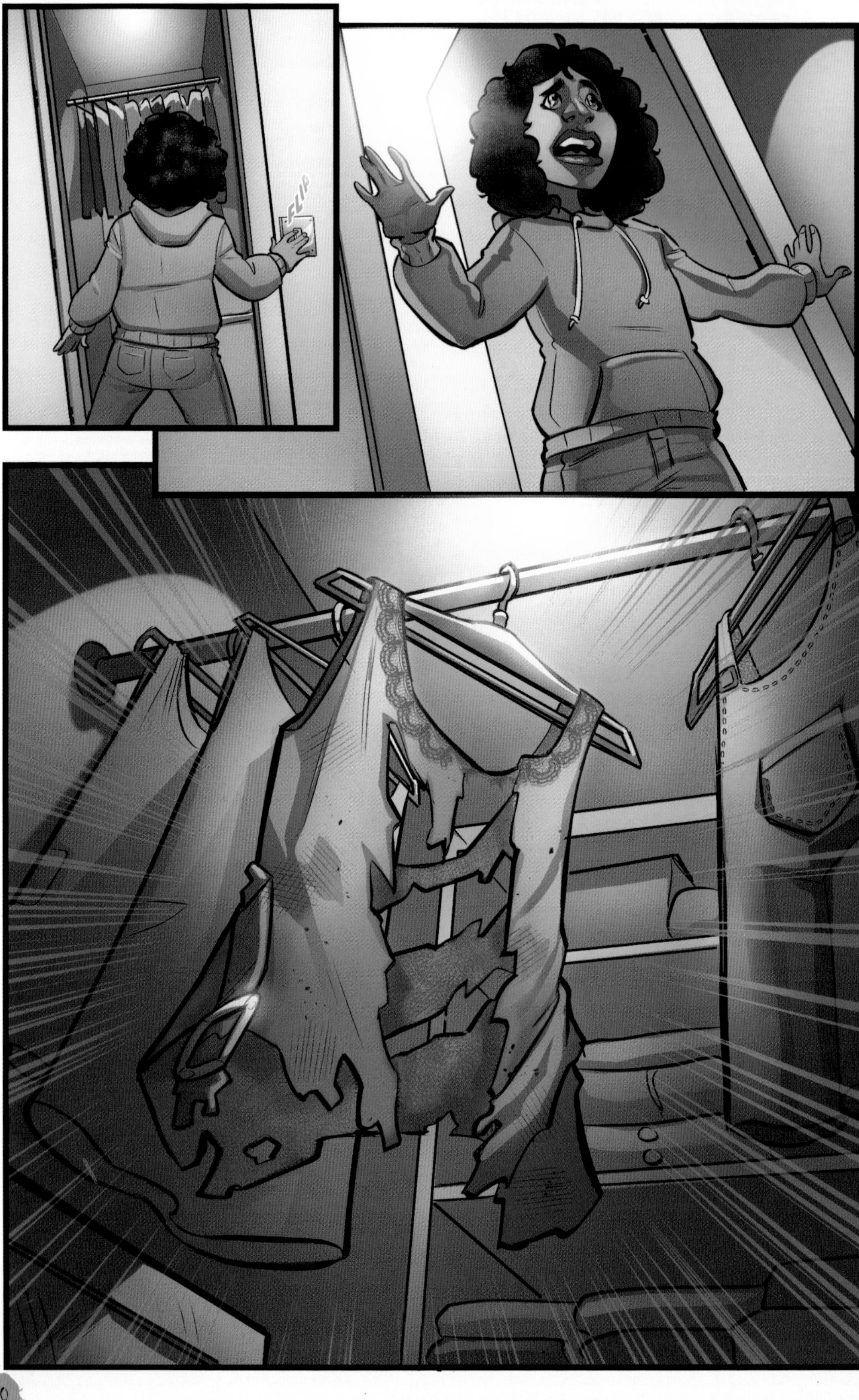
FLIP

CHAPTER 7

SOMETHING CRAZY IS DEF GOING ON! I JUST FOUND MY BRAND-NEW TOP RIPPED UP!!!

HUH?

I RAN OUTSIDE TO FOLLOW THAT GIRL, AND I THREW THE TOP ON MY BED, BUT WHEN I GOT BACK, IT WAS HANGING IN THE CLOSET, TORN TO PIECES!!

LEAH, SOMETHING REALLY SCARY IS GOING ON!

Ok, ok, calm down. There has to be a reasonable explanation for all this

Chester? Could he have chewed it up?

AND THEN HUNG IT UP IN THE CLOSET HIMSELF?

HE'S A DOG

DON'T YELL @ ME! I AM JUST TRYING TO HELP YOU

No offense, but it seems like U are trying to freak URSELF out

??

It's not enough for u that the guy u like asked u to the dance

Now u have to make up drama so u can be the center of attention?

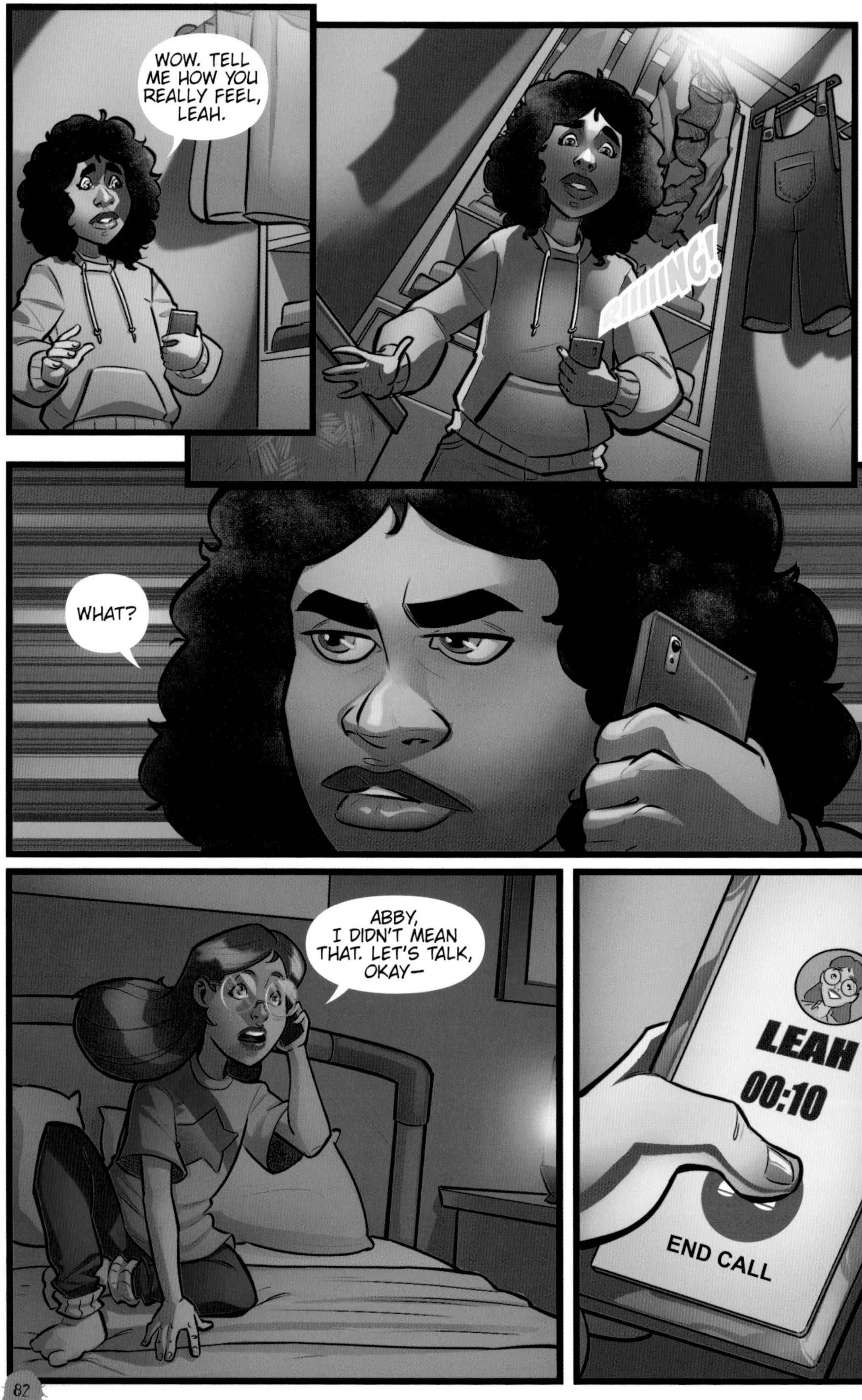
WOW. TELL ME HOW YOU REALLY FEEL, LEAH.
RIIIIIING!
WHAT?
ABBY, I DIDN'T MEAN THAT. LET'S TALK, OKAY—
LEAH
00:10
END CALL

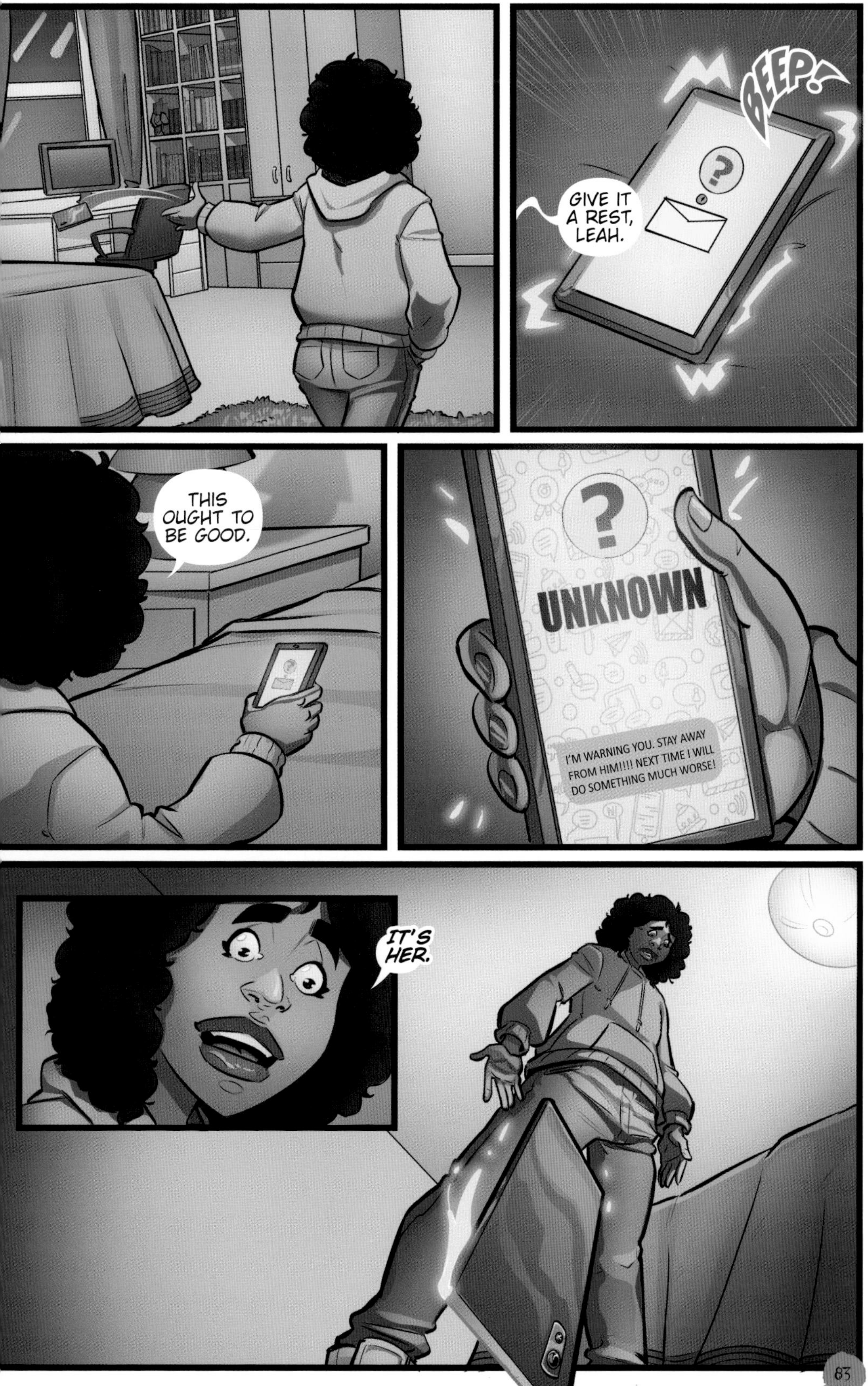
BEEP!
GIVE IT A REST, LEAH.
THIS OUGHT TO BE GOOD.
UNKNOWN
I'M WARNING YOU. STAY AWAY FROM HIM!!!! NEXT TIME I WILL DO SOMETHING MUCH WORSE!
IT'S HER.

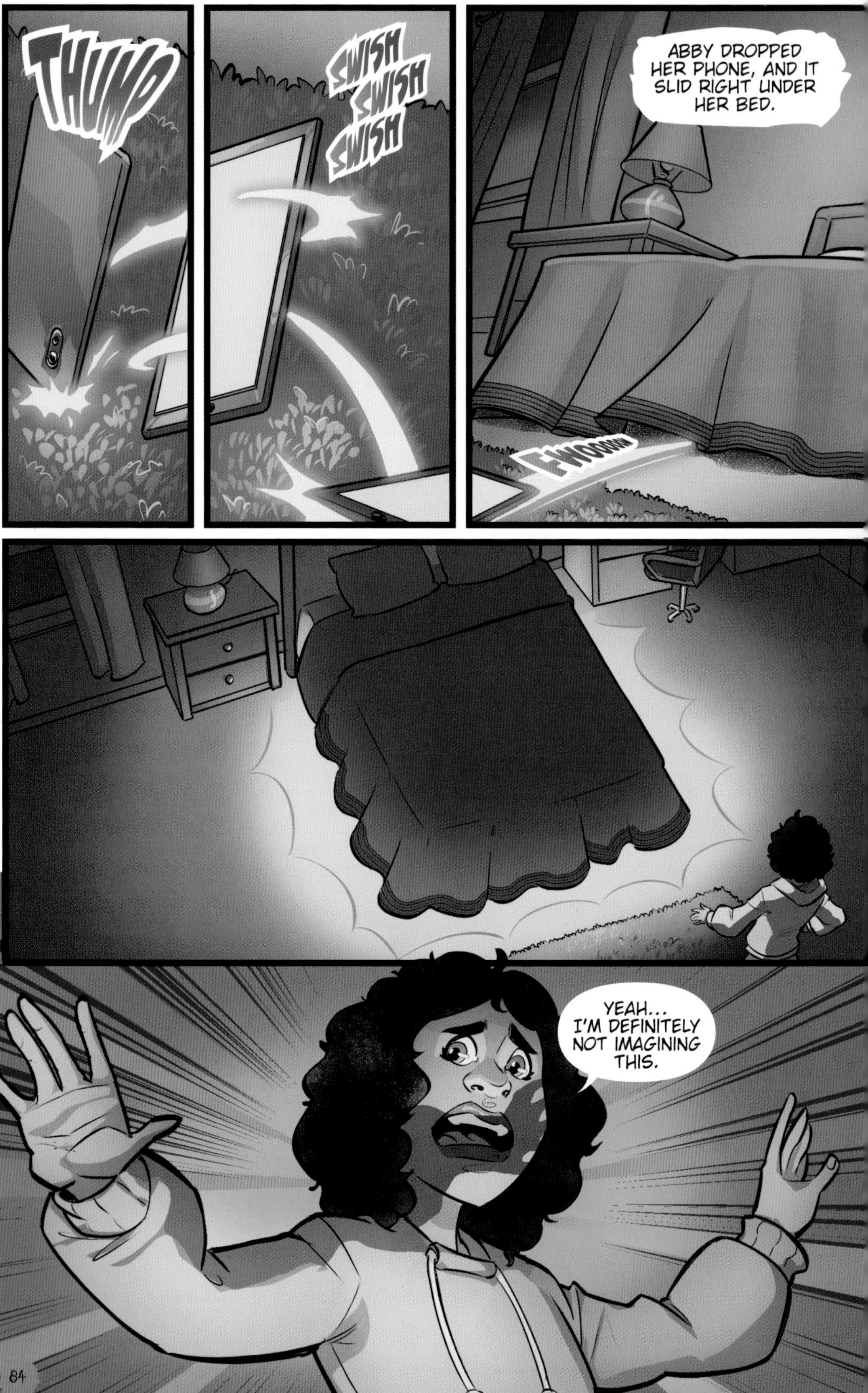
THUMP
SWISH
SWISH
SWISH
ABBY DROPPED HER PHONE, AND IT SLID RIGHT UNDER HER BED.
FWOOOOM
YEAH... I'M DEFINITELY NOT IMAGINING THIS.

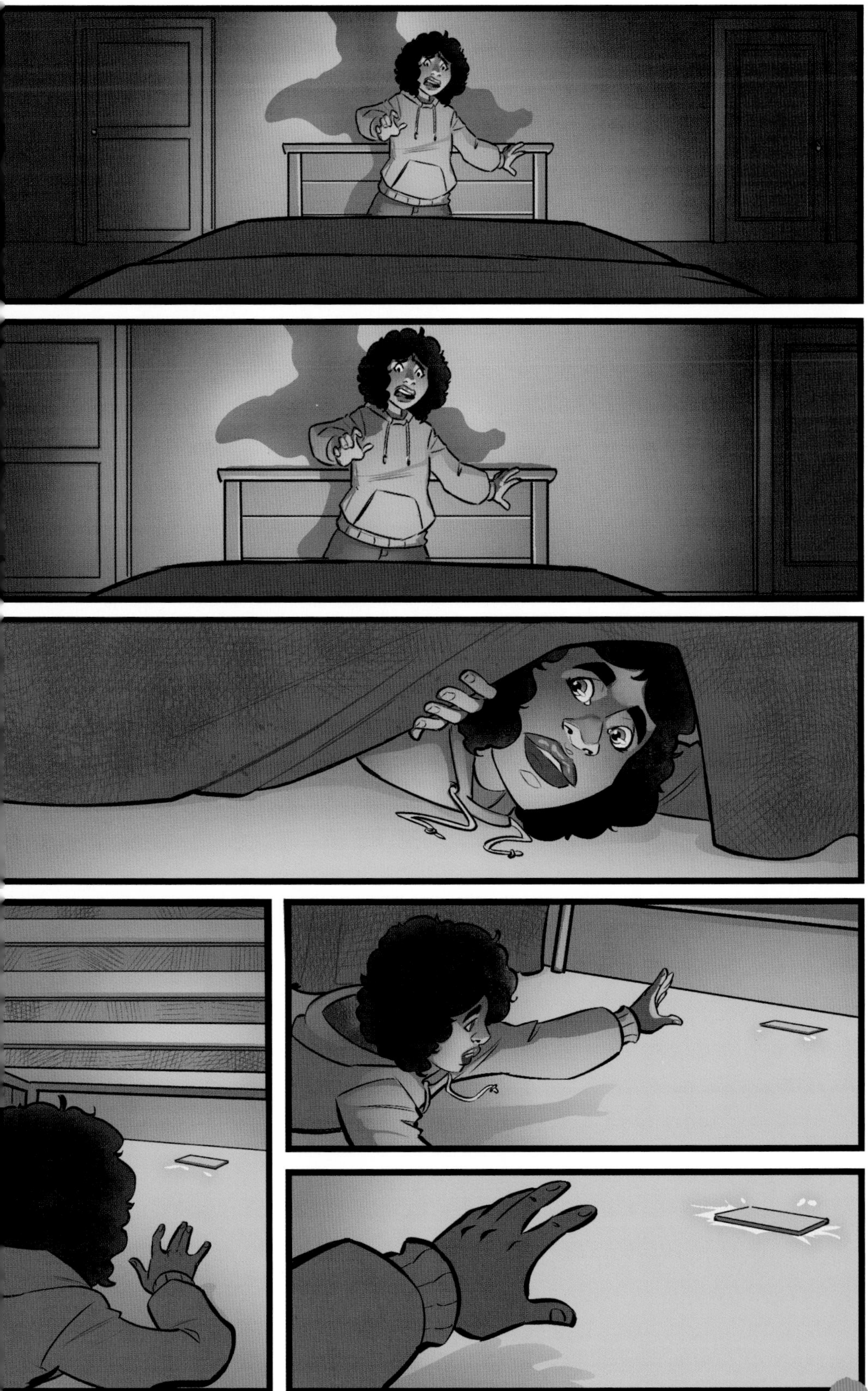

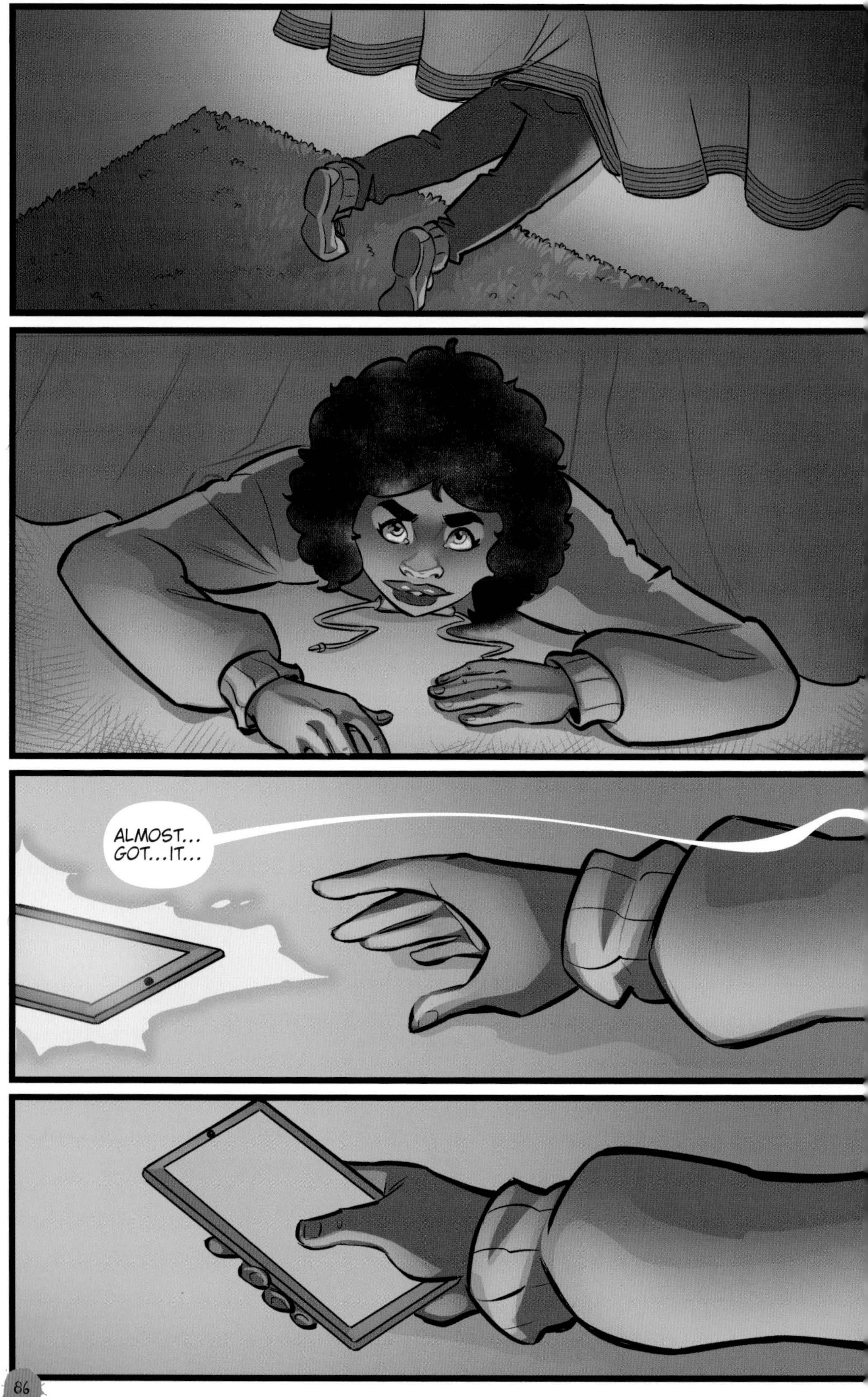
ALMOST...
GOT...IT...

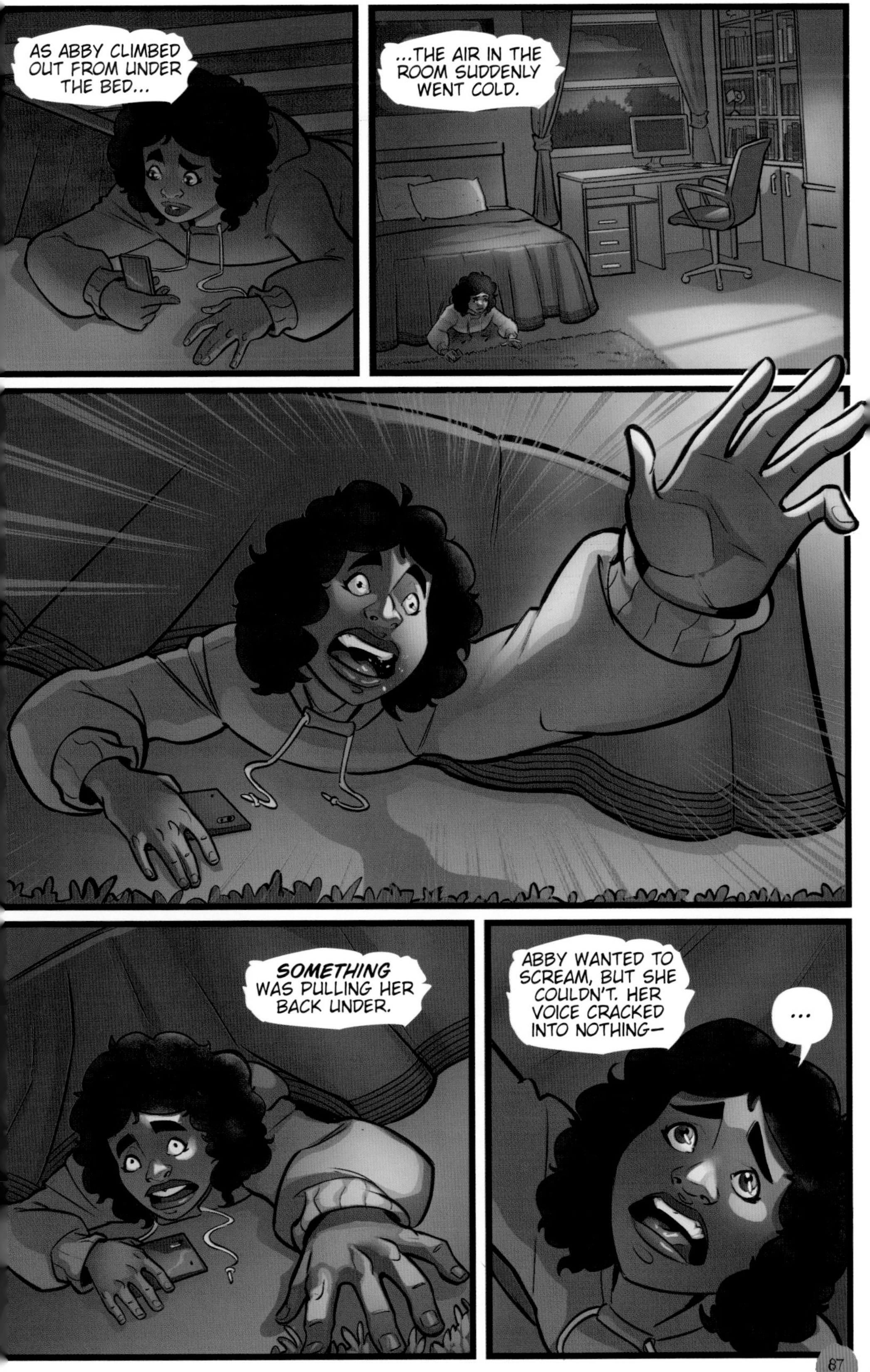
AS ABBY CLIMBED OUT FROM UNDER THE BED...
...THE AIR IN THE ROOM SUDDENLY WENT COLD.
SOMETHING WAS PULLING HER BACK UNDER.
ABBY WANTED TO SCREAM, BUT SHE COULDN'T. HER VOICE CRACKED INTO NOTHING—
...

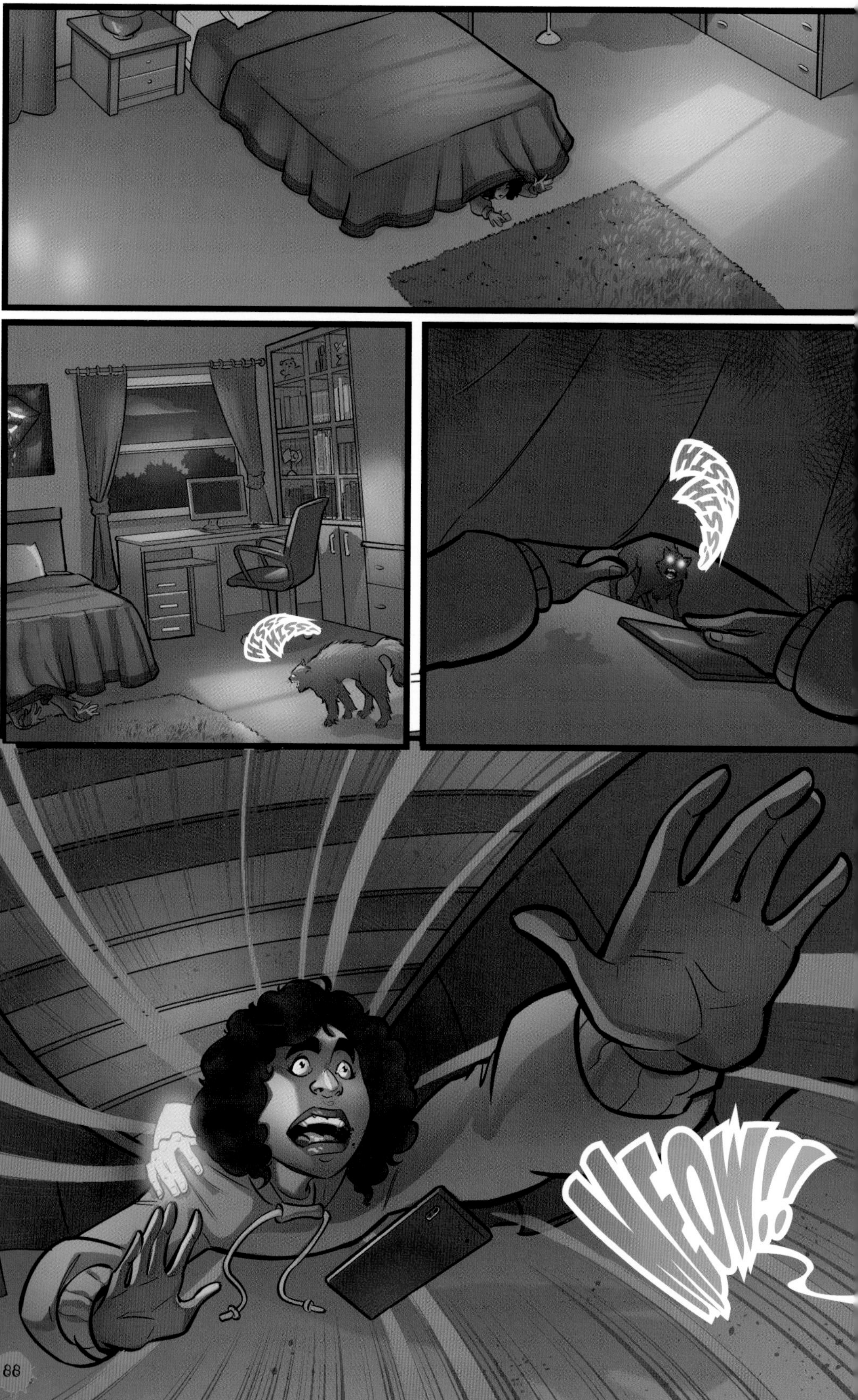
HISS! HISS!
HISS! HISS!
MEOW!!

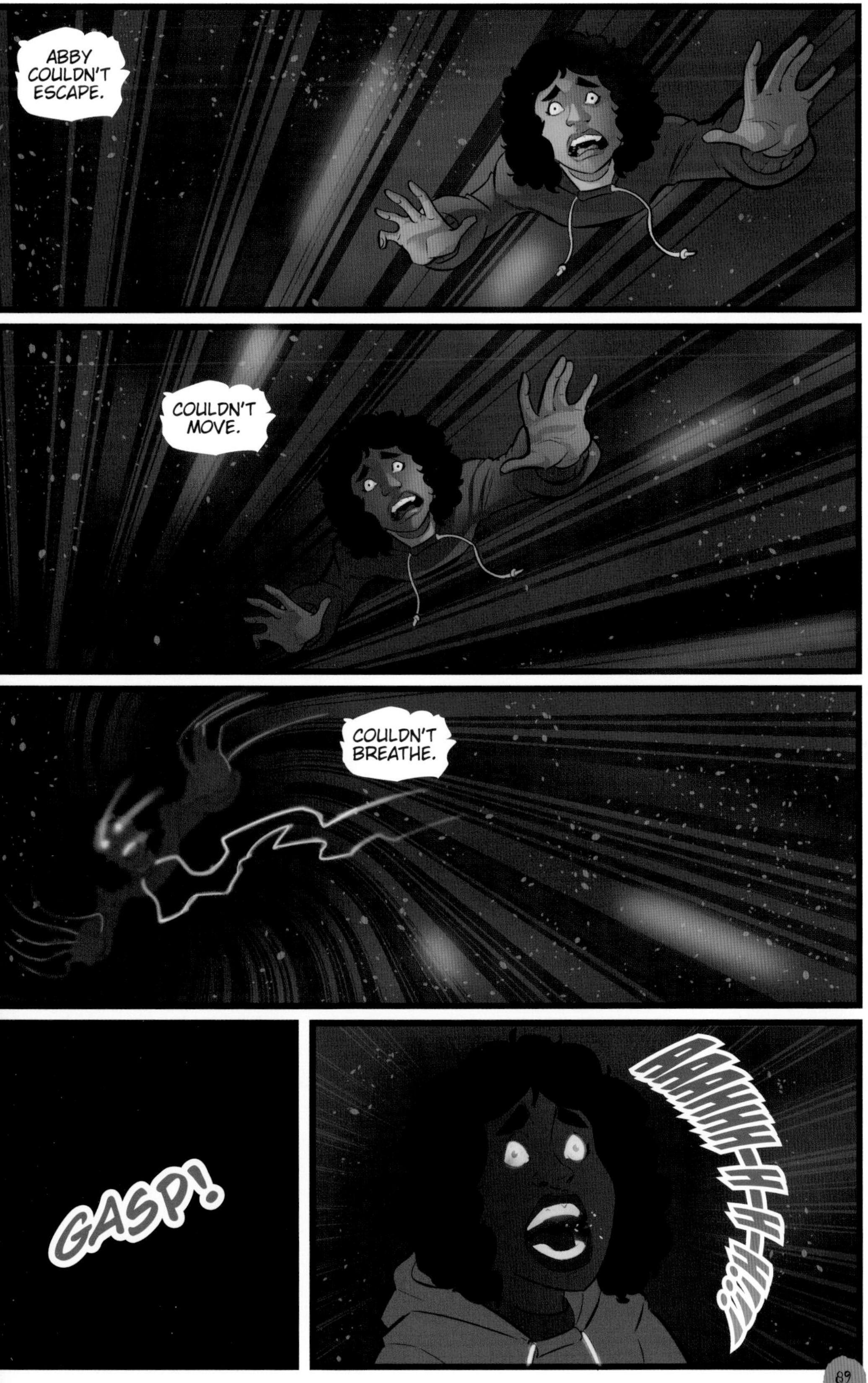
ABBY COULDN'T ESCAPE.
COULDN'T MOVE.
COULDN'T BREATHE.
GASP!
AAAHHHH–H–H–H...

CHAPTER 8

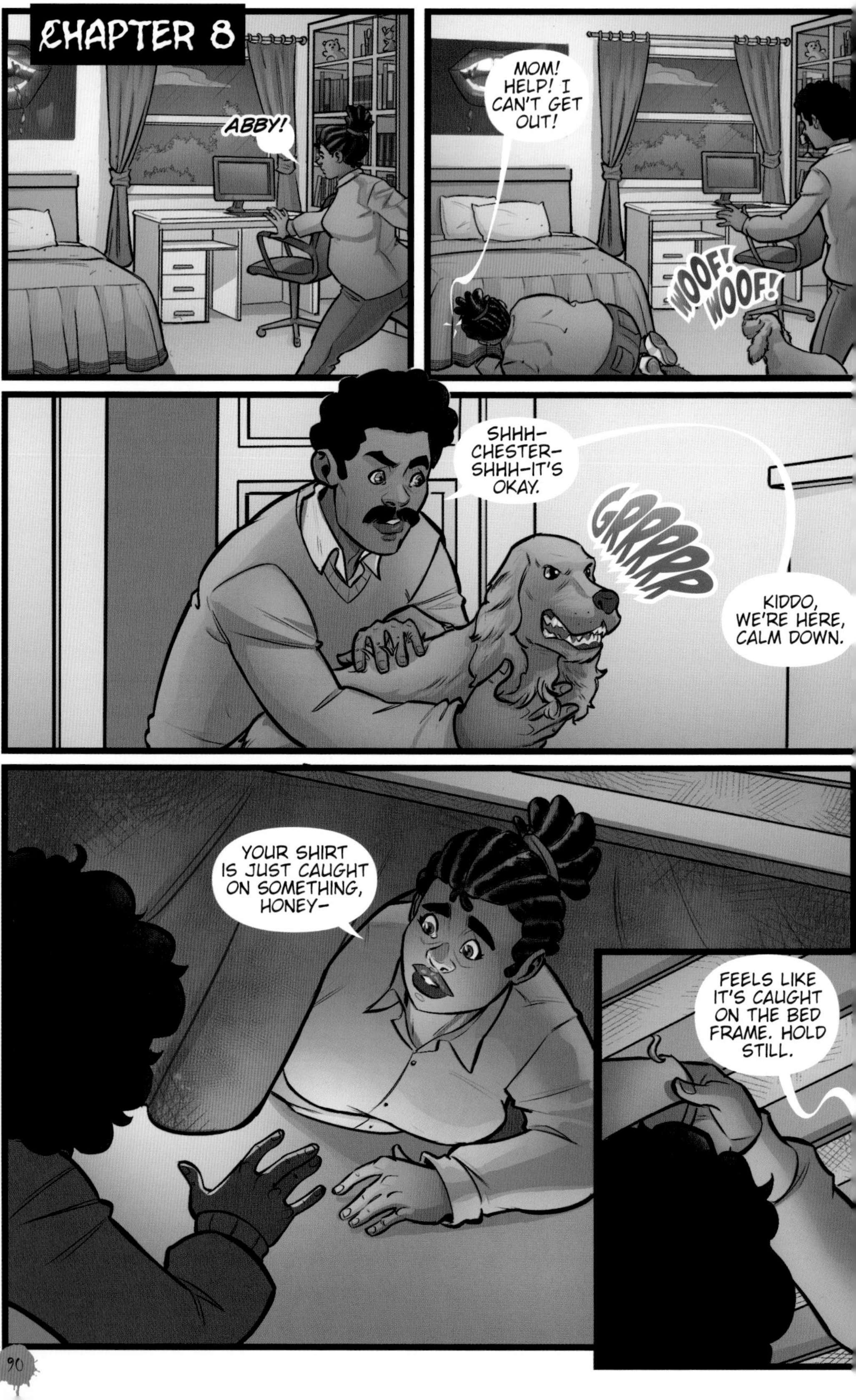
ABBY!
MOM! HELP! I CAN'T GET OUT!
WOOF! WOOF!
SHHH-CHESTER-SHHH-IT'S OKAY.
GRRRRP
KIDDO, WE'RE HERE, CALM DOWN.
YOUR SHIRT IS JUST CAUGHT ON SOMETHING, HONEY-
FEELS LIKE IT'S CAUGHT ON THE BED FRAME. HOLD STILL.

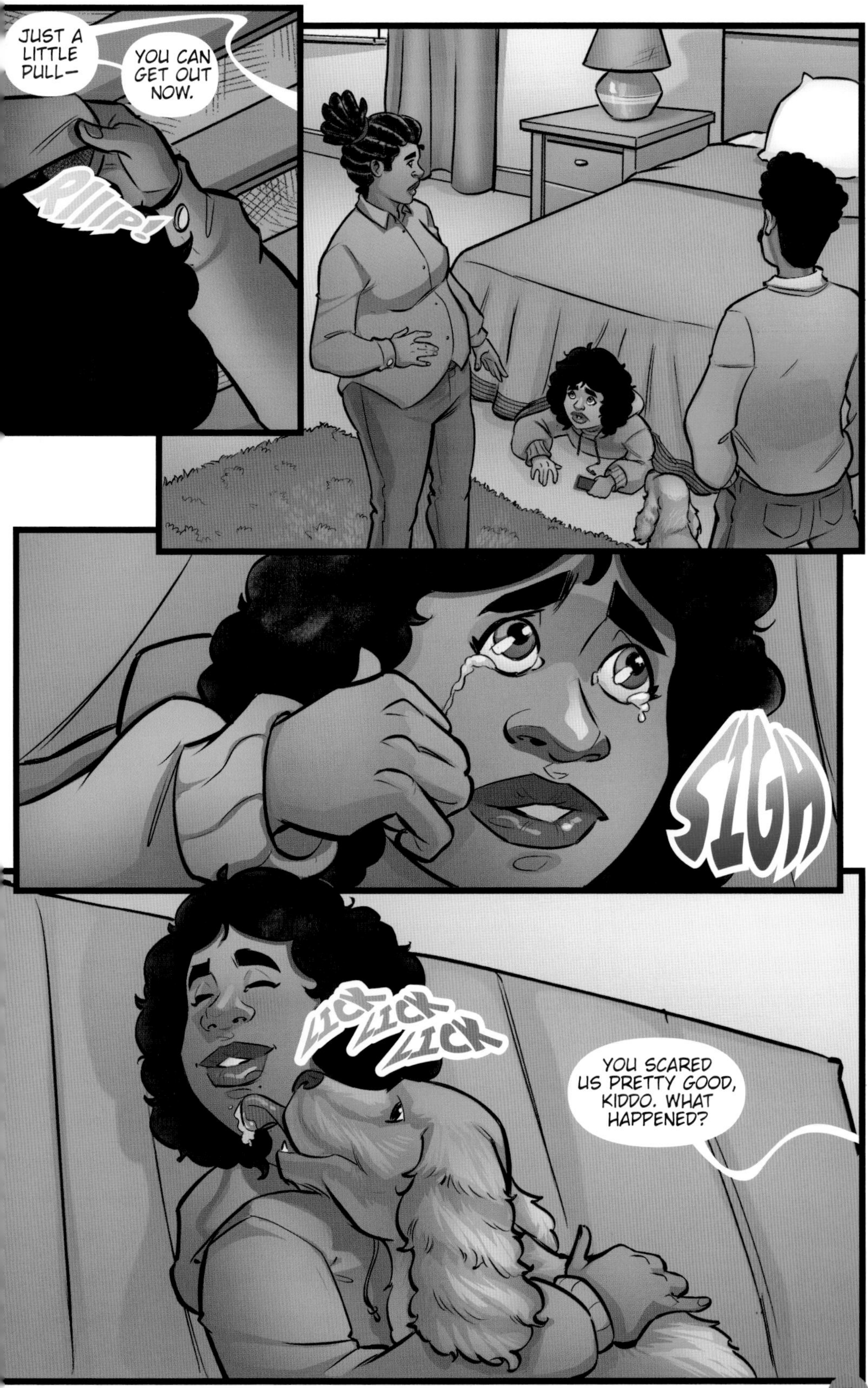
JUST A LITTLE PULL—
YOU CAN GET OUT NOW.
RIIIP!
SIGH
LICK LICK LICK
YOU SCARED US PRETTY GOOD, KIDDO. WHAT HAPPENED?

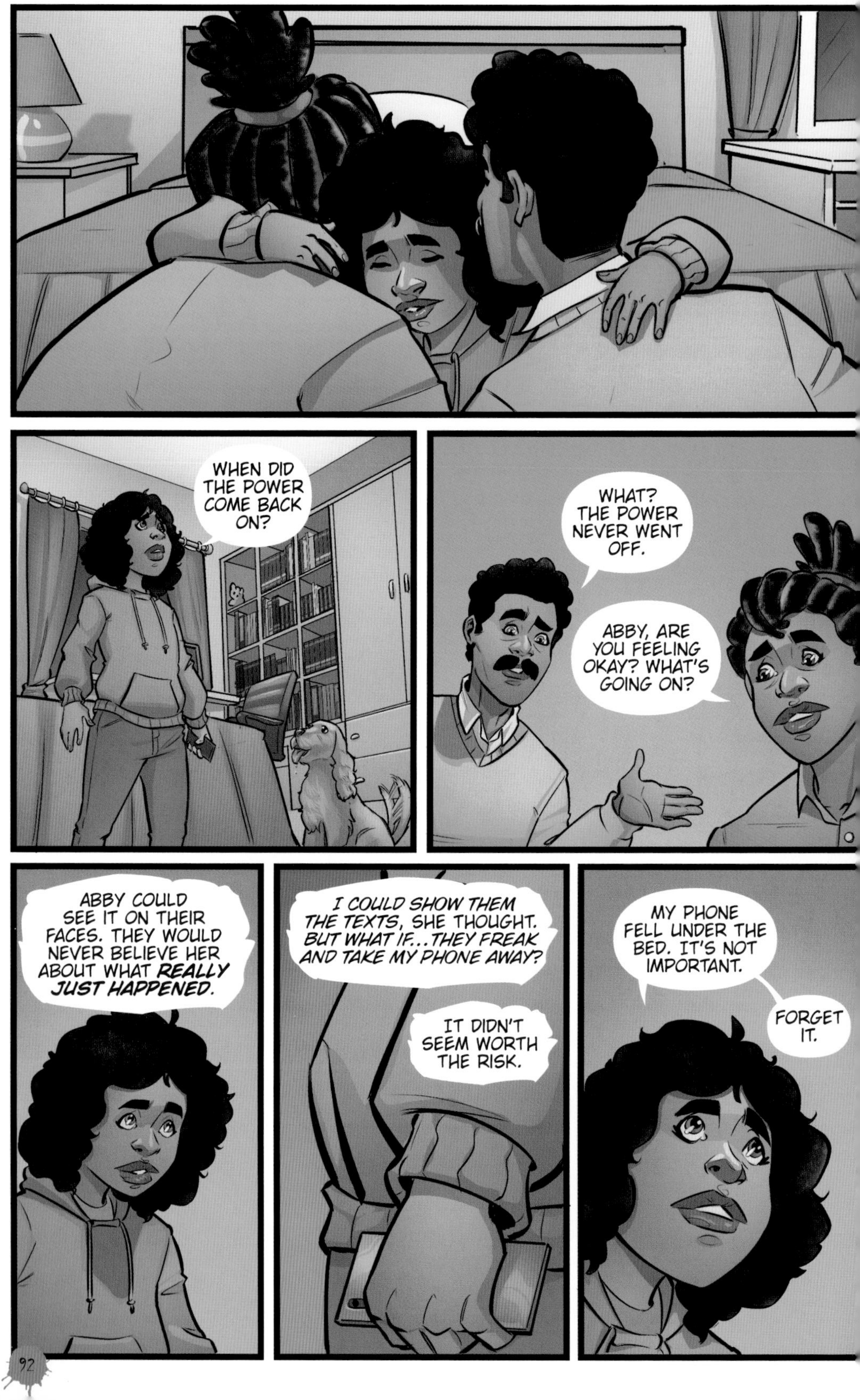
WHEN DID THE POWER COME BACK ON?
WHAT? THE POWER NEVER WENT OFF.
ABBY, ARE YOU FEELING OKAY? WHAT'S GOING ON?
ABBY COULD SEE IT ON THEIR FACES. THEY WOULD NEVER BELIEVE HER ABOUT WHAT ***REALLY JUST HAPPENED***.
I COULD SHOW THEM THE TEXTS, SHE THOUGHT. *BUT WHAT IF...THEY FREAK AND TAKE MY PHONE AWAY?*
IT DIDN'T SEEM WORTH THE RISK.
MY PHONE FELL UNDER THE BED. IT'S NOT IMPORTANT.
FORGET IT.

COME ON. SOME LASAGNA WILL HELP YOU FEEL BETTER.

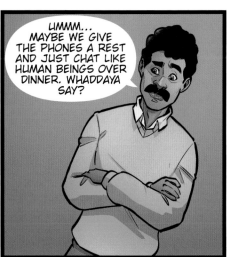

UMMM... MAYBE WE GIVE THE PHONES A REST AND JUST CHAT LIKE HUMAN BEINGS OVER DINNER. WHADDAYA SAY?

WITH PLEASURE.

WOW, I CAN'T BELIEVE THAT WORKED! YOU HIT YOUR HEAD UNDER THE BED, KIDDO?

FIRST A HUG? THEN WILLINGLY NOT TAKING YOUR PHONE TO THE DINNER TABLE?

WHO ARE YOU AND WHAT HAVE YOU DONE WITH MY DAUGHTER?

THUMP

OH HAHA. VERY FUNNY.

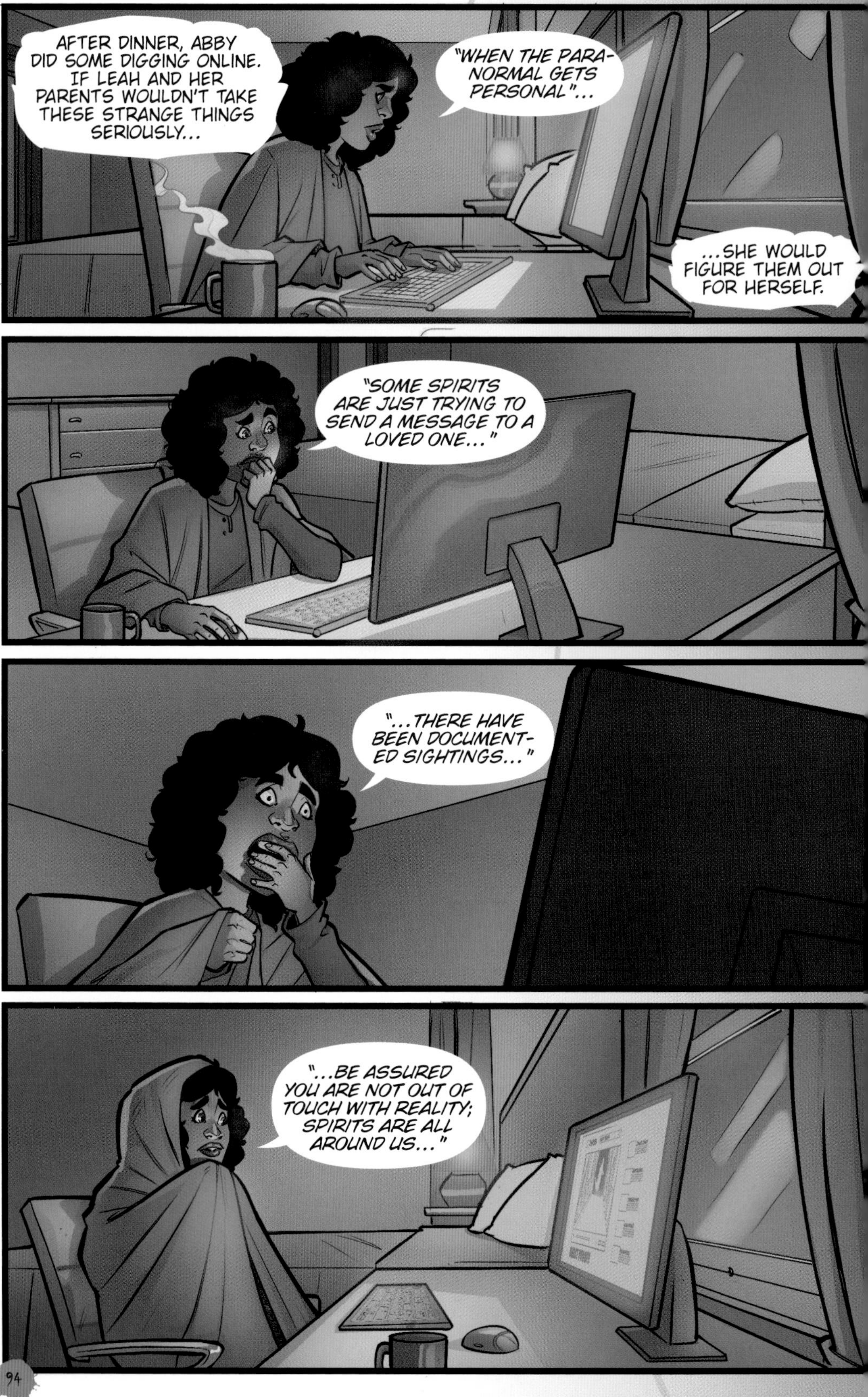
AFTER DINNER, ABBY DID SOME DIGGING ONLINE. IF LEAH AND HER PARENTS WOULDN'T TAKE THESE STRANGE THINGS SERIOUSLY...
"WHEN THE PARA-NORMAL GETS PERSONAL"...
...SHE WOULD FIGURE THEM OUT FOR HERSELF.
"SOME SPIRITS ARE JUST TRYING TO SEND A MESSAGE TO A LOVED ONE..."
"...THERE HAVE BEEN DOCUMENT-ED SIGHTINGS..."
"...BE ASSURED YOU ARE NOT OUT OF TOUCH WITH REALITY; SPIRITS ARE ALL AROUND US..."

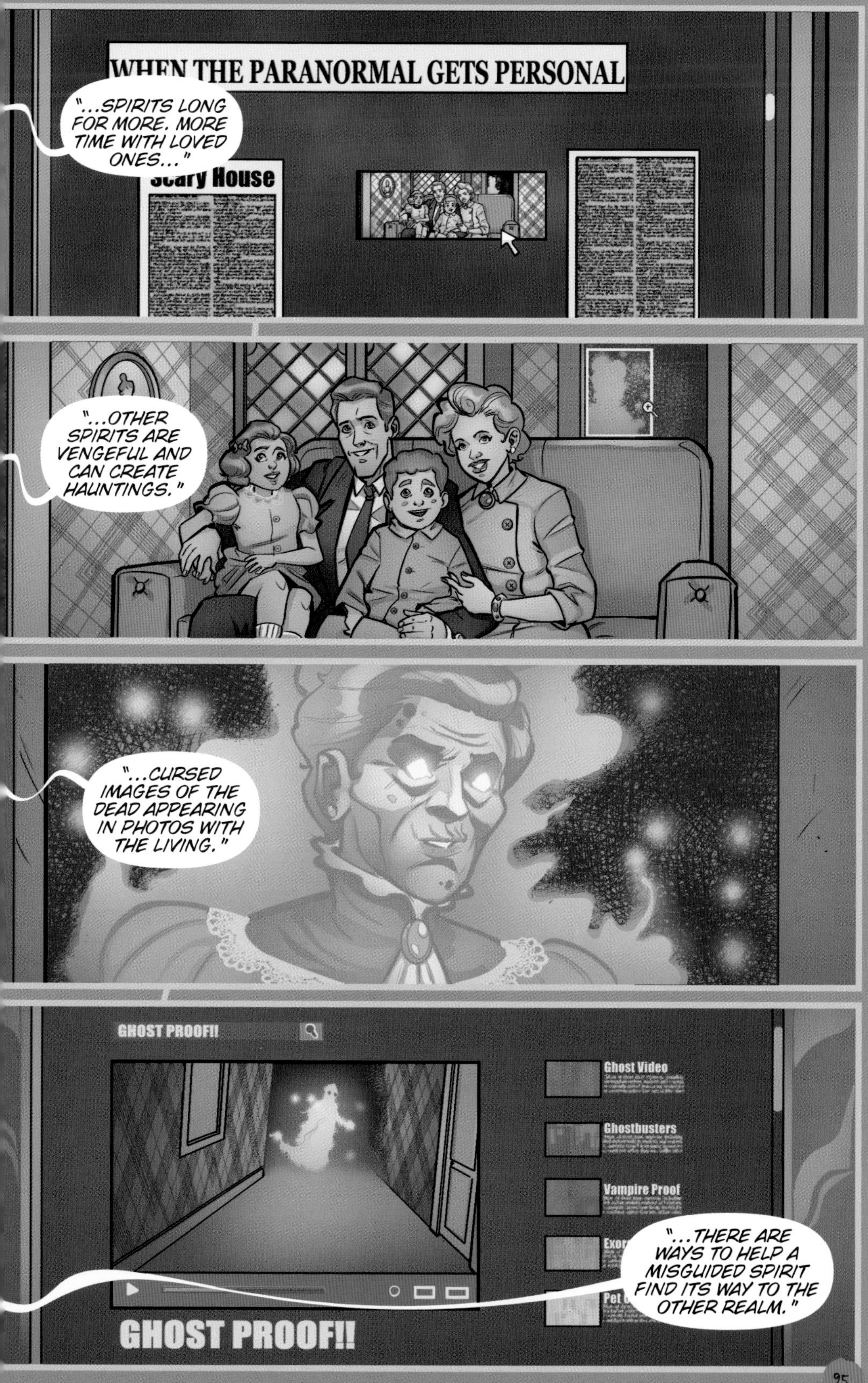

WHEN THE PARANORMAL GETS PERSONAL
"...SPIRITS LONG FOR MORE. MORE TIME WITH LOVED ONES..."
Scary House
"...OTHER SPIRITS ARE VENGEFUL AND CAN CREATE HAUNTINGS."
"...CURSED IMAGES OF THE DEAD APPEARING IN PHOTOS WITH THE LIVING."
GHOST PROOF!!
Ghost Video
Ghostbusters
Vampire Proof
"...THERE ARE WAYS TO HELP A MISGUIDED SPIRIT FIND ITS WAY TO THE OTHER REALM."
GHOST PROOF!!

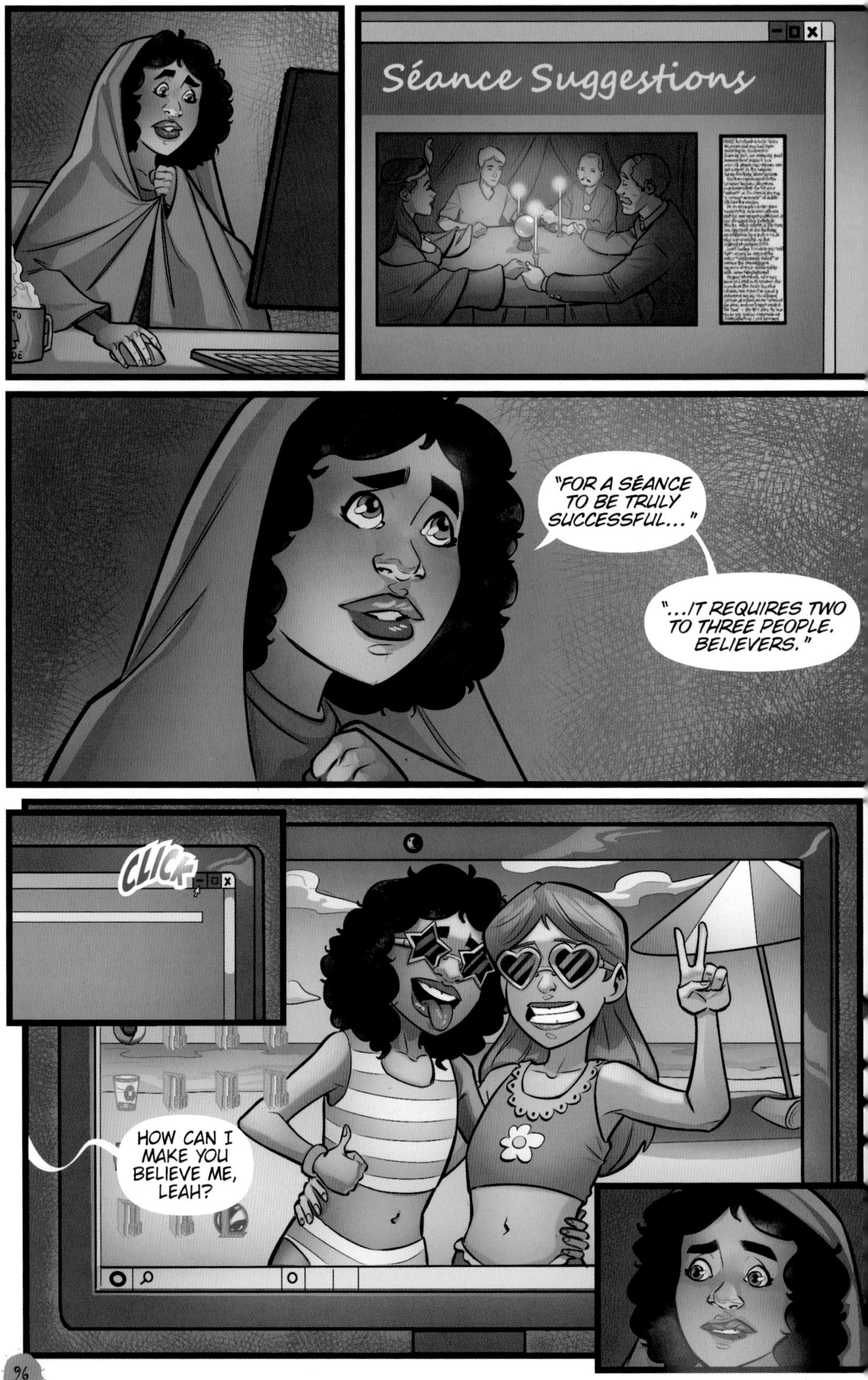
Séance Suggestions
"FOR A SÉANCE TO BE TRULY SUCCESSFUL..."
"...IT REQUIRES TWO TO THREE PEOPLE. BELIEVERS."
CLICK
HOW CAN I MAKE YOU BELIEVE ME, LEAH?

TO: Leah601

FROM: AbbyGirl

SUBJECT: Sorry

Hey Leah,

First, I'm sorry I hung up on you. I'm really stressing out. So many weird things have been happening, and some of them you don't even know about. So I'm going to tell you everything. Please hear me out before assuming it's just my imagination. I wish it was. Because then I could control it and make it STOP.

At my sleepover, I got a scary text message in the middle of the night. And my phone was on—not the way I left it when we went to sleep.

Then earlier, I saw a girl who looked like Sara running away from my window! When I got back to my room, my top was not where I left it, and I found it shredded in my closet. All that stuff is VERY weird. Don't you agree?

Then things got even scarier. I got another freaky text message from that same number today. After I read it, my room went icy cold. The phone got sucked under my bed, and when I went to grab it, I felt like something was pulling me under. I was terrified. If just one or two of these things happened, I would think it was a coincidence. Or maybe even my imagination. But all this together...I mean, how could I imagine those texts? Or my top getting ripped up? These things are completely real, and you can come see them for yourself if you don't believe me.

I need to make this stop NOW, and I have an idea. But I need your help. Can you meet me at school tomorrow morning before class starts? 8 a.m.? You are my best friend, Leah. Please help.

<3

Abby

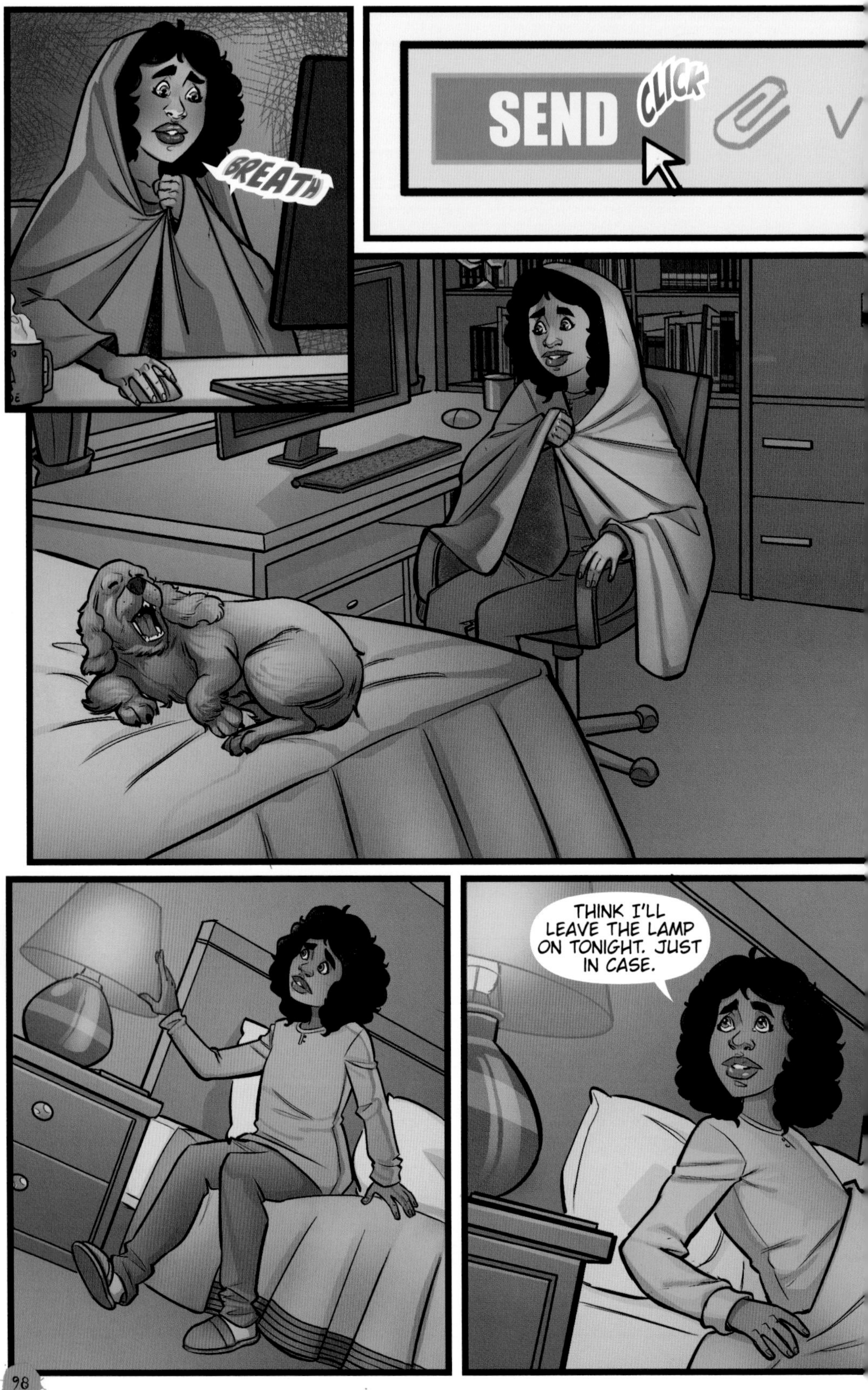
BREATH
SEND
CLICK
THINK I'LL LEAVE THE LAMP ON TONIGHT. JUST IN CASE.

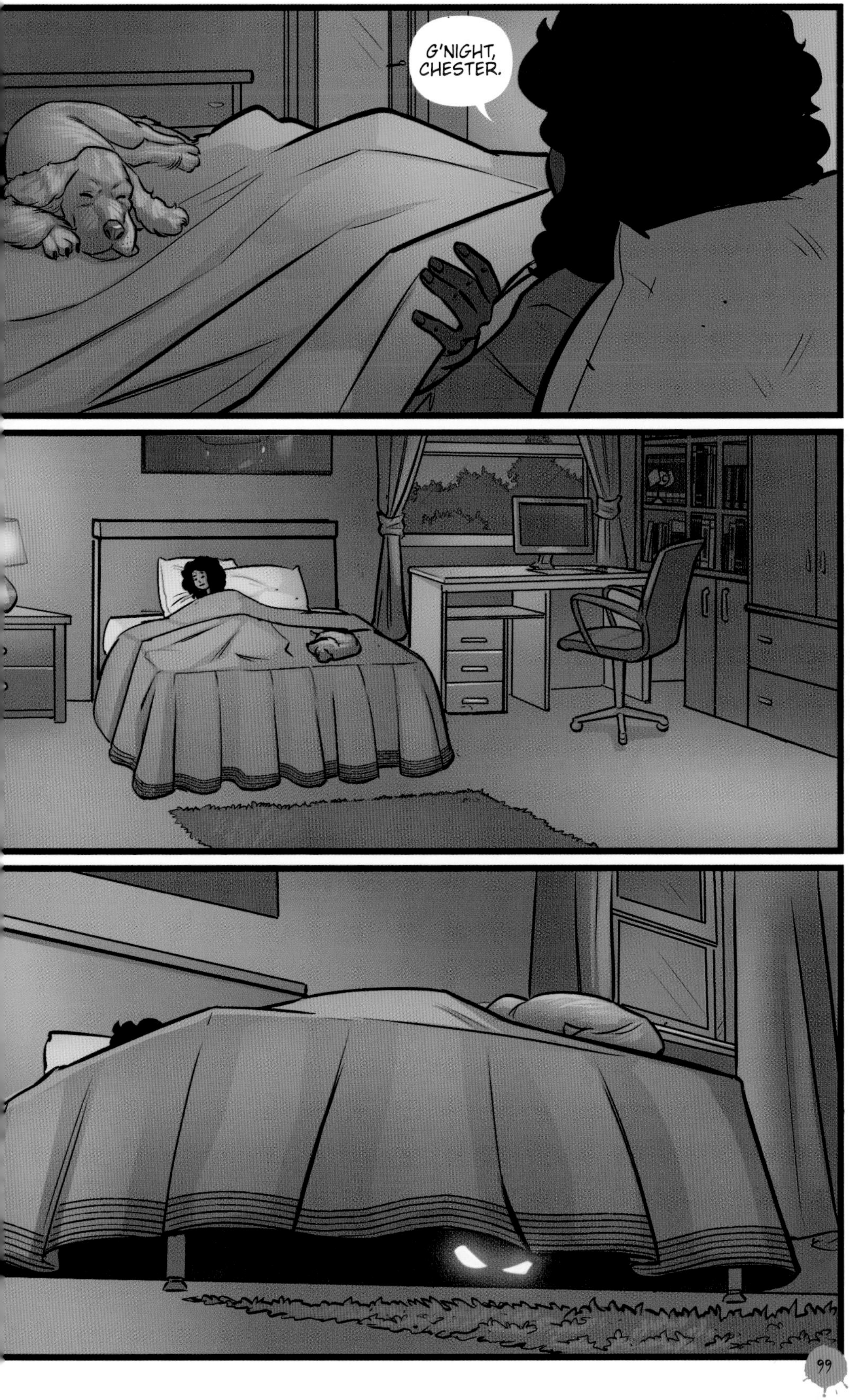
G'NIGHT, CHESTER.

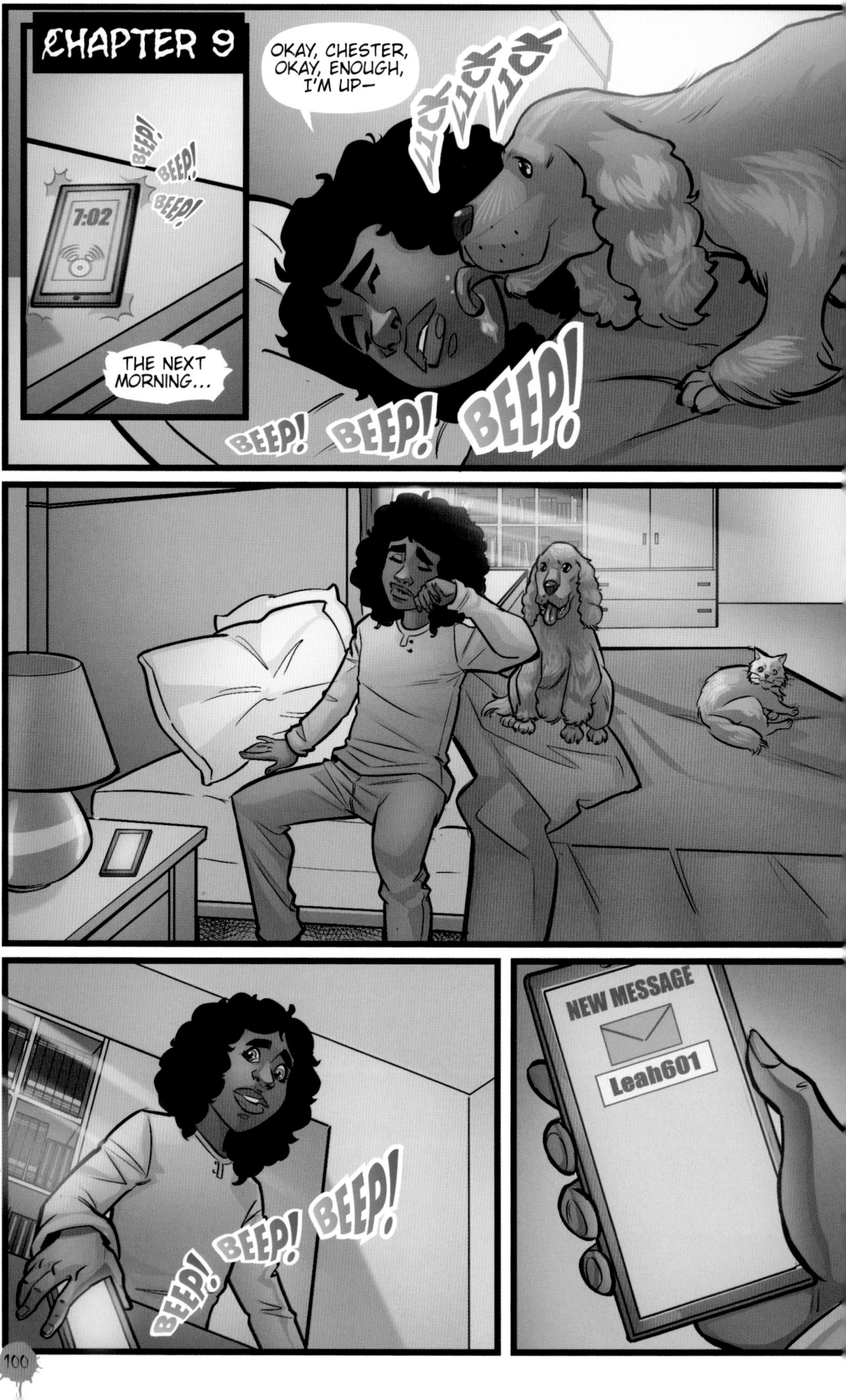
CHAPTER 9
BEEP!
BEEP!
BEEP!
7:02
THE NEXT MORNING...
OKAY, CHESTER, OKAY, ENOUGH, I'M UP—
LICK LICK LICK
BEEP! BEEP! BEEP!
BEEP! BEEP! BEEP!
NEW MESSAGE
Leah601

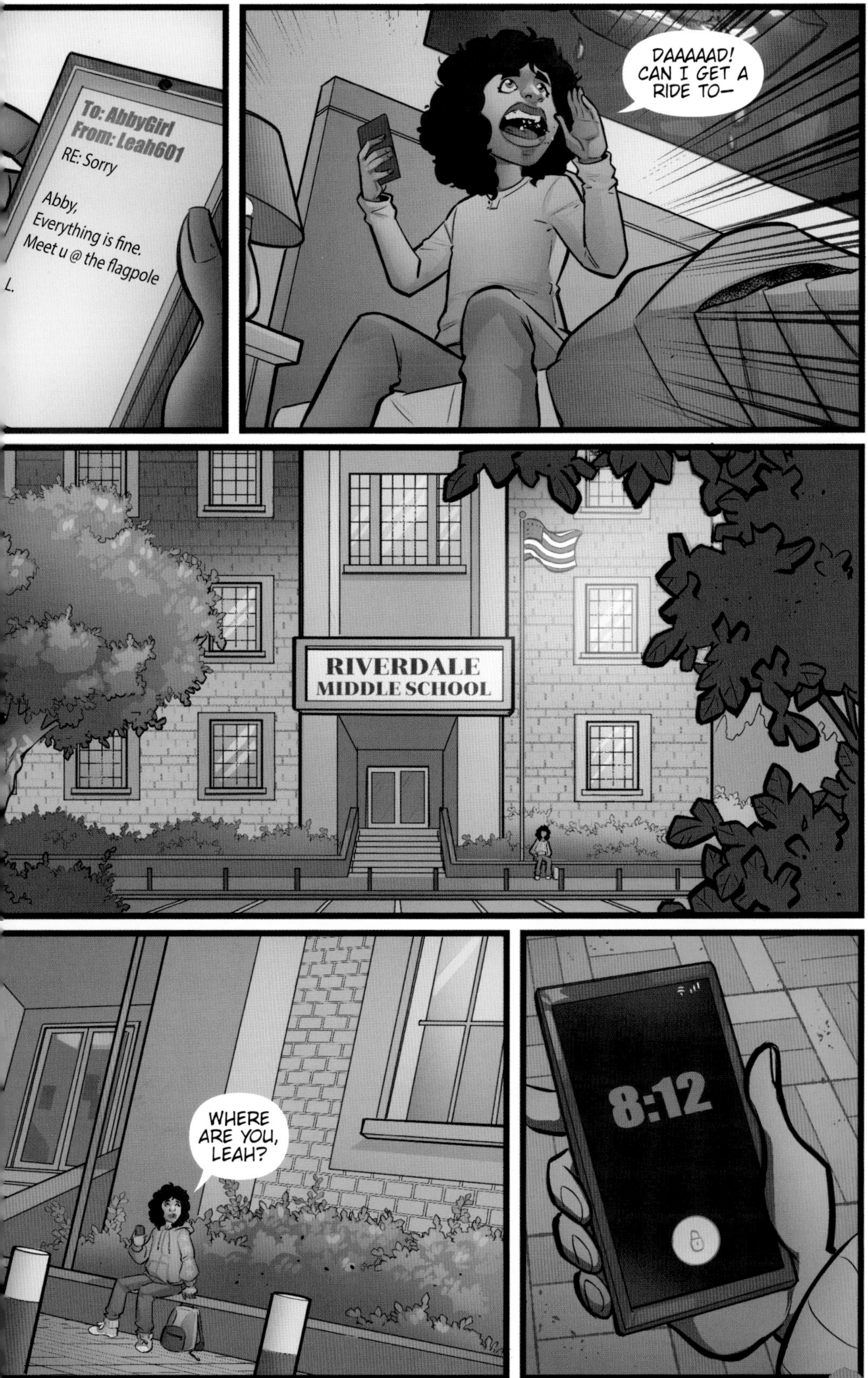
To: AbbyGirl
From: Leah601
RE: Sorry
Abby,
Everything is fine.
Meet u @ the flagpole
L.
DAAAAAD! CAN I GET A RIDE TO—
RIVERDALE MIDDLE SCHOOL
WHERE ARE YOU, LEAH?
8:12

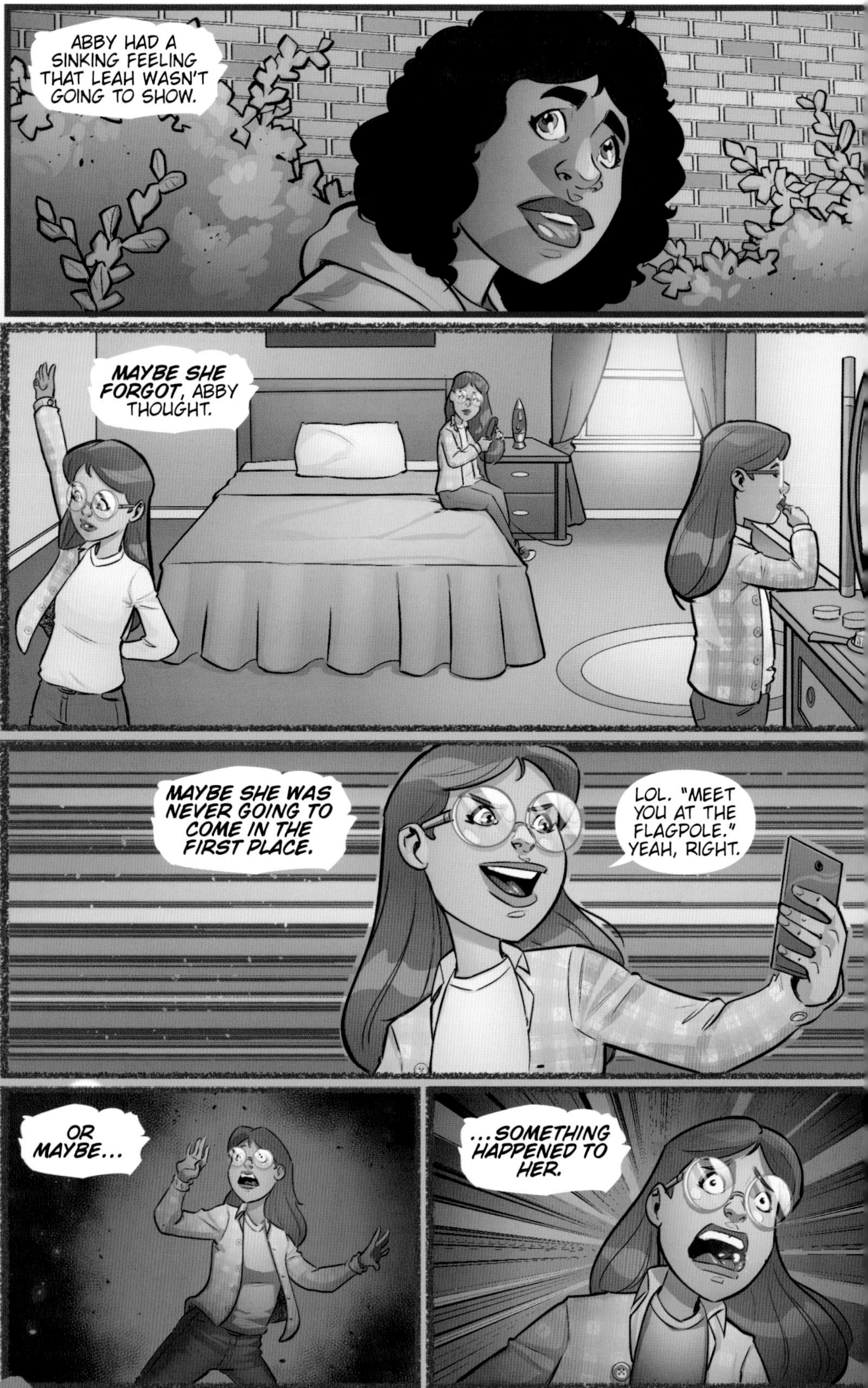

ABBY HAD A SINKING FEELING THAT LEAH WASN'T GOING TO SHOW.
MAYBE SHE FORGOT, ABBY THOUGHT.
MAYBE SHE WAS NEVER GOING TO COME IN THE FIRST PLACE.
LOL. "MEET YOU AT THE FLAGPOLE." YEAH, RIGHT.
OR MAYBE...
...SOMETHING HAPPENED TO HER.

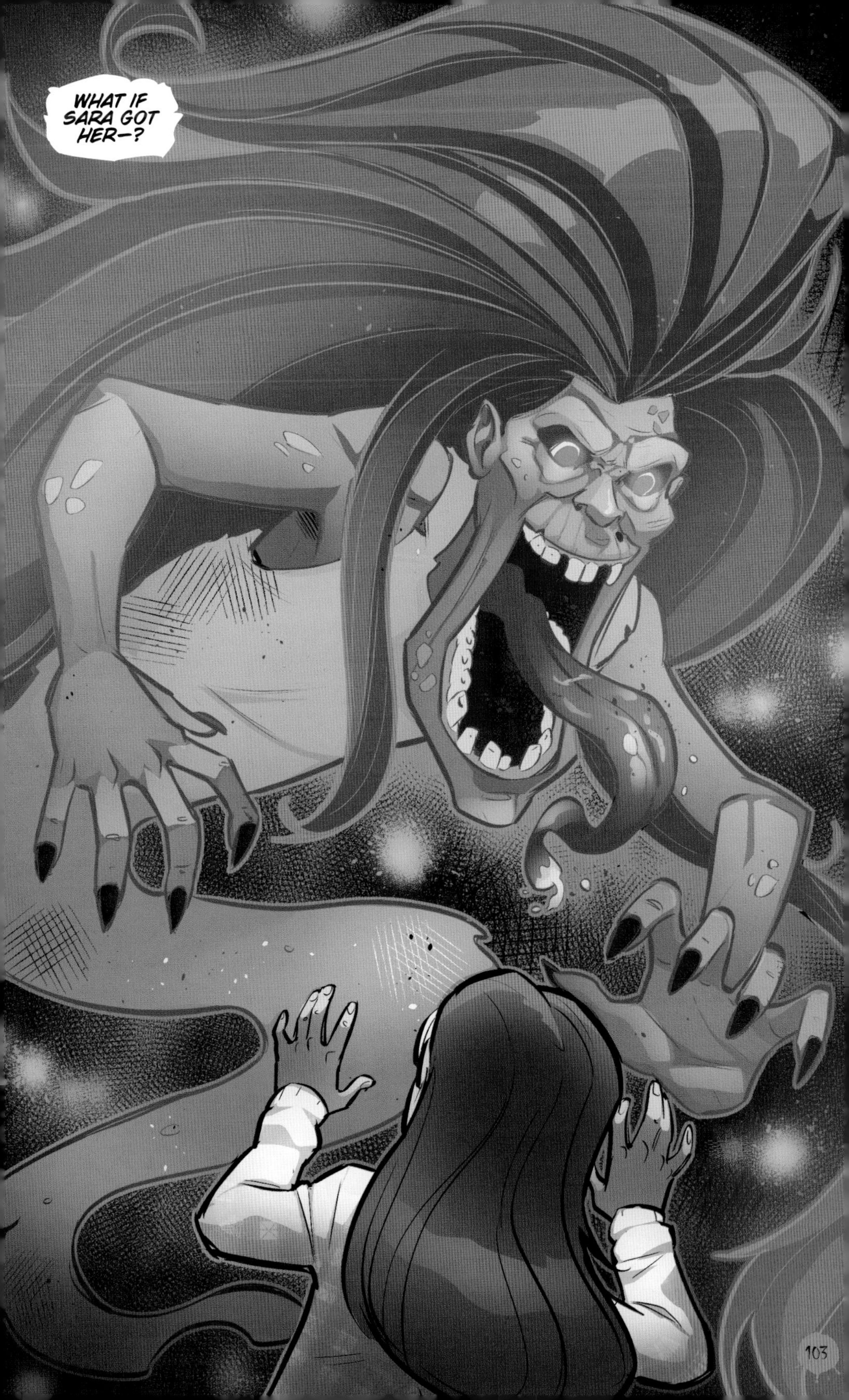
WHAT IF SARA GOT HER—?

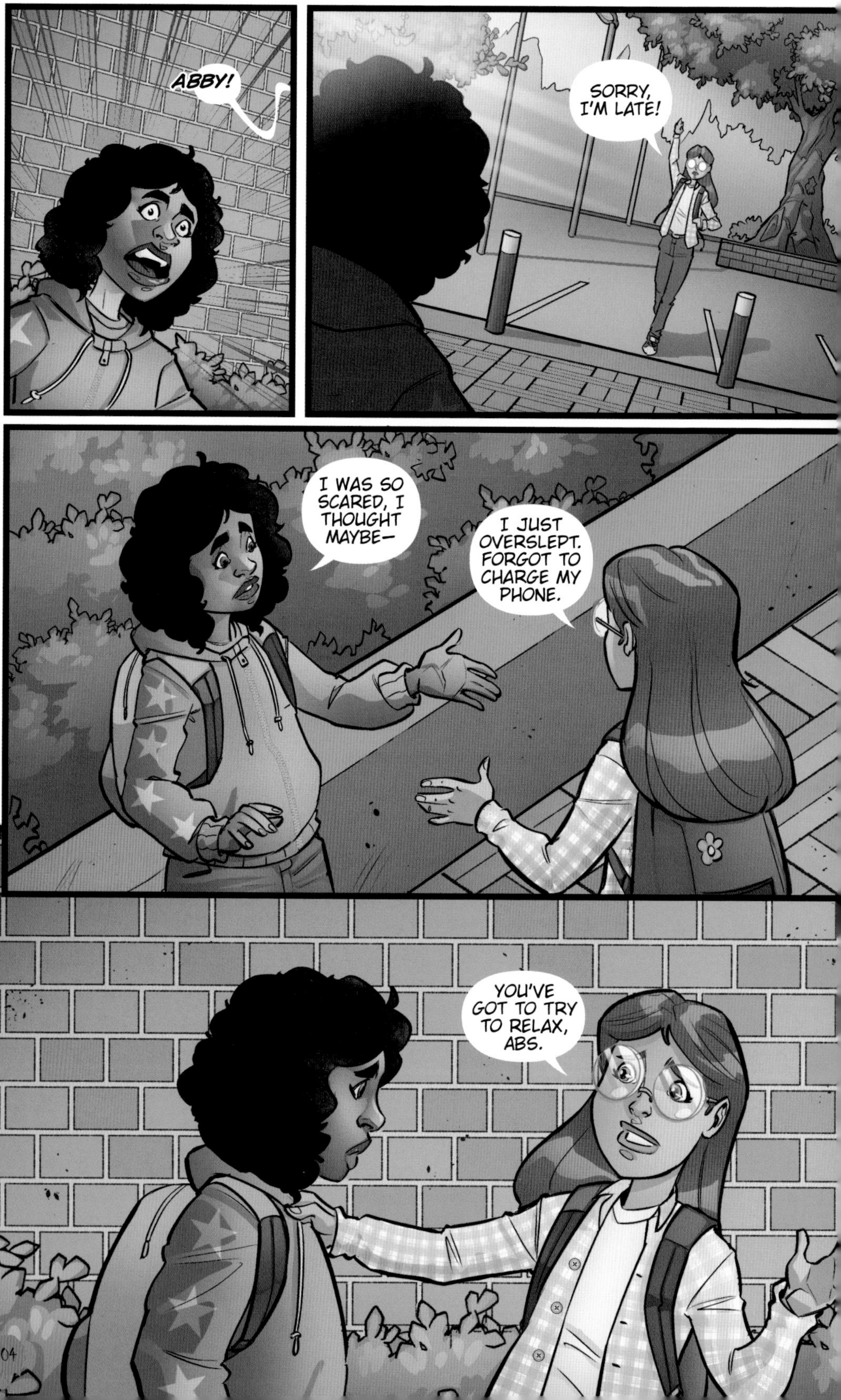
ABBY!
SORRY, I'M LATE!
I WAS SO SCARED, I THOUGHT MAYBE—
I JUST OVERSLEPT. FORGOT TO CHARGE MY PHONE.
YOU'VE GOT TO TRY TO RELAX, ABS.

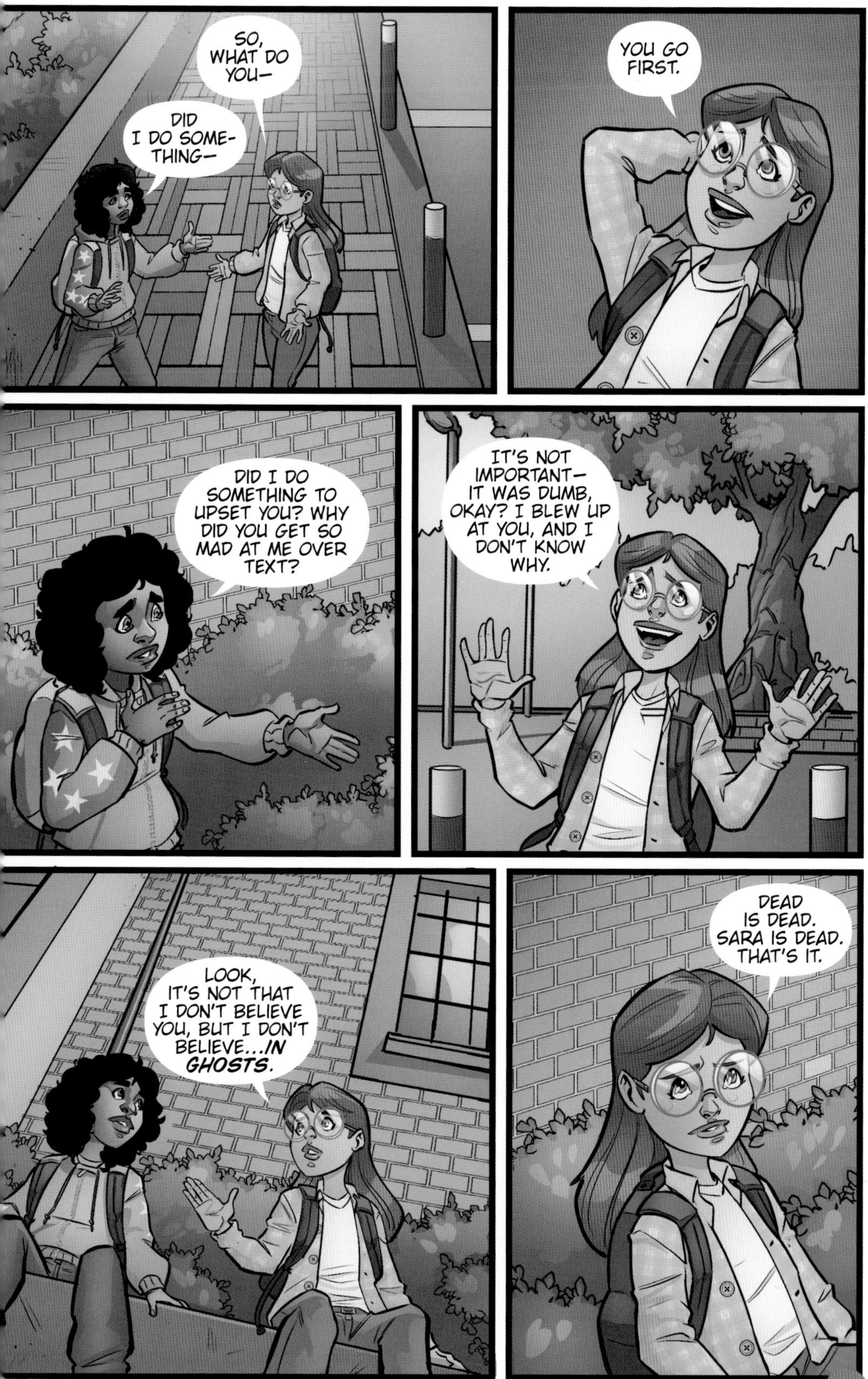
SO, WHAT DO YOU—
DID I DO SOME-THING—
YOU GO FIRST.
DID I DO SOMETHING TO UPSET YOU? WHY DID YOU GET SO MAD AT ME OVER TEXT?
IT'S NOT IMPORTANT— IT WAS DUMB, OKAY? I BLEW UP AT YOU, AND I DON'T KNOW WHY.
LOOK, IT'S NOT THAT I DON'T BELIEVE YOU, BUT I DON'T BELIEVE...*IN GHOSTS*.
DEAD IS DEAD. SARA IS DEAD. THAT'S IT.

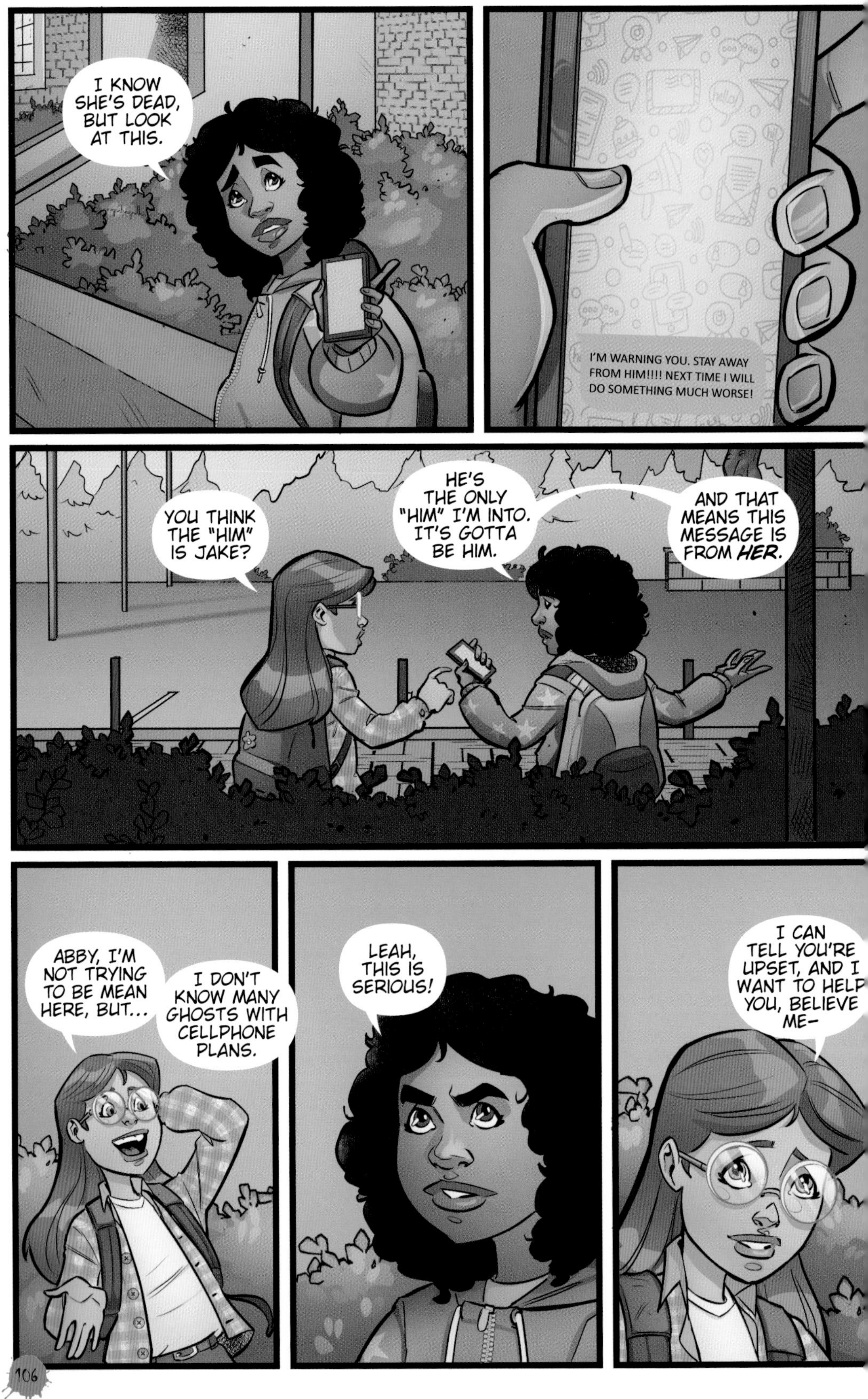
I KNOW SHE'S DEAD, BUT LOOK AT THIS.
I'M WARNING YOU. STAY AWAY FROM HIM!!!! NEXT TIME I WILL DO SOMETHING MUCH WORSE!
YOU THINK THE "HIM" IS JAKE?
HE'S THE ONLY "HIM" I'M INTO. IT'S GOTTA BE HIM.
AND THAT MEANS THIS MESSAGE IS FROM *HER*.
ABBY, I'M NOT TRYING TO BE MEAN HERE, BUT...
I DON'T KNOW MANY GHOSTS WITH CELLPHONE PLANS.
LEAH, THIS IS SERIOUS!
I CAN TELL YOU'RE UPSET, AND I WANT TO HELP YOU, BELIEVE ME–

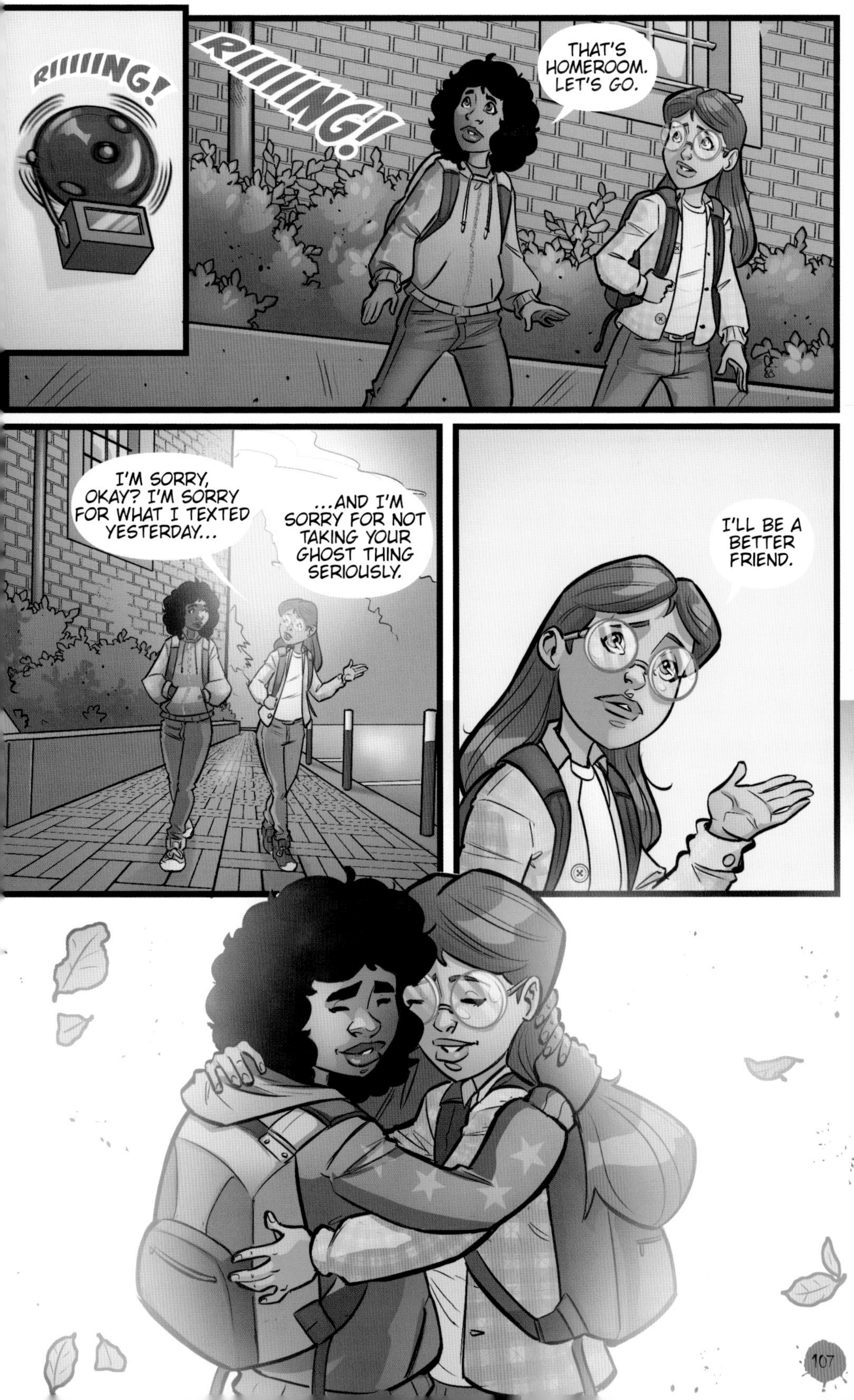
RIIIING!
RIIIING!
THAT'S HOMEROOM. LET'S GO.
I'M SORRY, OKAY? I'M SORRY FOR WHAT I TEXTED YESTERDAY...
...AND I'M SORRY FOR NOT TAKING YOUR GHOST THING SERIOUSLY.
I'LL BE A BETTER FRIEND.

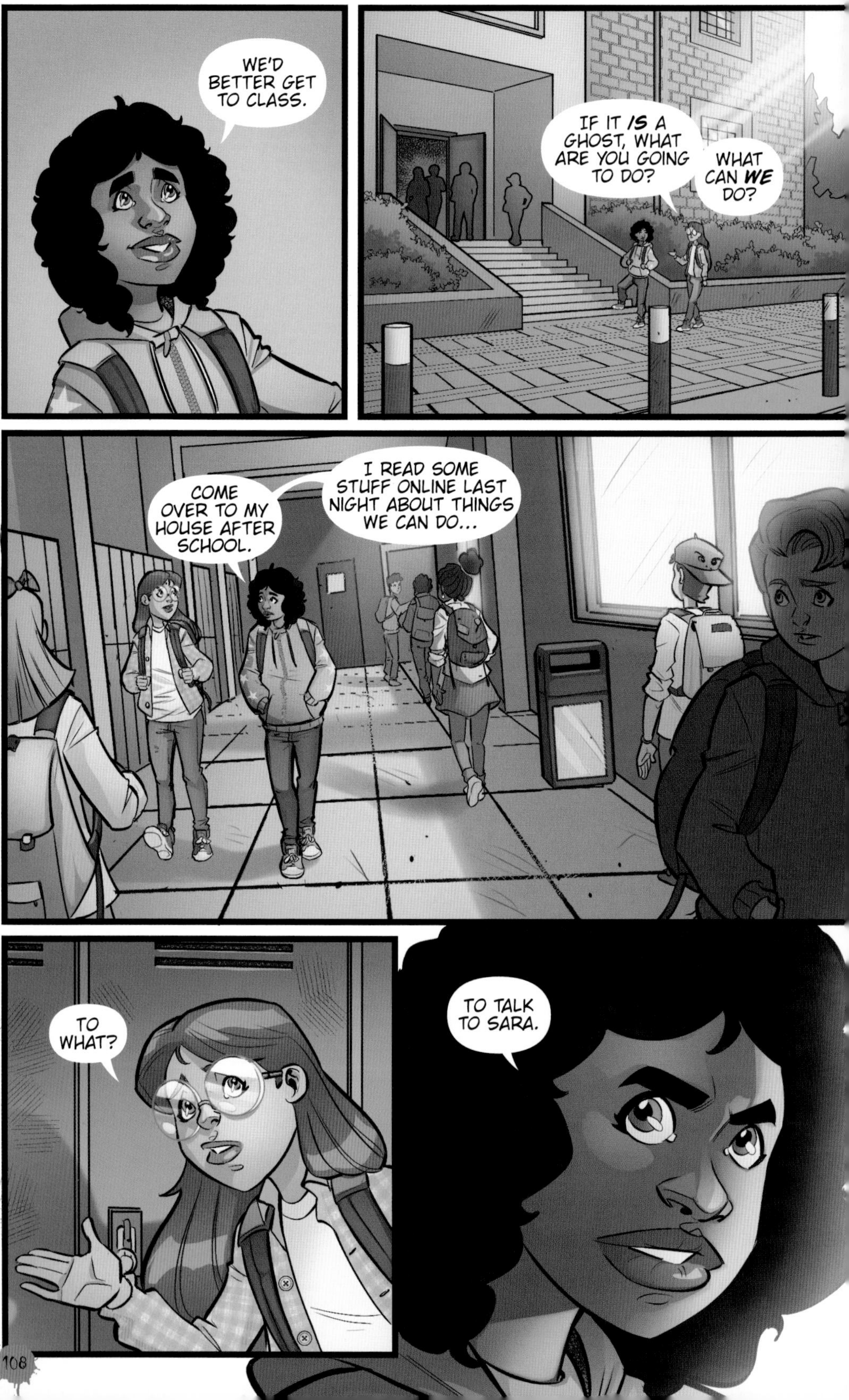
WE'D BETTER GET TO CLASS.
IF IT IS A GHOST, WHAT ARE YOU GOING TO DO?
WHAT CAN WE DO?
COME OVER TO MY HOUSE AFTER SCHOOL.
I READ SOME STUFF ONLINE LAST NIGHT ABOUT THINGS WE CAN DO...
TO WHAT?
TO TALK TO SARA.

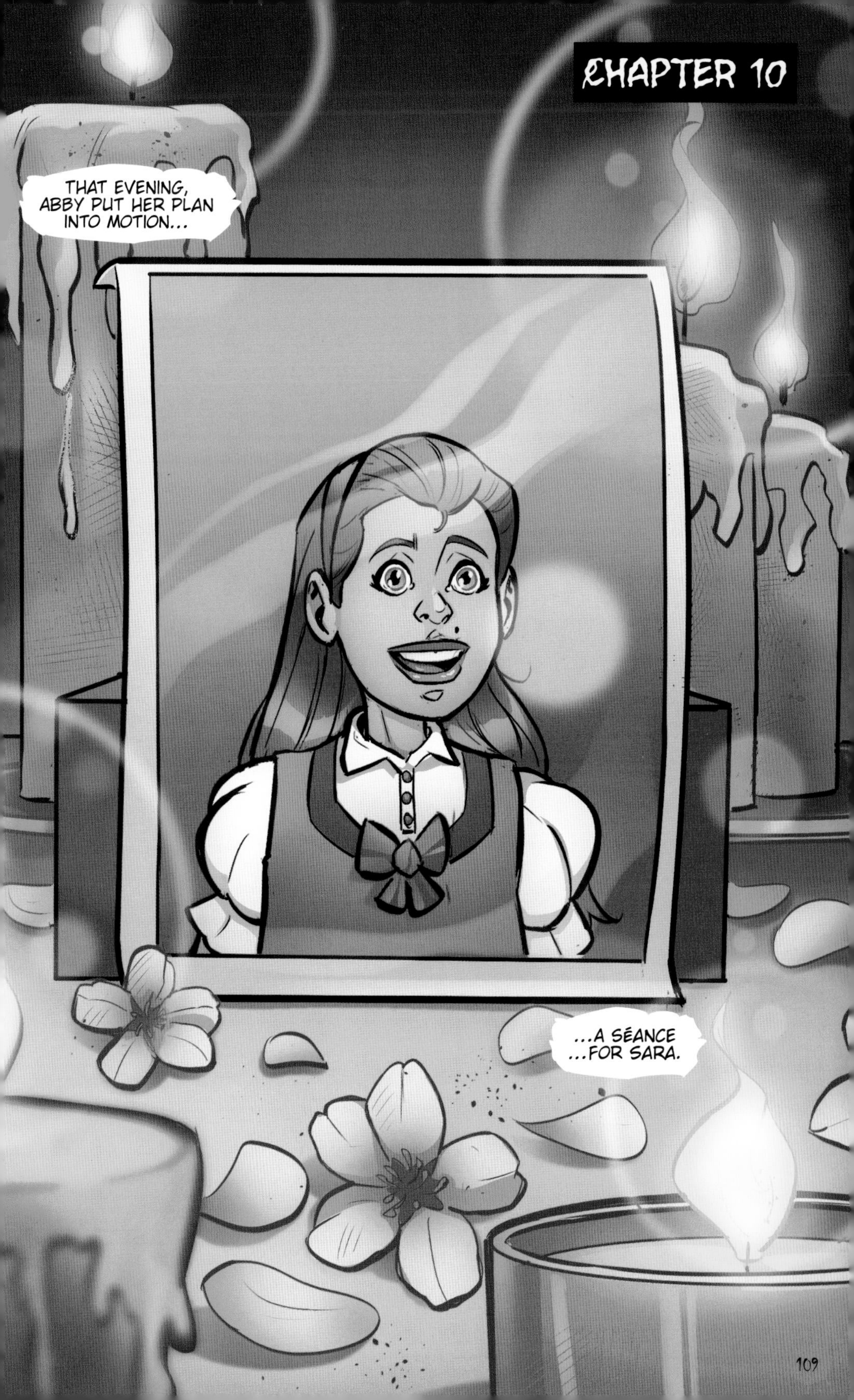
CHAPTER 10
THAT EVENING, ABBY PUT HER PLAN INTO MOTION...
...A SÉANCE ...FOR SARA.

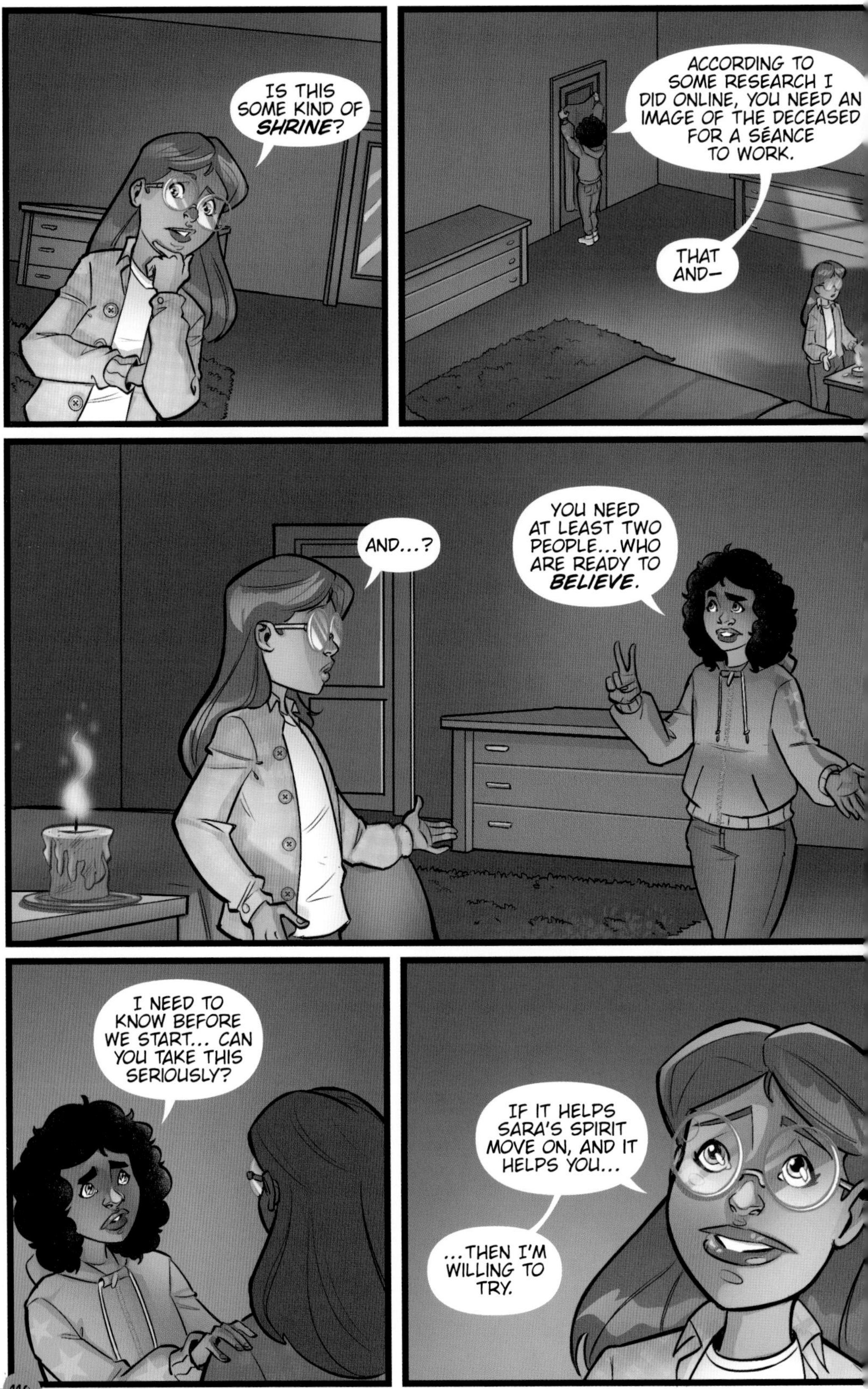
IS THIS SOME KIND OF SHRINE?
ACCORDING TO SOME RESEARCH I DID ONLINE, YOU NEED AN IMAGE OF THE DECEASED FOR A SÉANCE TO WORK.
THAT AND—
AND...?
YOU NEED AT LEAST TWO PEOPLE...WHO ARE READY TO BELIEVE.
I NEED TO KNOW BEFORE WE START... CAN YOU TAKE THIS SERIOUSLY?
IF IT HELPS SARA'S SPIRIT MOVE ON, AND IT HELPS YOU...
...THEN I'M WILLING TO TRY.

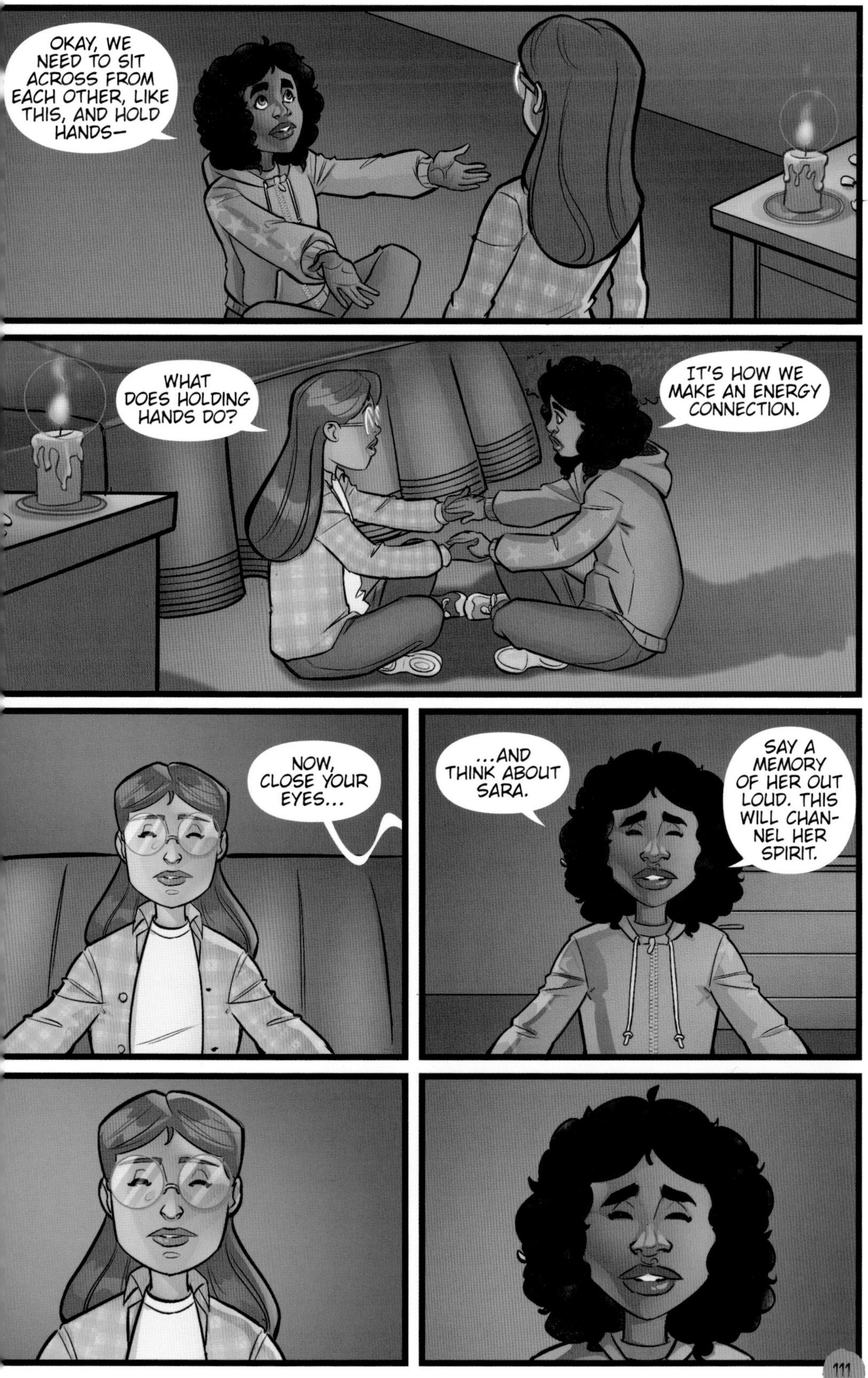
OKAY, WE NEED TO SIT ACROSS FROM EACH OTHER, LIKE THIS, AND HOLD HANDS—
WHAT DOES HOLDING HANDS DO?
IT'S HOW WE MAKE AN ENERGY CONNECTION.
NOW, CLOSE YOUR EYES...
...AND THINK ABOUT SARA.
SAY A MEMORY OF HER OUT LOUD. THIS WILL CHAN-NEL HER SPIRIT.

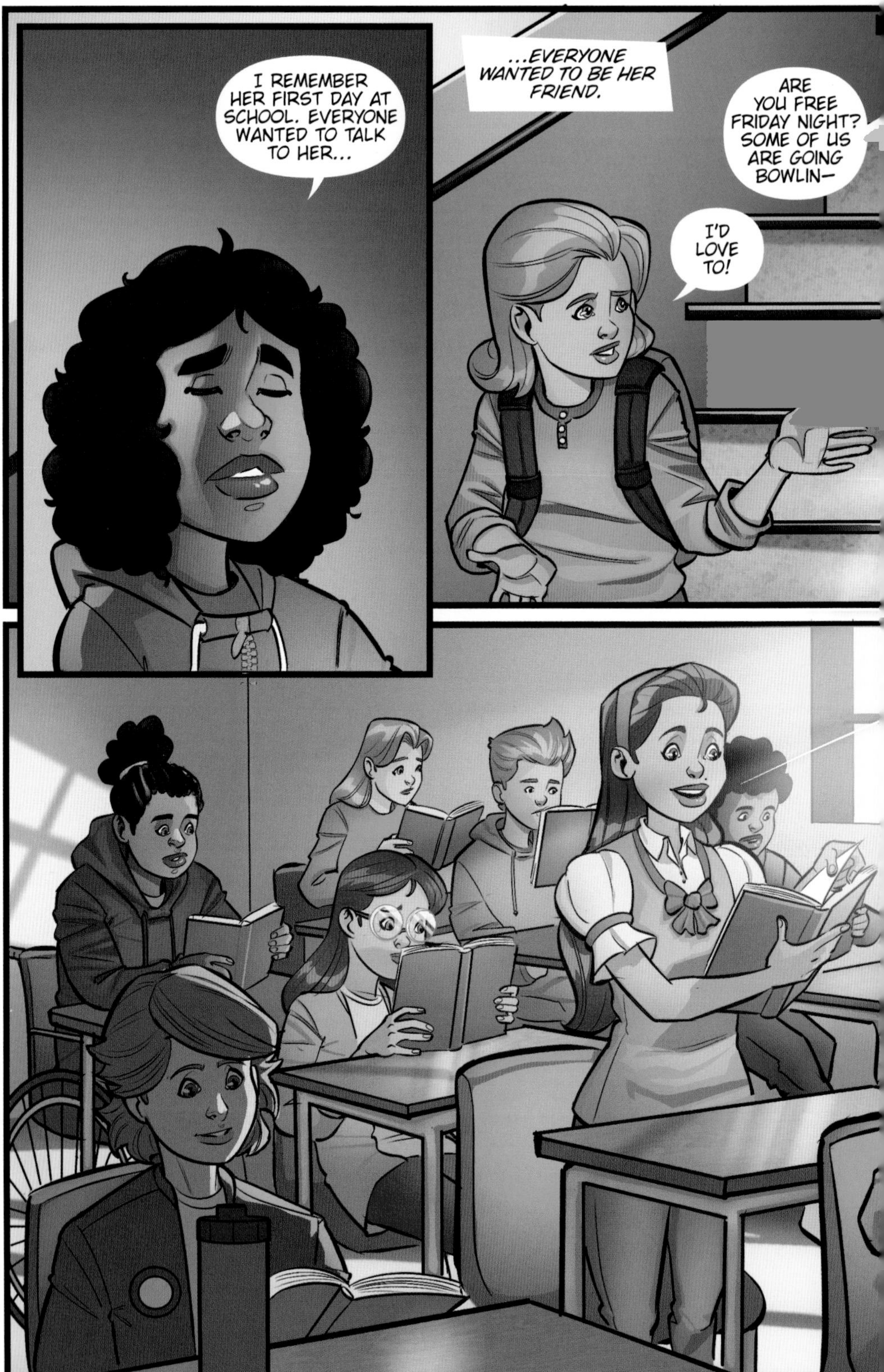
I REMEMBER HER FIRST DAY AT SCHOOL. EVERYONE WANTED TO TALK TO HER...
...EVERYONE WANTED TO BE HER FRIEND.
ARE YOU FREE FRIDAY NIGHT? SOME OF US ARE GOING BOWLIN—
I'D LOVE TO!

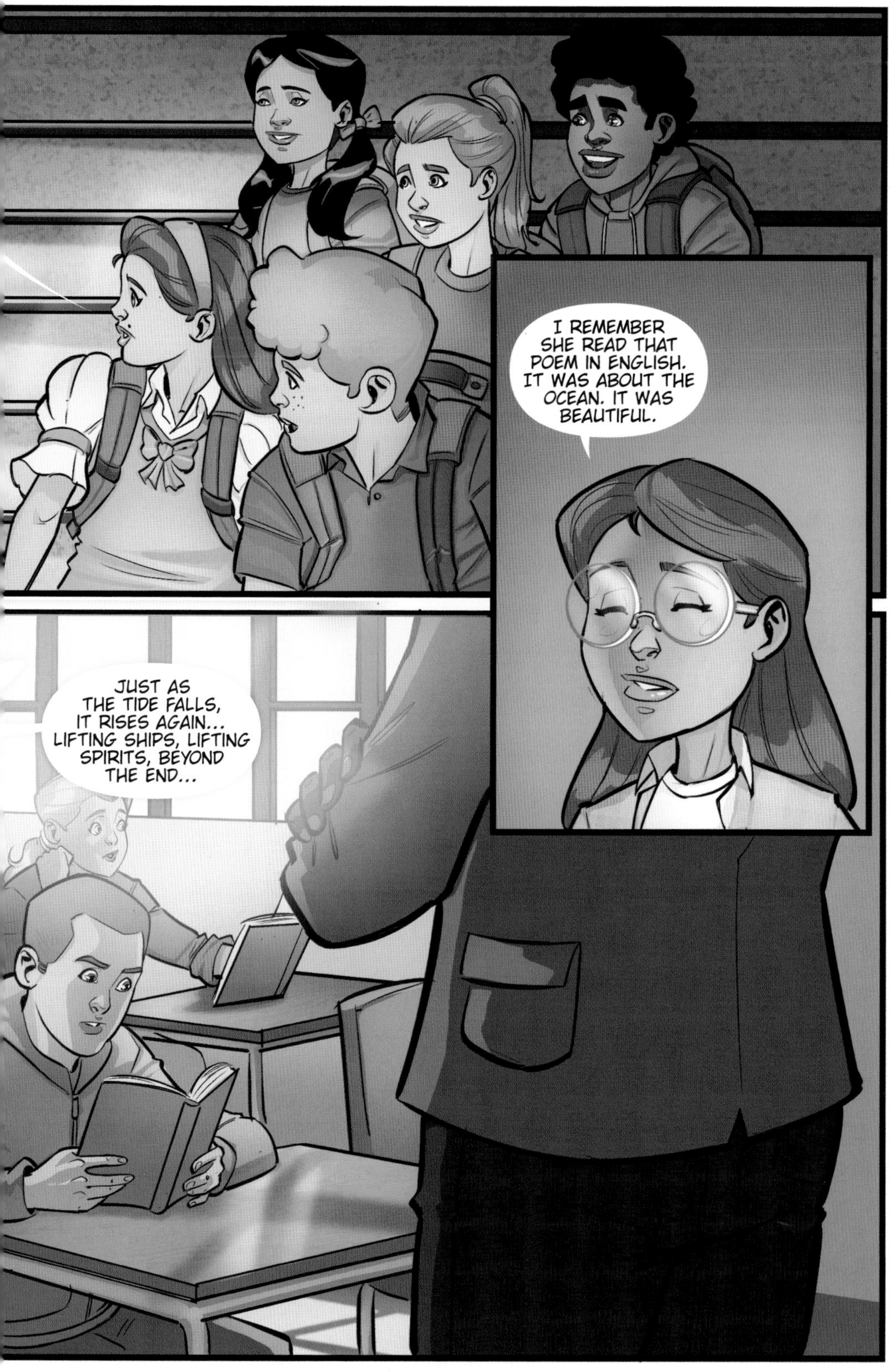
I REMEMBER SHE READ THAT POEM IN ENGLISH. IT WAS ABOUT THE OCEAN. IT WAS BEAUTIFUL.
JUST AS THE TIDE FALLS, IT RISES AGAIN... LIFTING SHIPS, LIFTING SPIRITS, BEYOND THE END...

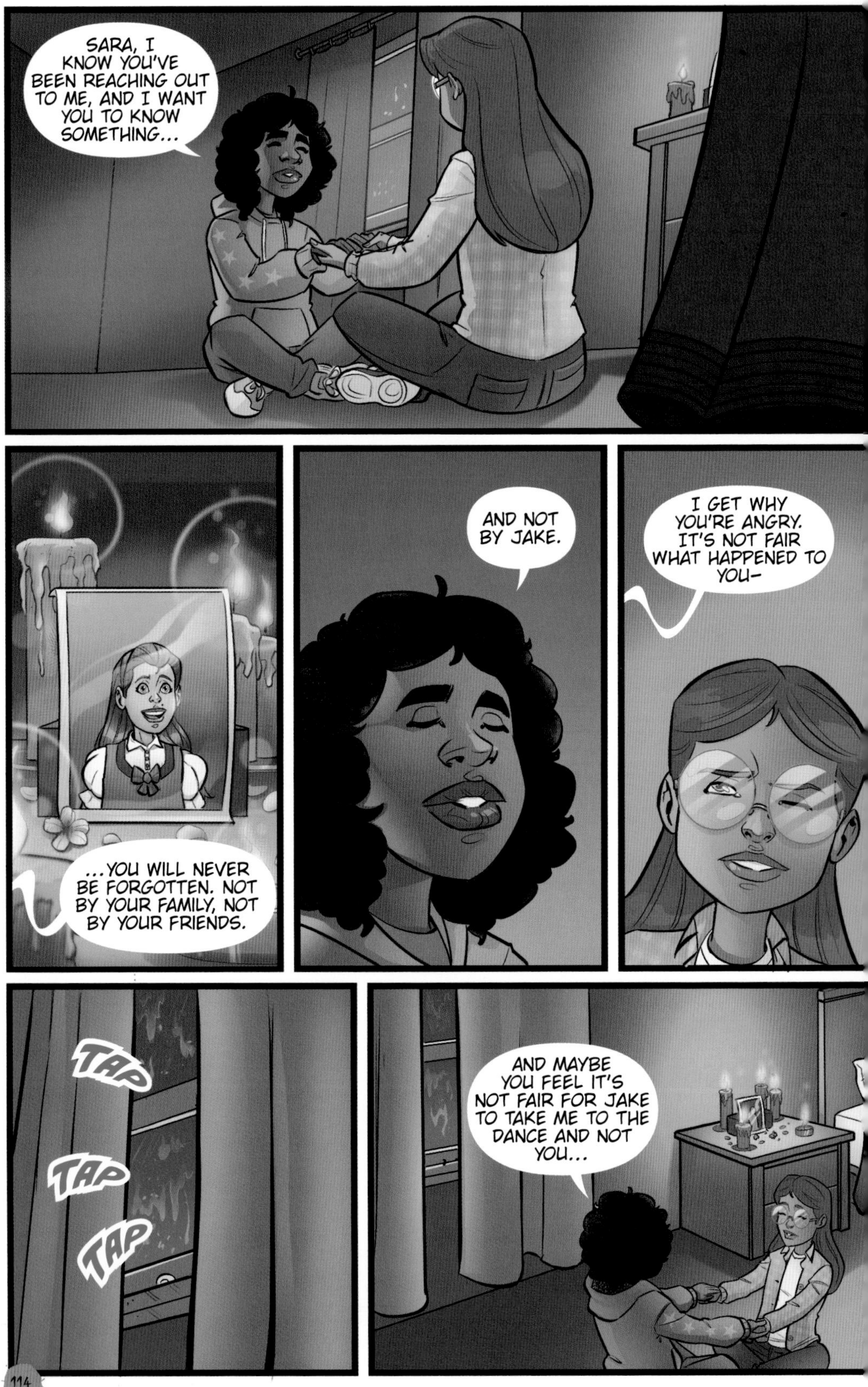
SARA, I KNOW YOU'VE BEEN REACHING OUT TO ME, AND I WANT YOU TO KNOW SOMETHING...
...YOU WILL NEVER BE FORGOTTEN. NOT BY YOUR FAMILY, NOT BY YOUR FRIENDS.
AND NOT BY JAKE.
I GET WHY YOU'RE ANGRY. IT'S NOT FAIR WHAT HAPPENED TO YOU–
TAP
TAP
TAP
AND MAYBE YOU FEEL IT'S NOT FAIR FOR JAKE TO TAKE ME TO THE DANCE AND NOT YOU...

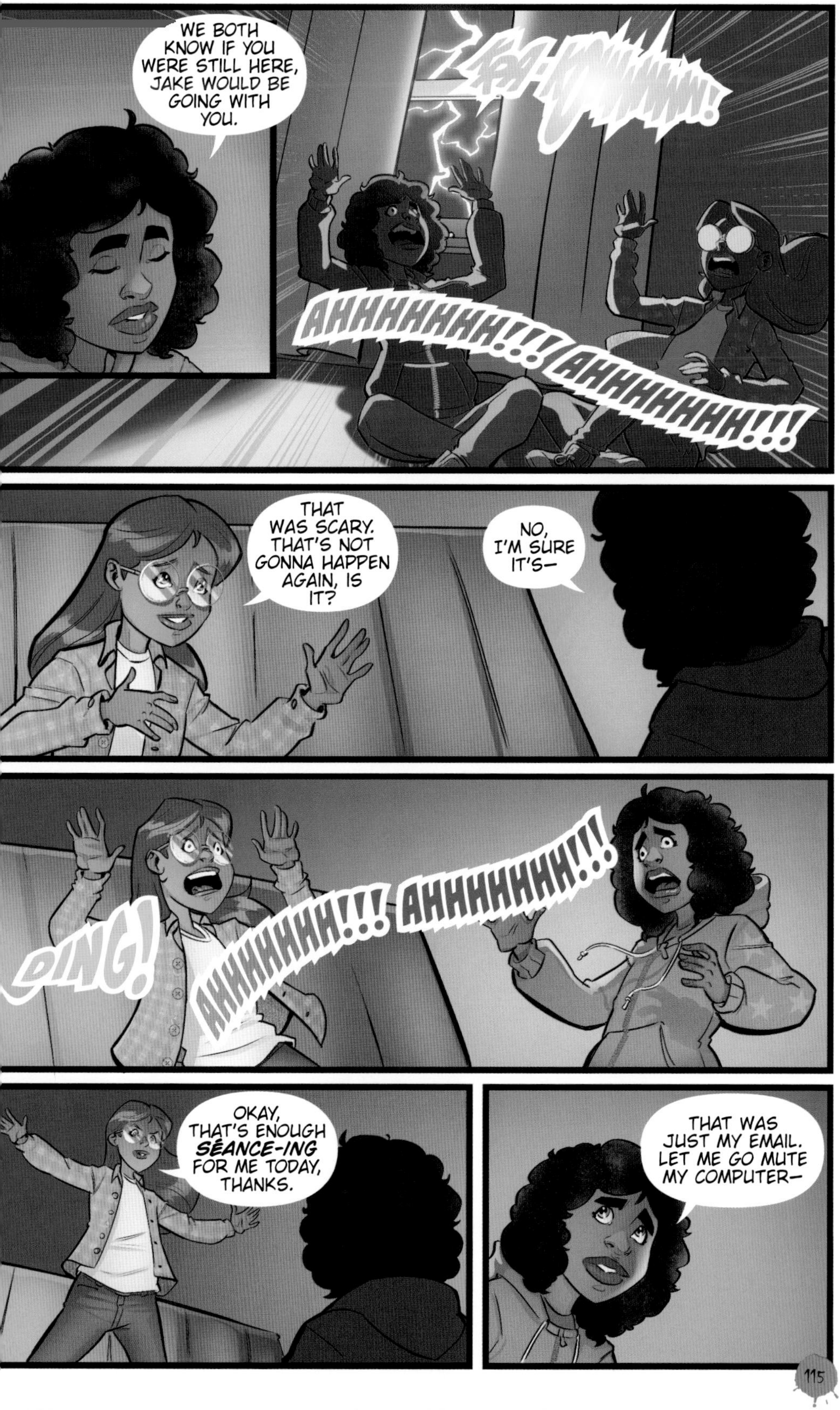
WE BOTH KNOW IF YOU WERE STILL HERE, JAKE WOULD BE GOING WITH YOU.
AHHHHHHH!!!
AHHHHHHHH!!!
THAT WAS SCARY. THAT'S NOT GONNA HAPPEN AGAIN, IS IT?
NO, I'M SURE IT'S—
DING!
AHHHHHHH!!!
AHHHHHHH!!!
OKAY, THAT'S ENOUGH *SÉANCE-ING* FOR ME TODAY, THANKS.
THAT WAS JUST MY EMAIL. LET ME GO MUTE MY COMPUTER—

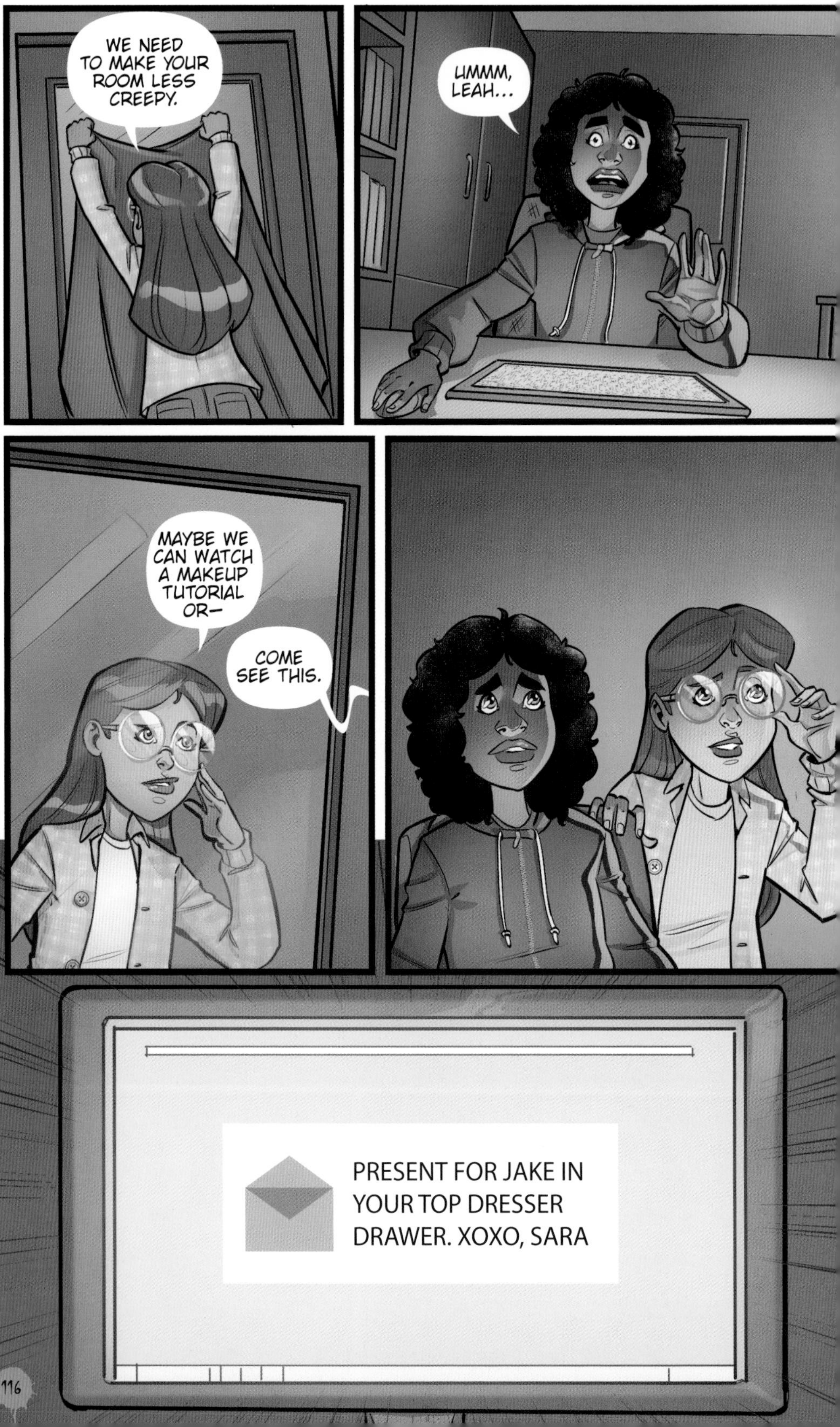
WE NEED TO MAKE YOUR ROOM LESS CREEPY.
UMMM, LEAH...
MAYBE WE CAN WATCH A MAKEUP TUTORIAL OR—
COME SEE THIS.
PRESENT FOR JAKE IN YOUR TOP DRESSER DRAWER. XOXO, SARA

ABBY, DON'T—

WHAT IF THERE REALLY IS SOMETHING IN THERE—?

I HOPE THERE IS. MAYBE THEN WE CAN ALL FINALLY MOVE ON.

I HAVE A BAD FEELING ABOUT THIS.

YOU WOULDN'T HURT ME, WOULD YOU, SARA?

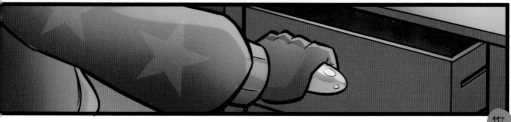

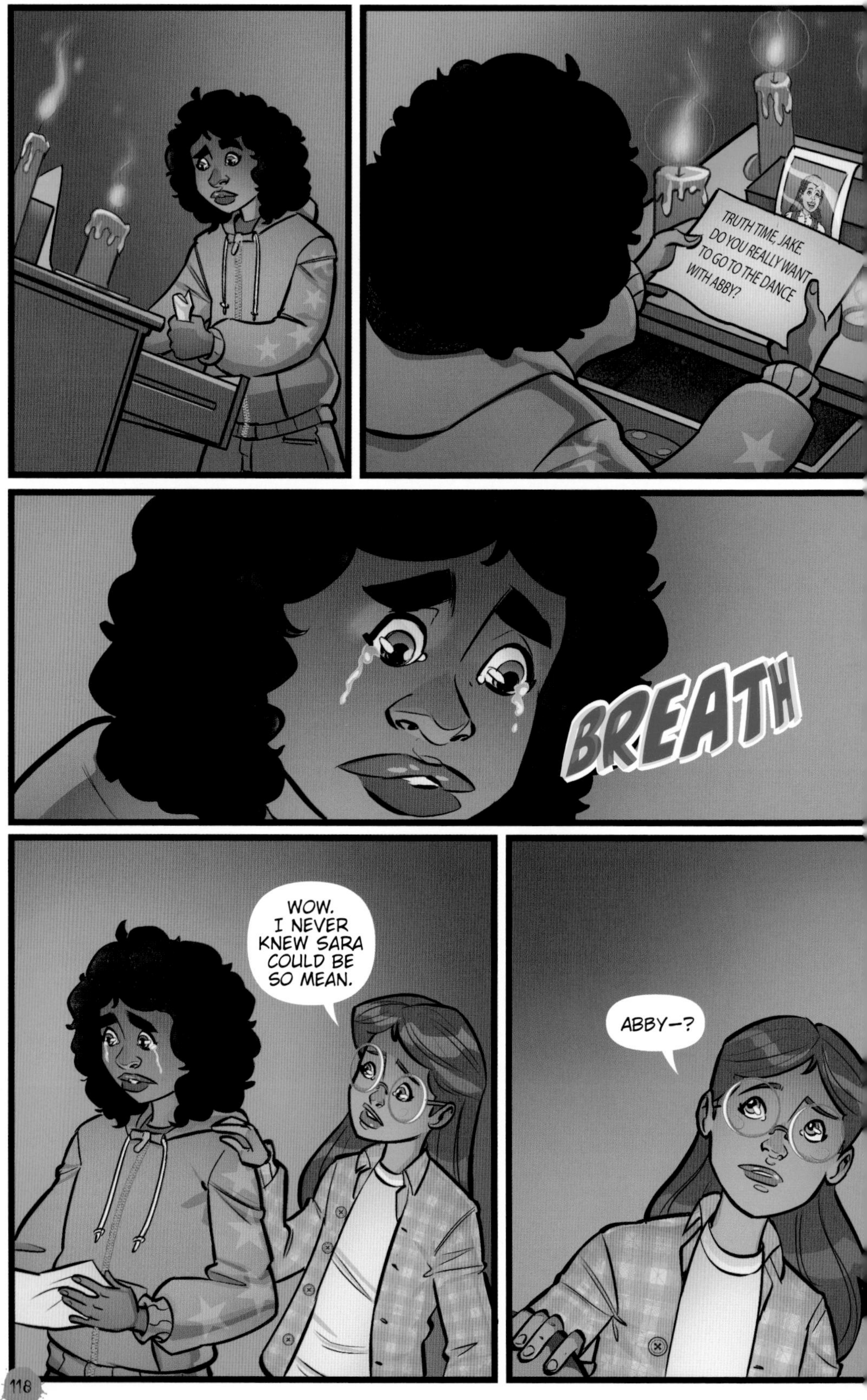
TRUTH TIME, JAKE. DO YOU REALLY WANT TO GO TO THE DANCE WITH ABBY?
BREATH
WOW. I NEVER KNEW SARA COULD BE SO MEAN.
ABBY—?

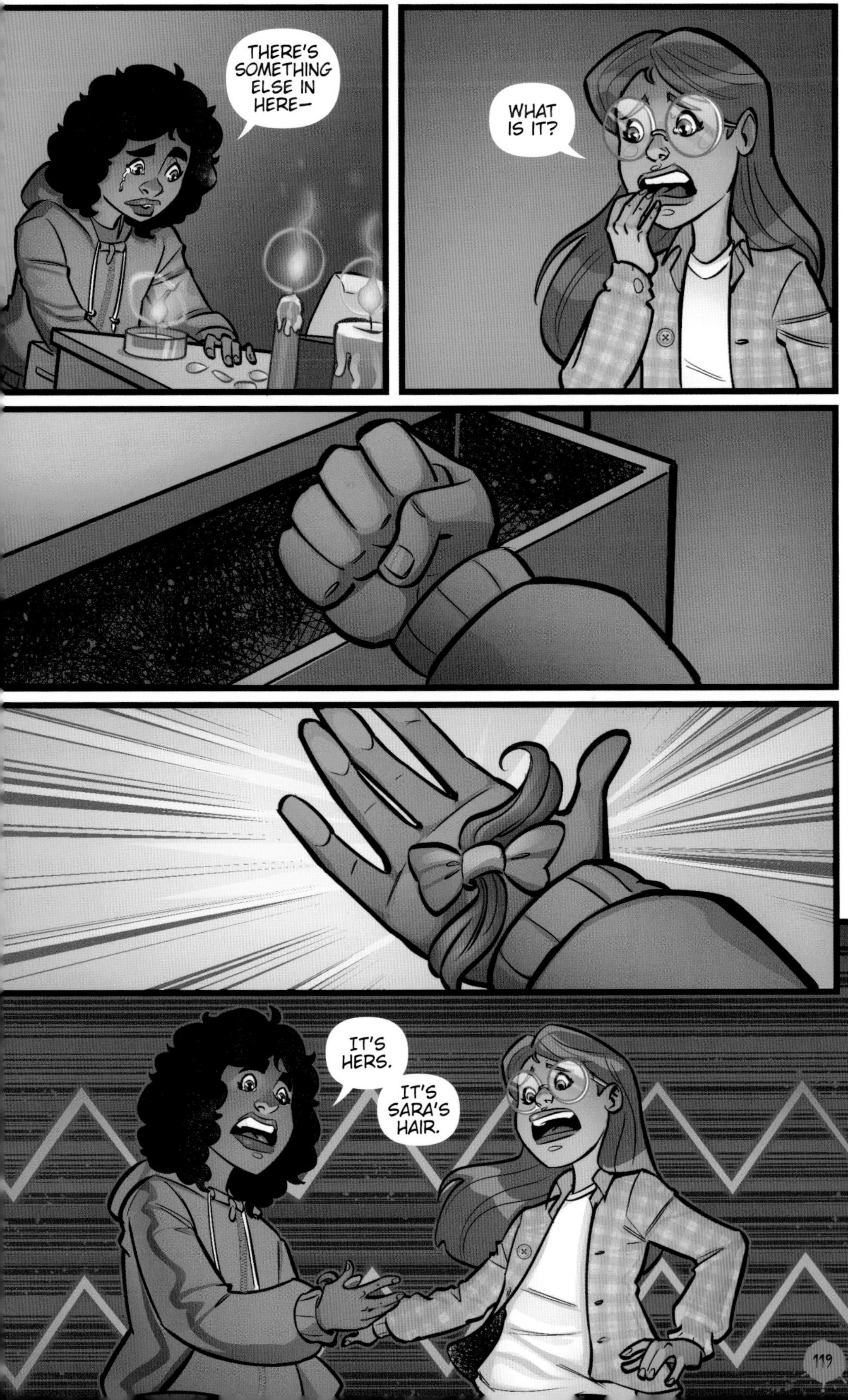
THERE'S SOMETHING ELSE IN HERE—
WHAT IS IT?
IT'S HERS.
IT'S SARA'S HAIR.

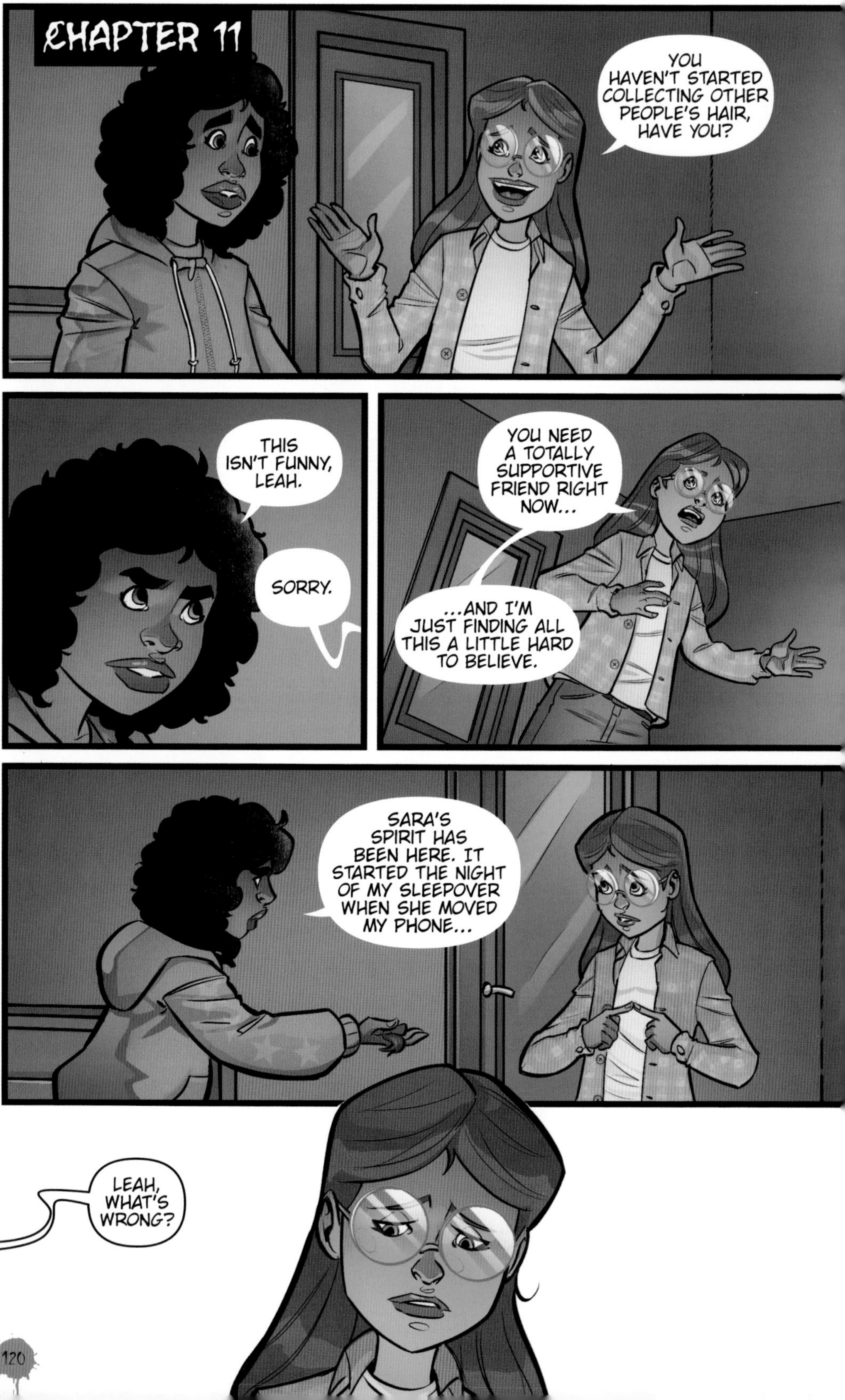
CHAPTER 11
YOU HAVEN'T STARTED COLLECTING OTHER PEOPLE'S HAIR, HAVE YOU?
THIS ISN'T FUNNY, LEAH.
SORRY.
YOU NEED A TOTALLY SUPPORTIVE FRIEND RIGHT NOW...
...AND I'M JUST FINDING ALL THIS A LITTLE HARD TO BELIEVE.
SARA'S SPIRIT HAS BEEN HERE. IT STARTED THE NIGHT OF MY SLEEPOVER WHEN SHE MOVED MY PHONE...
LEAH, WHAT'S WRONG?

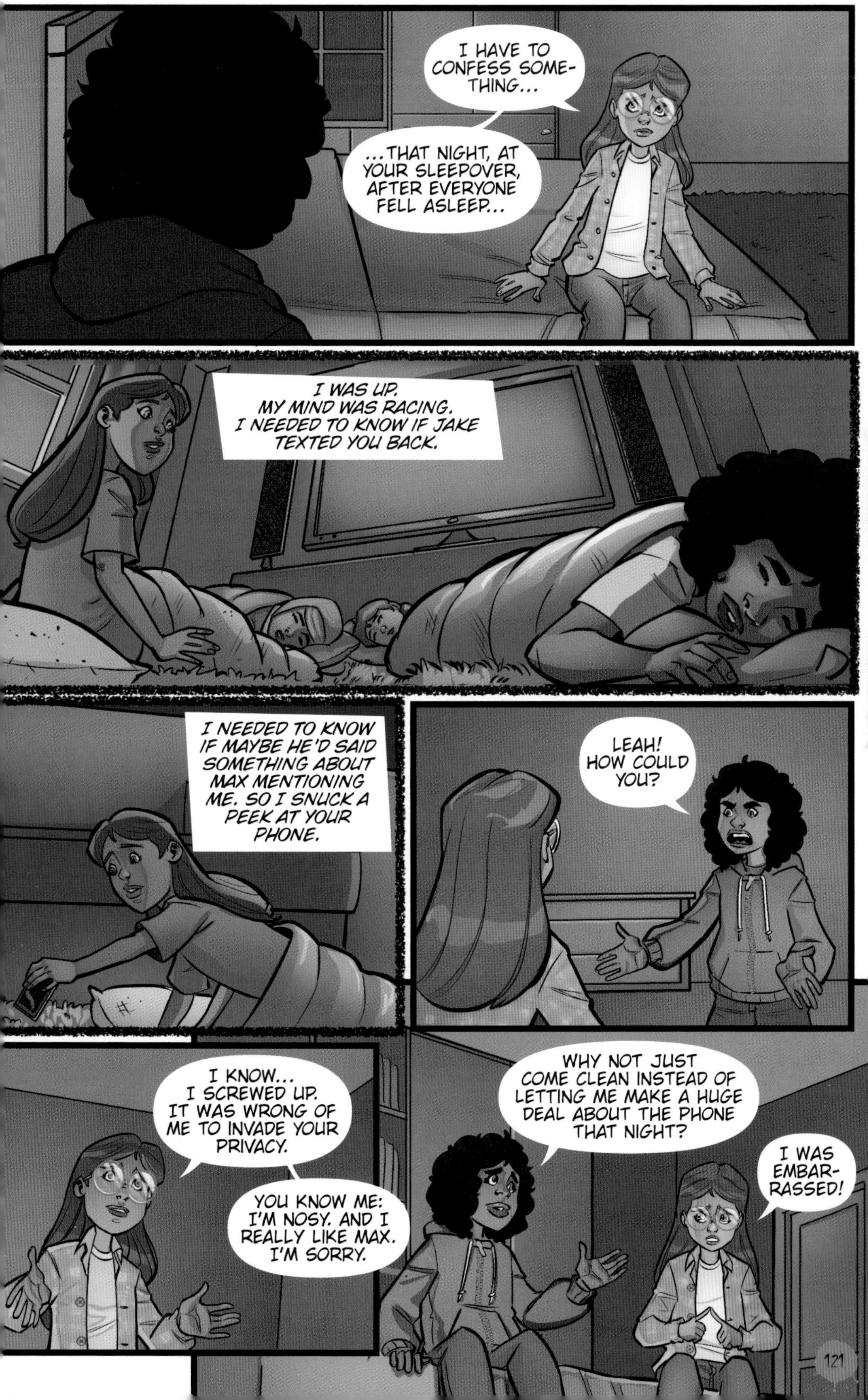
I HAVE TO CONFESS SOMETHING...
...THAT NIGHT, AT YOUR SLEEPOVER, AFTER EVERYONE FELL ASLEEP...
I WAS UP. MY MIND WAS RACING. I NEEDED TO KNOW IF JAKE TEXTED YOU BACK.
I NEEDED TO KNOW IF MAYBE HE'D SAID SOMETHING ABOUT MAX MENTIONING ME. SO I SNUCK A PEEK AT YOUR PHONE.
LEAH! HOW COULD YOU?
I KNOW... I SCREWED UP. IT WAS WRONG OF ME TO INVADE YOUR PRIVACY.
YOU KNOW ME: I'M NOSY. AND I REALLY LIKE MAX. I'M SORRY.
WHY NOT JUST COME CLEAN INSTEAD OF LETTING ME MAKE A HUGE DEAL ABOUT THE PHONE THAT NIGHT?
I WAS EMBARRASSED!

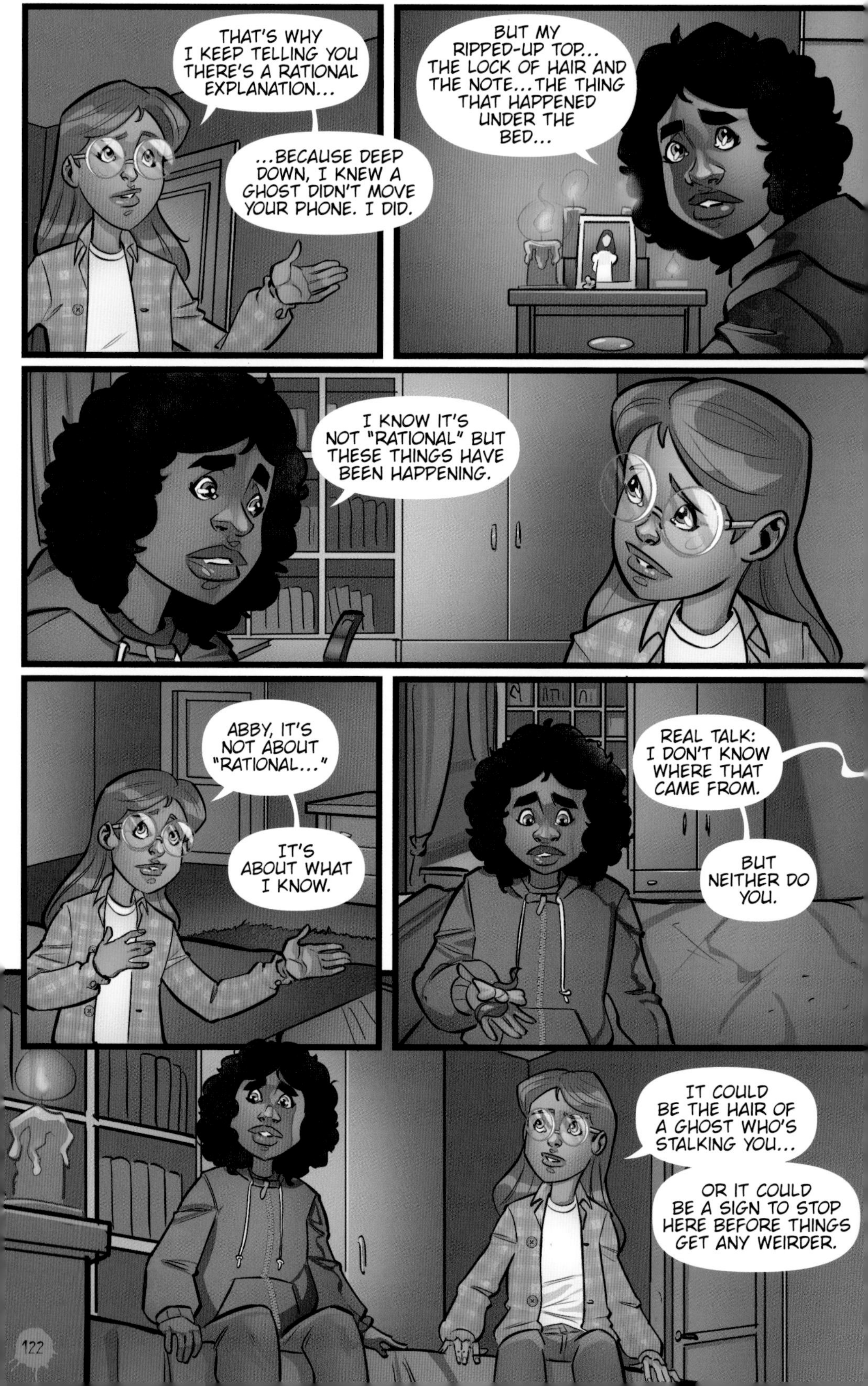
THAT'S WHY I KEEP TELLING YOU THERE'S A RATIONAL EXPLANATION...
...BECAUSE DEEP DOWN, I KNEW A GHOST DIDN'T MOVE YOUR PHONE. I DID.
BUT MY RIPPED-UP TOP... THE LOCK OF HAIR AND THE NOTE...THE THING THAT HAPPENED UNDER THE BED...
I KNOW IT'S NOT "RATIONAL" BUT THESE THINGS HAVE BEEN HAPPENING.
ABBY, IT'S NOT ABOUT "RATIONAL..."
IT'S ABOUT WHAT I KNOW.
REAL TALK: I DON'T KNOW WHERE THAT CAME FROM.
BUT NEITHER DO YOU.
IT COULD BE THE HAIR OF A GHOST WHO'S STALKING YOU...
OR IT COULD BE A SIGN TO STOP HERE BEFORE THINGS GET ANY WEIRDER.

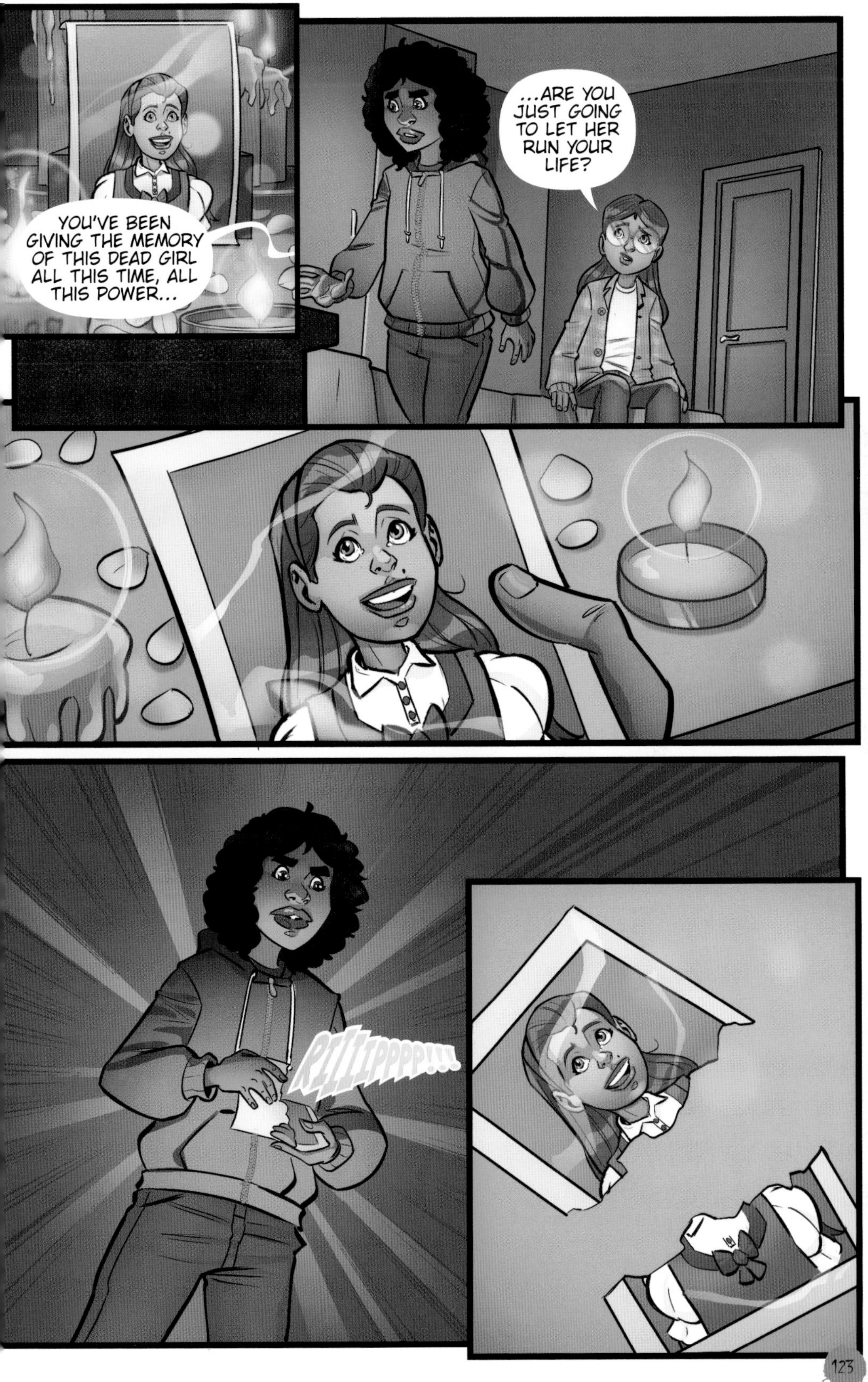
YOU'VE BEEN GIVING THE MEMORY OF THIS DEAD GIRL ALL THIS TIME, ALL THIS POWER...
...ARE YOU JUST GOING TO LET HER RUN YOUR LIFE?
RIIIIPPPP!!!

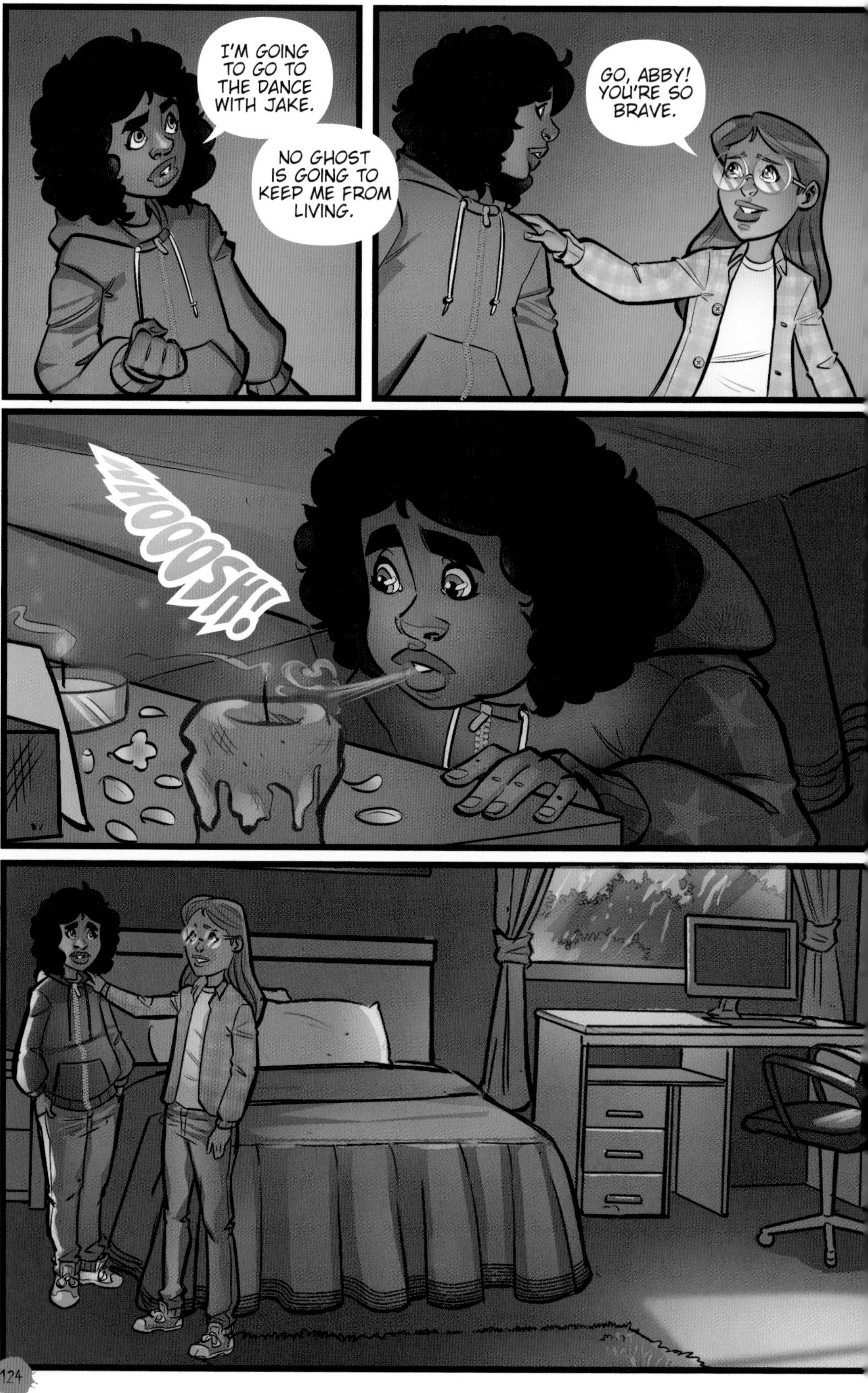
I'M GOING TO GO TO THE DANCE WITH JAKE.
NO GHOST IS GOING TO KEEP ME FROM LIVING.
GO, ABBY! YOU'RE SO BRAVE.
WHOOOSH!

THE NEXT DAY, ABBY DECIDED TO PUT THE WHOLE THING TO REST.

SHE REMOVED ALL TRACES OF SARA FROM HER ROOM...

EDNESDAY	THURSDAY	FRIDAY	SATURDAY	SUND
X	X	X	X	X
EDNESDAY	THURSDAY	FRIDAY	SATURDAY	SUND
X	X		THE DANCE!!	
EDNESDAY	THURSDAY	FRIDAY	SATURDAY	SUND
EDNESDAY	THURSDAY	FRIDAY	SATURDAY	SUND

...AND TOOK HER LIFE BACK WITH THE TOUCH OF A BUTTON.

DELETE ALL MESSAGES?

YES

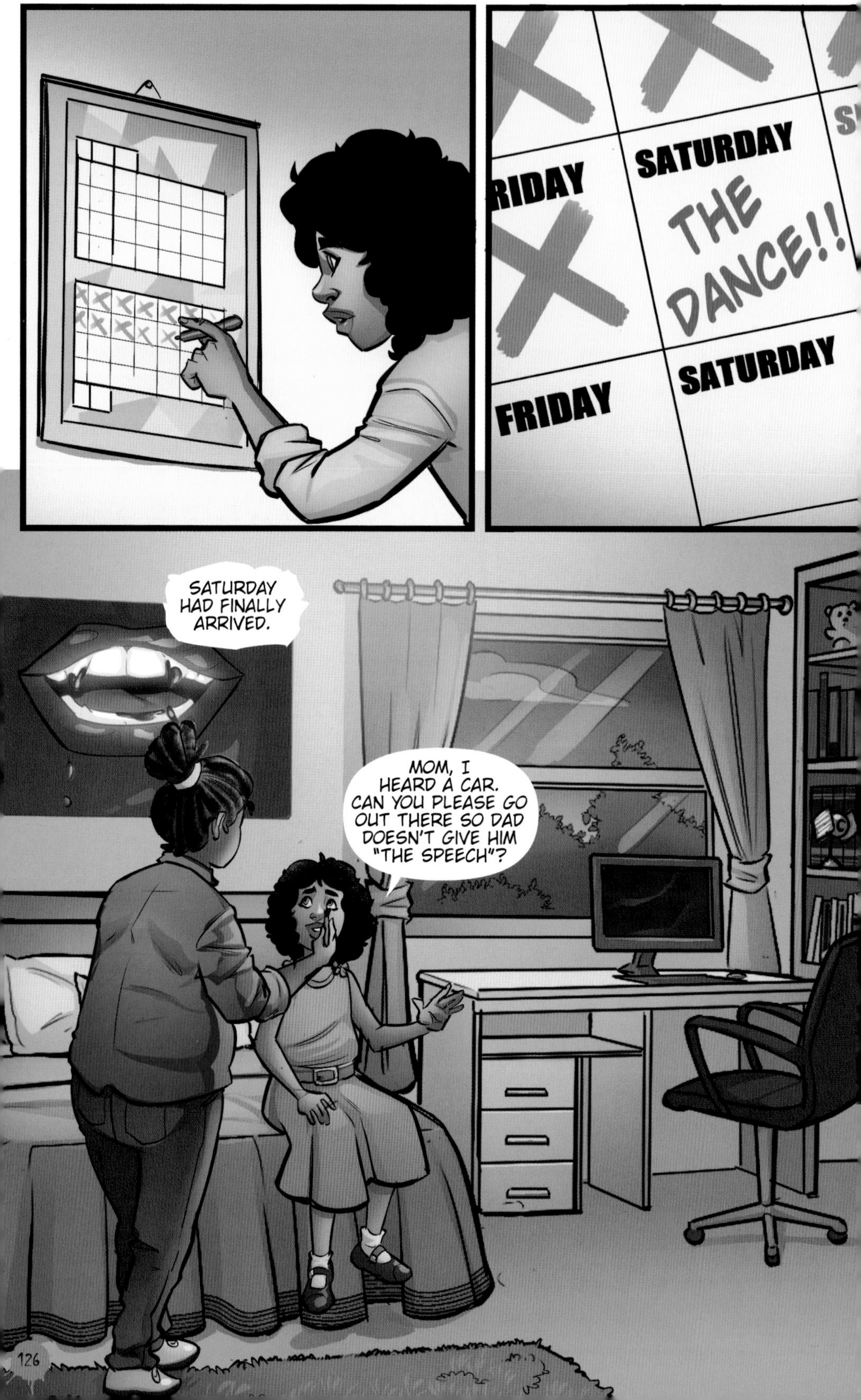
SATURDAY
THE DANCE!!
FRIDAY
SATURDAY
SATURDAY HAD FINALLY ARRIVED.
MOM, I HEARD A CAR. CAN YOU PLEASE GO OUT THERE SO DAD DOESN'T GIVE HIM "THE SPEECH"?

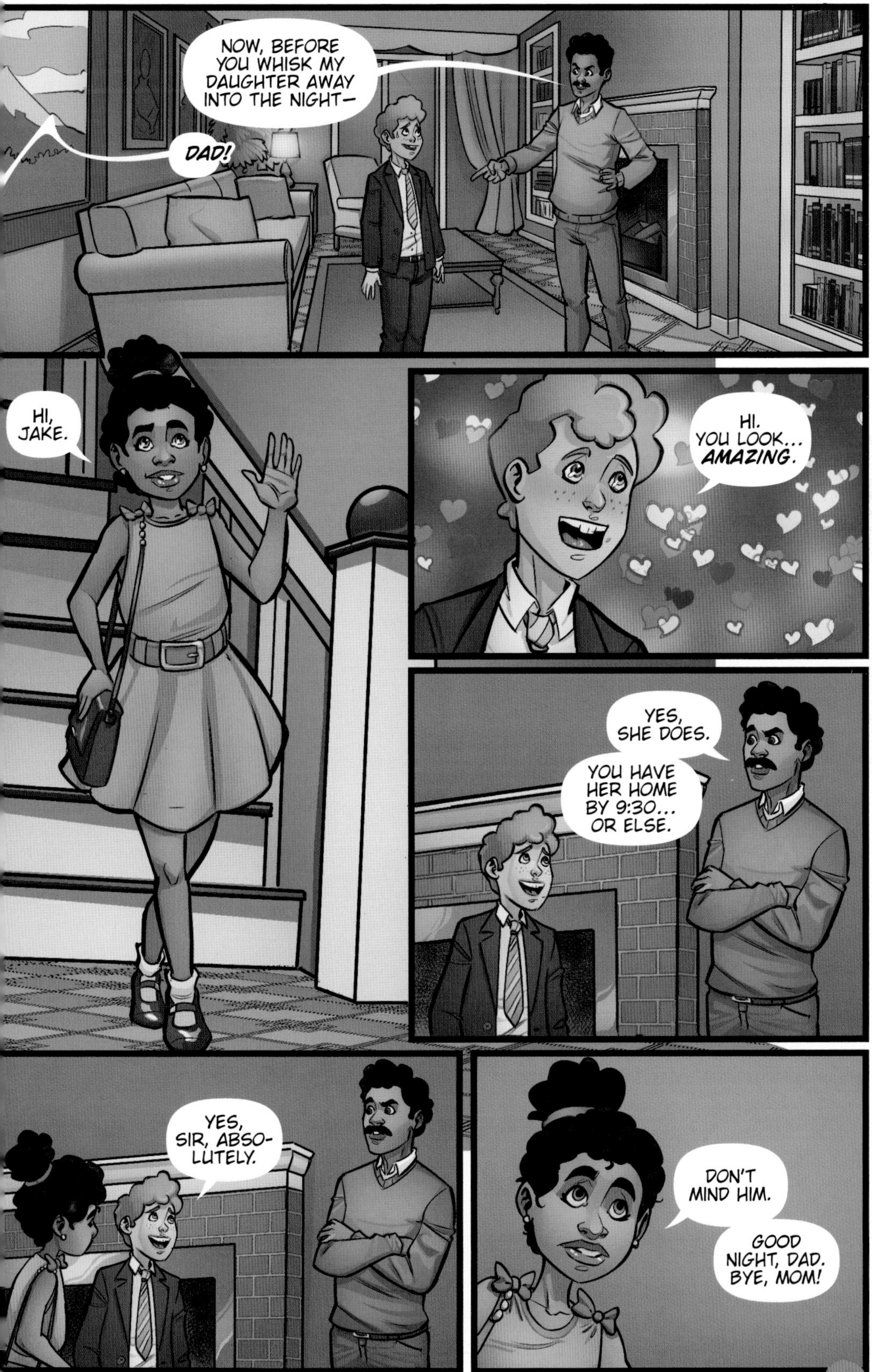
NOW, BEFORE YOU WHISK MY DAUGHTER AWAY INTO THE NIGHT—
DAD!
HI, JAKE.
HI. YOU LOOK... AMAZING.
YES, SHE DOES.
YOU HAVE HER HOME BY 9:30... OR ELSE.
YES, SIR, ABSO-LUTELY.
DON'T MIND HIM.
GOOD NIGHT, DAD. BYE, MOM!

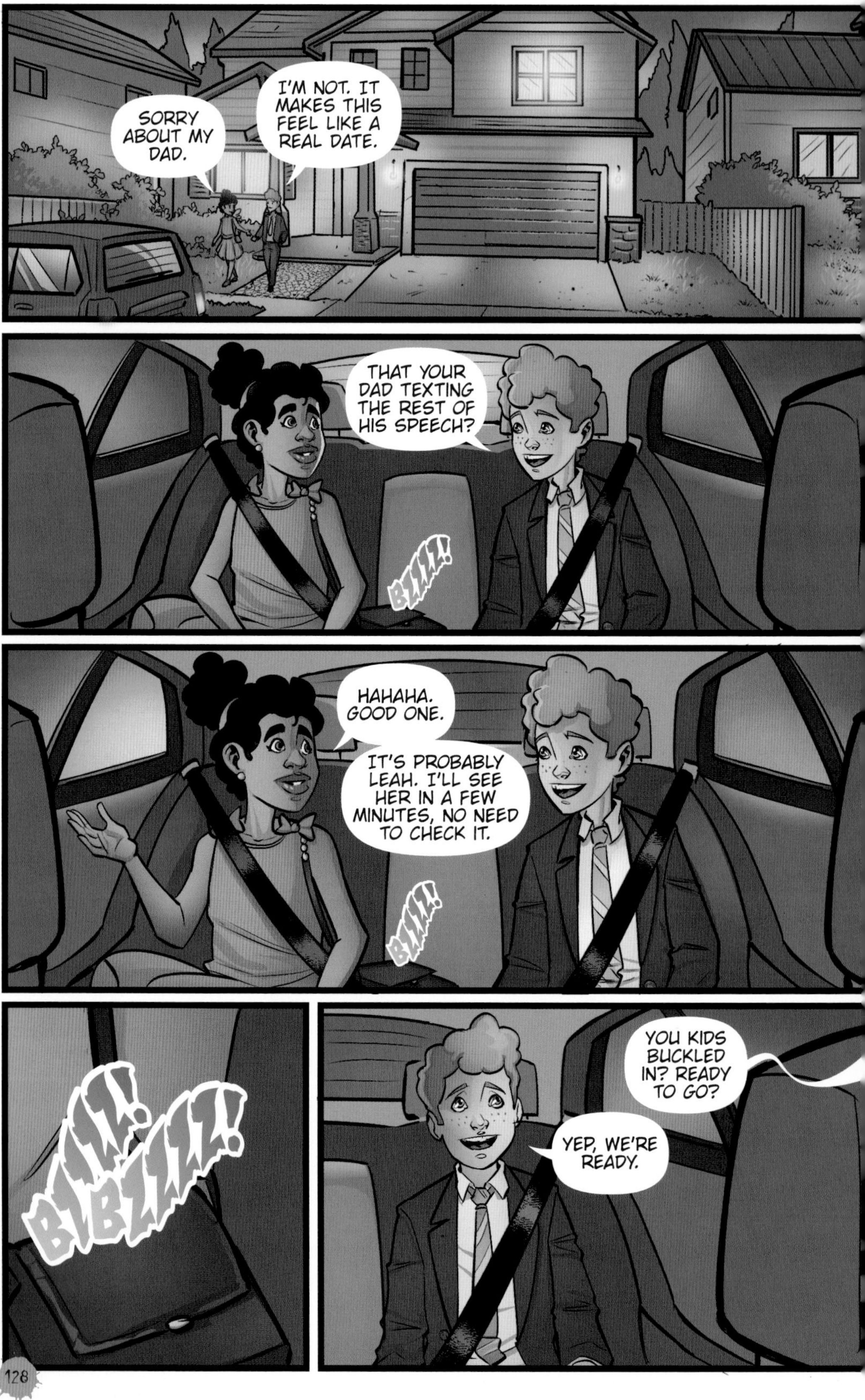
SORRY ABOUT MY DAD.
I'M NOT. IT MAKES THIS FEEL LIKE A REAL DATE.
THAT YOUR DAD TEXTING THE REST OF HIS SPEECH?
BZZZZ!
HAHAHA. GOOD ONE.
IT'S PROBABLY LEAH. I'LL SEE HER IN A FEW MINUTES, NO NEED TO CHECK IT.
BZZZZ!
BZZZ! BZZZZZ!
YOU KIDS BUCKLED IN? READY TO GO?
YEP, WE'RE READY.

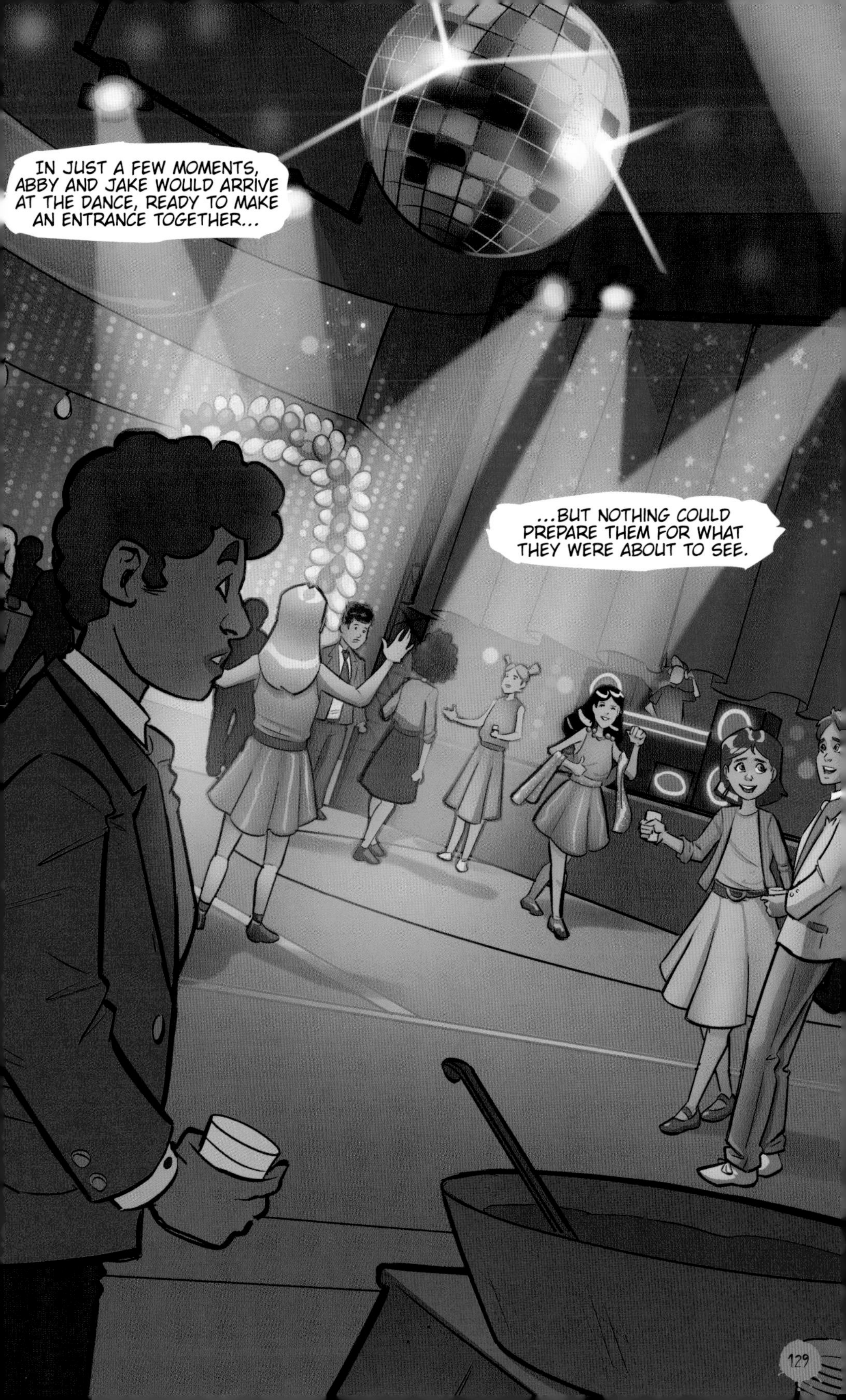
IN JUST A FEW MOMENTS, ABBY AND JAKE WOULD ARRIVE AT THE DANCE, READY TO MAKE AN ENTRANCE TOGETHER...
...BUT NOTHING COULD PREPARE THEM FOR WHAT THEY WERE ABOUT TO SEE.

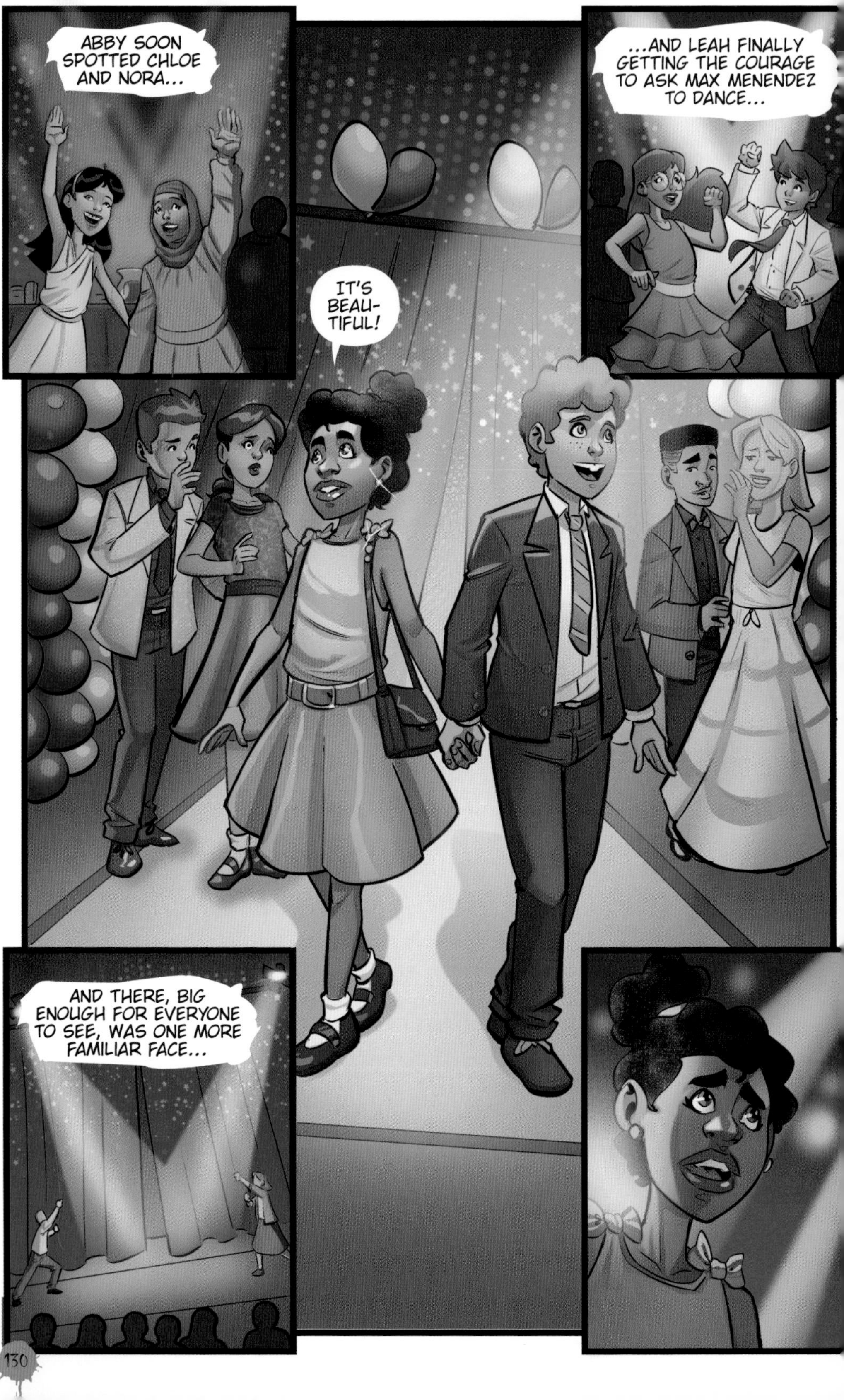
ABBY SOON SPOTTED CHLOE AND NORA...
...AND LEAH FINALLY GETTING THE COURAGE TO ASK MAX MENENDEZ TO DANCE...
IT'S BEAU-TIFUL!
AND THERE, BIG ENOUGH FOR EVERYONE TO SEE, WAS ONE MORE FAMILIAR FACE...

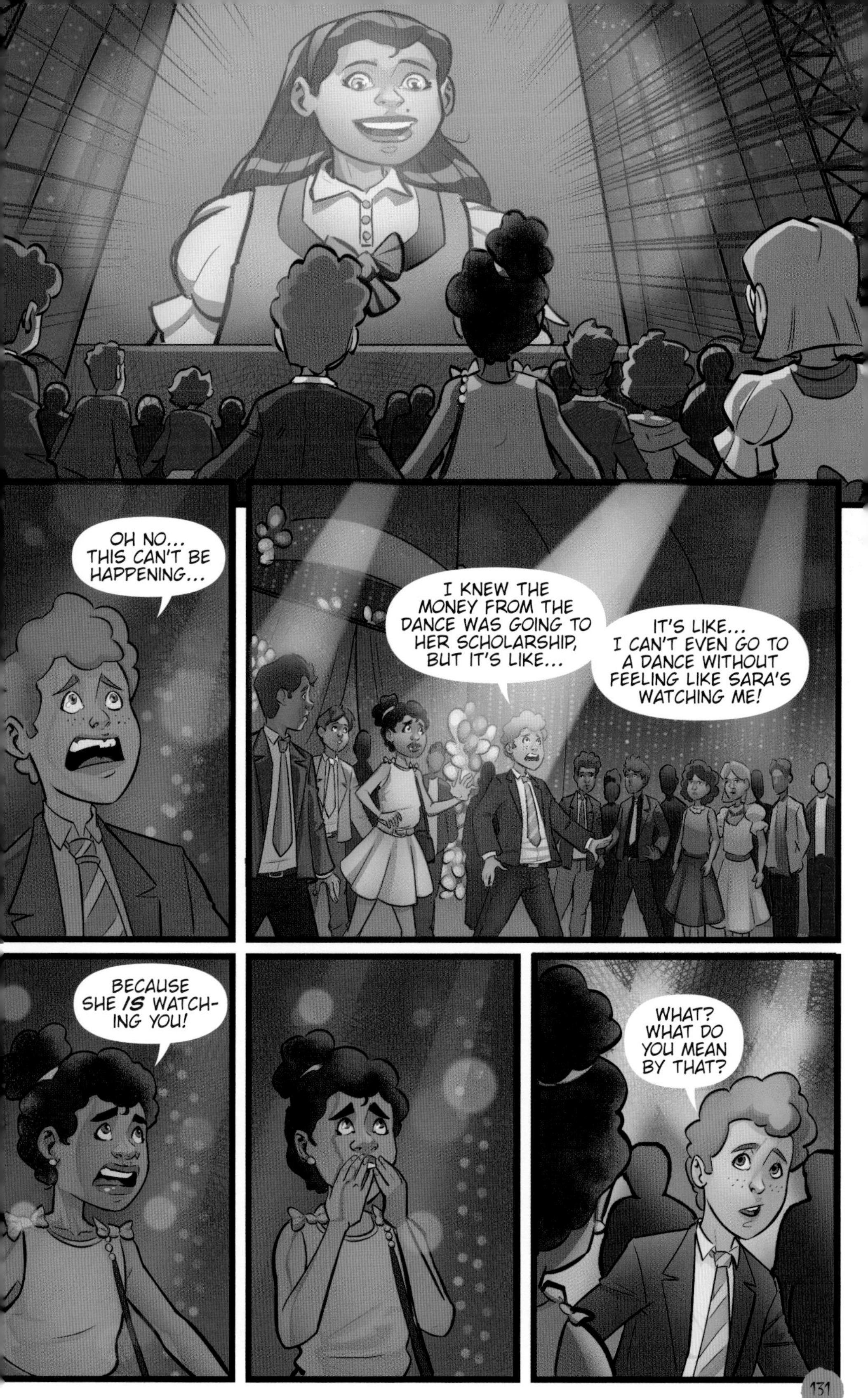
OH NO... THIS CAN'T BE HAPPENING...
I KNEW THE MONEY FROM THE DANCE WAS GOING TO HER SCHOLARSHIP, BUT IT'S LIKE...
IT'S LIKE... I CAN'T EVEN GO TO A DANCE WITHOUT FEELING LIKE SARA'S WATCHING ME!
BECAUSE SHE *IS* WATCHING YOU!
WHAT? WHAT DO YOU MEAN BY THAT?

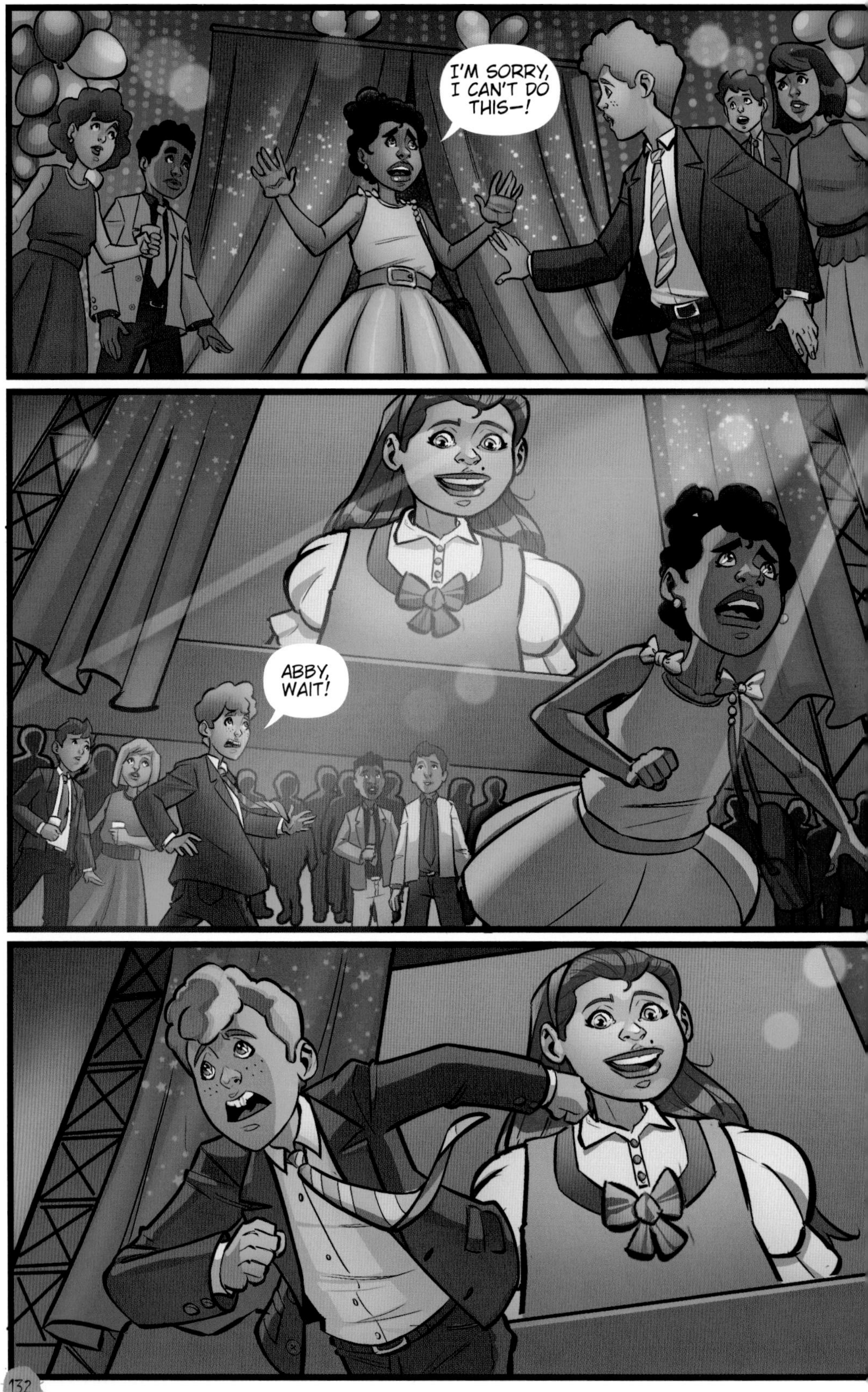
I'M SORRY, I CAN'T DO THIS—!
ABBY, WAIT!

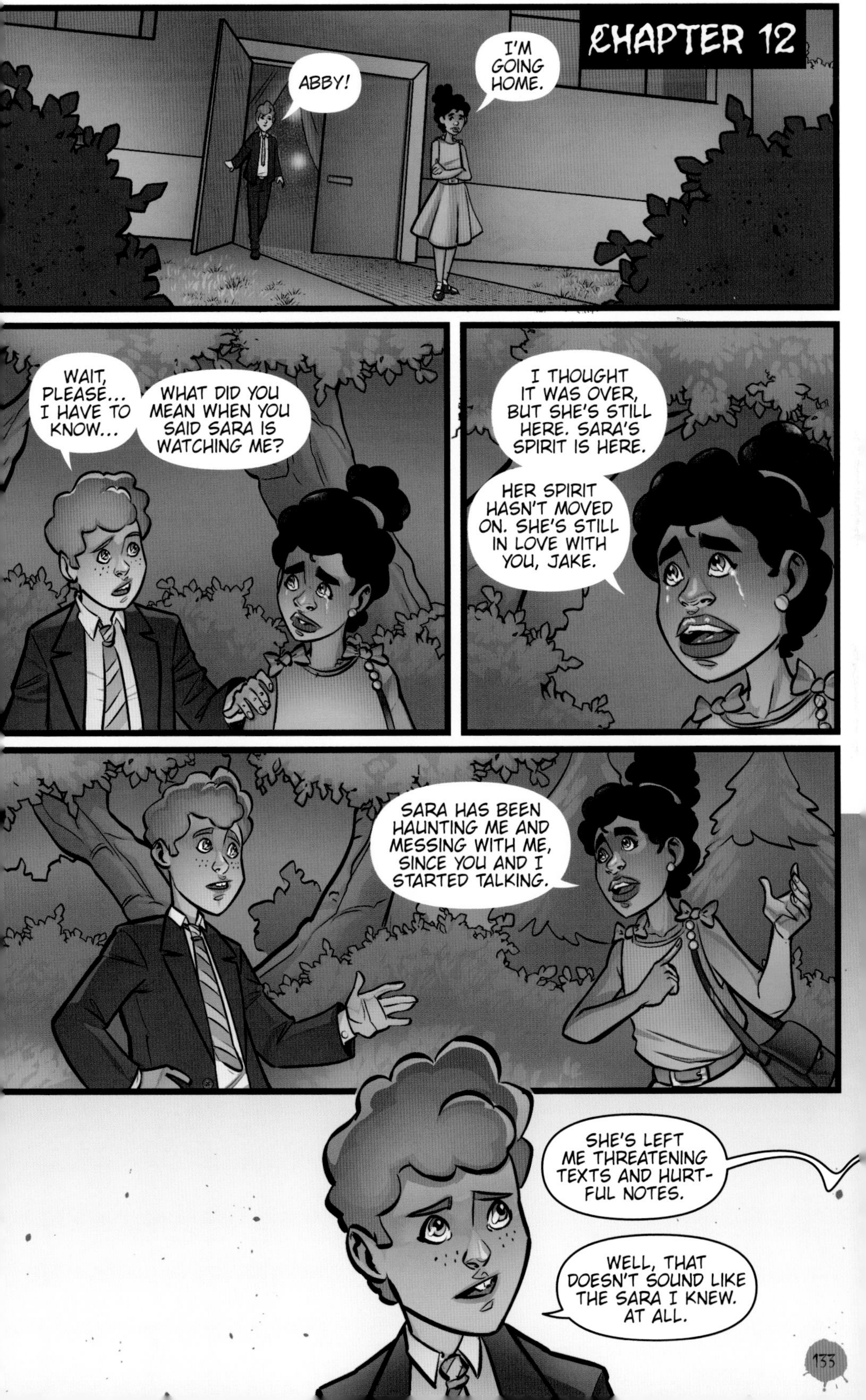
CHAPTER 12
ABBY!
I'M GOING HOME.
WAIT, PLEASE... I HAVE TO KNOW...
WHAT DID YOU MEAN WHEN YOU SAID SARA IS WATCHING ME?
I THOUGHT IT WAS OVER, BUT SHE'S STILL HERE. SARA'S SPIRIT IS HERE.
HER SPIRIT HASN'T MOVED ON. SHE'S STILL IN LOVE WITH YOU, JAKE.
SARA HAS BEEN HAUNTING ME AND MESSING WITH ME, SINCE YOU AND I STARTED TALKING.
SHE'S LEFT ME THREATENING TEXTS AND HURT-FUL NOTES.
WELL, THAT DOESN'T SOUND LIKE THE SARA I KNEW. AT ALL.

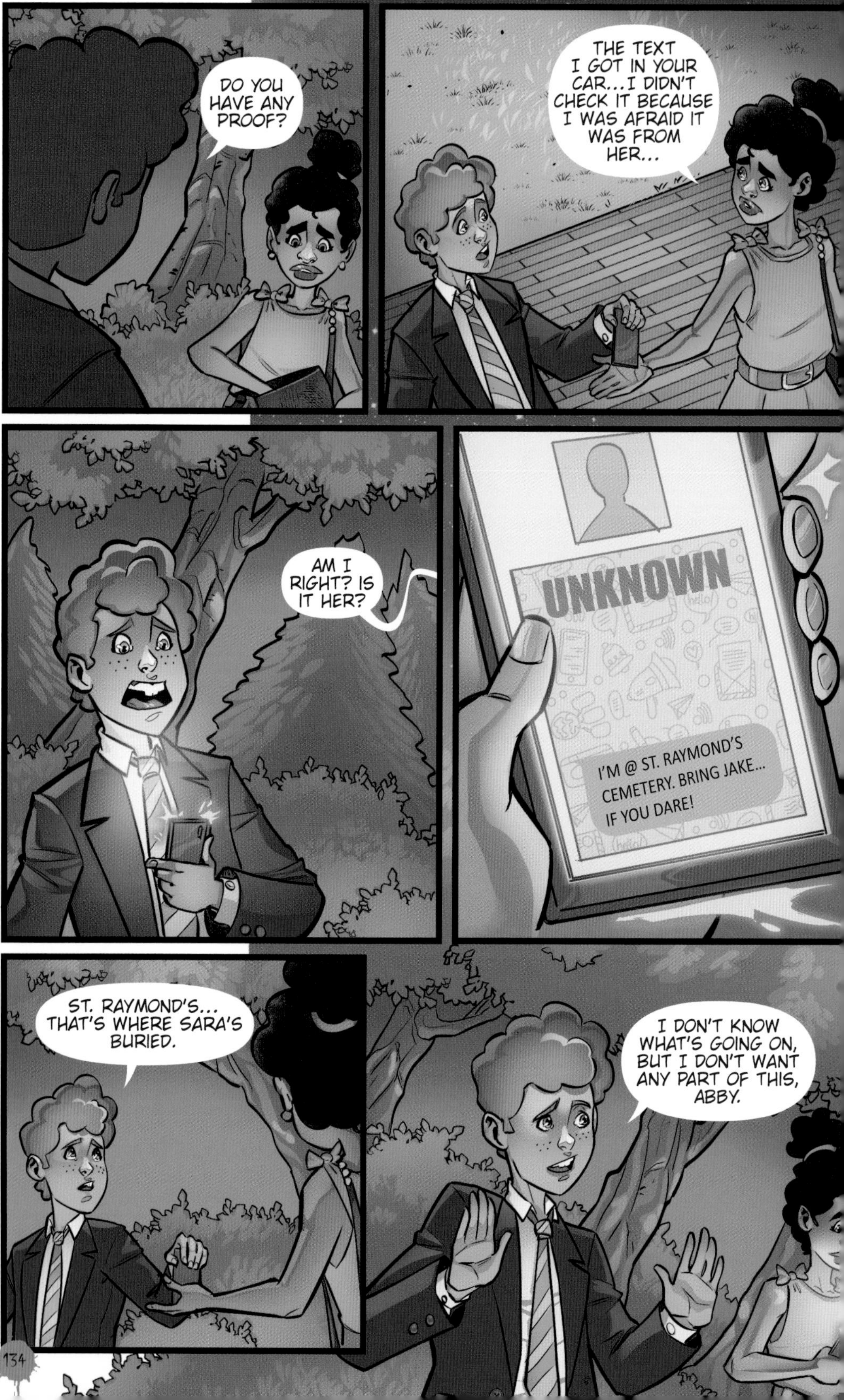
DO YOU HAVE ANY PROOF?
THE TEXT I GOT IN YOUR CAR...I DIDN'T CHECK IT BECAUSE I WAS AFRAID IT WAS FROM HER...
AM I RIGHT? IS IT HER?
UNKNOWN
I'M @ ST. RAYMOND'S CEMETERY. BRING JAKE... IF YOU DARE!
ST. RAYMOND'S... THAT'S WHERE SARA'S BURIED.
I DON'T KNOW WHAT'S GOING ON, BUT I DON'T WANT ANY PART OF THIS, ABBY.

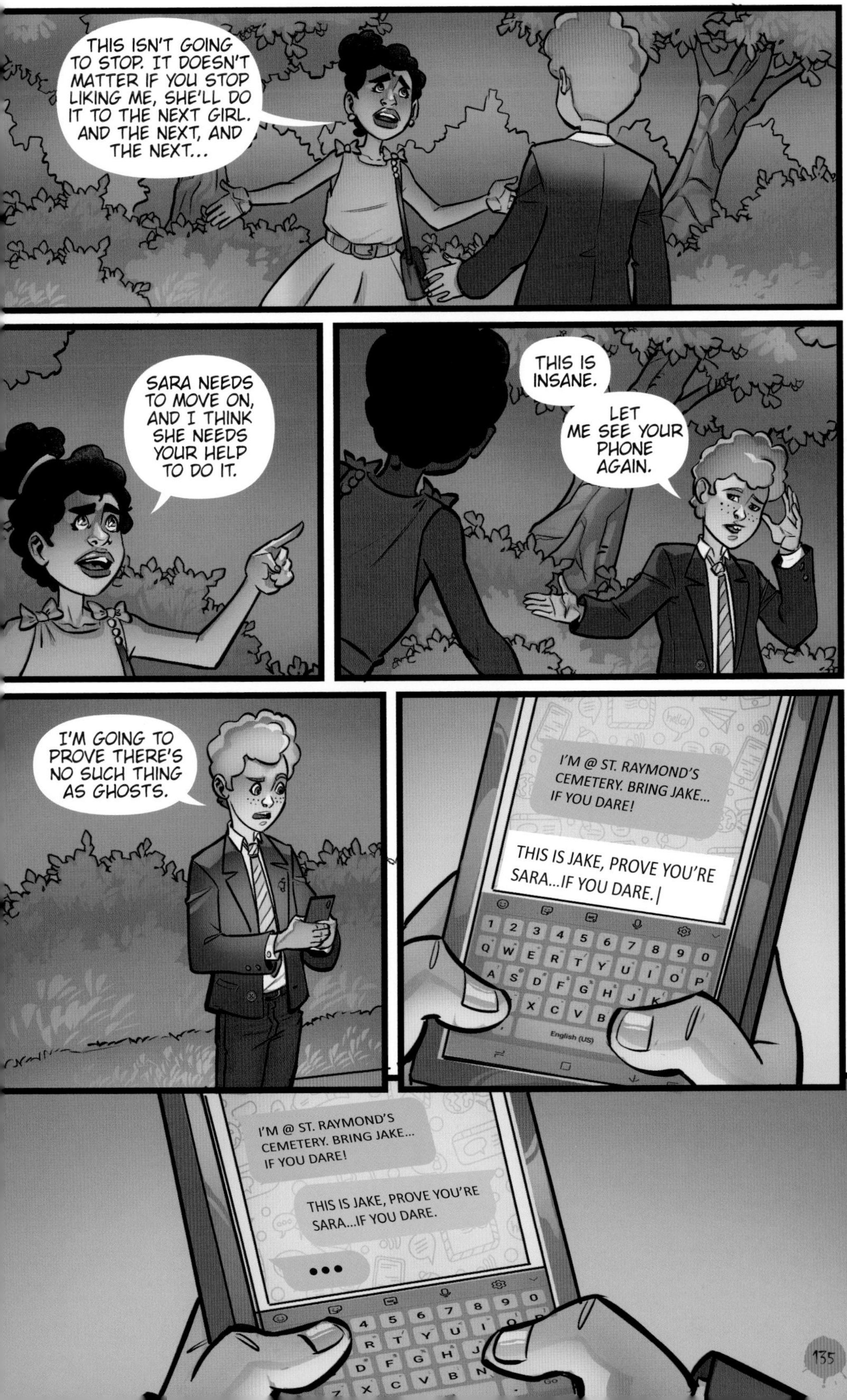
THIS ISN'T GOING TO STOP. IT DOESN'T MATTER IF YOU STOP LIKING ME, SHE'LL DO IT TO THE NEXT GIRL. AND THE NEXT, AND THE NEXT...
SARA NEEDS TO MOVE ON, AND I THINK SHE NEEDS YOUR HELP TO DO IT.
THIS IS INSANE.
LET ME SEE YOUR PHONE AGAIN.
I'M GOING TO PROVE THERE'S NO SUCH THING AS GHOSTS.
I'M @ ST. RAYMOND'S CEMETERY. BRING JAKE... IF YOU DARE!
THIS IS JAKE, PROVE YOU'RE SARA...IF YOU DARE.
English (US)
I'M @ ST. RAYMOND'S CEMETERY. BRING JAKE... IF YOU DARE!
THIS IS JAKE, PROVE YOU'RE SARA...IF YOU DARE.

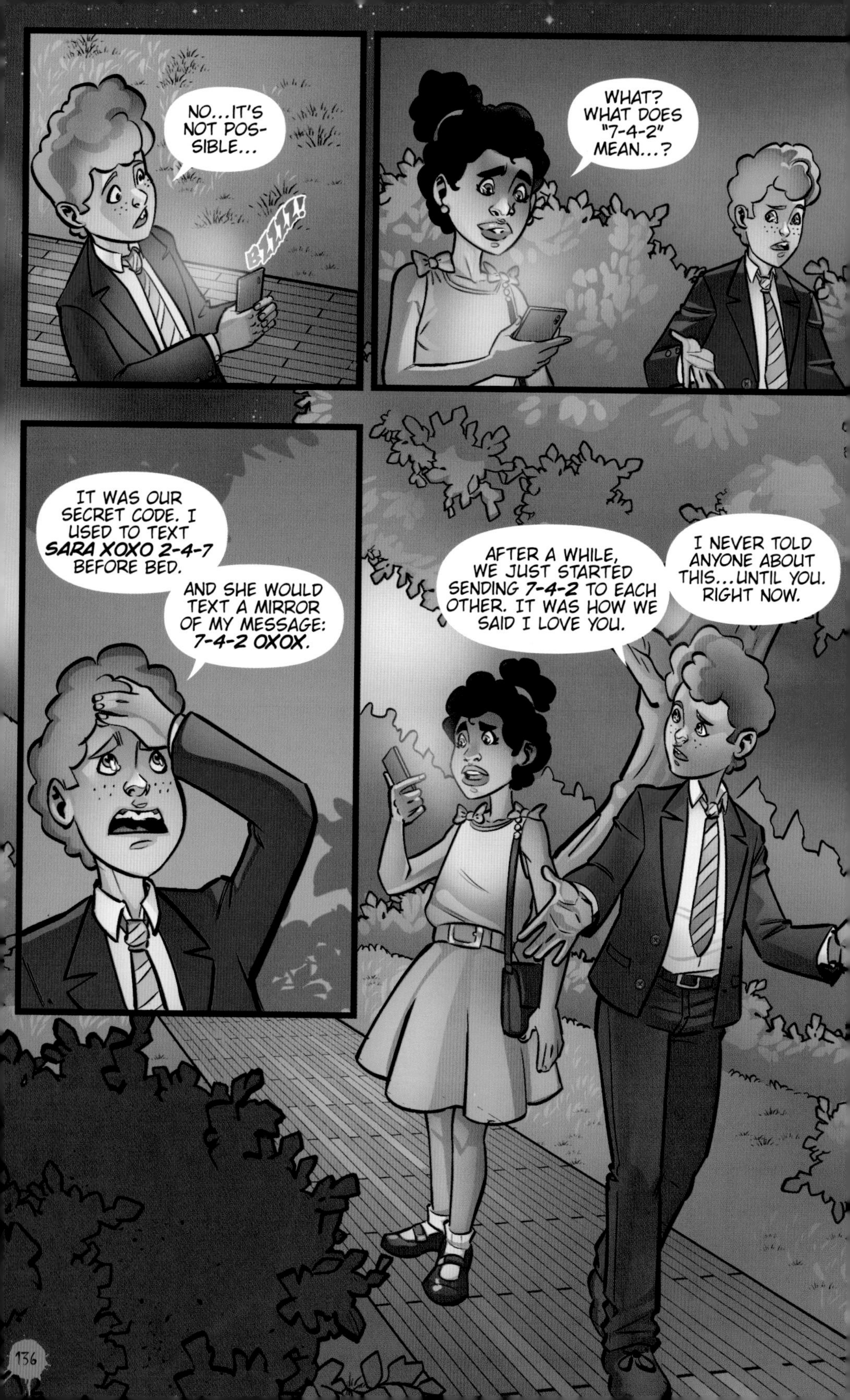
NO...IT'S NOT POS-SIBLE...
BZZZZ!
WHAT? WHAT DOES "7-4-2" MEAN...?
IT WAS OUR SECRET CODE. I USED TO TEXT SARA XOXO 2-4-7 BEFORE BED.
AND SHE WOULD TEXT A MIRROR OF MY MESSAGE: 7-4-2 OXOX.
AFTER A WHILE, WE JUST STARTED SENDING 7-4-2 TO EACH OTHER. IT WAS HOW WE SAID I LOVE YOU.
I NEVER TOLD ANYONE ABOUT THIS...UNTIL YOU. RIGHT NOW.

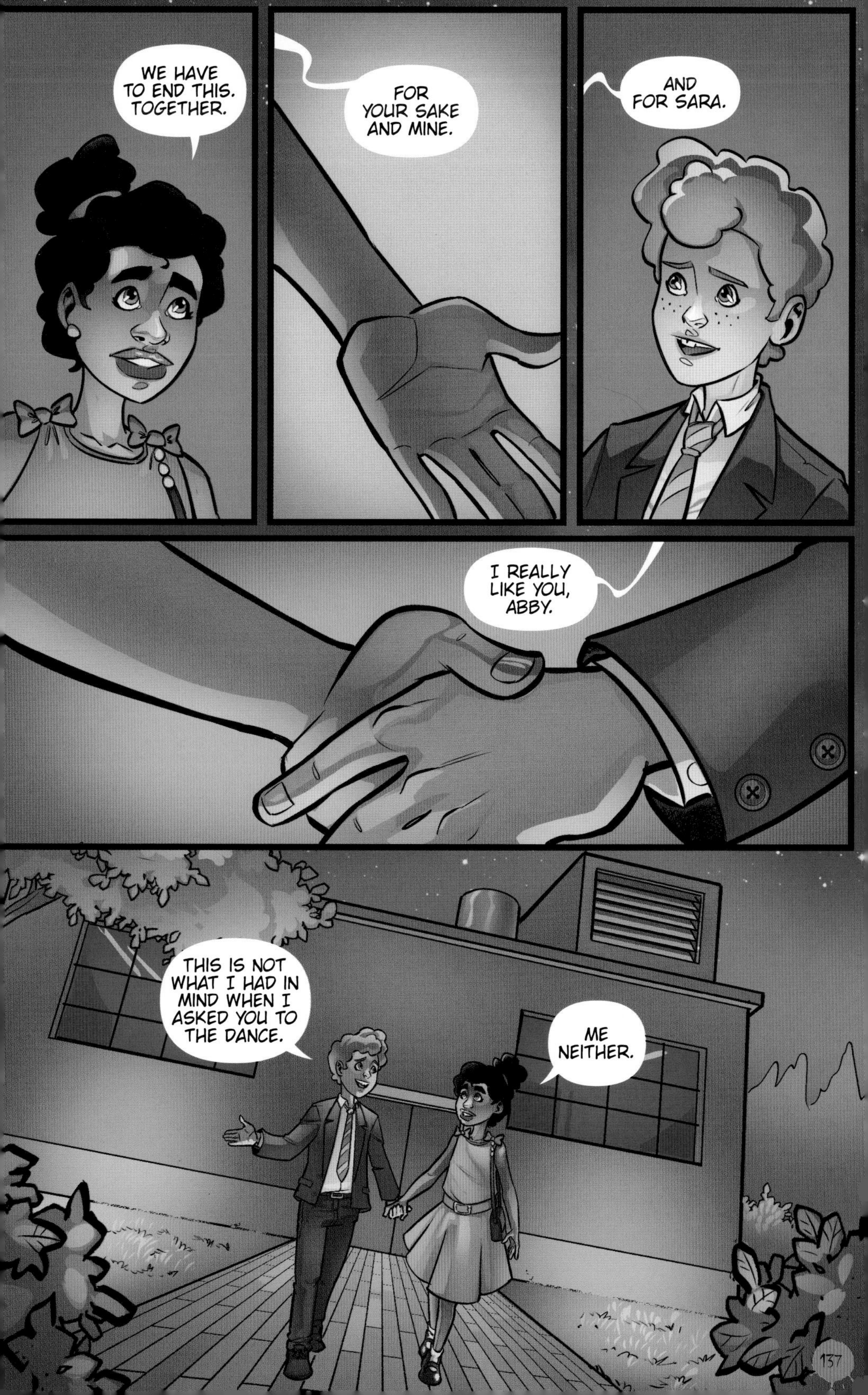
WE HAVE TO END THIS. TOGETHER.
FOR YOUR SAKE AND MINE.
AND FOR SARA.
I REALLY LIKE YOU, ABBY.
THIS IS NOT WHAT I HAD IN MIND WHEN I ASKED YOU TO THE DANCE.
ME NEITHER.

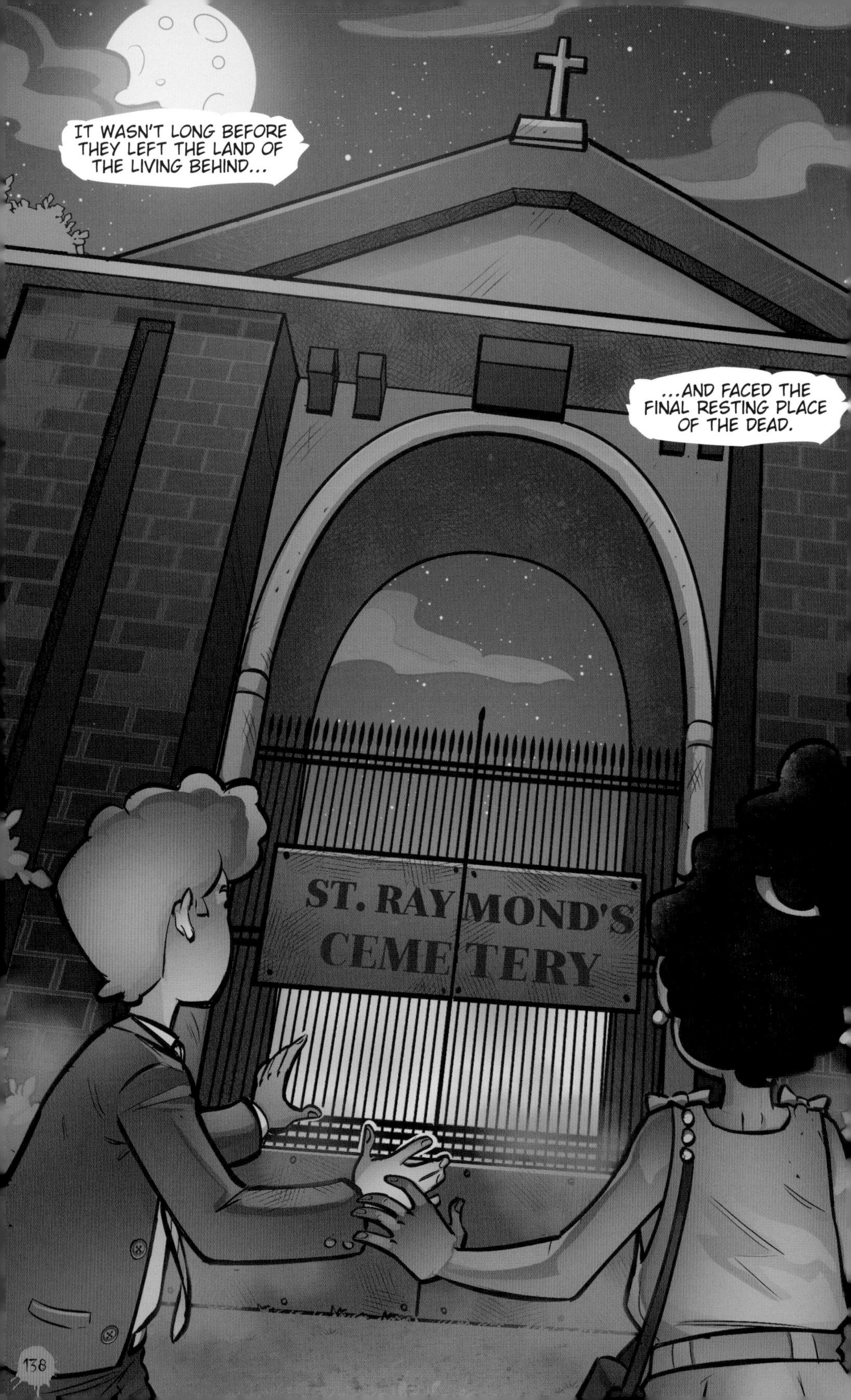
IT WASN'T LONG BEFORE THEY LEFT THE LAND OF THE LIVING BEHIND...
...AND FACED THE FINAL RESTING PLACE OF THE DEAD.
ST. RAYMOND'S CEMETERY

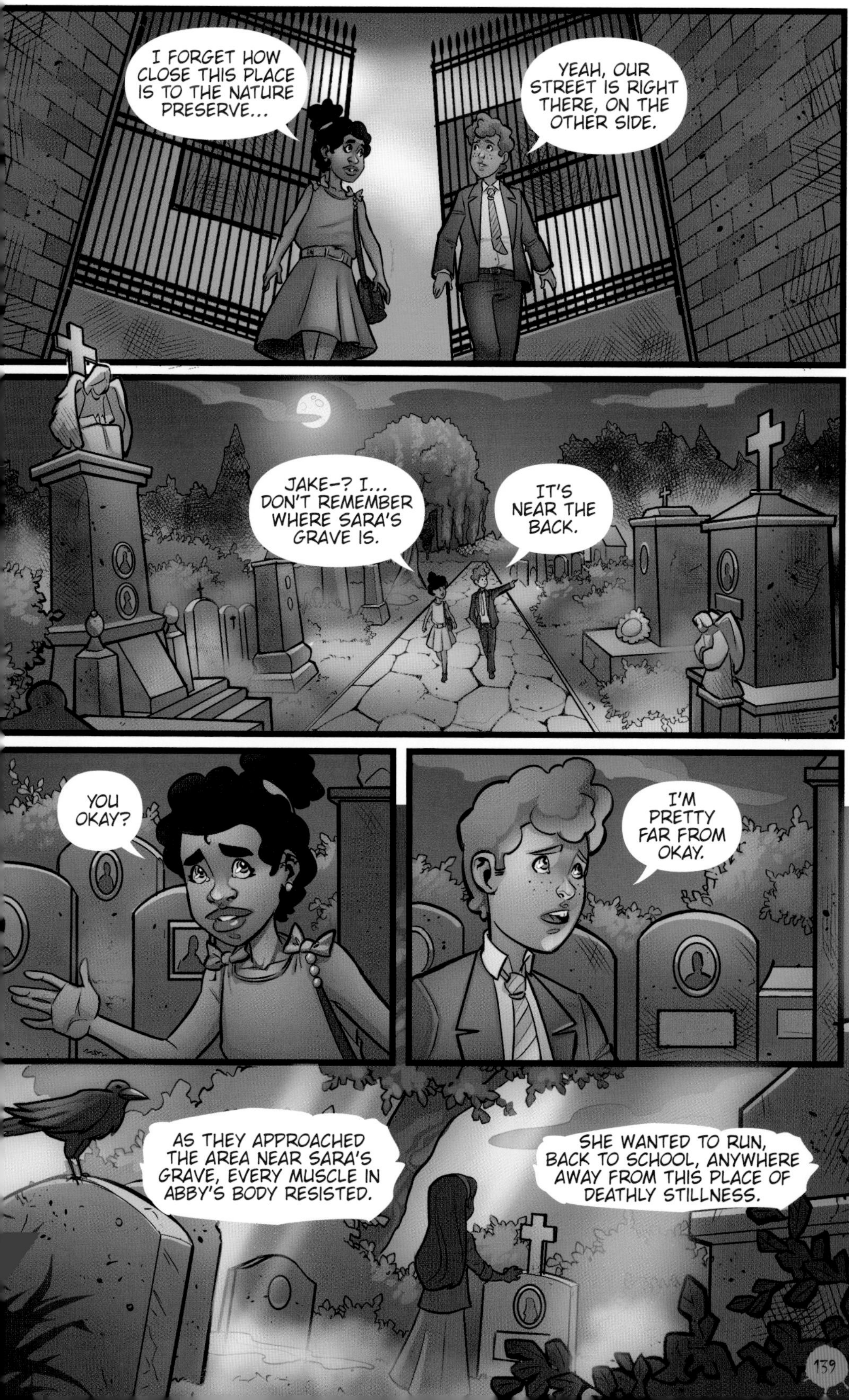
I FORGET HOW CLOSE THIS PLACE IS TO THE NATURE PRESERVE...
YEAH, OUR STREET IS RIGHT THERE, ON THE OTHER SIDE.
JAKE-? I... DON'T REMEMBER WHERE SARA'S GRAVE IS.
IT'S NEAR THE BACK.
YOU OKAY?
I'M PRETTY FAR FROM OKAY.
AS THEY APPROACHED THE AREA NEAR SARA'S GRAVE, EVERY MUSCLE IN ABBY'S BODY RESISTED.
SHE WANTED TO RUN, BACK TO SCHOOL, ANYWHERE AWAY FROM THIS PLACE OF DEATHLY STILLNESS.

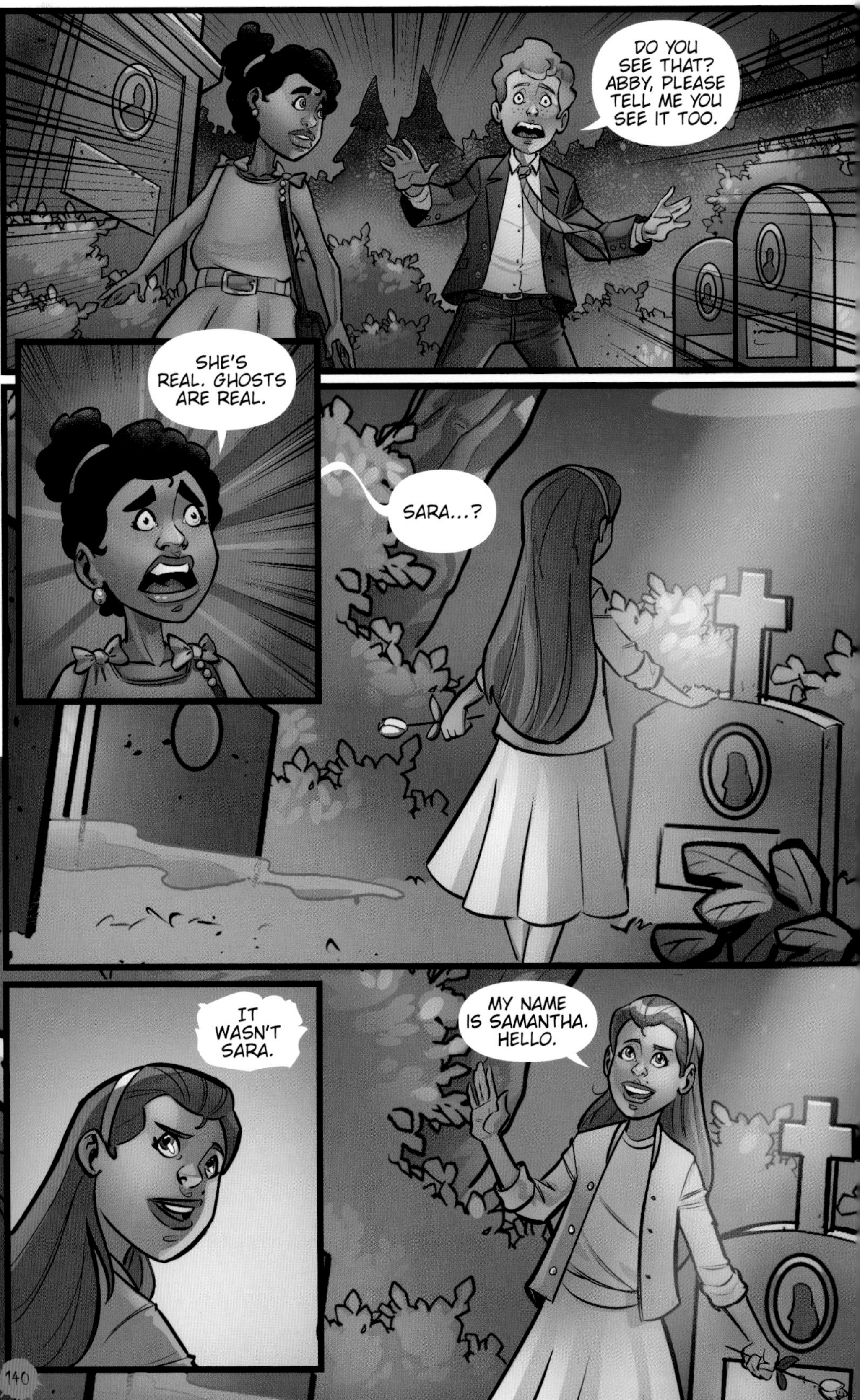
DO YOU SEE THAT? ABBY, PLEASE TELL ME YOU SEE IT TOO.
SHE'S REAL. GHOSTS ARE REAL.
SARA...?
IT WASN'T SARA.
MY NAME IS SAMANTHA. HELLO.

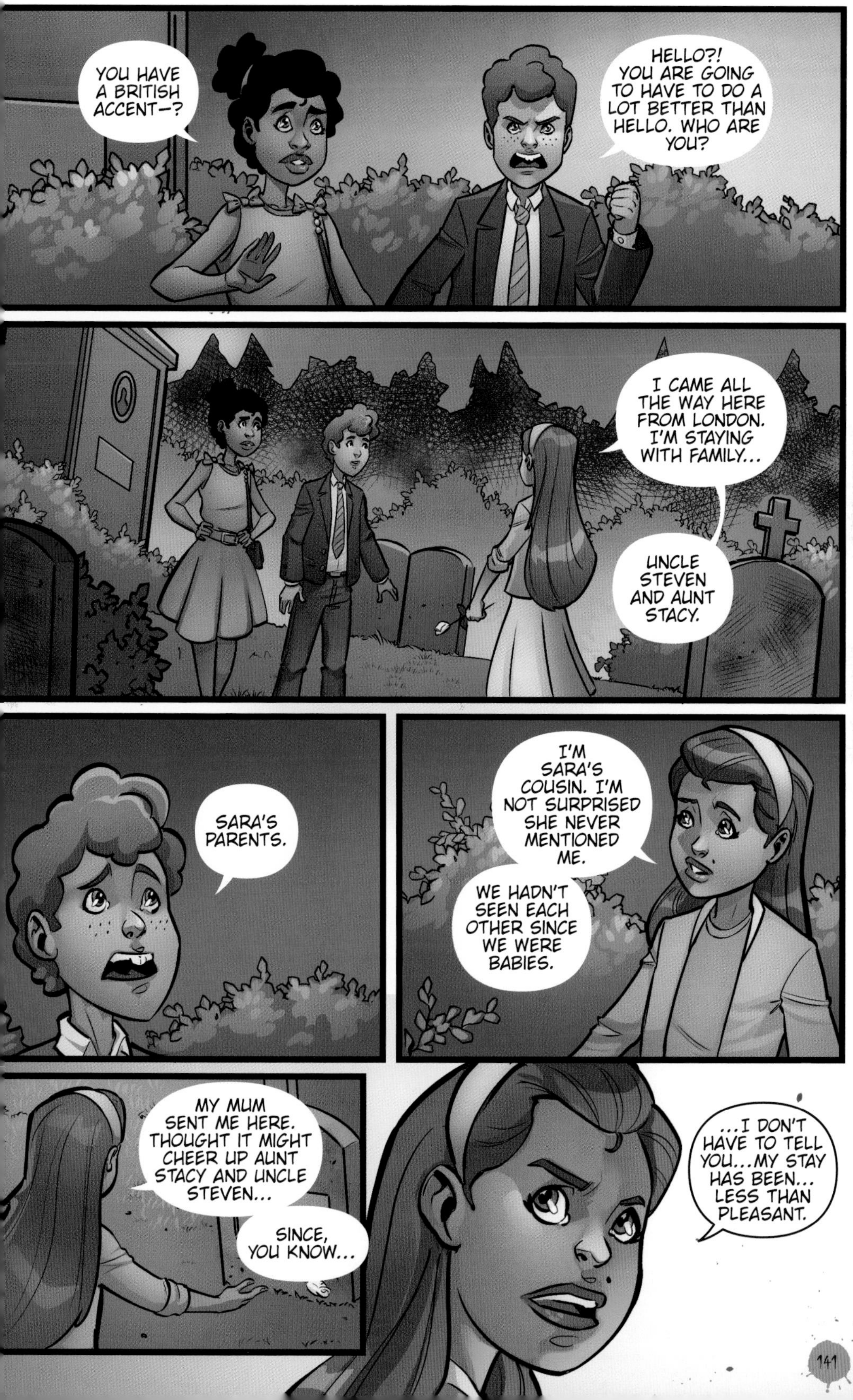
YOU HAVE A BRITISH ACCENT–?
HELLO?! YOU ARE GOING TO HAVE TO DO A LOT BETTER THAN HELLO. WHO ARE YOU?
I CAME ALL THE WAY HERE FROM LONDON. I'M STAYING WITH FAMILY...
UNCLE STEVEN AND AUNT STACY.
SARA'S PARENTS.
I'M SARA'S COUSIN. I'M NOT SURPRISED SHE NEVER MENTIONED ME.
WE HADN'T SEEN EACH OTHER SINCE WE WERE BABIES.
MY MUM SENT ME HERE. THOUGHT IT MIGHT CHEER UP AUNT STACY AND UNCLE STEVEN...
SINCE, YOU KNOW...
...I DON'T HAVE TO TELL YOU...MY STAY HAS BEEN... LESS THAN PLEASANT.

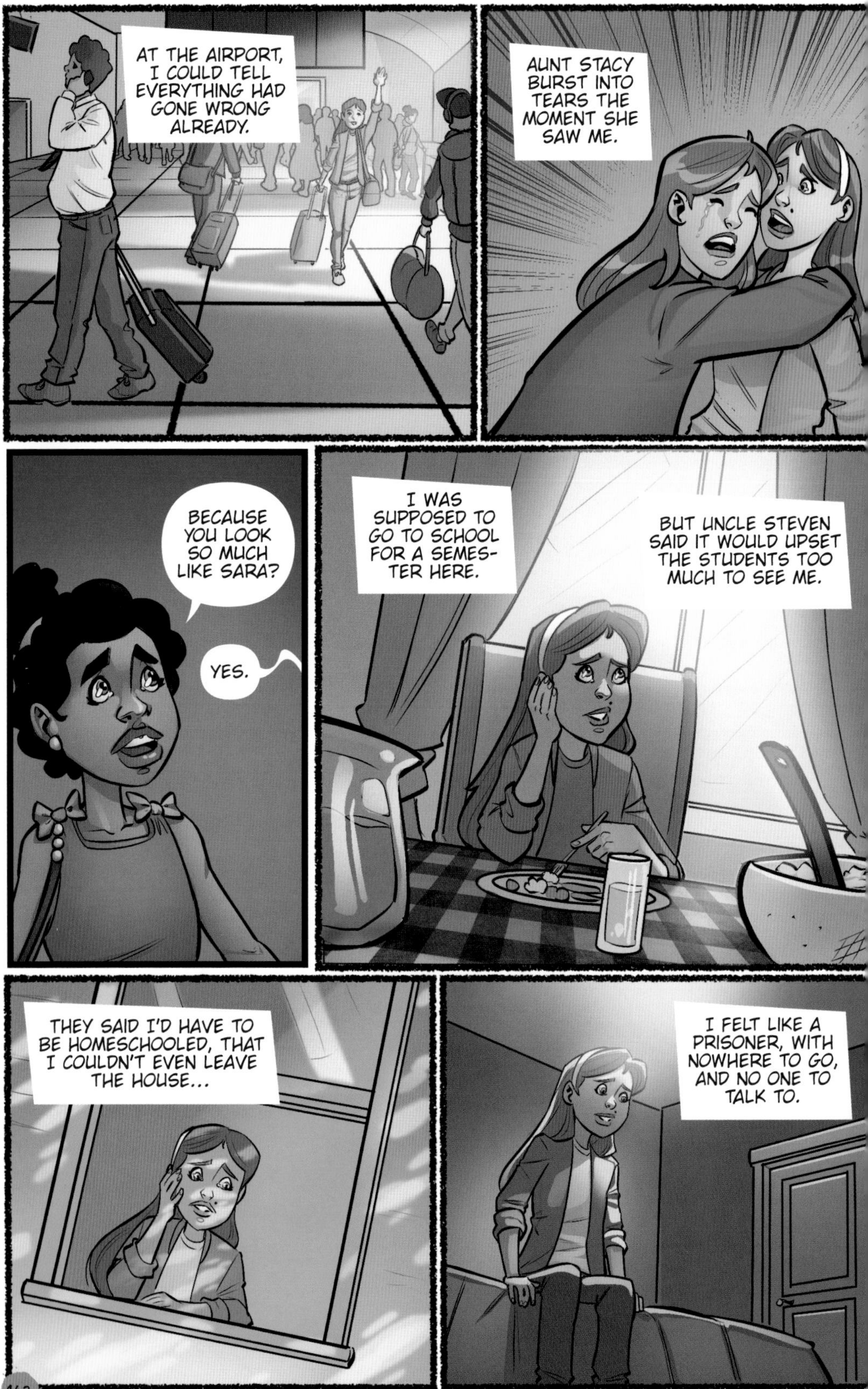
AT THE AIRPORT, I COULD TELL EVERYTHING HAD GONE WRONG ALREADY.
AUNT STACY BURST INTO TEARS THE MOMENT SHE SAW ME.
BECAUSE YOU LOOK SO MUCH LIKE SARA?
YES.
I WAS SUPPOSED TO GO TO SCHOOL FOR A SEMES-TER HERE.
BUT UNCLE STEVEN SAID IT WOULD UPSET THE STUDENTS TOO MUCH TO SEE ME.
THEY SAID I'D HAVE TO BE HOMESCHOOLED, THAT I COULDN'T EVEN LEAVE THE HOUSE...
I FELT LIKE A PRISONER, WITH NOWHERE TO GO, AND NO ONE TO TALK TO.

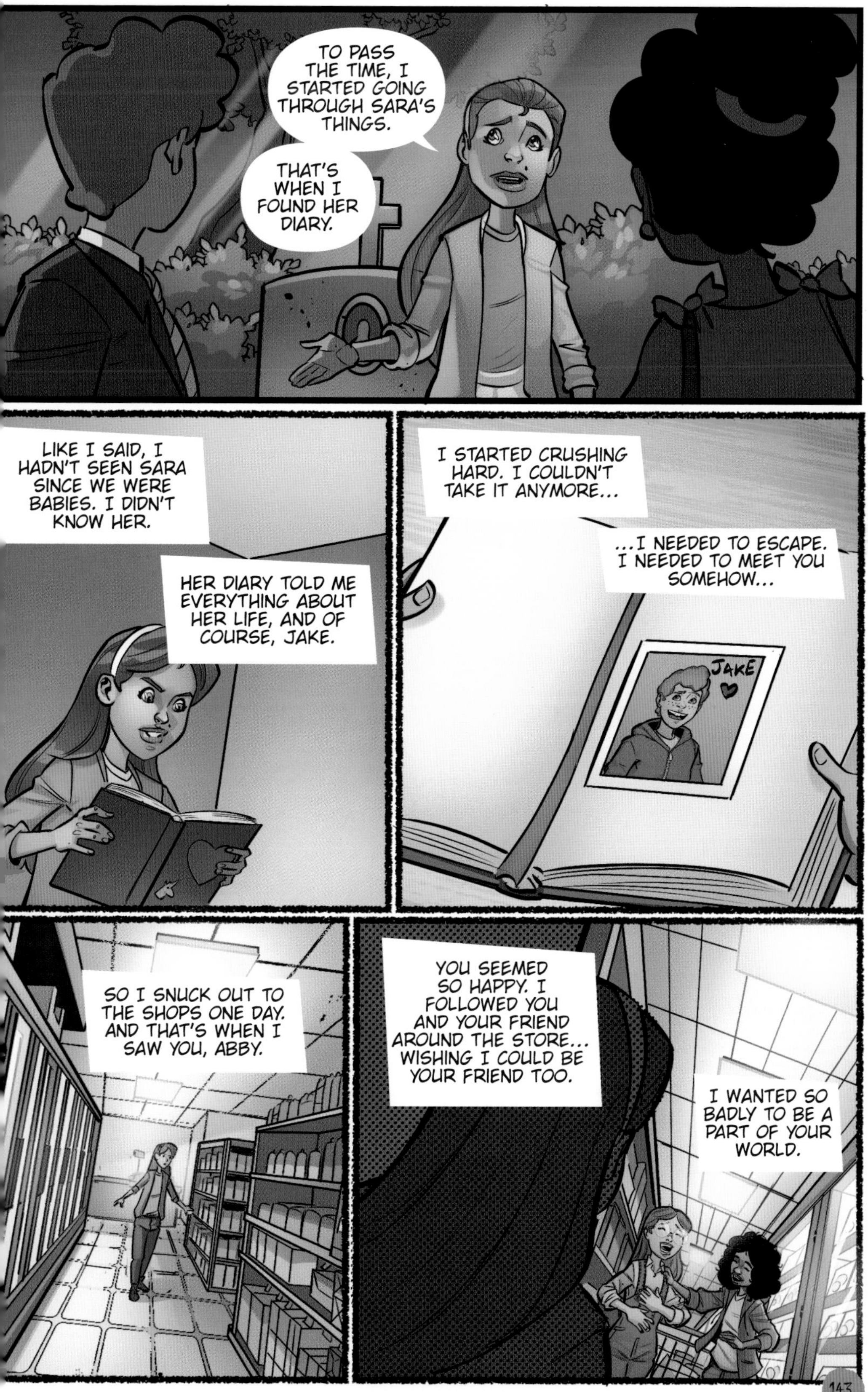
TO PASS THE TIME, I STARTED GOING THROUGH SARA'S THINGS.
THAT'S WHEN I FOUND HER DIARY.
LIKE I SAID, I HADN'T SEEN SARA SINCE WE WERE BABIES. I DIDN'T KNOW HER.
HER DIARY TOLD ME EVERYTHING ABOUT HER LIFE, AND OF COURSE, JAKE.
I STARTED CRUSHING HARD. I COULDN'T TAKE IT ANYMORE...
...I NEEDED TO ESCAPE. I NEEDED TO MEET YOU SOMEHOW...
JAKE
SO I SNUCK OUT TO THE SHOPS ONE DAY. AND THAT'S WHEN I SAW YOU, ABBY.
YOU SEEMED SO HAPPY. I FOLLOWED YOU AND YOUR FRIEND AROUND THE STORE... WISHING I COULD BE YOUR FRIEND TOO.
I WANTED SO BADLY TO BE A PART OF YOUR WORLD.

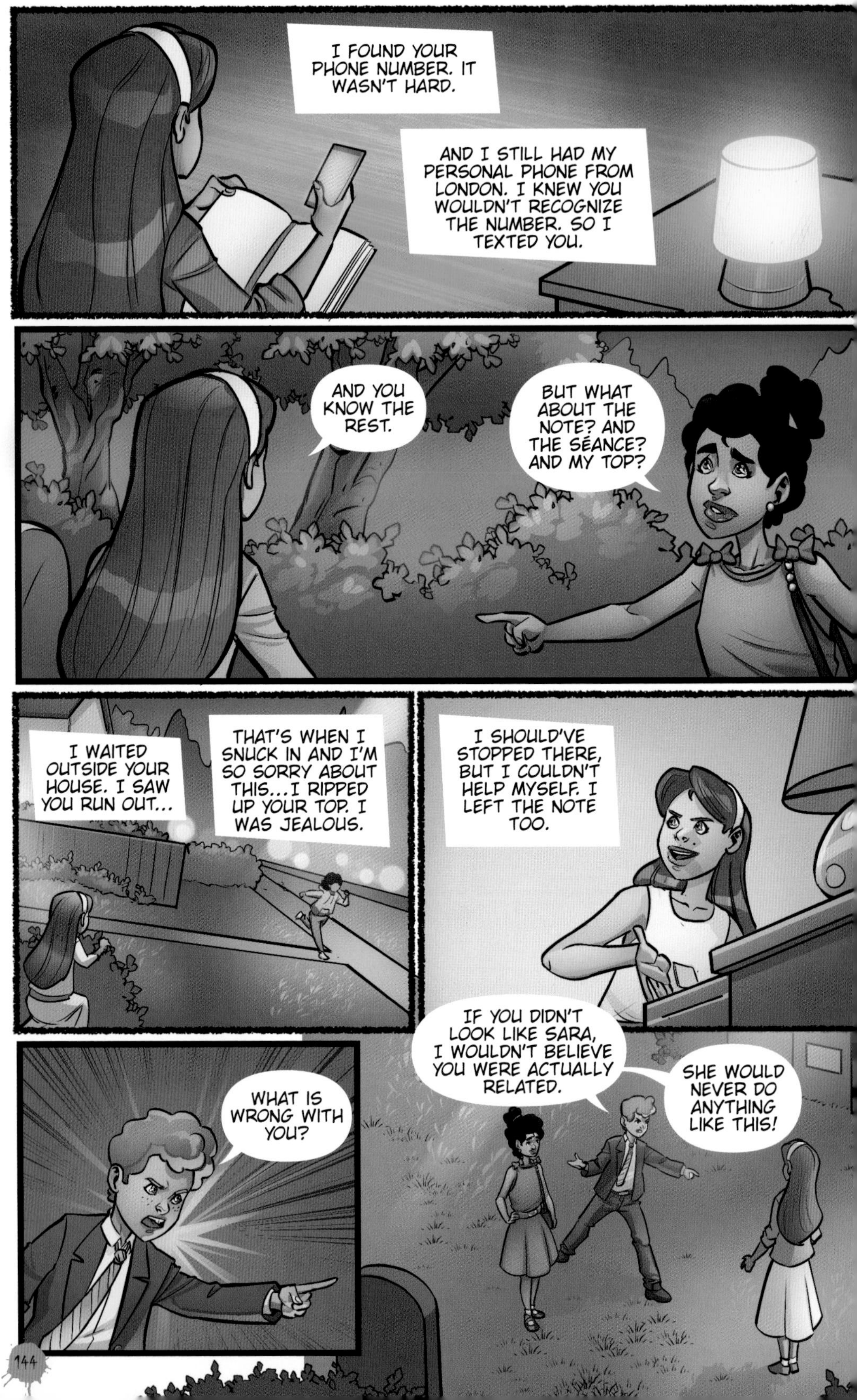
I FOUND YOUR PHONE NUMBER. IT WASN'T HARD.
AND I STILL HAD MY PERSONAL PHONE FROM LONDON. I KNEW YOU WOULDN'T RECOGNIZE THE NUMBER. SO I TEXTED YOU.
AND YOU KNOW THE REST.
BUT WHAT ABOUT THE NOTE? AND THE SÉANCE? AND MY TOP?
I WAITED OUTSIDE YOUR HOUSE. I SAW YOU RUN OUT...
THAT'S WHEN I SNUCK IN AND I'M SO SORRY ABOUT THIS...I RIPPED UP YOUR TOP. I WAS JEALOUS.
I SHOULD'VE STOPPED THERE, BUT I COULDN'T HELP MYSELF. I LEFT THE NOTE TOO.
WHAT IS WRONG WITH YOU?
IF YOU DIDN'T LOOK LIKE SARA, I WOULDN'T BELIEVE YOU WERE ACTUALLY RELATED.
SHE WOULD NEVER DO ANYTHING LIKE THIS!

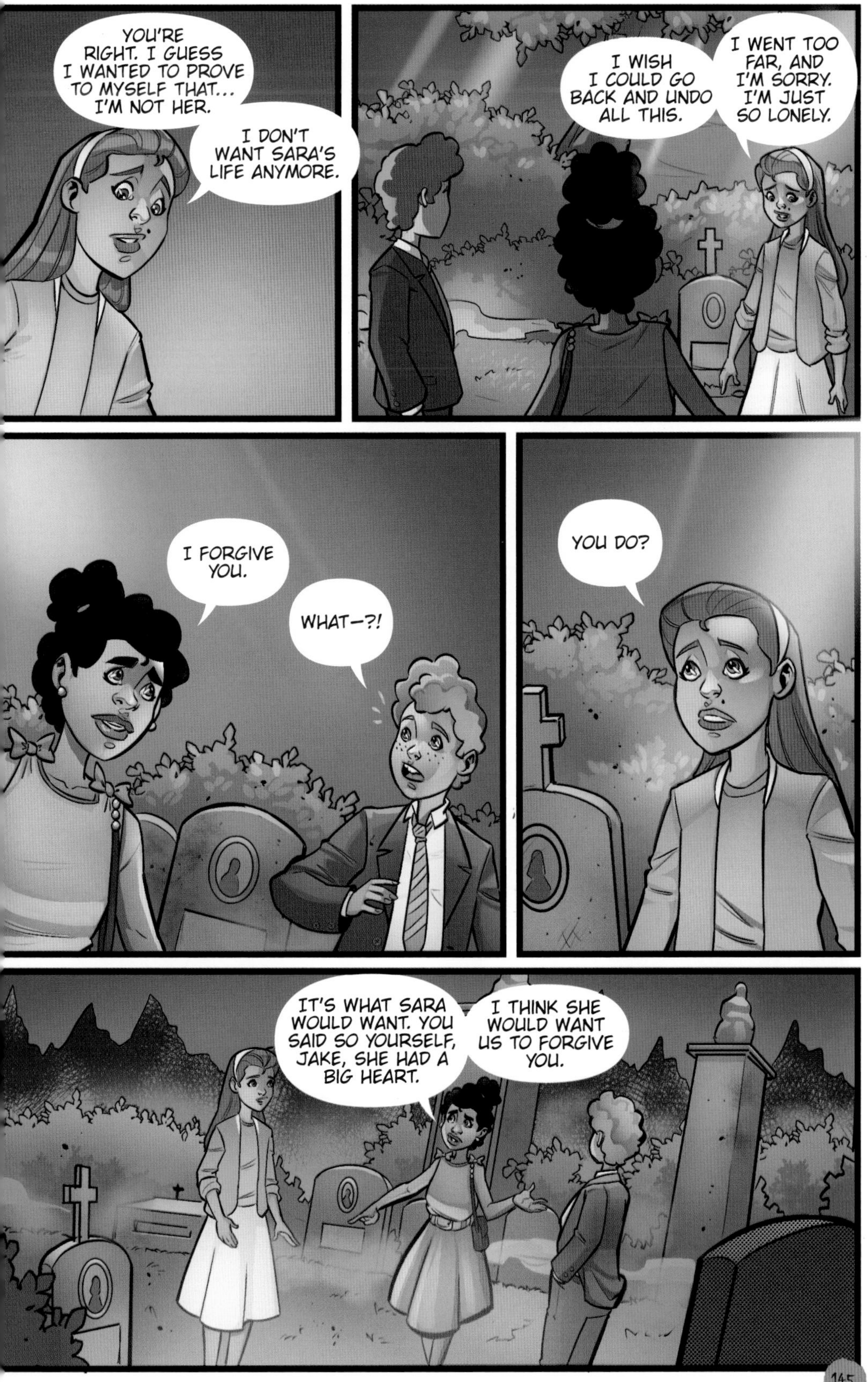
YOU'RE RIGHT. I GUESS I WANTED TO PROVE TO MYSELF THAT... I'M NOT HER.
I DON'T WANT SARA'S LIFE ANYMORE.
I WENT TOO FAR, AND I'M SORRY. I'M JUST SO LONELY.
I WISH I COULD GO BACK AND UNDO ALL THIS.
I FORGIVE YOU.
WHAT–?!
YOU DO?
IT'S WHAT SARA WOULD WANT. YOU SAID SO YOURSELF, JAKE, SHE HAD A BIG HEART.
I THINK SHE WOULD WANT US TO FORGIVE YOU.

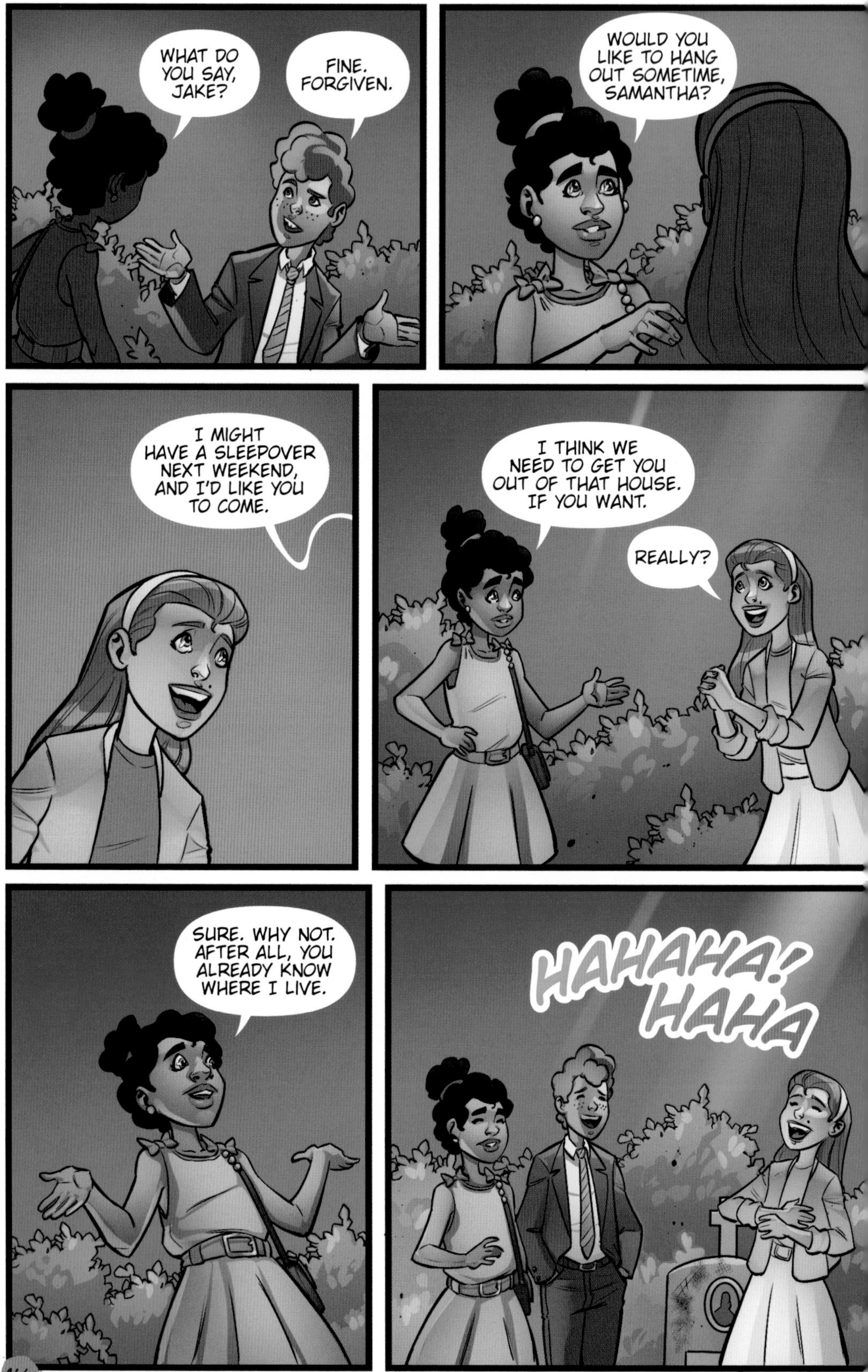
WHAT DO YOU SAY, JAKE?
FINE. FORGIVEN.
WOULD YOU LIKE TO HANG OUT SOMETIME, SAMANTHA?
I MIGHT HAVE A SLEEPOVER NEXT WEEKEND, AND I'D LIKE YOU TO COME.
I THINK WE NEED TO GET YOU OUT OF THAT HOUSE. IF YOU WANT.
REALLY?
SURE. WHY NOT. AFTER ALL, YOU ALREADY KNOW WHERE I LIVE.
HAHAHA! HAHA

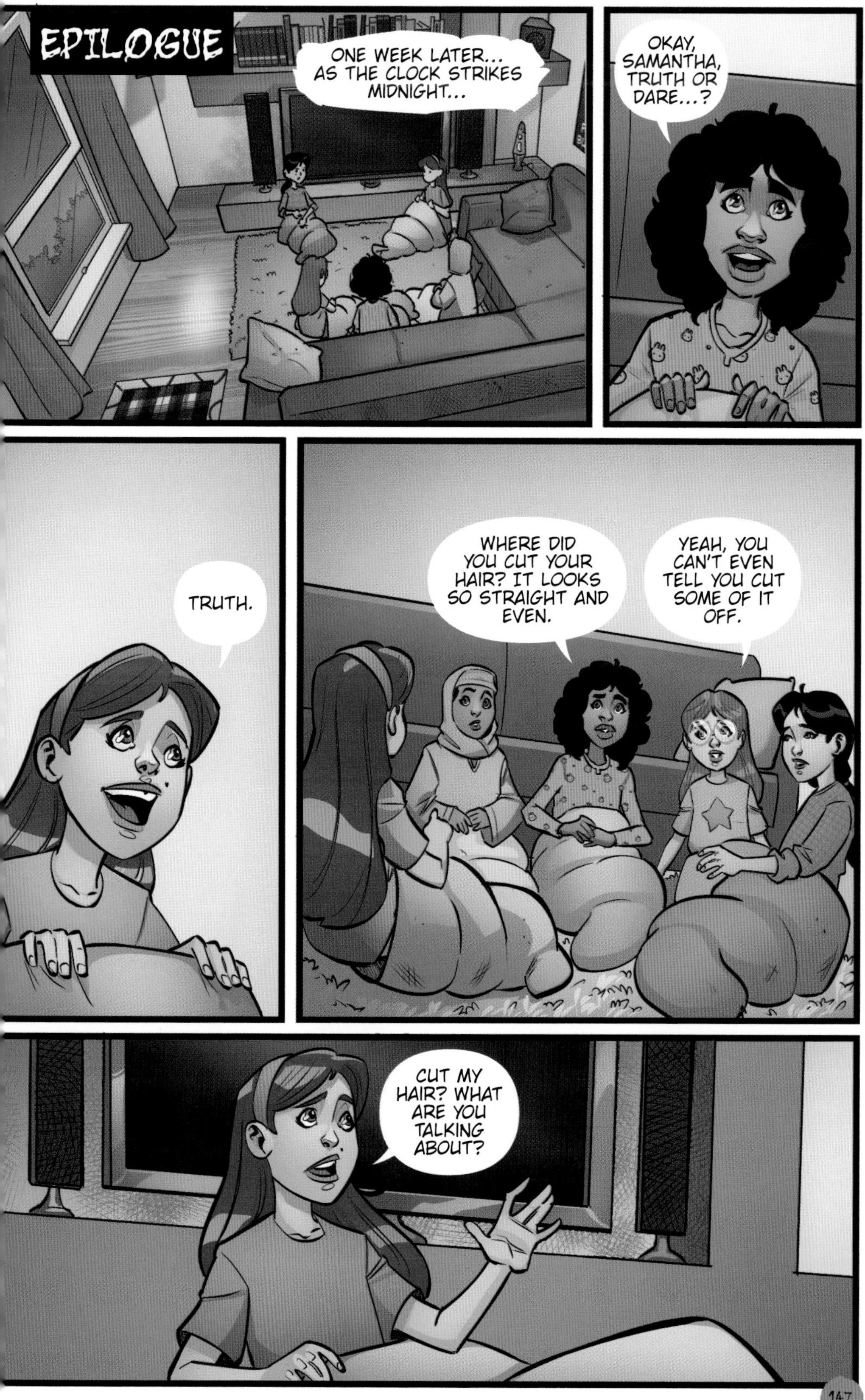
EPILOGUE
ONE WEEK LATER... AS THE CLOCK STRIKES MIDNIGHT...
OKAY, SAMANTHA, TRUTH OR DARE...?
TRUTH.
WHERE DID YOU CUT YOUR HAIR? IT LOOKS SO STRAIGHT AND EVEN.
YEAH, YOU CAN'T EVEN TELL YOU CUT SOME OF IT OFF.
CUT MY HAIR? WHAT ARE YOU TALKING ABOUT?

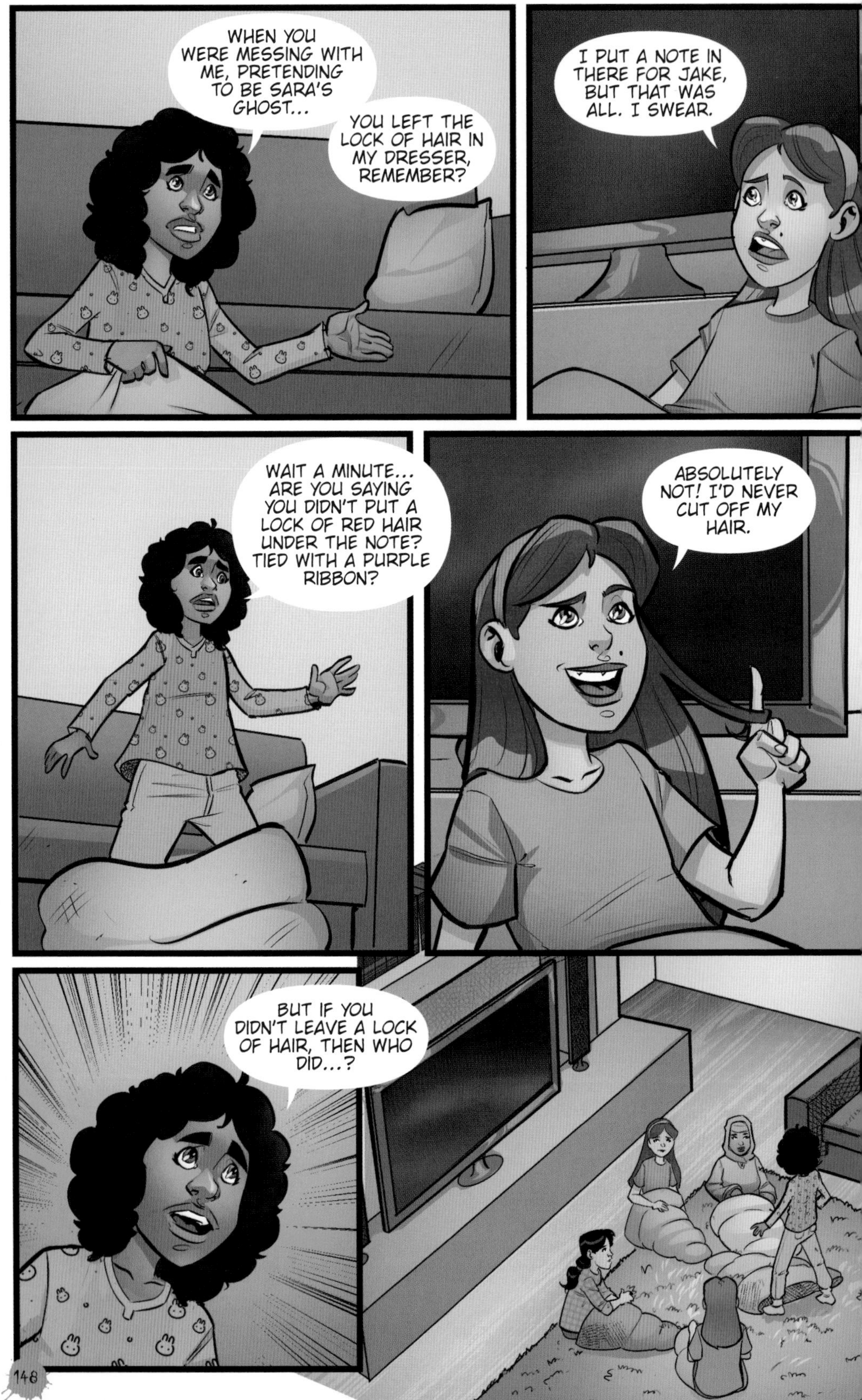
WHEN YOU WERE MESSING WITH ME, PRETENDING TO BE SARA'S GHOST...
YOU LEFT THE LOCK OF HAIR IN MY DRESSER, REMEMBER?
I PUT A NOTE IN THERE FOR JAKE, BUT THAT WAS ALL. I SWEAR.
WAIT A MINUTE... ARE YOU SAYING YOU DIDN'T PUT A LOCK OF RED HAIR UNDER THE NOTE? TIED WITH A PURPLE RIBBON?
ABSOLUTELY NOT! I'D NEVER CUT OFF MY HAIR.
BUT IF YOU DIDN'T LEAVE A LOCK OF HAIR, THEN WHO DID...?

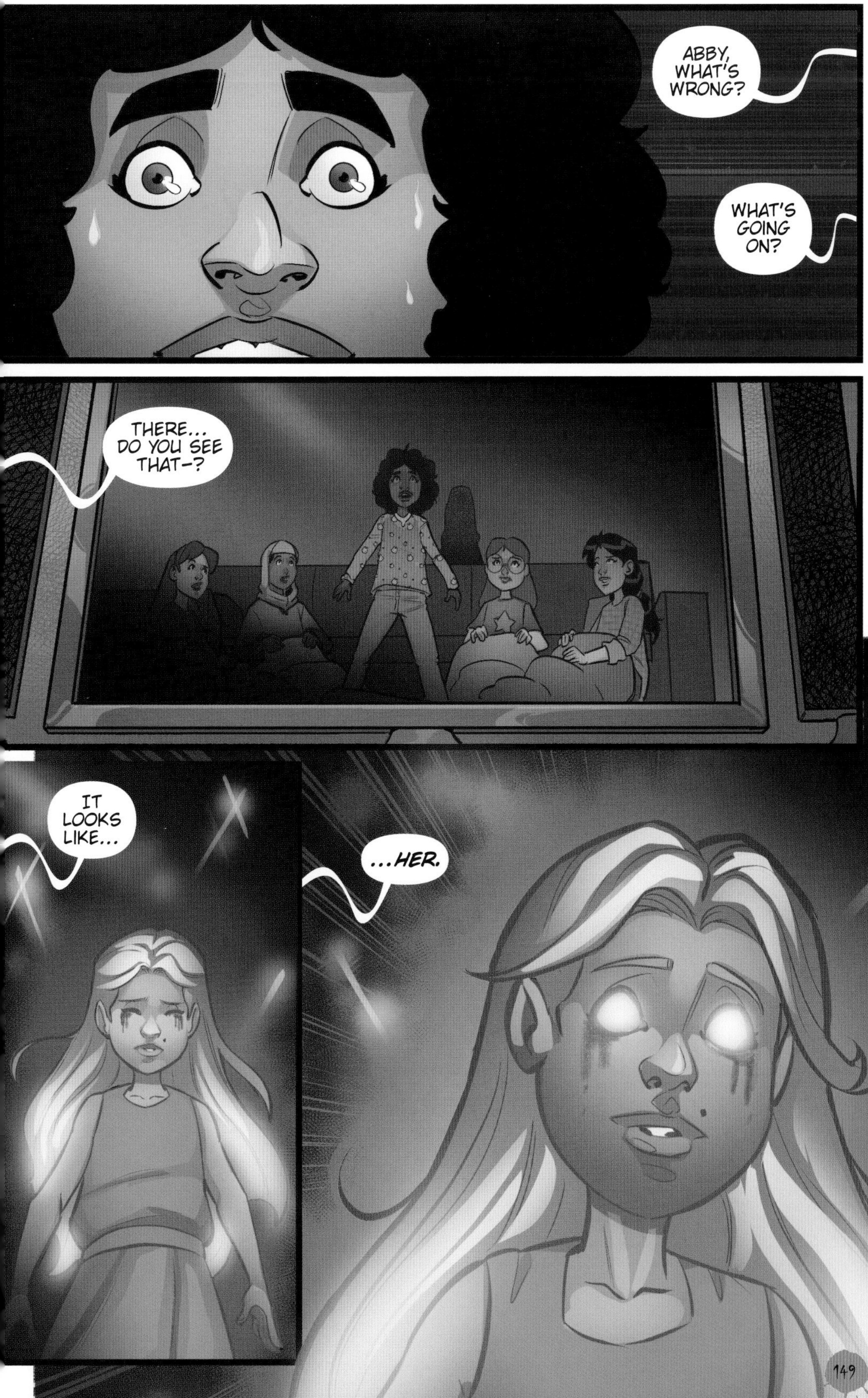
ABBY, WHAT'S WRONG?
WHAT'S GOING ON?
THERE... DO YOU SEE THAT-?
IT LOOKS LIKE...
...HER.

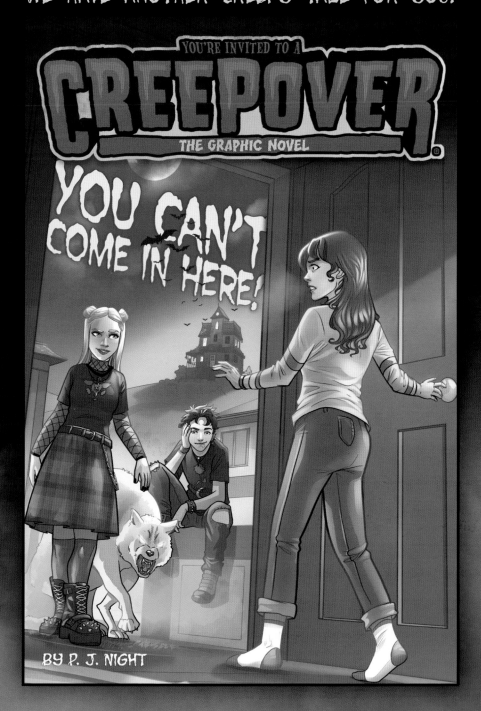

CHAPTER 1

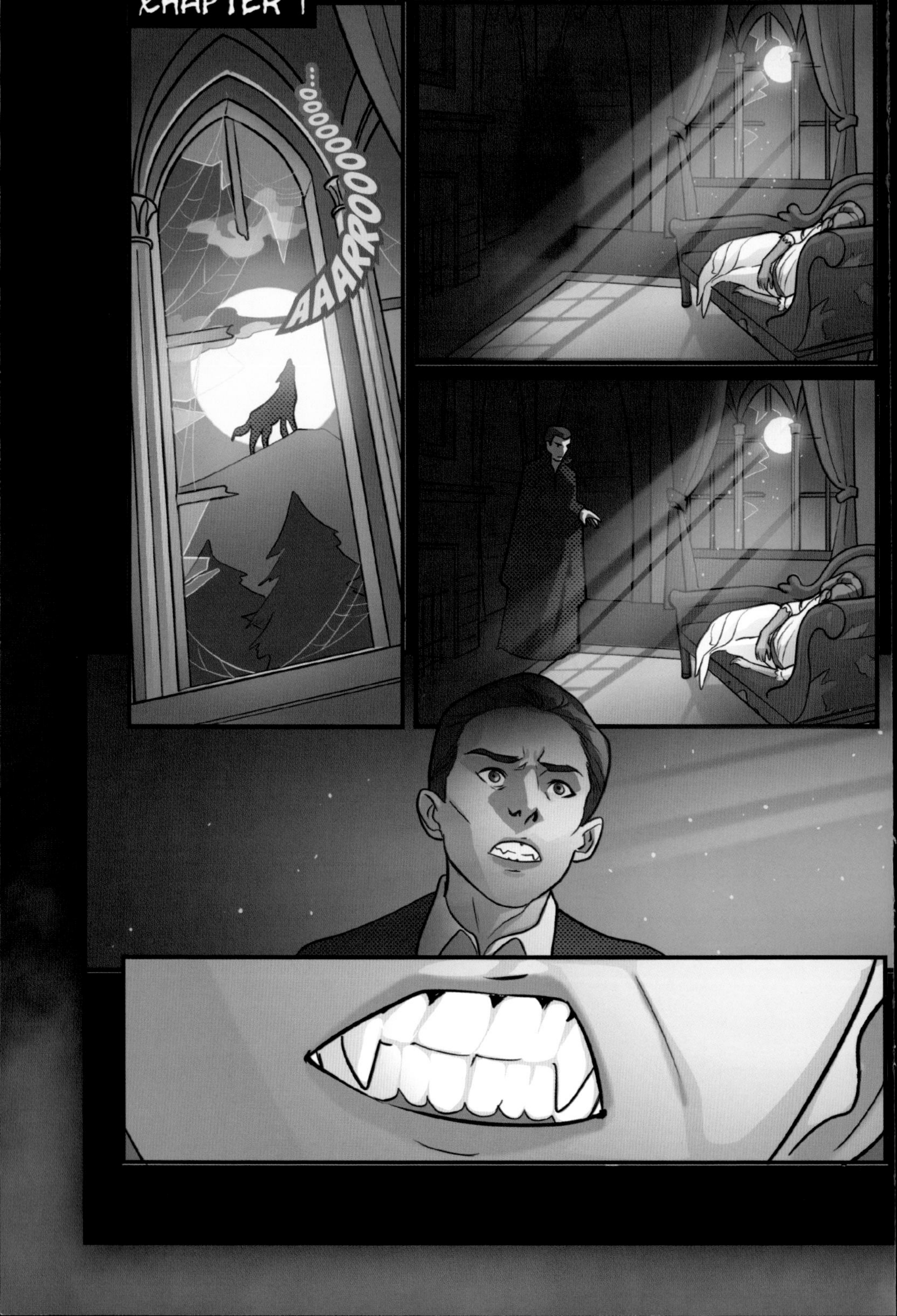

AAARROOOOOOOOO...

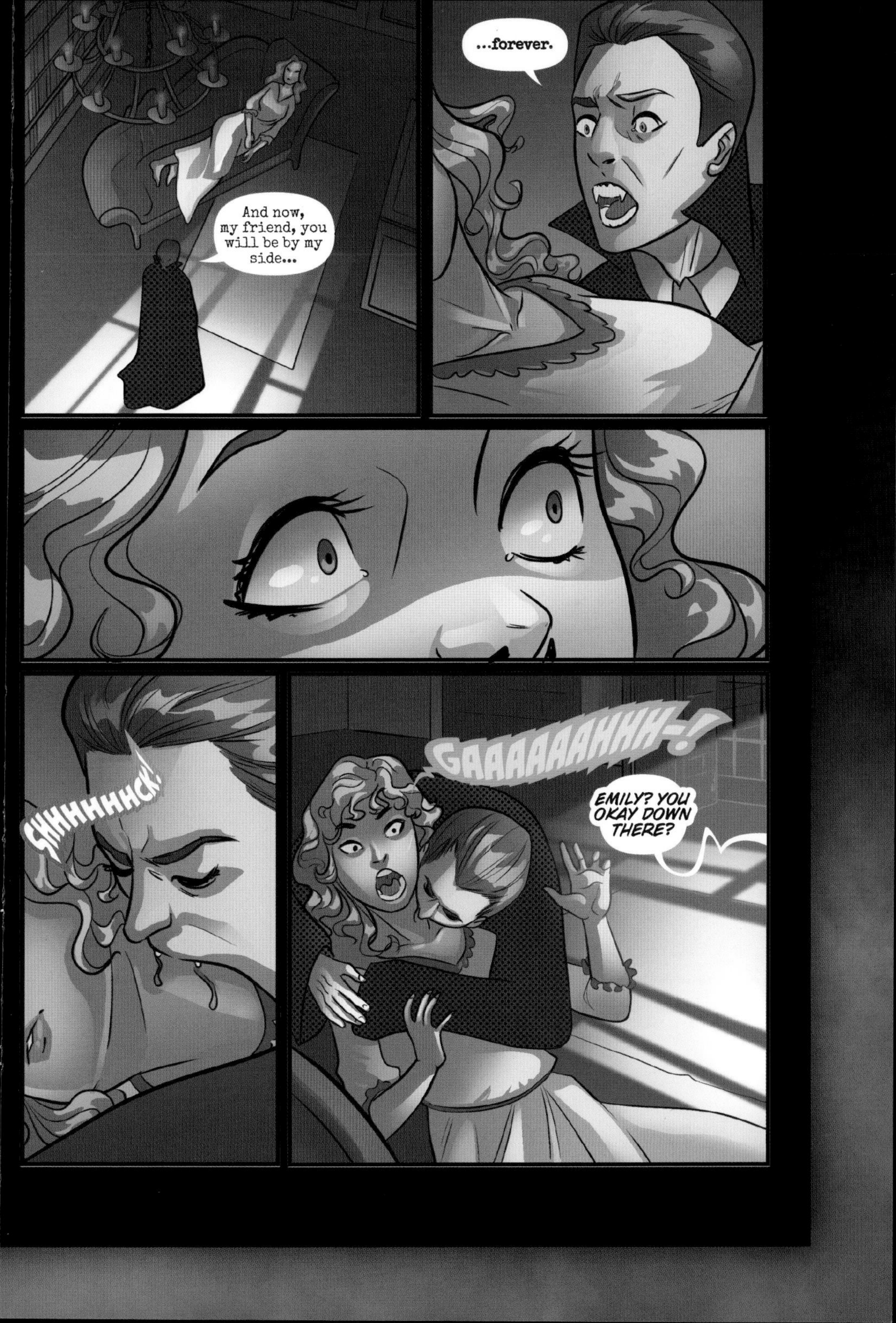
And now, my friend, you will be by my side...
...forever.
SHHHHHHCK!
GAAAAAAHHH-!
EMILY? YOU OKAY DOWN THERE?

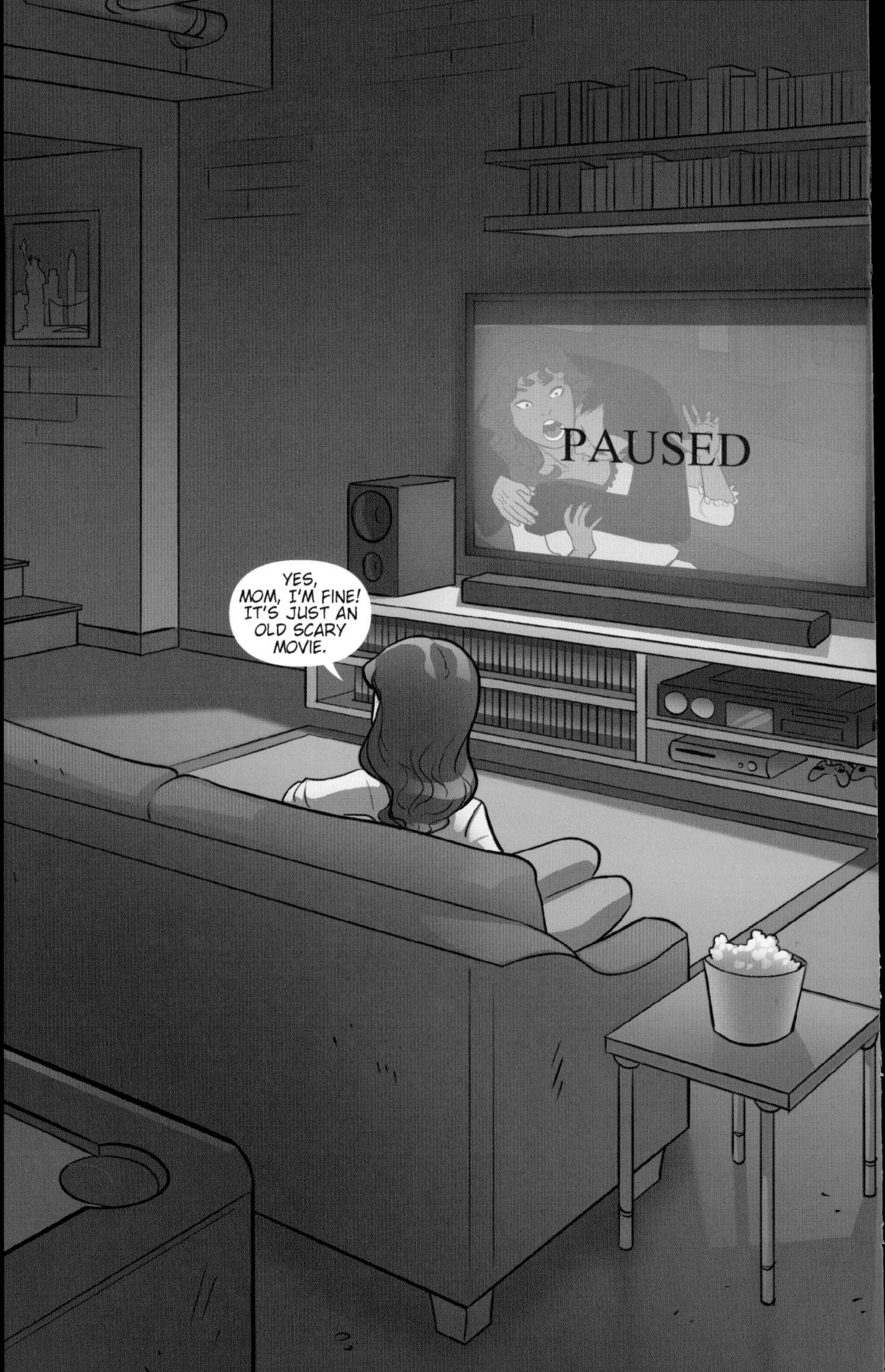
PAUSED
YES, MOM, I'M FINE! IT'S JUST AN OLD SCARY MOVIE.

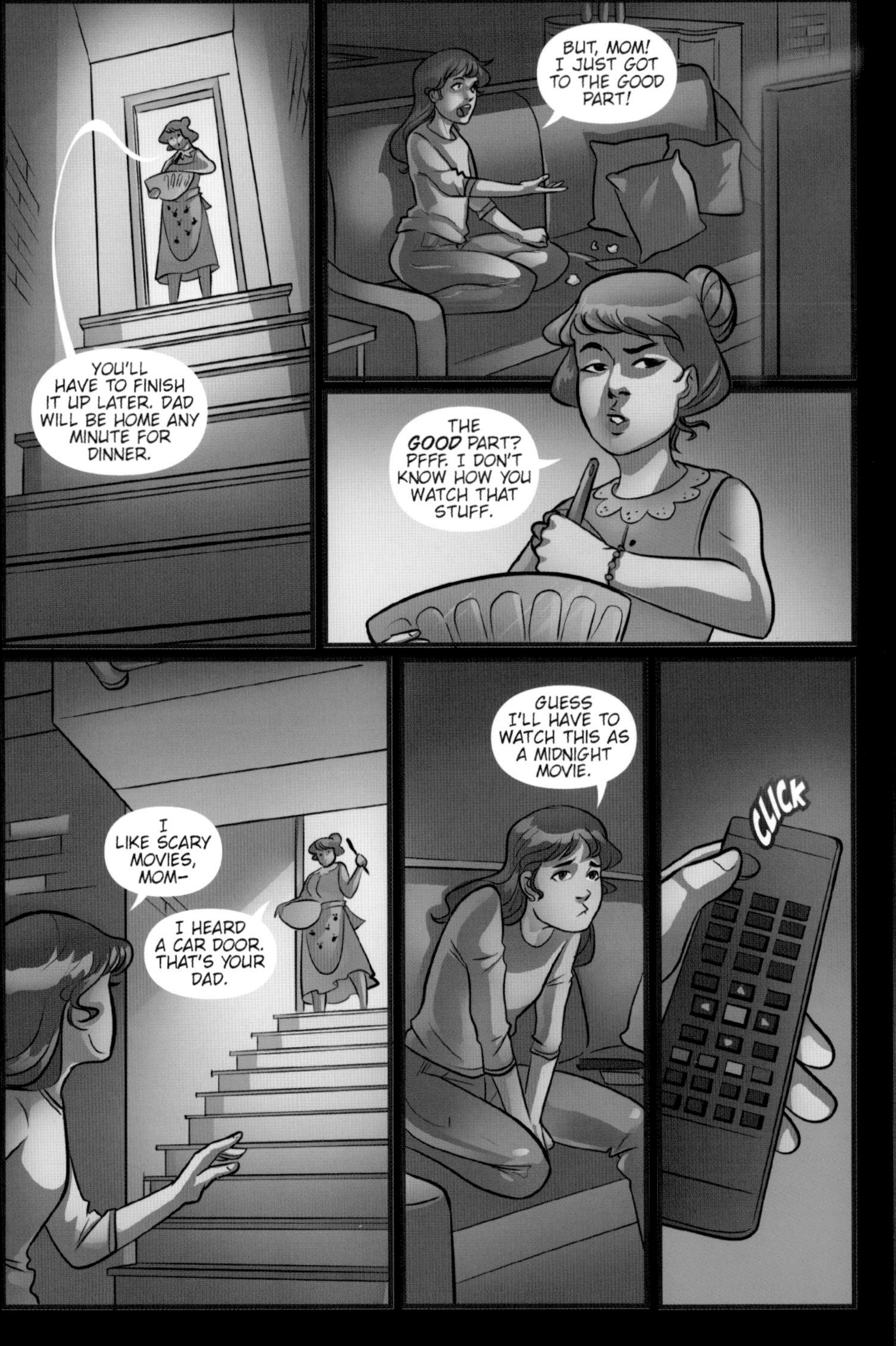
YOU'LL HAVE TO FINISH IT UP LATER. DAD WILL BE HOME ANY MINUTE FOR DINNER.
BUT, MOM! I JUST GOT TO THE GOOD PART!
THE *GOOD* PART? PFFF. I DON'T KNOW HOW YOU WATCH THAT STUFF.
I LIKE SCARY MOVIES, MOM—
I HEARD A CAR DOOR. THAT'S YOUR DAD.
GUESS I'LL HAVE TO WATCH THIS AS A MIDNIGHT MOVIE.
CLICK

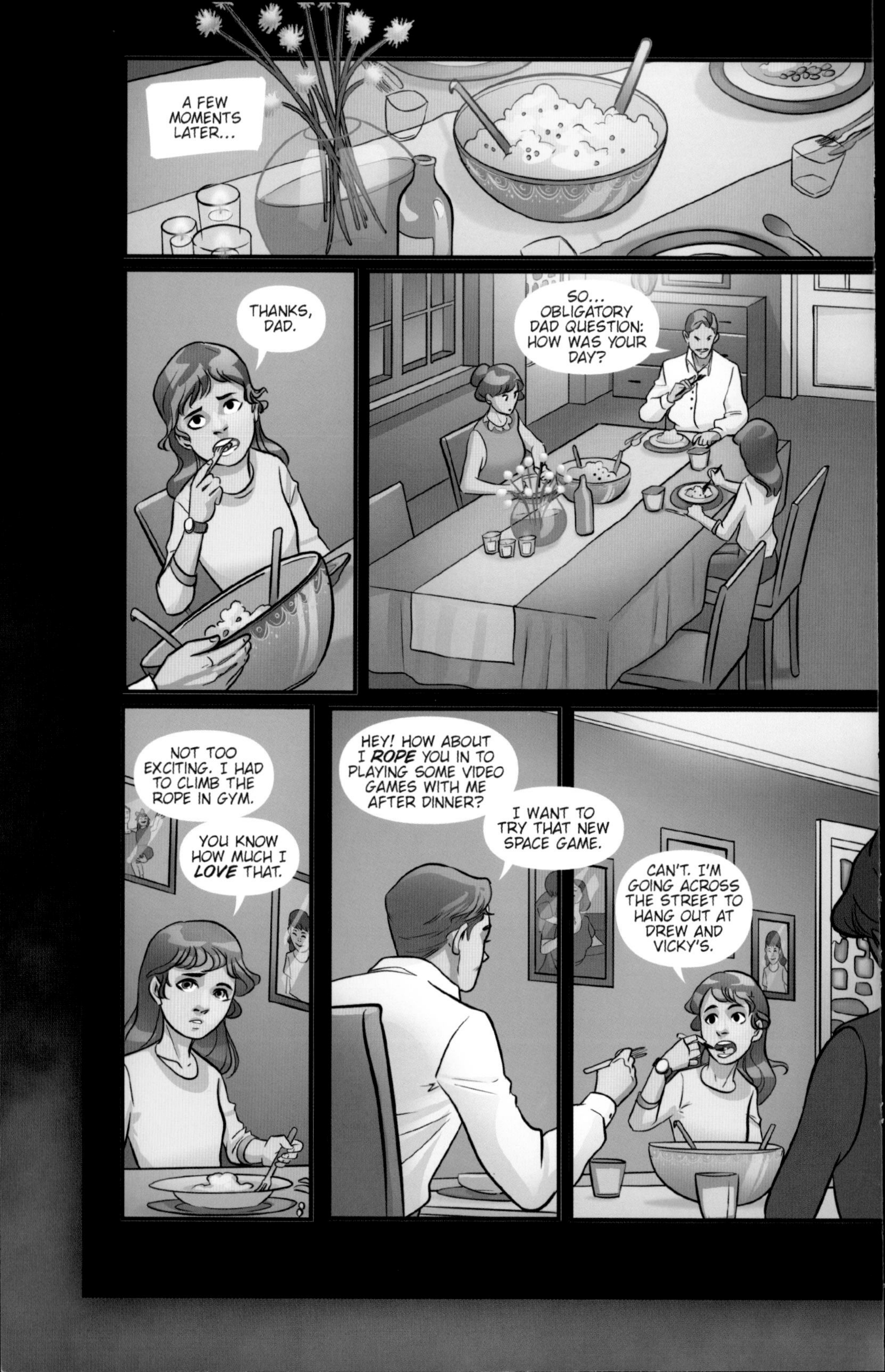
A FEW MOMENTS LATER...
THANKS, DAD.
SO... OBLIGATORY DAD QUESTION: HOW WAS YOUR DAY?
NOT TOO EXCITING. I HAD TO CLIMB THE ROPE IN GYM.
YOU KNOW HOW MUCH I **LOVE** THAT.
HEY! HOW ABOUT I **ROPE** YOU IN TO PLAYING SOME VIDEO GAMES WITH ME AFTER DINNER?
I WANT TO TRY THAT NEW SPACE GAME.
CAN'T. I'M GOING ACROSS THE STREET TO HANG OUT AT DREW AND VICKY'S.

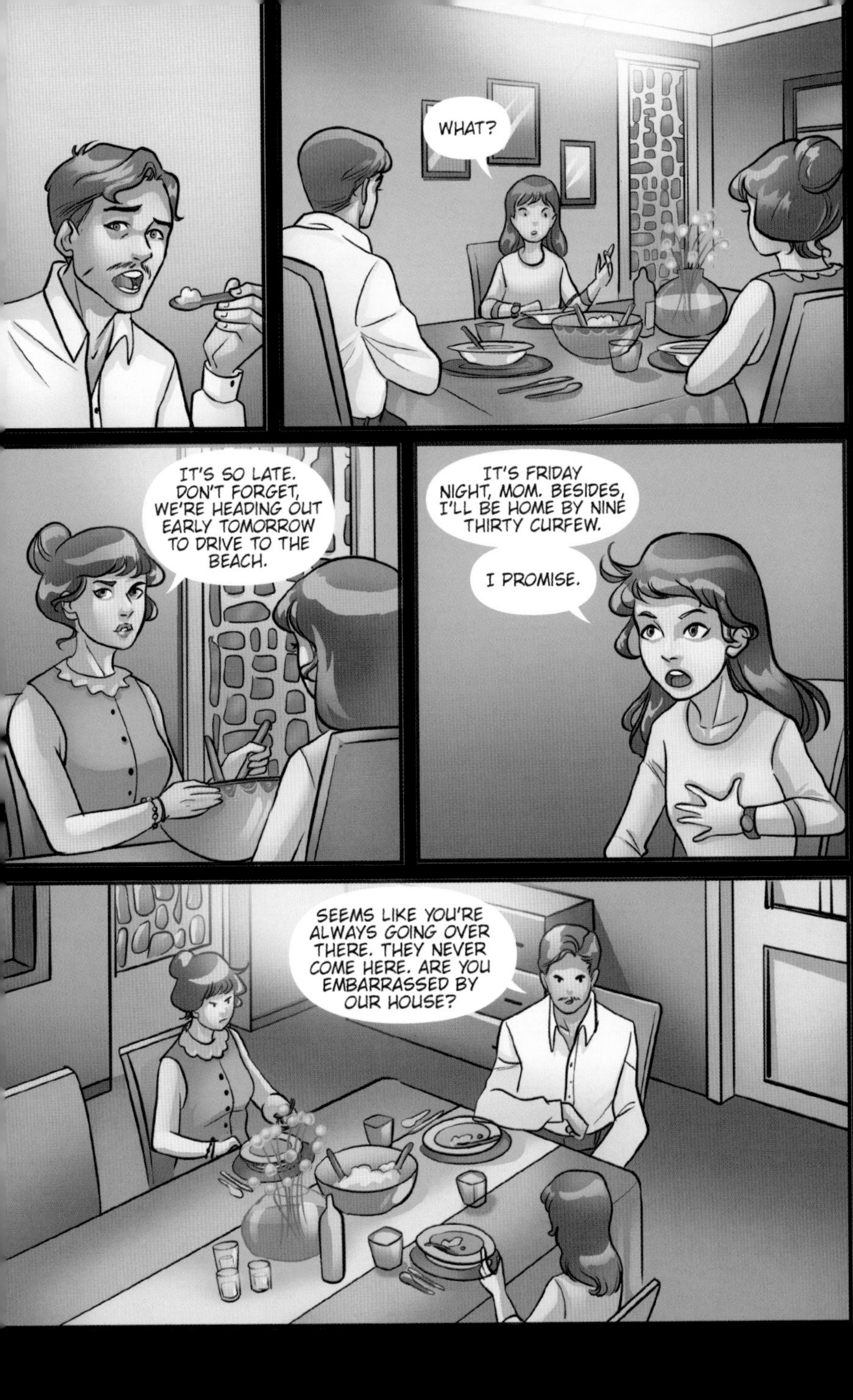
WHAT?
IT'S SO LATE. DON'T FORGET, WE'RE HEADING OUT EARLY TOMORROW TO DRIVE TO THE BEACH.
IT'S FRIDAY NIGHT, MOM. BESIDES, I'LL BE HOME BY NINE THIRTY CURFEW.
I PROMISE.
SEEMS LIKE YOU'RE ALWAYS GOING OVER THERE. THEY NEVER COME HERE. ARE YOU EMBARRASSED BY OUR HOUSE?

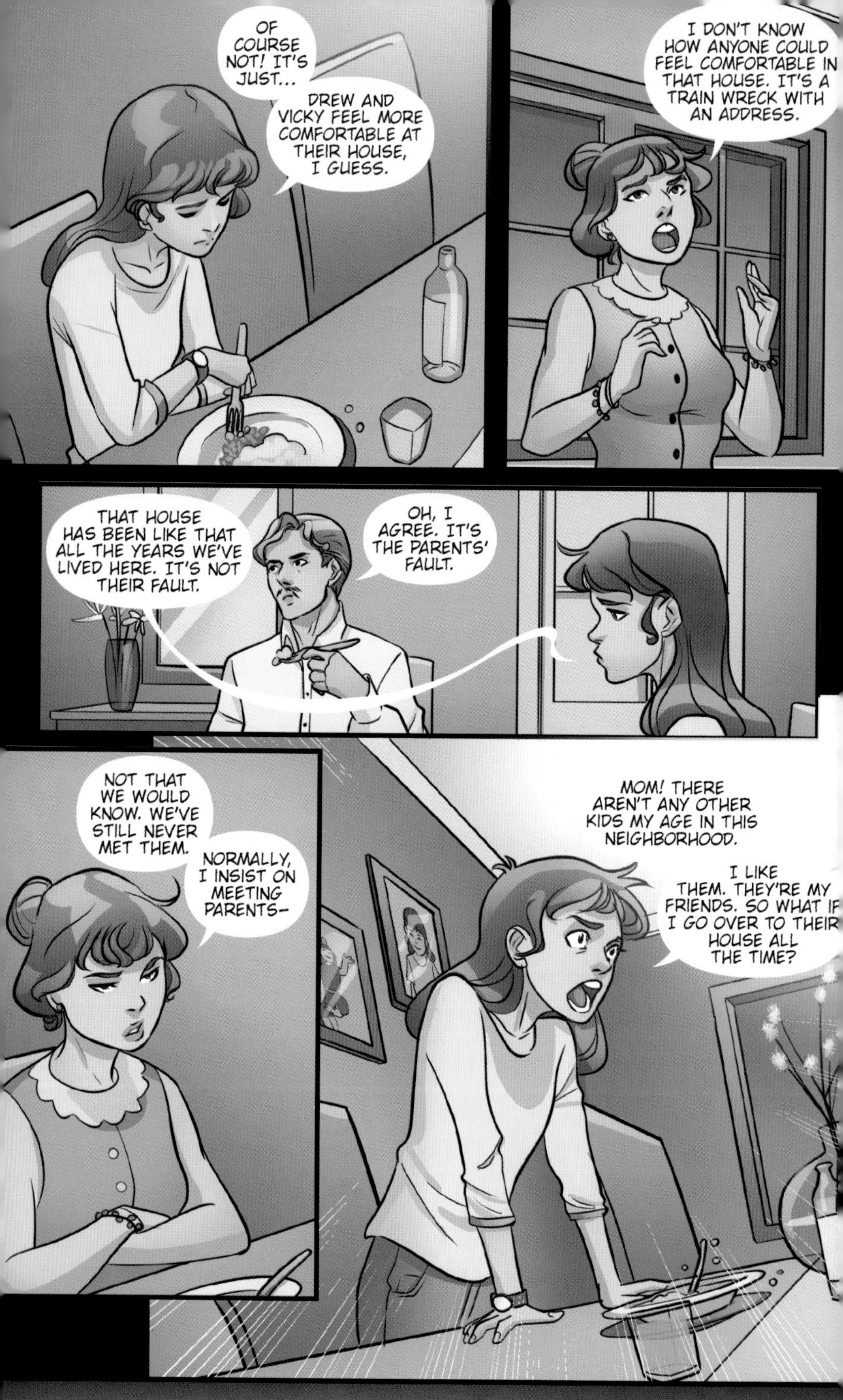
OF COURSE NOT! IT'S JUST...
DREW AND VICKY FEEL MORE COMFORTABLE AT THEIR HOUSE, I GUESS.
I DON'T KNOW HOW ANYONE COULD FEEL COMFORTABLE IN THAT HOUSE. IT'S A TRAIN WRECK WITH AN ADDRESS.
THAT HOUSE HAS BEEN LIKE THAT ALL THE YEARS WE'VE LIVED HERE. IT'S NOT THEIR FAULT.
OH, I AGREE. IT'S THE PARENTS' FAULT.
NOT THAT WE WOULD KNOW. WE'VE STILL NEVER MET THEM.
NORMALLY, I INSIST ON MEETING PARENTS–
MOM! THERE AREN'T ANY OTHER KIDS MY AGE IN THIS NEIGHBORHOOD.
I LIKE THEM. THEY'RE MY FRIENDS. SO WHAT IF I GO OVER TO THEIR HOUSE ALL THE TIME?

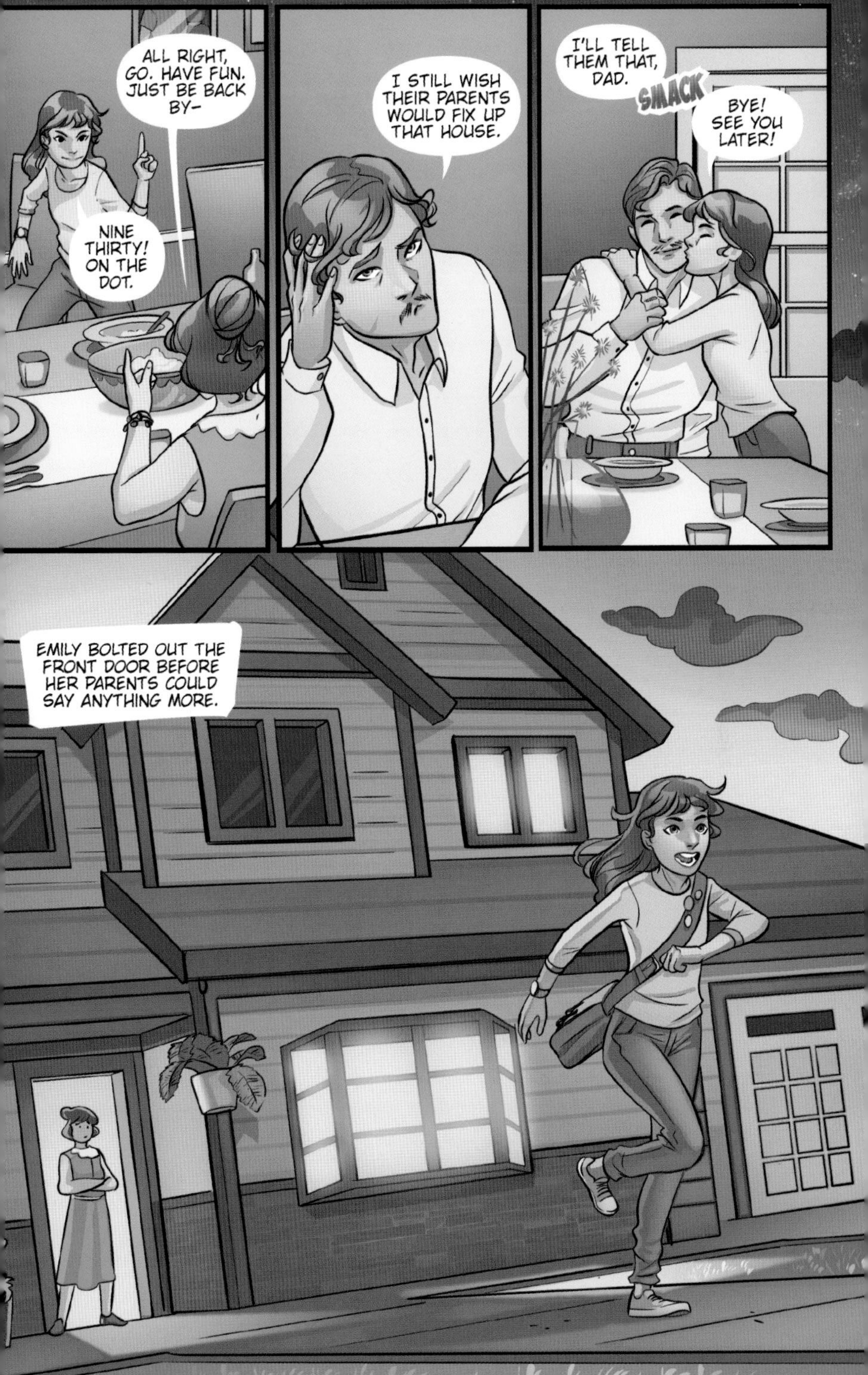
ALL RIGHT, GO. HAVE FUN. JUST BE BACK BY–
NINE THIRTY! ON THE DOT.
I STILL WISH THEIR PARENTS WOULD FIX UP THAT HOUSE.
I'LL TELL THEM THAT, DAD.
SMACK
BYE! SEE YOU LATER!
EMILY BOLTED OUT THE FRONT DOOR BEFORE HER PARENTS COULD SAY ANYTHING MORE.